DANCE OF THE BILLIONS

A Novel About Texas, Houston, and Oil

DANCE OF THE BILLIONS

GEORGE C. McGHEE

DIAMOND BOOKS   Austin, Texas

FIRST EDITION

Published in the United States of America
By Diamond Books
An Imprint of Eakin Publications, Inc.
P.O. Drawer 90159   ★   Austin, TX 78709-0159

ISBN 0-89015-692-1

Library of Congress Cataloging-in-Publication Data

McGhee, George Crews, 1912–
    Dance of the billions : a novel about Texas, Houston, and oil in the seventies / by George McGhee.
        p.   cm.
    ISBN 0-89015-692-1 : $17.95 ($22.95 Can.)
    1. Houston (Tex.) — History — Fiction. I. Title.
PS3563.C3638D3   1988
813'.54--dc20   89-16963
                                                                        CIP

Foreword

This was Houston as it was at the peak of its boom in the seventies, and about the oil men who made and shared in this boom.

Big, sprawling, driving Houston: Bursting with the energies of its 1.7 million people, the fifth largest city in the nation; spreading across 556 square miles of flat prairie, twice the area of New York City; thrusting its skyscrapers boldly and defiantly into the heavens; a city motivated, it has been said, by greed, by the scramble for the almighty dollar.

Fast-growing Houston: Leading the country during the seventies in growth of population, employment, retail trade, per capita income, residential construction and, at its peak, in total construction; the second largest U.S. port in foreign trade; providing sixty percent of the nation's basic petrochemicals and forty percent of its refined oil; with over 400 oil companies and 1,600 oil field supply companies and 550 foreign firms.

Ugly Houston: The Bottoms of the Fifth Ward and block after block of old, falling-down, half-painted frame houses; mile upon mile of garish, lugubrious, roadside drive-ins selling McDonald's Big Macs, Midas Mufflers, Dart Drugs, and the myriad of things Houstonians buy; huge signs, neon lights glaring out and blinking, demanding attention; and the king of all, the automobile, without which Houston could not exist, stretching in endless lines along the freeway, lined with dealers mothering their broods of pastel-colored used cars that dominated the landscape.

And yet there is beautiful Houston: The roses of the Houston Garden Center or a quiet glade in the inner recesses of Hermann Park; the elegant drawing room of the older Houston oil aristocracy replete with period French furniture; a gallery of the Houston Museum of Fine Arts, walls covered with priceless Old Masters; the fresh face and chic dress of a young attractive woman, swinging along Main Street to her public relations job; a dark-glass-covered double trapezoidal skyscraper silhouetted against the setting sun.

There are also, of course, mediocrity and provincialism in Houston: Dejected, staring "red necks" just moved in from the country; evidence everywhere of no zoning, little planning, inadequate transportation, poor schools, trash and abandoned automobiles in the streets, and cheap shops full of gaudy baubles.

However, Houston also contains much excellence and sophistication: The Texas Medical Center, the Manned Space Center; Rice and Houston Universities; corporations run so well they dominate world oil; leading firms in computer and electronic technology; ladies' clothing stores that attract the discriminating style-seeker from all over the world; the Post Oak Galleria, whose glass-covered shopping mall cuts out the cruel Houston sun from its fantasy world; smart hotels like the Warwick; the Alley Theater, the Rothko Chapel, and the Old Market Square restoration.

Houston has been called a "geographic term describing a congeries of villages," rather than a city. "What one misses in Houston are old things," said a European journalist. Said another, Houston has "little seasoning or distinction" as do older cities like London or Paris, or even contemporary American cities like San Francisco or Chicago: These can only occur where "famous men have lived, dined, talked with their friends or have written books and painted pictures or composed music."

Which was truly representative of Houston, or was all of it? Was Houston cause or effect? Was it a crucible imbibing raw materials and spewing out fine steel? Was it a catalyst that brought out from the group something better than the sum of the individuals who composed it? If so, what price did it exact in the process? Was the price too high? Would Houston in the end destroy, like the flame the moth, those attracted to its bright lights? Or destroy itself?

1

Jack

The letter lay on Jack Sanderson's desk like a rattlesnake poised to strike. As he read it for the fourth time, he felt sweat beading on his forehead and at the nape of his neck despite the chill of the air conditioning.

The letter was from Clay Phillips, vice-president of the First National Bank of Houston. In the most cordial and respectful language, Phillips stated that the bank would be happy to lend Sanderson Production Company another two million dollars *if* Jack would put up additional collateral.

But in fact Jack had none. Everything — the house he and Janet lived in, even the ranch in Central Texas he'd sworn he would never part with under any circumstances — was mortgaged.

Abruptly Jack wadded the offending piece of paper into a ball and threw it at the nearest wall, then jumped to his feet, and began to pace around his large office. A tall, ruddily handsome man whose athletic build belied his sixty years, he looked his age when he was worried, which lately had been more and more often.

"Two million dollars!" he growled, remembering when a simple phone call would have gotten him twenty million. It was painful acknowledging that his position had changed that much, that now, instead of increasing each year, his oil production and reserves were beginning to run out.

Swallowing a stream of curses, he seized the phone and brusquely told his secretary to get Clay Phillips.

Phillips' voice boomed in his ear almost instantly.

"Clay? Jack Sanderson here."

"Jack, good to hear your voice. What's on your mind?"

"I've got a loan from your bank on my mind, Clay. Your letter was a disappointment."

The banker sighed. "Jack, I hated to write it. You know how I feel about you. But my hands are tied. Money's tight. The board is reviewing all of our larger loans. Even though you've worked your loan down well, you still owe us twenty million dollars, and we just can't go any further without more collateral."

"Well, Clay, it's a rotten way to treat an old customer, especially over a lousy couple of million. You're holding my feet too close to the fire! Look, a few bills need paying . . . a temporary cash flow squeeze. You know I have plenty of reserves. Hell, that deep sand in Cameron will pay back every penny I owe." He paused.

"Perhaps so, Jack. But Cameron isn't producing yet, and perhaps it never will. I'm sorry, but the Board has to accept Alf Frazier's estimate of your reserves."

"Frazier! What the hell does he know? I'm the oilman, Clay! Are you going to take the word of some salaried engineer over mine? I've been finding the stuff for thirty years and made your bank a lot of money doing it. Never lost you a penny. That should count for something."

Jack knew very well the banks' position on risks: virtually out of the question since they lent depositors money at low rates of interest with no participation in profits. They would not lend for a "wildcat," or exploratory, well. However, the Houston banks had always been eager to make development loans to drill up proven fields, which loans were to be repaid out of oil production. An operator who found a good field could usually borrow his way through the drilling without additional capital. With his practical experience supported by solid data, Jack had always won his bouts with Frazier and gotten his loan. But now, in 1976, the economy was in an inflationary cycle, and bankers were worried that the boom might end.

The banker's tone grew cool. "Frazier's raised serious questions about your reserves. He says your Jackson County field is losing pressure. Twenty million is our limit, Jack. You can always try another bank, of course."

Jack gritted his teeth. Phillips' last remark was a slap in the

2

face. An Independent oilman couldn't change banks easily. An Independent's stock was skyhigh only as long as he was a winner. Then the banks fought like alley cats to loan you money, even when you didn't need it. You built credit with a bank in the good times to help you over the bad. Confidence was crucial in the oil business. Success was measured less by how much you had than by how much you could borrow. But there were limits, and once you reached yours things could change overnight. Jack shuddered. In the posh Petroleum Club, high atop the Exxon Building, the whispers would begin: "Poor Sanderson's overextended. First National won't lend him another dime."

Jack shook his head as if to clear it, then muttered, "It's Butler, isn't it?"

"Beg your pardon?"

"Bill Butler recently joined your board, didn't he?"

"Well, yes . . ."

"He's been out to get me for forty years. Is he behind this?"

Phillips' long silence was all the answer Jack needed. And then he surprised Jack by whispering, "Butler's a dangerous man." There was another pause. "That's all I can say, Jack. Good luck."

Jack put down the phone slowly and stared out at the bright blue Texas sky. His thoughts moved to the well that had gotten him into this jam just a few weeks ago. Was Butler the real enemy or was it just the oil business, this infinitely exciting, rewarding, albeit risky game he had set out to conquer so many years ago?

The well, in Louisiana's Terrebone Parish, had looked like his best bet in years. He'd watched that area a long time, and when Conoco dropped its leases he'd snapped up a ten-thousand acre block. He had "shot" it thoroughly and spent hours poring over the seismic records and subsurface maps. He'd had the data run through a new type of computer, a tool not available in the old days. His goal, a one-hundred-foot gas sand at twenty thousand feet, had been a prolific producer in nearby fields.

At first, everything had gone well. At twelve thousand feet, Jack had hit a fair sand which the electrical log indicated to be gas. True, it was thin, only twenty feet, but Jack figured it would be enough to pay for the well, no matter how the deep sand came out. He kept drilling, and took a risk by making the last six thousand feet in open hole, without setting protection pipe.

Jack could still taste the excitement he had experienced standing on the derrick floor as they neared twenty thousand feet. He'd never drilled that deep before, and it gave him the kind of thrill he'd rarely known since his first discovery as an Independent at West Bayou Bleu, thirty years before.

Right on target, at 19,980 feet, the bit drilled twenty feet of good sand. The log looked good and the well was drilling ahead, still in sand, when it "kicked" gas.

Jack had let out a whoop. There was a hundred million dollars worth of gas and distillate waiting for him in that deep sand. He was so sure, he could taste it — so sure he'd called Janet and told her she could buy out Sakowitz.

Then all hell broke loose.

The well started to blow out, shooting up gas and salt water. If unchecked, the flow could spread like wildfire, cratering into a vast boiling cauldron, spewing out gas and salt water like a runaway fire hose, opening up yawning vents, sucking in massive chunks of sandy Louisiana soil. Instead of his millions, Jack suddenly saw a disastrous bill for damages.

Once the well started to blow, an emergency call went out for all the drilling mud he could find in South Louisiana. Soon there was a long column of mud-trucks lined up by the well. It was like watching hundreds of taxis with their meters running. Before long a mountain of empty mud sacks were piled up beside the well, but still the trucks kept coming.

When the well was finally brought under control, Jack ran a 20,000-foot protection string of pipe. But just before that reached the deep sand, it got hopelessly stuck. Now Jack had no assurance that he could control another blowout.

He'd had no choice. The well was plugged and abandoned. Even the thin upper sand Jack had counted on to pay expenses also tested salt water. The prospect was a total loss.

Still, despite the expensive mistake, Jack continued to believe a huge gas field was waiting to be discovered in the sand at twenty thousand feet. He believed in the log. He was convinced the blow-out came from a thin, high-pressure saltwater sand they had encountered above it but had failed to shut off. However, the possibility of another blowout, coupled with the uncertainty of what was in the deep sand, meant he couldn't justify drilling a second well.

Now Jack owed the oil supply companies almost two million dollars, due within thirty days. And the First National Bank had refused him a loan. Perhaps the other banks would do the same, despite the reserves he owned across Texas and Louisiana.

An Independent oilman spent his life believing there was always another prospect to drill, always another million dollars to be borrowed, always another well to be brought in. But for some, Jack knew only too well, the dream ended in dust.

He'd seen them all his life, oilmen who one day were living in River Oaks, lunching at the Petroleum Club, driving Cadillacs, and the next day were wiped out. Afterwards, they turned up in the Milam Hotel lobby or the streets, wearing cheap seersucker suits, shabby and shrunken, waving tattered maps, touting deals, trying to hustle their way back to the big time. Sometimes, as a favor, you looked at what they were offering. More often, you crossed the street.

Could it happen to *him*, Jack wondered, because of one lousy blowout in Terrebone Parish? Could a lifetime of success be blown away like a house of cards?

No, he vowed, no! He wouldn't let that happen.

Jack's secretary buzzed, interrupting his dialogue with himself. "Mr. Butler's secretary wants to know if you're available."

Jack couldn't help laughing. First the polite letter, now the shark, smelling blood.

"Let him hold a minute," said Jack, and settled back in his chair.

Bill Butler. Who else but Butler? It figured. He and Bill had been enemies from the moment they faced each other in anger as youths, in the turbulent early days of the fabulous East Texas field. Later it had come to blows on a derrick floor. Their natural dislike for each other had spawned endless confrontations as they competed in the oil business, in Houston and Texas politics, even in Houston's social and cultural affairs.

At first, Jack had blamed Butler's arrogant, aggressive nature for the feud, but in time he had come to wonder if their hostility might not have been inevitable. So many of Jack's friends had pointed out what natural antagonists the two men were: one was an Independent, the other a Company man; one was from modest circumstances and had worked hard for his success, the other was heir to an oil fortune and the chairmanship of the biggest oil company in Houston; one was a political moderate who believed in giving every man an opportunity, the other a relentless reactionary who sought wealth and power for himself and his rich friends.

The question now was whether Houston, even the vast state of

Texas, was big enough for them both. He picked up the phone.

Jack's tone was polite — that was part of the game. "Bill, haven't heard from you in a long time. How've you been?"

"Never better. Just flew in from Kenya."

"Business?"

"Pleasure. Got me a lion. Great sport."

"What's on your mind?"

"Business. How'd you like to sell your interest in West Bayou Bleu? We both know the field has seen its best days. Texoil wants to buy out the minority interests there to simplify our operating problems."

Jack cleared his throat. "That field is where I got my start, Bill."

"No room for sentiment in the oil business."

"I don't like selling reserves, Bill. Never sold anything in my life. It goes against my grain."

"We can offer you a good price."

"Probably not good enough."

"You surprise me. I thought you could use the money."

"Not yours."

"Don't be so damn stubborn. Most people would say I was doing you a favor."

"Butler, you've done me no favors in forty years. I certainly don't need any now."

"You may be begging for favors before long, fella. Check your hole card and let me know if you change your mind."

Jack spoke softly. "Did you really expect to push me out of Bayou Bleu by getting the First National to turn down my loan?"

"Don't blame me if you're in hock to your eyeballs, Sanderson. You Independents all think the oil business is a game, but it's not anymore. The future of the industry is with the big companies. It's an international business, not a scavenger hunt. The Independents are relics, just like your precious Bayou Bleu. Hang onto your damn interest. It's your funeral!"

"Bill, your dad was a great oilman and he built a fine company. Hell, it's surviving even with you in charge, and all of Houston realizes that you wouldn't be there if you weren't his son."

"Damn you, Sanderson! I'll have that field and break you while I'm getting it."

"Careful, or it might go the other way," Jack said, and dropped the phone onto its cradle.

Jack sat back heavily in his chair, feeling his heart pump, his blood race. It had felt good to tell Butler off, but now he was drained.

The phone rang, his private line this time.

"What's up, darling?"

Jack felt the tension ebb. After forty years, Janet's voice still did that to him.

"Just a routine day," he said easily. "The bank turned me down and Bill Butler is after my scalp."

"Well, I'm glad it's nothing serious," she said lightly. "I just wanted to remind you that tonight is the Harrisons' party."

"Oh, Lord. Can't we beg off?"

"They'd be so disappointed, Jack. We *did* sponsor them at the club. Come on darling, don't let the bank and Butler spoil a perfectly fine evening." She paused. "Jack?"

"Hmnn?"

"We'll make out. We always do."

"You bet we will," he said, wishing he felt as sure as he sounded. After he hung up he stood up and stretched, ashamed of his self-doubt, and went over to stand by the window. He stared out at Houston, his city. It was a great city, and he believed in it utterly. The city of the future, he had often called it in speeches he delivered to civic groups. There was no question in his mind but that Houston was unique, the prototype for the great cities of the future. Now its vigor rebuked him for his pessimism. As he gazed out at this city he loved so well, he tried to draw strength from it once again.

But on this night it just didn't come. He had no doubts about the future of Houston; the question now was *his* future.

Jack Sanderson, a self-made millionaire at twenty-eight, once Houston's Independent Oilman of the Year, suddenly felt old and very tired. He'd been in tight spots before. After all, an Independent oilman was by definition a gambler, playing long odds, betting his skill and luck against demanding Mother Nature, and Jack had won the game far more times than he'd lost. But it got harder as the years raced by. Youth made anything possible; one's luck would run forever. Alas, with age came caution, an unwillingness to keep risking everything on the turn of a bit in a deep well. And then there was fear.

Jack pressed his forehead against the glass and willed the years to slip away.

2

Jack Sanderson was born to find oil, or so he believed. It was in his blood from the time of his birth in 1916 in the sleepy East Texas town of Tyler, cheek by jowl with what would become the greatest oil field the world had ever seen.

Tyler, founded in the 1840s, was at the western margin of the Old South, where the pine trees and the sandy red soil and the plantations, worked by darkies living in shanties, ran out. Its better homes were white-columned, ante-bellum colonial, as was its way of life. It was Baptist, still in deep mourning over the bitter loss of the War Between the States, which had crippled East Texas economically and robbed it of its best men.

Tyler was a jumping-off place for the new Texas that was being created beyond: the bald, cotton-rich Black and Grand Prairies of Central Texas, which led to the teeming cattle-rich, rocky plateau of North Central and West Texas and, to the north, the table-flat, dreary Staked Plains of the Panhandle. In the very center of Texas lay the lovely Hill Country, merging in the south with the flat, almost tropical Coastal Plain. Around the edges lay the brash, burgeoning cities of the new state: Dallas in northeastern Texas clearly faced the East and was a thriving banking and business center; nearby Fort Worth served the cattle ranches of West Texas; to the south lay Houston, the state's principal cotton and oil center, and Galveston, a declining cotton port; and finally, in the the southwest was the forerunner of them all, gentle, Hispanic San Antonio.

Jack felt deeply that he was both Southern *and* Texan. His family, like most of the other people who had settled in Tyler, had migrated there from the eastern reaches of the Old South. Mostly of English yeoman stock, they were a roving, restless people whose predecessors had landed in Virginia or the Carolinas or Georgia. When the best land there had been taken, the more adventurous had moved west in easy stages, looking for more and better land, opportunity, more space and more freedom. Jack's father, born in a small Mississippi town bankrupted by the Civil War, had come to Texas as a young man to seek his fortune. Jack's mother's grandparents on both sides had made the long trek to Texas in covered wagons from Georgia.

From boyhood Jack had loved the rolling, pine-covered, sandy countryside around Tyler. He swam and fished for catfish in its slow-moving creeks and small lakes, murky with pine needles and smelling of oil. He spent hours searching Caddo Indian relics. He walked endlessly up and down the long rows of cotton looking for the flint arrowheads. He even discovered the sites where they had camped beside streams. He spent many weekends scouring the fields for minerals and fossils. He studied the outcroppings of rock strata and, in time, began to understand how they had been laid down as sand or mud in the inland seas that had covered East Texas millions of years before. By the time he reached high school, he was self-educated in geology.

Like any young Texan, Jack was well aware of Texas' new oil fields and what they meant to his state. Sometimes he overheard his father and Dr. Wesley Crews, the Tyler dentist who was his father's best friend, talk about the great oil fields that had been found at Spindletop, Ranger, Desdemona, Vernon, and nearby Corsicana, The two men's voices would rise with excitement.

"By golly, Wes, we've got to get in on this oil boom," his father would declare.

"Men are making millions, all over the state. I'm keeping my eyes open, Frank," Dr. Crews would reply. "One day the right deal will come along."

Jack secretly hoped that his father would stay out of the oil business because he was well aware that his father was not a good businessman. He was the cashier at the Tyler bank, but his savings were periodically lost in land deals and other misguided business ventures. By the time the Depression gripped Tyler, there was precious little money for food and clothing for the family, much less for oil deals.

The night after his graduation from high school, Jack and his parents discussed his plans for the future. "You know I want to major in geology," he told them. "After all, I've got a head start. I've been messing around with it since I was a kid."

"Do you still want to go to the University?" Eula Sanderson asked. She was a handsome, big-boned woman with piercing brown eyes, who had graduated from the San Marcos Normal in South Texas and had taught school for a few years before marrying. Jack had grown up with great respect for her. She devoted her life to her family and helping other people, and she was a strong, determined woman. When times were hard, it was his mother who held the family together.

"I sure do. Texas has a good geology department," said Jack eagerly. "My general science teacher says so."

There was a long silence. Finally his father spoke.

"Jack, there's something we haven't told you. We thought it best to wait until after you'd enjoyed your graduation."

Jack stared at his father.

"Things have been very bad at the bank, as I think you know," his father said gravely. "Well, to make a long story short, I'm leaving the bank. I'm afraid there's just no money for your college right now."

Jack was speechless for a moment. "That's all right," he said slowly, though his heart was breaking. "Maybe I should stay home and work for a year and help you and Mother. College can wait."

His father nodded. "Yes, that might . . ."

"You'll do no such thing," Eula declared. "You'll go to the University of Texas and you'll study geology and you'll do it this September. Your great grandfather, Dr. James Wilkenson, left Georgia and came to East Texas by covered wagon because he believed this was a land of opportunity. When he arrived he founded the first private school in this county in Arp. My family insisted I go to San Marcos. Education is our family tradition, and you're not going to give up on college just because your father has suffered a minor setback."

"But, my dear, where will the money come from?" Jack's father stammered.

"The boy is a good scholar and a track star," Jack's mother

said evenly. "The University of Texas will be lucky to get him. Why, he'll outrun any miler they've got! Jack, you go down to Austin next week and talk to the dean of admissions. If he doesn't offer you a scholarship, you can go to A&M or Rice or SMU instead. Are we agreed?"

Neither son nor husband dared protest, and the next Monday Jack borrowed the family car for the three-hour drive to Austin. There, to his amazement, he found that his mother was right: UT was happy to give him student aid. He returned home with an athletic scholarship that covered all of his tuition and part of his dormitory costs, and the track coach had promised him help in finding part-time jobs to cover his living expenses.

In the summer of 1935, when Jack was nineteen, he made the rounds in Tyler, looking for work. But it was men with families who got jobs, not college boys with scholarships.

One Sunday, confused and discouraged, he went for a long walk on the farm owned by his father's friend, Dr. Crews. He took along a compass and a hand level, and using some of the knowledge he'd acquired at the university, he mapped the structure of the outcrop of a bed of hard sandstone. He was eager to see if it would indicate whether there was a dome beneath it that could contain oil. Absorbed in his task, he was startled by a familiar voice, "Found any oil on my land, son?"

"Oh, hello, Dr. Crews! No, just mapping the surface. You never know, these days."

"Have any plans for the summer?" asked the dentist, a plump genial man.

"Well, I'm looking for a job."

"Maybe you can help me."

"You mean working around the farm? Be glad to!"

"No, I've in mind something that will put your college education to work."

"No kidding!"

Dr. Crews smiled. "Did I ever tell you that I know Dad Joiner?"

"Lord, no," Jack exclaimed.

Joiner was the most talked-about man in East Texas. Now seventy, he had spent the last twenty years prospecting for oil in Texas and Oklahoma. In the late 1920s, Joiner's search had settled on Rusk County in East Texas, where he leased five thousand acres, announced plans to drill, and raised the hopes of the Rusk County citizenry that their fortunes would soon be made.

Oilmen laughed at Joiner's venture. The experts agreed that there were no structures in Rusk County that might produce oil. But Joiner went ahead and raised the money to start drilling, largely from the local residents. His long history of bad luck continued. Bits jammed and his machinery broke down. And yet he kept at it. The skeptics said they would drink all the oil Dad Joiner found in East Texas.

By the third year of unsuccessful drilling, Joiner was hustling twenty-five-dollar certificates for small interests in his leases to anyone who would buy. Still, the local people kept faith, and many worked for free on his well. His dream had become their dream.

Then, on September 12, 1930, Dad Joiner's Number 3 Daisy Bradford well came in, producing pipeline oil from the Woodbine sand of the Cretaceus era at 5,300 feet. The most colossal oil boom in American history had begun. In time the field he had discovered would spread over four counties, extending forty miles and covering 135,000 acres. Its thirty thousand wells would produce more than six billion barrels of oil.

"I'll tell you about Dad Joiner," Dr. Crews said. "Folks used to say he was a crazy dreamer. Now they say he's some kind of prophet. But you know what he really is?"

"What?" Jack asked eagerly.

"He's an old man with bad teeth," Dr. Crews said, shaking with laughter. "He came to me three years ago in a lot of pain. I did a good bit of work on him. Naturally, he didn't have any money. Said he'd pay me in leases. I knew they'd be worthless, but I liked the old fellow. Had to admire his perseverance. I met a waitress once who had a 1/3000th interest in his well that he'd given her in exchange for a cup of coffee."

Jack found himself wondering what 1/3000th of Joiner's millions would be worth.

"Well, anyway," continued Dr. Crews with the air of a man who knew he had a good story and enjoyed telling it, "Joiner ended up giving me six leases, and they're right there in the same block as Number 3 Daisy Bradford. One has already been drilled by Texoil, who gave me an overriding royalty, and now people are making offers to drill the other five. Trouble is, I don't know anything about oil, and unlike most around here, I'll admit it. That's where you come in."

"Me?"

"I want you to take my old Ford and drive over there. Get yourself a room and stay a few weeks. Get a map and locate my leases. Find out how Texoil's well is doing, how much it's producing. They won't tell me a thing. Find out if there are producing wells around my other properties, what kind of deals are being made. I've got no idea what those leases are worth. I'll pay you fifty dollars a week plus expenses."

Jack hesitated. "Dr. Crews, I'd love to do it, but you've got to understand, I'm no expert on oil."

"I realize that. But you know a little and you're honest. That's good enough for me."

Jack stuck out his hand. "You've got a deal."

"Just one thing, Jack," said Dr. Crews, his genial expression now becoming serious. "Remember, these boom towns can be dangerous. People go a little crazy around oil. You be careful."

Jack left the next morning, thinking it'd take an hour or two to make the short drive to Joinerville, the new boom town at the field.

It took him all day. The roads were clogged once he got within ten miles of the oil field. Thousands of cars, trucks, and horse-drawn wagons were pouring into the new town from all directions. Many of the license plates were from out of state — Oklahoma, Louisiana, Arkansas, Tennessee, and Missouri. News of the East Texas oil boom had given hope to thousands laid low by the Depression. But Jack knew the back roads, and by the end of the day, he'd reached the outskirts of Joinerville. When his car topped the last hill, he gasped in amazement.

Crude wooden oil derricks stretched toward the horizon as far as he could see, appearing more numerous than the pine trees surrounding them. Many derricks were so close together their bases touched, and where there was space between them, it was choked with men, mules, cars, and trucks.

The shantytown, Joinerville proper, still lay some distance away. Jack pulled the car into a stand of trees and set out on foot, suddenly apprehensive. The smell of the black jacks and the murmur of the pine needles in the breeze was familiar. That was East Texas. But the acrid smell of crude oil and the smoke of the countless flares from the gas produced with the oil, each gleaming bright

13

against the darkening sky, was new to him — and frightening.

In one of the jerrybuilt eating establishments, he wolfed down a bowl of chili and a beer. "Ain't this the damndest thing," an oil-soaked man next to him declared. "Sell a barrel of oil for ten cents, and a bowl of chili costs me fifteen! Ain't gonna get rich that way!"

Appalled by the sleazy flophouse in which he had sought a room, Jack tramped back to Doc Crews' car and stretched out on a blanket beside it. He fell asleep wondering whether he was cut out for the oil business.

The world looked infinitely better the next morning. After breakfast he set off in search of a map of the oil field. He passed numerous green-pine shacks touting "Good Deals for Good Leases" and piles of rusty drilling pipe and casing, some being offered in exchange for interests in wells. By midmorning he chanced upon a frame house with a sign that promised "Maps" and where, after a little dickering, he spent ten dollars for one that included Dr. Crews' leases.

Map in hand, Jack trudged the two miles to Dr. Crews' producing well, which was at the edge of a pine forest. A sun-bronzed man in overalls was fiddling with the pipes at the base of the derrick.

"How's she doing?" Jack called out.

The man rose, a wrench in his hand, and stared suspiciously. "Who wants to know?"

"My name is Sanderson. I work for Dr. Crews, a royalty owner in this well." Jack pulled out his letter of introduction.

The man glanced at it, then shrugged. "Don't mean nothin' to me."

"I just want some information," Jack said easily. "How is production holding up?"

The fellow spat tobacco juice at Jack's feet. "I can't tell you a thing, young fella. Texoil people'll be here at six; ask them. Now get on out of here. Visitors ain't allowed."

Jack stepped back, eyeing the man's wrench with respect. From thirty feet away, he studied the well carefully, noting the distance to the offsetting wells on adjoining properties. A flare was burning near each one. Gas was an unwanted byproduct with no economic use and so was piped away from the well and burned.

Jack noted that the flare from the Crews well was bigger and brighter than on the nearby offsetting wells, although all were presumably controlled by the same Railroad Commission quota "allowables of daily production." He examined the pipes that ran out from the Crews well, and he thought he saw signs of an extra, underground pipe in addition to the surface pipe.

"I said to get out of here!" the roughneck yelled. He advanced with his wrench held high, and Jack withdrew.

Back on the shantytown's main street, he saw a sign proclaiming "Geologist." Curious, he glanced inside the doorless shack and found a familiar face. "Hey! Don't I know you from UT?" he cried.

The red-headed fellow leaning over a drafting table looked up. "Yeah, I've seen you around the Geology building. I'm Sam Jackson," he drawled.

"Jack Sanderson. Boy, it's great to see a friendly face!"

Sam Jackson stood up, a rangy, open-faced young man with freckles and a lopsided grin. "What brings you to this hellhole?"

Jack explained his mission. "I'd like to make a structure map of Dr. Crews' leases to give him some idea of their value, but I need a lot more information. At the same time, I'd like to try figuring out why there's oil here when all the experts said there wasn't."

Sam Jackson laughed heartily. "Do that and you'll be a rich man."

"What are you up to?" asked Jack.

"Trying to turn an honest dollar by making structure maps and selling them. I've got a master map, and every time a new well comes in I add the new data needed to contour a structure map of the top of the Woodbine sand, and another showing its thickness. Like you, I'd like to learn more about how to find oil. Sometimes I think I see a pattern as to why there's oil here. Sometimes I think it's all a mystery. Anyway, landowners are buying my map for fifty dollars. Tell you what," he said eyeing Jack speculatively. "New data's pouring in faster than I can handle it. Help me spot subsurface points on my map and I'll give you a print covering the Crews leases and all the help I can."

"Fine with me," said Jack.

"You can start tomorrow morning," said Sam. "Come back at eight tonight and we'll get some dinner."

Jack returned to the Texoil well a little after five to find it deserted. He shouted, "Hello! Anybody here?"

There was no reply.

He eyed the few roustabouts on the offsetting wells a hundred yards away, then quickly ran to the Texoil well and followed the line of fill he had seen earlier, which suggested a buried pipe. The slight rise in the earth, with the grass not yet grown over it, paralleled the surface pipe that appeared to be carrying oil from the well. From the separator, both headed west.

Jack dropped to his knees. If there was oil flowing through a buried line, maybe he could hear it. He put his ear to the ground, but heard nothing.

Suddenly a rough voice said, "Put your hands up!"

The roustabout he had encountered that morning was pointing a shotgun at Jack's chest. Behind him were two other men, one middle-aged in a dark suit, the other about Jack's age, wearing some kind of college letter sweater.

The roustabout jabbed the shotgun two feet from Jack's face. "I said put your hands up," he barked. "And get up."

Jack held his hands up and tried to scramble to his feet, but lost his balance and pitched forward onto his face.

"He can't even stand up," the young man sneered.

"Dammit, boy, get up," said the man in the suit.

The second time, Jack made it to his feet. He kept his hands high and tasted warm, salty blood in his mouth.

"Who are you and what the hell do you think you're doing?" the man in the suit demanded.

"My name's Sanderson. Dr. Crews, a royalty owner, sent me. I'd appreciate your telling that man to point the shotgun somewhere else."

The older man nodded at the roustabout, who lowered the gun so that it aimed at Jack's feet.

"Young fellow, you are a damn fool," the older man said. "People get killed in oil fields for poking their noses into the wrong places. You tell Dr. Crews to write Texoil if he wants any information instead of sending out some dumb kid."

"I'm studying geology at the University of Texas," protested Jack.

The young man in the college sweater laughed. "Teach you to eat dirt there, do they?"

"That's enough, Bill," said the older man sternly. He addressed Jack again, "Get out of here, boy, and stay out. You don't know how close you came to getting yourself killed."

16

Jack was still smarting when he met Sam Jackson for dinner that night. In a crowded tavern, after a few beers and good T-bone steaks, Sam said, "The guy's right. Some of the people here might've shot you. They're all in the hot oil game and would figure you for some kind of government man."

"That's crazy," cried Jack, setting down his beer mug.

"Crazy's got nothing to do with it," said Sam. "We're talking big money. When a man's got a well that will produce a thousand barrels a day, and the state of Texas says he can only take out twenty, what do they expect to happen? That buried line leads to a tank somewhere. Tonight a truck will carry out a load to a refinery in Dallas. Even at a dime a barrel, that's not a bad night's work."

"Then Dr. Crews is being cheated?" said Jack.

Sam snorted, then laughed. "This is no place for righteous indignation, Jack. You're damn right he is."

"What can he do about it?"

"Send a lawyer to the Texoil people, threaten a suit. They'll probably say it's all a mistake and pay him to keep him quiet."

Jack sipped his beer. "Wish I knew the name of that wise guy college kid at the well."

"College kid? What did he look like?"

"Tall. Blonde. Arrogant jerk with a phony eastern accent. He wore some kind of college sweater."

"A 'Y' on it?"

"Yeah, that was it. A 'Y.' How did you know?"

"Must've been Billy Butler himself!"

"Who?"

"Big John Butler's kid. Big John founded Texoil. Didn't you learn anything at school? Anyway, word is that Billy is a spoiled, obnoxious son of a bitch."

"Like to meet him again sometime," said Jack. "Minus the guy with the shotgun."

Jack stayed a month in the oil fields, spending his mornings helping Sam Jackson and his afternoons working for Dr. Crews. By examining Dr. Crews' five other lease sites, he learned that one had been condemned because the Woodbine sand had pinched out, two were being drained by offset wells and should be drilled as soon as possible, and the other two had good prospects.

On his return to Tyler, Jack spent an evening making his re-

17

port to Dr. Crews. He suggested that the dentist not accept an overriding royalty for his lease, but should negotiate for a half working interest in the well, giving him half the profits after payout of drilling and production expenses. He had with him written offers from reputable drillers offering those terms. At the end, the dentist paid not only the money agreed on, but an additional five-hundred dollar bonus. Jack, though terribly grateful, could not help wishing he'd been given a percentage of the production from one of those wells instead. Someday, he vowed, he would get a percentage — or better still, own it all.

He returned to school with a new sense of purpose. Not one man in ten at Joinerville had any idea about how to find oil. Most just poked holes in the ground and hoped for the best. Jack was going to do better than that. He realized that the vast East Texas field had lain undiscovered until 1930 because geologists had not understood that the oil of the rich Woodbine sand would be trapped by its pinchout over the Sabine Uplift. It had been discovered only by chance and its early development had been without scientific guidance. Jack was going to improve on that. In fact, he was going to become the best damn geologist in the business!

3

Ralph

Days that decide your fate do not necessarily seem fateful at the time. To Ralph Harrison, Thursday, May 20, 1976, was a day like any other, except that in the evening he and his wife Anne were giving a formal dinner party at the River Oaks Country Club, their first since becoming members.

Ralph would have been amused, to say nothing about apprehensive, if someone had told him his life was due to change beginning at 5:14 that afternoon. If anyone had asked him, he would have said that he liked his life the way it was. He liked his job as Assistant General Counsel for Texoil, known to oil business insiders as "Bill Butler's company." He was happily married and had two children of whom he was particularly proud. He had a pleasant house on the fringes of Houston's most prestigious suburb. He was a member of the bar in Virginia, the District of Columbia, and Texas. He served on the Art Museum Board, and he and his wife Anne held season tickets to the Houston Symphony and the Oilers.

In actuality, he was beginning to feel stuck in his job, his wife was impatient for his next promotion, he felt he was losing touch with his children, he only went to the Oilers' games because his son loved football, and he had begun to suspect he didn't like Houston.

At five o'clock on this particular day he pushed back the pages of the wearisome oil leases he had been working on, stretched, sighed, and got up reluctantly, wishing he did not have to face Houston's rush hour traffic.

He sighed again, tidied up his desk, then picked up his brief-case. In the outer office he paused to speak to Martha, his secretary. "I'm off," he said and managed a smile. "Will you lock up?"

"Glad to," she said brightly. "Good luck with your party."

"I'm sure it will be fine. Mrs. Harrison is a pro at this sort of thing."

Martha, it would have surprised him to know, had a little crush on him. She admired his quiet good looks, his dark well-tailored suits and striped rep ties, his nice manners, his considerateness. In a city where men prided themselves on their profanity, she had never heard him utter so much as a goddam. Mistaking formality for intimation, she assumed that his wife was cold to him because he always referred to her as "Mrs. Harrison." Being of a certain age, however, she contented herself with mothering him. "You just relax and have fun, hear?" she said, as Ralph headed for the door.

"Thank you, ma'am, I'm sure we will."

The party was particularly important because it was the culmination of four years of adapting to Houston since Texoil had transferred him from Congressional Relations in Washington, and Anne seemed convinced that their social position and his professional future depended on its success. Ralph liked to think that their background and competence counted more than dinner parties, but he had to admit he too was anxious for things to go well that evening.

The express elevator from the top tier of the Texoil Building was crowded, but he spied his immediate boss, Harry Colt, Texoil Vice President for Exploration and Production, who signaled "See you later," as they crossed the lobby.

The air outside was hot and muggy, a nasty slap in the face after the air conditioned office. Ralph was glad the parking garage was only a half block away, and headed for it quickly.

"Ralph? Ralph Harrison?"

He was so intent on beating the heat and traffic that he hadn't noticed the man who had fallen into step beside him. The man was middle-aged with wisps of untidy gray hair showing beneath an old fedora that was pulled down almost to his eyes. Seedy, thought Ralph, and didn't recognize him at first. Suddenly it came to him. It was Chuck Ames, the party chief of the Texoil seismic exploration crew that had shot the Gillette property when Ralph was commuting to Lake Charles, working out the land deal with Maude Gillette. He remembered Ames well, a diffident, eccentric fellow, who was a real genius at seismic work. Ralph had liked Ames, and since he was interested in learning more about how oil was found with the seismograph, he had spent a lot of time with him after hours. He hadn't seen him for years; for reasons Ralph hadn't fully understood, Ames had been separated from Texoil.

"Well, Chuck, Chuck Ames! Hello, how are you? Nice to see you! Are you living in Houston?"

"Oh yes, several years now," the older man said hurriedly. "It's good to see you, too. Listen, I've got something I want to talk to you about. Do you have a few minutes?"

Ralph thought Chuck looked decidedly furtive as he glanced around himself apprehensively.

"I really don't, Chuck — I have to get home. We're giving a party tonight, and I promised my wife —"

"*Please,* Ralph. It won't take long. Besides, I'm afraid if I wait I'll lose my nerve."

Ralph's first thought was that Chuck must want to borrow money, poor devil. He looked at his watch. "Well . . ."

"Half an hour, that's all, I promise. There's a bar around the corner and down a couple of blocks, the Blue Tavern. I'd better go ahead. We shouldn't be seen together."

Ralph hesitated, then followed at a discreet distance, feeling both foolish and curious. It certainly didn't take a half hour to ask for a loan.

The Blue Tavern was a dimly lit bar where office workers dropped in for a drink before heading home. Chuck led Ralph through the noisy crowd to an empty booth at the back. There was a red-checked paper tablecloth and some pretzels in a basket on the table, and a strong odor of stale beer. Seedy, like Ames, thought Ralph.

"Sorry to be secretive," Chuck said when they'd sat down, "but I don't think it would be wise for anybody from Texoil to see you with me. You probably know they fired me."

Ralph shook his head, "No, I didn't. I knew you'd left, but I didn't know the company had any hard feelings against you."

"Oh, they had their reasons. See, I bought royalty under the Bayou Bleu play, when the company was taking leases there. Everyone does it, even if it is against the rules. I was careful, but they found out. The ironic thing is *how*. They were looking for royalty to buy for the Texoil Executive Royalty Pool, and they found a recent sale in my sister's name. That blew it."

"Now come to think of it, there *was* some talk at the time." Ralph frowned. "The way I heard it, they drilled a bad first well at Bayou Bleu on account of the pool owning royalty there. Almost lost the field. But I didn't know you were involved. Frankly, I can't see any difference between you buying royalty and the big boys doing the same. After all, that royalty is supposed to be the landowner's share. Company's supposed to keep hands off. Anyway, what you did couldn't have hurt the company any." He paused. "What a damned shame . . . must have been hard on you."

Ames exhaled audibly, then shrugged. "Well, like I said, Texoil's vindictive. They blacklisted me. No oil company or geophysical outfit will hire me. I've been scraping by by working records for independents now."

Ames' sudden bitterness made Ralph uncomfortable. "Is there anything I can do?"

"Actually, there is," said Ames, "and it could make you a pile of money. I've got a proposition. All I ask is that you listen and if you say no, you keep it quiet. Okay?"

Ralph, thinking "Here comes another of the crackpot schemes Houston's full of," said, "I'd be glad to listen and I certainly won't tell anybody. But why come to me?"

"You're the only man in this business I really trust. And you were the one who persuaded Maude Gillette to give Texoil a lease in the first place. It's too bad you're still with Texoil, but that can't be helped."

Ralph was flattered, but Chuck's appearance, attitude, and general shadiness were still making him uneasy.

"I surely remember Miss Maude *and* her lease," said Ralph. "The production people were all for it, but we ended up with only two small fields at 10,000 feet. Nobody got rich on that deal."

"That's because they didn't go deep enough."

"They took it down to twenty thousand as I recall," said Ralph, puzzled.

"Only one well, and it was badly located. Rather than do the additional deep seismic work I recommended, they decided to save money and deepen a well that had been dry in the shallow sands. This well missed the deep structure because they didn't know the top was further south in the deeper sands. In that area, the sands that could produce oil occur only on top of structures, and these sands were missing where the well was drilled. That dry hole was damned expensive, and it caused a lot of recriminations in Texoil. The chief geologist *had* to believe there were no deep sands at all. He was so committed to that idea that he refused to get a new seis picture of the deep structure."

Ames leaned forward, the tone of his voice was conspiratorial now. "But there *are* deep structures there — big ones that can be mapped down to twenty thousand feet. There are good seismic reflections to this depth, which means there must be sands. In that area, only a bed of sand lying between beds of shale can reflect the sound recorded on the seismograms."

Ralph was worried now. As a lawyer for Texoil's Exploration and Production Department, he shouldn't even listen to what was probably an improper proposal.

"Even if you're right," he said slowly, "Texoil has the lease."

A smile spread across Ames' face and his voice dropped again, making it almost impossible for Ralph to pick out his words amid the din in the restaurant. "Texoil let the lease go. It expired today."

Ralph was beginning to see why Ames had chosen the Blue Tavern. "If they let it go, they must have had a damned good reason," he said, trying to close off the conversation. "They've got a good Exploration Section."

Ames snorted. "Geologists try to cover their mistakes like everyone else. They're on record saying there's nothing there. But I've got information they don't have."

Ralph's inner alarm went off. Industrial espionage was rife in the oil business, but if you got caught in that game, blackballing would be just the start.

Evidently, Ralph's misgivings showed, for Ames said quickly, "It's not what you think. I didn't steal any dope. I just picked it out of the trash basket after they threw it away. Since the records weren't labeled, no one bothered to shred them."

Ralph said nothing.

"I know, I know," said Ames. "It sounds crazy, but it's true."

A harried looking waitress finally appeared to take their order for a cup of coffee and a Bud.

Ralph waited for her to leave before speaking. "Well now, you surely have roused my curiosity, I'll admit. So let's hear the rest of it. I won't say anything, but you have to understand that I do have responsibilities to Texoil. If your proposition sounds improper, I'll swear I never heard it."

"Okay," said Ames, exhaling heavily as he reached into his briefcase and pulled out a dogeared seismic record of the type used years ago. He handed it, carefully covered up, to Ralph, who immediately saw that it was only the end of the record. All the routine data regarding the Shot Point Number, the location, the depth and the amount of charge, the instant of blast, as well as the initial ground wave reception and the early reflected sound waves, were missing.

Reading his thoughts, Ames said, "I had the sense to scribble enough info on them to identify the location and make computations possible."

Ralph had read books on seismic prospecting, which had come out of German efforts in World War I to locate enemy guns by measuring the arrival time of the first sound from the gun traveling through the earth. By using the velocity of sound through the path, the distance of the gun could be calculated. After the war, this technique was adapted by American oil companies, with the help of the Germans, for finding shallow oil-producing salt domes in South Texas and Louisiana. Since sound travels about twice as fast through salt as through the surrounding rock, the first arrival of sound from a dynamite charge that came through salt had a "lead," or faster arrival time. The location of the salt dome, even its depth and dimensions, could be calculated from the seismic data.

Starting in 1928, an improved seismic technique used a small dynamite charge placed in a shallow drill hole, to record sound which went straight down into the earth and reemerged after being reflected from the contact between rock beds of different velocity, usually sandstone and shale. From these reflections, the depth and dip of the reflecting strata could be mapped, showing the structure of the rock beds at different depths. And from these, a geologist could locate traps for oil. Oil being lighter than water, it floats on the water between the tiny grains of a porous sandstone bed and rises over thousands of years to the highest part of the trap, waiting there until it is released by the drill.

"I don't get this, Chuck," said Ralph. "These are tail ends of records. Where's the rest?"

"Believe it or not," said Chuck, "these came from a Texoil trash can. They have the late arrivals of the reflections from the Texoil shooting on the Gillette lease. We mapped the shallow structures from the early arrivals on the same records. In those days, we didn't have those fancy new devices for filtering sound waves and reinforcing reflected energy with computers. When I was working these records for Texoil, I studied them night after night. Sometimes I thought I could see deep reflections coming across, but they were never good enough to convince anyone else. From the beginning, the brass didn't believe there were sands below 10,000 feet on the Gillette lease. None had ever been found in that area. That meant no reflections beyond 2.5 seconds. When I gave my report as party chief, I recommended that we try to get deep reflections below 10,000 feet, but they wouldn't do it."

The waitress arrived with their order. Ames paused long enough to take a swallow of beer while Ralph paid. "I remember the very words of Jerry King, the supervisor. 'There's nothing there,' he said, 'no sands, no reflections. Forget it.' We were packing up to move our office to the next prospect, preparing the records for shipment to Houston. By chance the boxes we had took the records, laid out, only to 2.5 seconds, a little below 10,000 feet. Several seconds of deeper recordings remained on each record. I told King we should get longer boxes, but he just said, 'Cut 'em off,' so I did. The ends were left lying on the floor when the boxes were packed and sent to geophysical storage."

Ames took another swallow. "Well, I can be stubborn myself. I pulled those records out of the trash and took them home. For years, I tried to make some sense out of them. I'd just about given up when I found out about a new computer program on a consulting job. The new method could take the old records and, by reinforcing the reflected energy, make interpretations possible that couldn't be done before. I managed to use the machine in my off-time. It took me weeks, but when I was finished I had an entirely new structural picture. Below 14,000 feet there's an unconformity, a break in the sediments which marks a recession and regression of the old sea. Below this level, I found large gentle structures, domes pushed up by deep-lying salt intrusions. There are at least three enormous structures which should provide traps for oil on the Gillette lands. Because there were good reflections, I know there must be sands. To top it off, I found out that fifty miles west, in Texas, a new deep discovery produced from sand at an equivalent depth. I'm sure the Gillette structures will produce. I've been sure for two years."

Ralph's interest had increased as Chuck's story unfolded. He knew enough geology to appreciate the value of the find. "But why didn't you do something about this before? Why didn't you get someone to try to make a deal with Texoil? While they held the lease to the Gillette land, you had no alternative."

"That was true," Chuck said quietly, "until today. You haven't followed the Gillette lease as well as I have. I've kept track of it all these years. Three months ago, production ran out from the last of Texoil's shallow wells. Your Lake Charles office had no new ideas as to where to drill to hold the lease. Since they failed to make a new location within ninety days, you were forced to reassign the lease back to Maude Gillette. That was done today. It's open. That's why I came to you. I trust you. I know you can get a new lease if anyone can. I want you to get it and get someone to drill a well on my best structure to 14,000 feet, anyone, that is, except Texoil. You know this could make hundreds of millions.

"Because of the way Texoil treated me, I want nothing else to do with them. I can't show anyone else the seismic records on which my map is based — there's too great a risk that Texoil would find out and claim the lease. They'd refuse me any interest, and they might even charge me with theft. You can show the map, but it has to be to someone who has enough confidence in you to accept your word that it's based on good seismic data. I won't show anyone else my records and seismic sections. You know me well enough to reach a conclusion as to whether my work is good. Texoil loses nothing, because I would never under any circumstances let them see my dope. I want $25,000 and 15 percent of the profits from production after payout. You can keep anything over that you can get from whomever you persuade to drill the deep structure. What do you say?"

Ralph applied himself to his cooling coffee before replying. His first instinct was to turn Chuck's proposition down and excuse himself. From a professional viewpoint, he should tell Texoil what he had just heard. They would immediately take the leases again and shoot them for the deep structure. This was certainly the ethical thing for him to do. And then there was the legal side. If Chuck's story were true, he had merely picked up records which Texoil had discarded against his advice. He felt no personal obligation to Texoil, who had fired him, and was determined not to make a deal with them. Unless Ralph told them, Texoil would never know how the deep field, if it was there, was discovered. He had promised Chuck not to tell Texoil if he was convinced the information had been obtained legally, which appeared to be the case.

Ralph knew that he had signed an agreement with Texoil that he would not own oil interests. It might be a technicality, but what he got out of Chuck's deal as an intermediary could be contingent on production being found. It could be only an oral agreement. If the first well was dry, he could forget the whole affair. If production *was* found, it might be so big that he would not have to work again. He stood a chance of making millions; he could resign from Texoil, and who was to know how his windfall came about? It had already crossed his mind how he could provide a cover. Maybe he could even buy back Fairmont, his family home in Virginia.

Nevertheless, he had to admit he was, frankly, afraid. He considered himself an honest man, and accepting Chuck's proposition, if not technically dishonest, would still be unethical, to say nothing of the risks involved. That was it, he thought wryly, the risk, not his undying loyalty to the company.

Finally he said, "Chuck, I'm flattered that you trust me, and I think you've got something here. But I am, after all, a company man, and I've got problems with that. Don't worry, I certainly won't say anything to anyone — but it's going to take me some time to decide whether I'm really in a position to help you. Let's meet here, same time, next Monday?"

"Would you mind coming over to my house instead? It's not that far, and I can lay everything out for you there."

"That'll be fine. Just give me the address."

He sounded a lot calmer than he felt. Take it easy, he admonished himself. No need to start jumping until you see the hedge. He'd have to think this through, talk to Maude Gillette, and Jack Sanderson — Jack would be just the man, with his vast experience and know-how as an Independent producer, his honesty, his shrewdness. And besides, he was a friend. And, of course, he would have to talk to Anne.

He accepted a card from Chuck and shook his hand. "Now I really have to go," he said. "We're giving this party . . ."

"You told me," said Chuck. "Thanks, Ralph. I know I can count on you." By the time Ralph had picked up his briefcase, Chuck had melted into the crowd at the bar.

4

It was Ralph's curse that he *always* saw both sides of every question. One of his law professors had seen this as a talent — "You'd make a hell of a criminal lawyer, Harrison, you could play all the parts," he had said. To Anne it smacked of indecision; she had sometimes called him "Hamlet," not always affectionately. As he climbed into his aging Mercedes, he was seeing himself alternately as hero and scapegoat, riding high on oil millions or out on his ear. At least this was not going to be boring, he thought, addressing himself to the rush hour traffic.

As always, he was offended by what he saw. The ugliness of the details of the surrounding scene was in sharp contrast to the overview he enjoyed from his office on the twenty-fifth floor of Texoil's sleek skyscraper. Along the streets he had to travel were garish signs and dilapidated store fronts left over from the struggling cotton town Houston had been in the twenties. Cars literally poured out of parking lots, and pedestrians crowded the littered sidewalks. Ralph was happiest in the country; commuting rendered him misanthropic.

After a few blocks he turned off Main onto a quieter street. Now there were houses, also leftovers of early Houston, alternating haphazardly with liquor and fast food stores. Houston prided itself on having no zoning; zoning was considered an impediment to progress. Ralph knew that the swarms of newcomers from the small towns along the Gulf Coast, raised in sun-scorched, nondescript wooden houses with paint cracking and planting given up to sea spray, could hardly be expected to rank aesthetics high on the list of considerations — all they wanted out of Houston was a job, a place to live and make money. But he often wondered why those who had grown to power didn't try to improve things for those who hadn't. If he made millions on an oil well . . . Better not think of that while he was driving!

Slowly the view improved. Here, further out, houses had been restored, new ones built. People cared about lawns and shrubbery. Even so, there persisted the ubiquitous corner drugstore or shopping mall, noisy with traffic and gaudy with neon. How did anyone sleep with "Jax Beer" blinking through the window all night? What a contrast to Washington's orderly Mall and the neat strips of eight-story buildings along Connecticut Avenue.

He was homesick. Sometimes he thought he would never get used to Houston. If he made millions of dollars on an oil well, though . . . His mind went back to Virginia.

Two more turns and the shops disappeared. Ampler houses and greener lawns announced the approach to the sacred precincts of River Oaks. The architecture of these homes was eclectic: an occasional colonial, some modern boxes, a good many bogus Tudors, reminiscent of a bygone fad totally out of place in subtropical Harris County.

Just beyond the columns marking the entrance to River Oaks, Ralph turned into the curving drive of a pleasant, two-story, Georgian clapboard. It was not imposing, but as good as they could afford. So far.

It was Anne who had dreamed of living in River Oaks, which had been founded in 1923 by Will Hogg, son of Governor Jim Hogg. With its country club and private school it had been developed under the leadership of Hugh Potter as a residential area largely during the 1940s and early 1950s for the affluent of Houston who valued home and family life. The first houses built were not pretentious, but by 1976 prosperity from cotton and oil had added more and more elaborate mansions. The Harrisons' house was at least on the edge, and Ralph liked it as well as he would ever like anything in Houston, but Anne was ambitious to move up.

He sat in the car for a moment, watching his son John, who was ten, shagging balls with a friend. He knew he should rush in and tell Anne all about Ames, but he was leery. He knew what she would say — "Go for it!" — and he wasn't ready for that. What he had told Chuck Ames was true: he had to think it over, consider every angle. This is the way I am, he thought, for better or for worse.

In the dining room he found his daughter Kate doing her homework, notebooks and texts strewn all over the table. "Hi, Missy," he said. "How's my girl?"

"Terrible. I hate math, Daddy."

"Don't despair. I'll help you with it tomorrow."

"This *is* for tomorrow!"

"Golly, I'm sorry, but you know we're having that party tonight."

"You always have something else." She looked thoroughly dejected, pretty even in her pout, and Ralph was struck simultaneously with wonder and inadequacy — to have a daughter!

"I'm sorry, I really am, but I promise I'll help you this weekend. We'll do a review."

"Daddy, by this weekend, it'll all be over!" she wailed.

"Math is never over," he said, wanting to laugh but not wanting to insult her. "Just do the best you can, Sweetie. That's all anyone can ask. Okay?"

"Okay," she sighed and went back to chewing her pencil.

"Give us a kiss," Anne said as he walked into their bedroom. "You're late!"

"I know, something came up," he said wearily. "I'll tell you about it later. Everything set?"

"I think so. For a while it looked as though we'd lost the Comptons. Brad was up at his ranch and there was a storm, but his office sent his plane up. Everything else seems fine. I went over to the club to check the menu with the chef, and I think you'll like it — good steaks. And I talked to Jones about our table. He's giving us the one in the corner. I have the place cards and the chart — I've got you between Diane Compton and Sue Colt. I think we should put Sue on your right, since she's your boss's wife."

"Sounds good to me. My, don't you look nice!"

She did. Ralph was always proud of Anne, but never so much as when they dressed for a formal occasion. She looked regal in a long gown, her ash blond hair swept back, her customary trace of a smile cool, almost mocking. He liked the way other men stared when they appeared arm in arm, and the way she glanced at him as if they shared a secret. For her sake more than his own, he hoped this party would be a success. She had worked hard to make a place for them in the social life of Houston. From a prominent New York family, she took such things seriously. At thirty-eight she was seven years younger than he, and when she put on a long gown he was strongly aware of that.

"Do I have time for a drink?" he asked, loosening his tie.

"If you have it while you dress. We should get there early so I can put the place cards around and check on everything."

There was a tiny butler's pantry between the dining room and the kitchen which they used as a bar, and Ralph hurried down to make a mint julep. As a Virginian he regarded bourbon as the wine of his country, and a touch of mint and sugar muted the strong taste of the whiskey. Anne always left a few sprigs of fresh mint from the garden for him. He crushed the top tender leaves with his fingers — not the right way to do it, but there wasn't time to soak them properly in the drink in the refrigerator. He put the mint in a silver Jefferson mug, then added a hefty pinch of sugar and ice pounded to snow in an old canvas money bag. The ritual gave him pleasure; he always carried this bag with him when he traveled. He filled the mug with Virginia Gentlemen whiskey from Fairfax County, next to his Loudoun, stirred vigorously until the first frost appeared, then took a long, appreciative swig before carrying the mug upstairs.

He liked dressing for dinner. He wasn't particularly vain, but he enjoyed good clothes, and he always had a well-tailored dinner jacket, his current one being a carry-over from Washington, where formal dinners were more frequent. Even at home he always changed clothes before dining and put on a bright jacket and a fresh tie. Tonight he changed quickly, sipping at his drink as he did so. After applying double brushes to his still thick hair, he reentered the bedroom.

"I'm ready," he said, a smile creasing his face.

"Well, I'm not," said Anne crossly. "See if you can do something about these damned buttons. I can't get hold of them."

She was wearing a new dress by a Japanese designer who worked deftly with silks and chiffons, sliding one over the other. The colors were clear and stingingly bright, and the dress set off Anne's patrician good looks to advantage. She had spotted the dress months before on a model at Neiman's and had known how becoming it would be to her and how much too expensive. So she had sought out her favorite saleswoman and said, "If this doesn't

31

sell and is reduced as much as a third, let me know."

In due time she was notified that the dress would cost her only half the original price, and she had bought it immediately.

"Whatever happened to zippers?" Ralph complained as he fumbled with the tiny cloth-covered buttons and their delicate little loops.

"This dress was made by nimble-fingered Japanese who disdain zippers as the easy way out. Or in and out. I can do the top and the bottom, if you do the ones in the middle."

"Done," said Ralph.

Ann stepped back and twirled. "Well?"

"You're prettier than a field of clover. Are we off?"

"We're off to make our mark on Houston!"

"When you look like that, how can we miss?"

5

Anne

When they arrived at the club, the maitre d' seemed to have forgotten Anne's visit, and showed her a different table, not the one overlooking the wide lawns outside the main dining room, but with a view of the tennis courts instead.

"I'm sorry, Mrs. Harrison. I've gotten myself mixed up today. Accept my apologies, please," he said with a slight bow.

I don't believe you, Anne thought in a burst of fury. You nincompoop, ruining my dinner party! But she knew the man was not stupid, that he knew what he was doing. Someone else, someone more important had wanted her table. She gave him a cold stare, wondering who it was, not wanting to give him the satisfaction of telling her.

"I wouldn't want this to happen again," she said coldly.

"Nor would I, Mrs. Harrison," he answered smoothly.

In the short time she'd been in Houston, similar incidents had already made it clear that, although there were exceptions, Houston's society operated mostly on a blatant power base — not the subtle demarcations of the East, where little nuances of network and background mattered more than money. There, things were measured and changes were slower. Here, everything was out in the open. Now you had money, now you didn't, now you had the table, now someone else did. Anne was inclined to receive this latest evidence as a challenge, not a threat. All she needed to know was who her rival was. Who could be having a more important party?

Mentally, Anne ran down her own guest list. Jack and Janet Sanderson, of course; they had gotten them into the club. Although a generation older, they were perhaps their closest friends in Houston. Ralph and Anne had met them while they were still in Washington.

Doug Blount, the influential owner of the *Petroleum Journal*, and his wife Agnes, were solidly popular in Houston, though Doug's editorials sometimes got Ralph's back up even as an oil company man; Doug was always so blatantly on the side of the oilman, and against government.

Alastair Crane, the director of Houston's Fine Arts Museum, and his wife Sally, were part of the city's chic artistic circles. English-born and Harvard-educated, Crane mingled easily, charming the wealthy into support for the museum. Anne, although herself somewhat aggressive, considered Sally a little too "pushy."

And then there was Harry Colt, Texas A&M, high up in Texoil's Executive Suite, and Ralph's boss. Harry was highly respected among oilmen. And everyone liked Susan, his Texas-little-town wife, for her sincerity and friendliness.

Finally, they had invited Brad Compton and his wife Diane. Brad and Diane knew the other guests but were not close to them. The Comptons moved in a quite different circle. It was small, but its members had not the slightest doubt that they *were* Houston, that it was they who had created and now ruled Houston like a medieval barony. Brad's grandfather had founded Southwell Oil. He had hit a good well at Spindletop and had parlayed it into a small company that he and others had made into a major one. The Comptons, like other descendants of Houston's "big oil," had gone east to school and university: Foxhollow and Smith for her, Hotchkiss and Yale for him.

Although Brad himself had never done much except listen to his financial advisers and nod his head occasionally, he associated himself with the bigness of Southwell Oil. Others did, too, even though most considered him a pain in the ass. In his early years he had "played" around the edges of Southwell, getting information from company geologists as to likely prospects and cutting them in on the royalties he bought. He had developed small "throw away" fields that the company didn't want, but that could still be quite profitable. There were many supply companies doing business with Southwell in which he had managed to gain an interest.

Everyone who wanted Southwell to be nice to them was nice to Brad. He wasn't on the Board, but an uncle was chairman. People in Houston knew where the power was.

When Anne came into the lounge after her tiff with the maitre d', Ralph, who always said he could read her mind through her eyebrows, said, "Anything wrong?"

"Not really. There was a mixup about our table, but it's all right. It won't happen again."

"Why don't we wait on the terrace? I arranged to have drinks served out there."

"Lovely. Oh look, there's Jack and Janet."

"Hey, I'm glad you're first," said Ralph. "Come on outside and let me buy you a drink. After all, if it weren't for you we wouldn't be here."

"Nonsense," said Jack. "You'd have found plenty of other sponsors. Anne, you look lovely, as usual."

"Thank you, sir," said Anne, smiling. Well, and I do, she thought. Wrong table or no, I'm going to have a good time.

Other guests drifted out into the fresh evening air and, provided with drinks, began to create a happy party murmur. Anne kept her eyes open, making sure everyone was included in a conversation. She compared herself to the pet border collie she had heard about, who persuasively nudged a whole cocktail gathering into one corner of a living room. She took as a good sign that Doug Blount had begun expostulating about his favorite subjects, Houston and oil, after one swallow of bourbon. He wasn't tipsy, it was the party starting to work.

Doug had embarked on one of his favorite subjects, the ineptitude of the armchair petroleum experts in Washington. Although those bureaucrats had never found a barrel of oil, they were trying to dictate to oilmen how to run their business. "Pretty soon there won't be enough oil produced to lubricate a watch," he said. "It's a damned shame we can't get a government that understands the businessman!"

He was only interrupted by the late-arriving Comptons. Brad's tie angled to one side and his shirttail looked as if he'd stuffed it into his cummerbund two minutes ago. For effect, thought Anne. She smiled ruefully, thinking that her father had had a word for men like Brad: "blowhard."

"Hey, you all, sorry to keep you waiting," he called, as if the party hadn't started without him. "You wouldn't believe the mess we had up at the ranch, a royal washout. Bridges out, half the cattle stranded without feed — we had to haul in hay with a tractor. No way I could get my car out. Thank God the radio worked. The office sent my Lear up and here I am to tell the tale. How about a drink — ah, there you are," he said, accepting a double bourbon from a waiter who had obviously known him a long time.

"This is like home," he said happily, and waved his hand in the direction of the river. Everyone knew what he meant. Across the river from the club's terrace was a stand of pines that marked the boundary of the 3,000 acre Compton family farm.

"How does it feel to own a view?" asked Anne.

Brad rolled his drink on his tongue. "Good, good. Just recently some smartass offered me fifty million for that land, just mentioning in passing that that included the oil rights. Hell, the minerals themselves are worth more than fifty million. I've shot it, I know how much oil is there, and someday when the price of oil is right I'll drill it up. And when the last barrel is produced, Houston will have more space to grow in. And at a damned good price."

"My husband the philanthropist," Diane remarked drily. "Hello, Anne. What a gorgeous dress!"

"Thank you. Can I get you something to drink?"

"Ralph's coming with some white wine. Or rather, I'll go get it — Alastair has waylaid him, it seems."

Alastair Crane was talking museum, as usual. "Finest pre-Columbian show I've ever seen," he said to Ralph. "The Rotans have given us their Mayan collection, you know. We're having a big opening on the tenth with a super catalogue. I'll send you a reminder. Oh, there's Diane — 'scuse me a minute."

"Get her a glass of white wine, will you? I'm afraid I'm remiss — "

"My pleasure."

Escaping, Ralph drew Anne aside. "I can't imagine what's happened to the Colts. Harry left the office when I did."

"There they are now," said Anne, nodding toward the door.

Harry Colt looked worried. "Hi, fella, sorry we're late," he said quickly to Ralph. "Our Webb Number Two at Sunburst blew out at twelve thousand feet an hour ago. It's a hell of a mess. I've been on the phone getting relief organized. I'm having a telephone conference at midnight. You may have some big suits to take care of."

"Well, that's what we're paid for," said Ralph genially. "We appreciate your coming. Sue — " He kissed her on the cheek. "How's my favorite boss's wife? And what is your drinking pleasure?"

Anne frowned slightly when she heard Ralph offering Harry a mint julep as he led him to the bar. Sometimes she found Ralph's attachment to Virginia way out of place. Of course, Harry declined. Houstonians liked their drinks hard and fast, and her guests were downing theirs briskly. And the drinks were doing their work, releasing reserves and inhibitions, loosening tongues. Anne could sense the pleasure of the group at being together. She knew her party had developed a being of its own, and a tempo that quickened with each empty glass. She was proud to have created it, happy to be a part of it.

Occasionally, Anne guided the conversation around her, but mostly she flowed with it, adding a laugh here, a question there, and complimenting whenever she could. She had heard these tones and enthusiasms before, as a girl at her parents' home. Like New York, Houston was on the move. And the evening was convincing her that she very much wanted to be part of it.

Brad's loud voice shattered her reverie, damning the President and praising Houston's favorite political son, Clark Russell, a lawyer who had been Secretary of Commerce in the last administration. "Old Clark will show them when he gets in the White House," he said. "I'm putting up a hundred thousand for his campaign this year and trying to get everyone else to do as much as they can."

"Good for you," said Colt, leaning forward. "As a company man I can't do much, but I'm for him. We've got to get some sense back in Washington if we're ever going to find more oil. We spend half our time filling out forms. Red tape accounts for most of what it costs to find oil. I'll never understand why those idiots in Washington don't realize that."

Blount joined in. "Bunch of silly bastards. How could the country ever have gotten hoodwinked by them?"

This theme was echoed from voice to voice, heard but not really listened to by the women, who seemed detached from the men's frustrations. The women were animated, flirting a little, trying to please. But Anne knew that was a facade — these women were just as savvy as the men. I like them, she thought, as she walked over to join the group.

"Lord, I'm sick of the Chicken Little syndrome," Agnes remarked as Anne approached, turning her back on the men. "The sky falls forty times a day. It's a wonder they all don't have blood pressure coming out of their ears."

"Brad does," said Diane, "but if it weren't the government, it would be something else. I think they enjoy crying doom."

"Let's let them worry about it," said Anne. "Sally, when do I get to see your new painting? I hear it's quite a departure from your usual style."

"Yes, it is, and high time," said Sally Crane. "I've been in a rut — I was getting lazy. I still want to do abstracts, but I'm trying to paint with more character and structure, using more contrasts of color. I'd love to show you my latest stuff. I'll call you for lunch."

"Great," said Anne, but she didn't really want to lunch with Sally. Sally was too much of a hustler, too obviously "on the make." Everything she did or said seemed keyed to helping her husband's career in the museum and her own in art circles. Of course all the women were supposed to support their husband's professional efforts, but no one did so as blatantly as Sally. Her favorite trick was to corral big name visitors to Houston. Somehow she managed to get control of them and entertain them, to great fanfare in the society pages. "My dear, you must come meet the Gotrocks," she would say, dropping a famous name. "They're coming next month, and I'm planning a little soiree . . ." Her guests were invariably people who might buy, or help her sell, her paintings.

"My husband is giving me the high sign," Anne broke in, waving her hand. "Shall we go in?"

Carrying the last of their drinks, they drifted through the lounge and into the high-ceilinged dining room where the unrepentant maitre d' guided them to their table. They examined Anne's place cards and after being seated, exchanged opening gambits with their dinner partners.

Social reasons aside, it was natural that Anne had put Ralph next to Diane. By coincidence Diane had gone to a fashionable boarding school near Ralph's home in Virginia, and they had known each other there when they both rode in the Middleburg hunt. They had been so young that neither had made much of an impression on the other, but there remained the bond of a shared way of life. They also shared a love of art, and their work on the museum board had deepened their friendship.

"What do you hear from Middleburg?" Diane asked. "I read in my Foxhollow Bulletin that there's been an epidemic of rabid foxes. One of the girls was bitten on a hunt and had to take that dreadful treatment. Do you get back there at all?"

"No, not for years. There's nothing for me to go back to anymore. Family's gone, all the people I grew up with have moved on. Can't blame 'em — there's not much to do in Middleburg but real estate and horses. All that publicity when the Kennedys bought a place there — that didn't change a thing. It takes more than a couple of dignitaries to make an impression on the locals. Thank God!" They both laughed. "How's our museum? I'm afraid I haven't been much help lately. Texoil's a jealous master."

"Don't worry, I'll nab you pretty soon. We're getting ready for our big capital drive, and I'm counting on you to loosen up the oil companies. For all their money, they're a stingy bunch of bastards."

"I'll do my best," said Ralph gallantly.

"If you've got any bright ideas on strategy, I'd love to hear them."

On Ralph's right Susan Colt was talking to Jack Sanderson. Ralph suddenly remembered his encounter with Chuck Ames. I wonder if I should get him aside tonight, Ralph thought. No, this whole Ames thing sounds crazy. Be careful, think it over . . .

"Have you heard from the Simpsons lately?" Jack was saying to Susan.

"The last time Mary wrote, she said they were building a pool house at Cypress Point. Remember where the arbor was?"

"On the river side?"

"Yes. Mary said she's going hog wild, as she put it. She's going to build a Japanese pagoda."

Jack laughed. "That's Mary for you. When did you last see them?"

"Not for over a year. We keep talking about a visit, but something always comes up. I miss that Cajun country. Sometimes I wish Harry had never been promoted to Houston. You and Janet lived there once, didn't you?"

"Before you were born, it seems like. Before the war, when I was with Coastal. I still get down there occasionally because of Bayou Bleu, and I always see the Simpsons. Pagoda or no, nothing really changes. Does Harry miss the life there?"

"You know, he'd never admit it, but I think he does miss getting his hands dirty. It was a good place to start out. I don't think I could have coped with Houston when we were first married. I was just a country girl from Waco! And Harry was the typical 'hard-assed Aggie,' if you'll excuse the vulgarity. Always practical and direct."

"He's always had the reputation of being a real production man," said Jack, "and you know that's a special breed."

"Oh yes. Harry was always the first one up the ladder to the derrick floor when the drill stem got stuck. He used to come home covered with mud."

"Not many make the transition from mud to paper as well as he did."

"I know. I'm proud of him."

Jack noticed that Ralph had turned their way. "Sue and I were just talking about the Simpsons," he said. "Have you heard from them lately?"

"No, but I'll be seeing them in a couple of weeks. I have some business in Lake Charles." This was true enough. It was also true that he would stop in to see the Simpsons, as he always did when he was in the area. And Maude Gillette. It wouldn't hurt to sound her out, whatever he decided to do. After he thought it through, of course.

"Last time I saw them was — oh, March, I guess," said Jack. "Mary was in her usual form, ticking off the latest books and records. Makes even me want to go out and buy a novel."

"Golly, when I remember!" said Sue. "Cypress Point was just heaven back then for us company people. Here were Randy and Mary with degrees from fancy eastern universities I'd scarcely heard of, with the *Saturday Review* and the *New Yorker* on the coffee table — I was terribly impressed. But they always made everyone feel so comfortable."

"You were in Lake Charles too, weren't you, Ralph?"

"Yes, for six months, when I first came to Houston. I was assigned there temporarily to get an important lease for Texoil. I never thought it would take that long or I'd have had Anne and the kids come with me."

"Six months in a good cause," said Jack. "That was the Gillette lease, wasn't it?"

"Yes. But not worth all the time it took, as it turned out."

Indeed, this had been Ralph's first big success with the company. It was then that he had worked with Chuck Ames. Maude Gillette, who was the local dowager and widow of Senator Bob Gillette, owned a hundred thousand acres of the most promising oil land along the Louisiana coast, and it was this land that Ralph had managed to lease.

An hour later, sensing a break in the conversation, Anne got to her feet. "I think we ladies will leave you gentlemen to your brandy. We'll be in the lounge, if you find you can't do without us."

She let the other women go ahead and paused to order after-dinner drinks for the men, then made a detour through the dining room to see who had gotten the table she had wanted.

Her surprise was palpable. The table was occupied by none other than Bill Butler, chairman of Texoil, presiding over a boisterous party of twenty. The sight of him, powerful and confident, glass in hand, rekindled her anger. She glared at him as she passed, and to her extreme discomfort, he turned and caught her at it.

She felt a stab of alarm when he put down his glass, rose, and came toward her. He seemed huge. When he kissed her cheek, his presence blocked out the whole room.

"Anne," he said, "how lovely you look! If I'd realized you were here, I would have invited you to join us."

"It would have been the least you could do," she said, annoyance overcoming awe, "since you took the table I reserved four weeks ago for my own party tonight."

He laughed. "My dear girl, I had no idea."

She was suddenly appalled at her own behavior. He probably didn't know about it, and here she was, making a fool of herself in front of her husband's big boss. But her injured pride was not yet satisfied. "Do you always get what you want, Mr. Butler?" She flavored the question with a smile and a sidewise glance. Damn female instinct! Now he probably thought she was trying to flirt with him.

"Always," he said with a wide smile. "But I wouldn't have inconvenienced you for the world. The dinner arrangements were made by my staff. I'll instruct them in the future to make sure nothing I do interferes with any of your plans. And I'll find a way to make it up to you, I promise. All right?"

"That won't be necessary. You're forgiven," she said primly. As she turned and walked away, her hand brushed against his, shocking her with the exciting tingle that resulted. Must be static electricity, she told herself, regaining her composure before she pushed open the door to the ladies' parlor. She ignored the appraising looks of the other women as she sank into a chair of fine dove-gray corduroy, soft as velvet, and looked into the pier mirror, surprised at her glowing face and sparkling eyes. The door opened and Sally Crane hurried in, a mischievous grin lighting up her features.

"What was that all about between you and Bill?"

Anne smiled. "Just giving the great man a piece of my mind." She paused. "He stole the table I had reserved four weeks ago."

Sally raised an eyebrow. "That's a first. How did he take it?"

"He apologized and assured me it wouldn't happen again."

"Well," Susan Colt sighed. "I do admire you, Anne. Harry's worked for Butler for fifteen years and I'm still scared to death of him."

"Where's Alicia?" asked Diane Compton from the chair next to Anne's.

Sally, who knew everything about everyone important, said, "Off on a trip again. Italy, I think. I don't believe she's been home one month out of twelve for the last four years."

"I doubt he cares," offered Diane. "From what I've heard, Alicia's a cold fish. And he spends half his time in New York anyway. Maybe they meet between planes."

There was an appreciative chuckle. Anne was glad the conversation had moved away from her confrontation with Texoil's chairman. For her it was a private matter, to be thought about later. She sensed, however, that she had made an impression on the man. This was the first time he'd paid any attention to either her or Ralph. Maybe, just maybe, this was her chance to help Ralph in the company, something, she mused, Ralph never would have done for himself.

The men were talking, as they always did, about Houston and the oil business. Ralph had heard it all before, yet tonight he listened with new interest. Jack, Brad, and Harry were all oil men, and Doug Blount made his living observing them and reporting what they did. It came to Ralph that he himself might always be an outsider in this group, almost as much as was Alastair Crane, who was listening politely and probably thinking about how much they could be inveigled into donating to the museum. I deal only with the paper side, Ralph thought; they all deal with the real thing — oil. They've felt it and smelled it and tasted it and gotten dirty with it — black gold, out of the earth. They've actually *found* it, which must be almost more exciting than the money it brings.

Ralph forced himself to concentrate on his guests' conversation, shaking off the persistent memory of Chuck Ames with some difficulty. "It's simple," Jack was saying. "Houston is just a good place to do business in. People here have an instinct for a good deal. It's a question of putting your money in the right place at the right time. Men here know it's better to make a deal, even if you have to give a little, so you can get on with the next deal. If you haggle too long, both parties lose. Business in Houston is not a zero sum game, where one side just takes from the other. It's good because it's to the advantage of all concerned."

Lord, thought Ralph, warmed by the drinks and the obvious success of the party, what would it be like to "make a deal," find oil, to have plenty of money to "put in the right place at the right time . . ."

After some more desultory conversation Alastair Crane was looking at his watch, and the women were coming toward them from across the now empty room. It was past eleven, late by Houston's standards. Harry Colt got to his feet, followed by the others and announced that he had to leave to check on Texoil's troubled well. The other guests joined him in moving toward the door, complimenting Anne, exchanging promises for lunch and dinner.

On impulse Ralph took Jack aside. "I've got something I'd like to talk to you about, something confidential," he said. "Think we could get together next week sometime?"

"We're going up to the ranch on Friday. If you're not doing anything, maybe you and Anne would like to join us for the weekend. Bring the kids, too."

"That sounds fine. I'll check with Anne and let you know," said Ralph.

The Harrisons' first River Oaks dinner party was over.

6

Ralph

On the Sunday after the party Ralph spent the day in his library. He still had said nothing to Anne about Ames, and the longer he waited, the harder he found it to broach the subject. In a sense he was hiding, but in a deeper sense he was doing what he always did when he was uneasy about something — he was browsing through his many books on the history of Virginia. These included Douglas Southall Freeman's six volumes on George Washington and twenty-one volumes of the Princeton papers of Thomas Jefferson. Ralph had read all of them and was proud when he found references to early branches of his family. He enjoyed reading descriptions of historic places he had known since boyhood, even though now encumbered by motels, highways, and antique shops.

Virginia was to Ralph the center of the world. Among the fifty family names of ancestors of which he had records, all except three came from England, mostly of yeoman stock though a fair number were from the "gentry." Dissatisfied with the wars and oppression in England, the first had come to King William County, Virginia, in 1640, seeking a new life.

Eager for more land, the Harrisons had moved from the Tidewater into Loudoun County in the Virginia Piedmont, then a part of Fairfax County, around 1730. There they built a small stone house in the midst of 1,200 acres between the Blue Ridge Mountains, a wispy, whitish-blue apparition of hills stretching beyond rolling green fields to the west, and the Bull Run Mountains to the east. Thomas Jefferson's plantation lay fifty miles to the south, near Charlottesville, where he founded in 1819 the University of Virginia.

The rocky soil of the Piedmont is not rich by Tidewater standards; however, as virgin territory it was well adapted to growing tobacco, and it produced wealth for the Harrison family. They also grew corn and mixed grasses: blue grass, orchard grass, and clover as feed for cattle and horses. The growing prosperity of the Piedmont farmers was reflected in their homes and in the education of their children. This was a natural thing, since there had been no break between their English traditions and the new life they had created in Virginia. Many had come from cultivated English families and had brought with them their household furniture, books, silver, linen, and crockery.

Ralph's family had occupied an important position in Loudoun County. James Harrison had been sheriff of the county and a member of the governing Committee for Loudoun during the Revolution. He had a son named Joseph. In the early days many Virginia families had sent their young men back to England to Eton and Harrow, Oxford and Cambridge, but Joseph's father had chosen to send his son to "Prince Town in New Jersey." The records showed that he had become a member of the college in the fall of 1772 and had graduated in 1776. He married a young lady of Middlesex, New Jersey, and returned to Loudoun County, where he inherited the property of his father in 1791. The couple had two sons and a daughter.

Joseph built a fine residence, Fairmont, the first brick house in Loudoun County. This was the house in which Ralph had grown up. Although it was not pretentious by Tidewater standards, Fairmont was designed with impeccable taste. Joseph had visited Williamsburg often when he represented Loudoun County in the Virginia Assembly. Brick for the house was fired with great care on the grounds, and its Georgian architecture was copied from the residence of the revolutionary leader George Wythe, built in Williamsburg thirty-six years earlier.

The Harrisons had lived in the house that Joseph built from that time until 1947. They were planters, officials of the county, and vestrymen of the Episcopal Church. Their life in Loudoun was close to the soil. Generations of Harrisons had supervised the planting; had bred and ridden horses; and had hunted for quail, dove, and deer. Social life centered in the manor houses of the seventy families of the "gentry" in the area surrounding Middleburg. Harrisons rode to hounds with the Piedmont Hunt, as had Ralph when Diane Compton was at the Foxhollow School. There were hunt breakfasts and hunt balls and elaborate weekend house parties. Guests sipped juleps on the terrace of Fairmont as the sun set over the Blue Ridge. There was a tradition at Fairmont that any visitor would find an open door and the makings of a toddy on the sideboard.

Only the Civil War had disturbed the even tenor of their ways. Middleburg was the scene of bitter guerrilla fighting, led for the South by the colorful Colonel John S. Mosby, but no large-scale engagements took place there. Northern raiders had been ordered to take the animals and burn the barns but spare the manor houses, so the end of the war found Fairmont almost intact. The Harrisons by then were poor, but they still had their land and they still had 300 years of unbroken Virginia tradition.

Ralph's family consisted of his parents and his younger brother Josh. Henry Harrison had married late and his weather-beaten face reflected years of outdoor life, supervising his farm and riding to hounds. He was the prototypical Virginia gentleman — soft spoken, courtly, polite. No one had ever succeeded in going through a door behind him.

Miss May, Ralph's mother, was not beautiful, but she had a powerful personality and was known far and wide for her wry wit and enthusiasm. From an old Richmond family, she had met Henry when he was in "The University," and it was she who provided the spark for the family. Whenever Miss May was there, people said admiringly, "There was a party." It was she who saw to it that guests were always offered one more drink for the road. The boys adored her.

Since it had six hunts within "hacking" distance and was the home of the horse breeder's bible, *The Chronicle of the Horse*, Middleburg considered itself, perhaps overambitiously, "The Horse Capital of the World." Ralph and Josh had, as had all youngsters in the Middleburg community, started riding at three. At six they were jumping, and at nine they had gone on their first hunt. Once a week in summer they practiced their riding and competed for prizes in the Pony Club run by the mistress of nearby Foxhollow School.

One October, when Ralph was sixteen, breakfast was early because it was a special day — the beginning of the cub-hunting or "cubbing" season. The purpose of the hunt was to teach young hounds how to chase foxes, particularly to teach the young foxes, called cubs, to run in front of the hounds. Not many adult hunters went, but all the youngsters did. The hunt started at Fairmont at eight in the morning.

"Now you boys take good care of yourselves," their mother admonished them. "Watch your form. Don't get ahead of the field, and obey the Master. Take good care of the young hounds. They need to learn a lot about how to find and chase the cubs today; they'll be hunting them as grown foxes next year.

"Hold your heads high and never forget you're Harrisons of Virginia, and that you must always be a credit to your family. 'Deed you must. Ralph, you look fine in that new hunting outfit. Josh, you'll have one next year. Sorry your father and I aren't going with you, but this is young folks' day."

"Look! The first riders are coming up the road," Henry cried. "Let's get the sherry and cookies out for them and give them a good sendoff."

After a good start over the jump by the lake, the pack had circled an oak wood and turned north toward the neighboring Windrush Farm, which they entered on their second jump. Three of the young hunters couldn't make this and had to open the gate. On the other side they picked up a cub that didn't last long. After that they picked up a mature fox that led them a merry chase all the way to Goose Creek. The hounds finally got their fox, and the youngest hunter was given the honor of being "bloodied" with its blood. But since it was the beginning of the season, the hunters and hounds were not in shape, and all turned toward home around ten.

"Race you to the first barn," said Josh to Ralph as they entered Fairmont by the East jump. It was nip and tuck until after the last jump, when Ralph edged him out. "For that you can help me with my saddle, upstart," said Ralph, secretly admiring how well Josh had ridden.

They rubbed down and hand curried their ponies, Ralph's a fine young Arabian called Alashan that he had ridden since he was ten. "I sure do like hunting," said Josh. "It's super, 'deed it is. I can just feel my pony trying to get at that fox."

"I like it too," said Ralph. "I'd never like to live any place except Fairmont. I've been thinking, though. In a couple of years I'll finish Hill School and I have to start planning my future. I liked working with Uncle Charles in his law office in town this summer — made me think I might become a lawyer. If you're a lawyer, you can help settle a lot of people's problems. And you could still ride and hunt on weekends, even if you had to live in Washington." Saying this to Josh made it seem not only possible, but inevitable. Later he would remember it as the moment he made his first mature decision, one that shaped his life and those of all the others.

A few weeks later his father brought the subject up with Ralph while they were out counting the heifers in the south field. "Son, your Uncle Charles was talking to me about how well you did last summer. He says he even used some of the briefs you wrote with hardly any change. I'm right proud of you, boy. Maybe you'd like to study to be a lawyer. I've always hoped you'd follow the family example and go to The University. Why don't we drive down there next week and look it over?" They did, and Ralph's decision was confirmed. Two years later he entered the University of Virginia in pre-law.

Ralph had always felt completely at home in Charlottesville. It was still Piedmont. The same Blue Ridge Mountains were only six miles away. The university was part of his family tradition; he belonged there. As a matter of course, he joined his father's fraternity (the best) and formed the casual friendships which were comfortable to him within the safe circle of "brothers," one of whom was a distant cousin, two others sons of family friends. He avoided the more aggressive sports, but went out for tennis, winning a letter in men's doubles in his senior year. He applied himself to his studies with a true enjoyment which he found it politic to disguise as dutiful diligence among his peers, and was rewarded with the editorship of the Law Review in his second year of law school. It was not in his nature to make an effort to become a leader, but he won a reputation as an excellent student who was also a good sport.

He dated girls whose brothers he knew and whom he had known at home, none seriously. He knew he was not ready for anything serious.

During his last year of law school, Ralph fulfilled his ambition to live on Mr. Jefferson's version of an Oxford quad — the Lawn. He didn't mind the austerity of his cubicle, with its wood fire. It looked out on a spacious greensward bordered by Jefferson's stately white columns, with the view of his Rotunda beyond. The head of the law school lived in the Pavilion next door. He often sat with Dr. Hoskins on his second story porch, sipping bourbon in the setting sun.

"You've done well here, Ralph," said Hoskins, "but I don't feel you have the 'fire in your belly' to do much with the law. Some go on to be a judge, or run for political office, or go into business. Or you could just find a quiet niche in the legal bureaucracy turning out tidy briefs for a Richmond law firm, or working away in a small town solving the unending little legal problems of the average people there. What's the story? What do you really want to do?"

"I don't know, sir," said Ralph. "I don't believe I'm all that ambitious. I see the law mainly as a means of earning a livelihood, and raising a family in a country setting like I've always been used to. I really would prefer a career that led to a quiet, orderly life, and at the same time make some contribution to society. I'm not very competitive or aggressive, I know that."

But Ralph's even tenor of life was not to last long. In the middle of the first term of his last year his mother died, without warning, from a heart attack. Ralph was shocked and shaken. He had never fully realized how much his own confidence in himself had depended on Miss May's strength. He was even more shaken by the effect of her death on his father. He was drinking and he seemed to have lost his grip.

Ralph's father tried to put up a good front, but when Ralph and Josh came home for Christmas it was evident that Henry couldn't carry on alone. Josh volunteered to help his father run the farm, which wasn't producing enough to keep both boys in college — a move they all insisted would be temporary. Ralph protested that he should drop out too, but it was obvious that he was too close to finishing to interrupt his studies now. Unless he earned his degree, he wouldn't be able to help later.

"Don't worry a bit, boy," his father said. "Josh is going to drop out just for a while to help me over a bad spot. We're going to train hunters for some of our friends here. The Bolands have already given us an order for two for the fall season. Why, we'll be back on top in no time. Fairmont will be booming."

But when he graduated in June and his father walked back to the Lawn with him, he found Henry had been covering up. They sat in Ralph's little room with a bottle of bourbon and Henry told his sad tale. Without Miss May the house had become run down.

Despite Josh's help, so had the farm. One of the best hunters they had in training had hurt a leg and had to be put down. To keep the boys in college Henry had secretly borrowed from the Middleburg Bank. Times were bad, and when his note came due the bank foreclosed; now they had found a buyer. The Harrisons were to lose Fairmont.

Ralph knew, of course, he would have to get some sort of job, perhaps in Washington if not Richmond. But he was burdened with the grief that because of him, because the cost of his education had forced his father to borrow, Fairmont, seat of his family for almost two hundred years, had been lost, as far as he knew, forever. Ralph felt as if his umbilical tie with Virginia, and with his family, had been broken. His deep feeling of guilt shook his confidence just at the time he had to start a new life. And deep inside he resolved to get Fairmont back some day.

The week after graduation he moved into Washington, checked in at his father's club, and started looking for a job. In the years that followed he visited Middleburg twice, when his father died of a stroke, and again when Josh was killed in an automobile accident. After that he pledged never to return to Fairmont unless it could be his.

7

Anne and Ralph

Anne pried Ralph out of the library for dinner, and after the children had gone up to do their homework she said, "Let's have coffee out on the patio."

"I just don't see how you can spend so much time digging around in those old tomes," she said a few minutes later, setting cups and saucers on a tray.

"I'll have you know, ma'am, that those 'old tomes,' as you so elegantly put it, contain the history of my family."

"They wouldn't if your ancestors had spent as much time reading them as you do." Unfortunately, this didn't sound like the joke she had intended. Ralph's mouth tightened and he looked away from her, but he got up and followed her outside. "I'm sorry," she said quickly, thinking she'd been saying that far too often lately. "It's just that I don't understand how you can spend so much time — "

"Wallowing around in the past?" Ralph sat down and accepted a cup of coffee. "There are worse vices. Besides, there's something very satisfying about keeping in touch with the past. It makes me feel real, somehow, part of something permanent."

"I can understand that," she said quietly. "What worries me is that sometimes I think you prefer it to real life. Life here, in Houston."

"Houston's all right."

"But not like Virginia. You really don't like Houston, do you?"

"I can't say I'd like to die and be buried here."

"It was your decision to come, don't forget." She sounded defensive.

"I thought we decided together."

"Well, you *were* at a dead end in Washington."

He sighed. "I'm not saying it wasn't a good move." He remembered her excitement when he had broached it to her; how he had envied her anticipation when all he had was a sense of dread, a fear of failing. "And don't misunderstand me — I like it fine. It's just that it's so . . . different, so energetic, so mixed up. It won't stand still long enough to have its picture taken. Do you think we made the right decision, coming here? You know, we've given up a hell of a lot, a whole way of life, and friends with backgrounds like ours who think the way we do. Houston is just plain different from Virginia and Washington and New York, more different than they are from each other. This place is so sprawled out. It has all the disadvantages of a city and few of the advantages."

"What do you mean?" said Anne uneasily.

"Houston has just grown too damned fast to sort itself out. In Virginia and New York our families knew where they stood! The pattern of our life was made for us. Everything was orderly. Here in Houston no one knows where anybody stands, except by how much money they have. The city is a mélange. People from the same backgrounds are scattered all over the suburbs. You get your neighbors by chance. Your social life is completely haphazard."

"But there are clubs," protested Anne. "We've been admitted to River Oaks. We know a lot of people there."

"But the clubs are all full and have long waiting periods," said Ralph. "River Oaks has less than a thousand members. It took us three years to get in! At least in this neighborhood most people are well off, so there's the beginning of some common ground. But even here people often have such different backgrounds and outlooks. Take that fellow down the street who tried to sell me an insurance policy. No matter where you go you run into someone vulgar or pushy or both. You have to be constantly on the alert. In Washington the people we knew were all pretty much alike. You could relax with them." He paused to sip his coffee, then said softly, "I'm a country boy, remember. I like things to go slowly so I can think them through." I should tell her about Ames now, he thought.

"Stand still, you mean," Anne said.

That annoyed him. "There's something to be said for stability."

"Yes. It's dull. Houston's on the move, it's mixed up because it's seething with ideas, it's fun! People are looking to the future, not the past!"

He looked at her for a long moment, her ready smile — like The Last Duchess, she smiled for everyone. "I sound like an old fogey, don't I?" he said.

"I didn't say that. It's just that I wish you were more — "

"Interesting?"

"No, no, don't put words in my mouth. It's just that you're so . . . reserved. You don't put your best foot forward. I'm always afraid people don't appreciate you. At work, for instance."

"What about at work?"

"I don't know, I just wonder where you're *going*. It's been three years since your last promotion. Maybe it's time you did something, said something . . ."

"There's not much I can do except the best job I know how."

"But that's what I mean! You do such a good job nobody notices!"

"You don't understand, Anne. There's only so much I *can* do as a Texoil attorney. It's an oil company, after all, and though I've learned to talk a good line, I'm just not an oilman like Jack or Harry, and I never will be. I don't have the background."

"Darling, I'm not complaining. I love you, and I know you're a good lawyer and good at your job, and you take wonderful care of us. I should be perfectly satisfied, and it's probably a flaw in my character that I'm not. But we're still young! I just wish . . . I just hate the idea that we're standing still, treading water, while other people with less talent and brains are doing the Australian crawl and grabbing the brass rings!"

He had to laugh, and after a moment she did too.

"Mixed metaphor," she admitted.

"Very mixed. But you're right, as usual. I know I'm inclined to take things as they come. I'm sure if our roles were reversed you'd be cracking a whip around Bill Butler's ears, demanding a piece of the action."

"As a matter of fact, I did."

"Did what?"

"Cracked a whip around Bill Butler's ears. He was the one

who took our table Thursday night, and I told him what I thought about it."

"My God, when was all this?"

"On my way to the lounge, after dessert. I was going to tell you about it, but I was afraid you'd disapprove. I went right by the table and there he was, so I gave him a dirty look and he got up and came over."

"What did he say?"

"He was very abject, apologized all over the place, said he didn't know anything about it."

Ralph could not picture Bill Butler as "abject."

"He said he'd make it up to me," she went on. "This is the kind of thing I mean — I could help you, you know. It's time he knew who you are. There's more to business than the board room. Maybe we should give another party and invite him."

"I'd be careful of that. Butler's a tricky man. Dangerous, even. I'm not sure getting together socially is a good idea."

"Oh, Ralph, don't be so timid! He was perfectly charming. I don't know why everybody's so scared of him. He's probably sick of people licking his boots."

"Maybe," said Ralph. "On the other hand, he may enjoy it. He's also known to enjoy women other than his wife. You have a tendency to oversimplify."

"Oh? Well, you have a tendency to hesitate. Maybe that's why you're where you are — you're afraid to take a chance."

That stung. How had they gotten into this from a little casual conversation about his preoccupation with the past?

Anne was wondering the same thing. She was shocked at herself for having hurt him, but at the same time she knew she would have said this sooner or later. She jumped to her feet and walked to the edge of the patio. With her back to him she said again "I'm sorry," but it sounded as if she weren't.

Ralph took a gulp of cold coffee and waited. He never had to wait long. Anne could not abide rifts between them and rushed to patch them whenever they occurred. But as the silence continued he became increasingly uneasy, and the thing that was bothering him coalesced and became Chuck Ames.

Finally he addressed her stiff but graceful back, nonetheless. "Funny you should mention hesitation. Something happened last week I should have told you about before now. But in my own defense, sometimes hesitation is a good thing. A man with a wife and children can't afford to take risks."

She turned and came over to stand in front of him. "I know, I know," she said softly. "I'm sorry I said that. I love you and I wouldn't have you any other way — I guess! Now, what happened?" She drew her chair closer to him and sat down.

"Someone propositioned me."

"Anyone I know?"

"A business proposition. Do you remember Chuck Ames? Actually, I don't think you ever met him. I knew him when I was working on that Gillette lease. I ran into him on Thursday, or rather he made a point of running into me. He caught me on the way to the car and inveigled me into having a drink with him, and he told me the damndest story . . ." He quickly elaborated Chuck's proposal. "Mind you, I haven't seen his data, but if by chance he's got something solid, it could mean getting in on the ground floor of something big, and without putting up any money or taking much of a risk."

"Let me get this straight," said Anne slowly. "He thinks there's a lot of oil deep down on the Gillette land that Texoil knows nothing about?"

"That's it in a nutshell."

"And all you have to do is take up the lease that Texoil dropped?"

"He also wants me to arrange for digging a deep well."

"And you get a big share of the profits?" Anne inhaled sharply.

"Now, wait a minute, ma'am, this is a little like putting a blue chip on number twenty-two on the roulette wheel. Nobody knows whether there'll be any profits. That's the oil business — you never do know. I mean, look at Texoil — they're sure there's nothing there."

"Yes, but you said they never looked at the tail ends of the records the way Chuck did."

"As I said, the supervisor threw them out. That was Jerry King. I knew him — a hard-headed son of a gun. I think he's in Venezuela now — "

"*Ralph!*"

"What?"

"I don't know what you're waiting for! You said you don't even have to put up any money."

"Well, no, but I haven't seen the records yet."

"But you *are* going to see them?"

"Yes, after work tomorrow."

"Do you think you can tell anything?"

"I'm no expert, but I've picked up enough to know whether they're the real thing or not. But it still raises a lot of questions."

"Ralph, do you hear yourself? But, but, but! Here someone has just dropped this wonderful idea in your lap and you're not even sure you're going to do anything about it, are you? *Are you?*" she shouted.

"Look," he said slowly, trying to keep a firm rein on his anger, "it's not quite as simple as you would like to think it is. Please give me a little credit for at least knowing more about this than you do. You are forgetting one important fact — I'm a Texoil employee, a company man. By all rights I should go to them and tell them to renew the lease. I'm withholding information. People have gone to jail for less."

"But you said legally there was nothing wrong!"

"Technically, I don't believe there is."

"Well then, what are you worried about?" she challenged.

"Have you ever heard of ethics?"

"*Ethics?* With Texoil? Look what they did to Chuck Ames! You call that ethics?"

"Listen, damn it, if Texoil found out I could lose my job? They could see I never got another job with an oil company, possibly have me disbarred! But look here, what are we fighting about?" said Ralph sadly.

"We're not," Anne said quickly. "We're on the same side." She shrugged. "Whatever you decide is all right with me." But if he doesn't go for it I'll never forgive him, she vowed.

Why *do* I hesitate? he thought. She wouldn't. Not for a minute. "Come to think of it," he said smiling at her, "it does seem to be a risk worth taking, doesn't it?"

"You mean you'll do it?"

"I'll do it *if* it looks promising after I've seen all the evidence."

"Oh darling, I know it will! I feel it in my bones. And when we get all that money, I'll throw a party and reserve the whole dining room at River Oaks, and we won't ask Bill Butler!"

"Oh, we could ask him — then seat him next to the dining room door," he chuckled.

8

Ralph

The next day Ralph went to work with little on his mind but Ames. He prided himself on being early, but as usual Martha, his secretary, had gotten there first.

"Good morning," she said. "How was the party?"

"Fine, just fine," said Ralph. "Everybody seemed to have a good time and nobody got drunk."

"You have a message to call Mr. Pickering."

As Martha got Pickering's secretary on the line, Ralph prepared to wait the requisite three or four minutes which was considered proper by most bosses, or at least bosses' secretaries. Ray Pickering was Texoil's Chief Counsel, and as such Ralph's immediate supervisor.

"Ralph, you're in early," said Ray, sooner than Ralph had expected.

"Not as early as you, sir. What can I do for you?"

"Other way around, Ralph, other way around. Hope you don't mind a last minute invitation, but are you free for lunch? I've been meaning to set this up with you for some time, and I've just had a cancellation."

"Let me look at my calendar," said Ralph, who had been planning a quick snack in the cafeteria. "Let's see — yes, I'm free."

"Good. See you in the Executive Dining Room at 12:30."

Suddenly all thoughts about Chuck Ames took a backseat to this latest development. Ralph had had lunch with Pickering three times in seven years: once when he was hired and twice when he received promotions. He had climbed about as far as he could in his division, and though he wouldn't admit it to Anne, he himself had begun to feel stuck.

An ironic coincidence seemed to be shaping up, Pickering with a Texoil proposal at noon and Ames' proposal, which seemed increasingly tempting, after work. He had thought his mind was made up the night before, but now he realized he still wasn't sure of what he should do. Perhaps Anne was right — he *was* afraid, and not just of the specific risks involved, but of change, any change.

Pickering's manner had hinted at favorable developments concerning Ralph's future. Ralph had been hoping for something like this ever since Texoil had transferred him to Houston.

He had enjoyed his work with Texoil. He was by instinct a true professional; he was conscientious and he set high standards for himself. His transfer to Houston had made him think that Texoil was grooming him for something important. Indeed, over the years Ralph had become a good lawyer. Salary increases and hints of more to come had made this clear. This was important to him, but beyond his own achievements he respected the "majesty" of the law itself.

Ralph was proud to be a member of a profession that helped create order out of man's chaos. Within its terms of reference the law comprised a complete and satisfying system. To Ralph, it reflected the rigor and tidiness of the human mind in man's search for justice. In a sense, subject matter was irrelevant. He was pleased to be a part of the legal process and to be able to contribute to it.

Business, however, Ralph considered a different affair. When his legal work involved him in business deals, he found it much less satisfying, even distasteful. The office was often a cruel place. Harsh things were said. Men could be inhuman, insensitive to the feelings of their fellows. Competition could be ruthless. To Ralph, business in the modern era seemed pretty much a "dog-eat-dog" affair. Everyone was out for himself. Money was everything, money was power. Ralph admired many of his associates and tolerated all of them, but the process of "pulling and hauling" that was called business was not to his liking. It was different from the law.

He and Pickering lunched in the senior executives' penthouse dining room, normally restricted to the half dozen of Texoil's top command and their guests. Ralph usually ate in the junior executives' room below, whose clientele numbered some thirty. Although he had been in the penthouse before, the dramatic view through the fifteen-foot-high glass panel still awed him. Half of Houston lay below. The left foreground was dominated by a glistening, pink, glass-sheathed building of equal height. To the right was the prize-winning, dark glass, double trapezoidal Pennzoil building. The new, square Shell building, which had cost $200 million, lay to the left.

The view from Pickering's table, near the big table Bill Butler normally occupied, looked out beyond the business district, over the slums and older residential areas of the city, to the park-like wooded enclaves of the wealthy. In the far distance lay the precisely laid-out middle-class suburbs, as treeless as the prairie. The view gave Ralph a false sense of power, as if being able to look down on the city gave him control over it. He wondered if the top Texoil executives might not feel the same way, and if such a feeling could be a dangerous illusion.

Over daiquiris, Pickering asked routine questions about Ralph's work involving purchases, leases, and drilling deals. Ralph was the expert in this area, but was always subject to review by Pickering. Intensive exploration along the Gulf Coast in recent years meant that the larger, more profitable fields had already been found, and Texoil now purchased more oil than it discovered. The difference in cost per barrel was not great, and purchases were fast becoming almost the only way for a company to add substantial reserves.

For the small company, a sale of oil in the ground permitted it to get off the income-tax avoidance treadmill, the marginal tax was at its high point, 92%, and realize cash through the favorable capital gains tax which was at that time only 50%. The leases from landowners, which provided the oil company the right to produce these reserves, were the principal assets purchased. Since Ralph was responsible for assuring the land titles were good, his role was an important one. He had just completed acquisition by Texoil of a mid-sized producing company, Southwest Oil and Gas.

During the shrimp cocktail, Ray said, "I can't promise you anything today, Ralph, but I'd like to tell you about an interesting possibility that may open up. Colt thinks highly of you, and I've been impressed with your work, too. You've got a good grasp of the broad issues as well as the legal details. And we both know that many a deal has been won or lost on the fine print." Pickering smiled with the air of a man pleased with his ability to coin apt phrases. "Bill Butler and the top brass have been pleased with your work on Southwest Oil. Finding the flaw in the title of the Williams lease helped shave Southwest's price and, as you predicted, we were able to cure the title."

Pickering paused to sip from a glass of white wine, an Auslese Moselle. Ralph did the same, enjoying its fruity flavor and wondering what it cost. Pickering continued, "There'll be an opening soon for my principal assistant. I plan to take early retirement as soon as someone is ready to assume my place. It may be a year or several, but the idea is, if all goes well, that my assistant will succeed me on the Texoil Board. That would be quite a plum for a man your age."

Pickering paused and smiled, but before Ralph could comment, he went on, "You should understand that the work would be quite different from your present responsibilities. You'd be operating on a completely different level, weighing political as well as legal considerations. Texoil's chief counsel is also Bill Butler's personal lawyer. And Bill's interests go far beyond Houston and the oil business. He operates on Wall Street and with the New York banks, where they would sacrifice their mother for a half a point of bond interest. As you know, he and I spend a lot of time in the New York office. As vice president for finance, Jed Cullom has primary responsibility for our dealings with the banks, but I have to approve the SEC statements and the bond indentures."

At that moment, the filet mignons arrived. With well practiced efficiency, the waiter refilled their glasses from the bottle sitting in its caddy nearby. Between mouthfuls, Pickering talked on. "Whatever Bill wants to do, he's always right. My job isn't so much to tell him he can't do it as to find a way he can without his getting into trouble. Sometimes I get a chance to advise beforehand, but more often I have to come in after the fact to pick up the pieces. More than once, I've had to stretch the law." He looked at Ralph as if trying to gauge his reaction. "Occasionally, Bill's personal matters are involved, and that's not always pleasant."

The coffee arrived and Ralph busied himself by adding cream and sugar. With what he knew of Butler's reputation for womanizing and high living, he could well imagine the unpleasantness. He looked up and found Pickering watching him, as if expecting a comment. Long ago Ralph had learned that well-placed silence was often more effective than words. He looked back and waited.

Pickering's expression indicated that he appreciated Ralph's wisdom. "I don't have to tell you about our interests with the federal regulatory agencies and Congress. You've worked in Washington and you know what that's all about. But the game has gotten a lot rougher. Since we lost the 27.5 percent tax depletion fight, we've doubled our efforts on every issue affecting the oil industry. Bill being head of the American Petroleum Institute helps, and Wilf Jones has led our lobbying activity ever since he resigned his Texas House seat. We try to anticipate every fact and figure our friends in Congress might need, and we have a horde of researchers to see they get answers that put the oil industry in the best light."

As their waiter cleared the table and refilled their coffee cups, Pickering let out a sigh. "Of course, we don't buy anyone. It wouldn't be proper." He paused. Then, as if remembering he was talking to one of his own, or maybe just assured that the waiter couldn't hear, he added, "Besides, it's too risky. We don't want a repeat of the Eisenhower era gas bribery scandal. But we do make substantial political contributions. Bill's active in Republican politics and our Political Action Committee funds go to friends of the industry. And this means friends as demonstrated by votes on the floor, not because of their political party or professed philosophy."

Buying politicians is out, thought Ralph. Leasing them is in.

Again, Pickering dropped his voice, his manner conspiratorial. "It doesn't hurt to take care of the creature comforts of our government friends, either." Pickering looked around, as if he was imparting a secret which not all the inner circle shared. "That's why we have Greenfield Farms near Warrenton, Virginia, as the country club of the Texas delegation." He cleared his throat and resumed a normal conversational tone. "Right now, we have a real knockdown, drag-out going on in Washington to save tax deferral, which saves us tens of millions a year on interest during the period of delay. In Austin, we have another fight to stop a threatened severance tax for gas. Austin is more primitive than Washington. Votes are easier to control, and we know whom we can count on. I'm sure we'll beat the severance tax increase all right."

Ralph sipped his coffee. As described, the functions of the chief legal counsel seemed to him to involve not just law but business, politics, and legal babysitting. Advancement in the corporation would mean frequent conflict with his personal principles, Ralph realized. Still, that's where the big money was, and the company was certainly doing as much for him as he had a right to expect.

Pickering leaned back in his chair. "Well, I've done a lot of talking. What do you think?"

Ralph fixed Pickering with a steady gaze. "Well sir, I am flattered to be considered for such an important position, 'deed I am. I'm glad to know my work is appreciated. I like Exploration and Production fine, but I'm no engineer and I've always known my future there is limited. This position you're describing sounds very challenging. I've always liked working with you and I'd welcome the chance to learn something about other aspects of the oil business." Ralph paused, not so much for effect, but because his next statement, which he thought was required, did not reflect his real feelings. "I pride myself on being a realist. I don't believe you or Bill Butler would get into anything that would trouble my conscience."

Pickering smiled over the rim of his coffee cup. "Of course, there'd be a substantial increase in salary. We're not blind to the fact that headhunters are everywhere. At your age, you're a prime target. As you know, we have a very comprehensive program of executive incentives: bonuses, stock options, retention payments, and extra bonuses tied to long term company growth. There's another sweetener, but I'll let Bill tell you about that when he's ready." Pickering winked. "A little royalty can be a good thing in your old age."

Not if that's all you got, thought Ralph, remembering Chuck.

Pickering rose and Ralph followed suit, saying "I'll certainly think about what you said and talk it over with Anne. And when it's time to get specific, I'll have an answer for you, sir."

Perhaps it was his imagination, but Ralph thought that some of the other company officers looked up and smiled at him as he passed. He liked the attention. Also, he was looking forward with relish to the expression on Anne's face when he told her they now had a choice.

The meeting, however, only served to confuse his feelings about meeting Chuck Ames. Ralph had always been a company man, and Texoil had been good to him. It wasn't really right for him to help rob it of an oil field, even one it had stupidly thrown away. But Anne's words about his hesitation echoed in his memory. And, as the lunch with Pickering suggested, being a company man would become more distasteful as he moved up the corporate ladder. A share in an oil field offered an alternative. Didn't he owe it to Anne and the kids to try? And to himself, for that matter.

But he still had to find a way to participate in the deal with minimum risk to his job. One or two ideas were already forming as he drove to Chuck Ames' place after work.

Ralph found Ames' boxy, white clapboard house sitting between a TV repair shop and a gas station. Like all Houston houses of the period it had a front porch, held up by four-by-four posts, broad enough to accommodate sleeping pallets, as was the Houston custom in the hot summers. Despite the commercial surroundings, the yard was pleasant and shady, with colorful flower beds attesting to hard work and care. Ames must have mowed the lawn, recently, judging from the long rows of cuttings.

Bess Ames, a trim, cheerful woman, answered the door. Her hair was all gray now and her face more lined than Ralph had remembered. The house was small and the furniture old and scarred from countless moves, yet the place was spotless and homey, giving off a warmth that made Ralph feel comfortable at once. Chuck was a lucky man, he thought, despite his financial misfortune.

Over a bottle of chilled burgundy, which had been ceremoniously produced to mark his visit, Ralph answered questions about the doings of various people within the company. Obviously the Ames' had not been able to maintain the friendships they had formed during their twenty years with Texoil. Houston was a company town, and Ralph suspected that many of their old friends were scared to be involved with Texoil outcasts. He felt sorry for them and apprehensive that the same fate might befall him and his family if he were not exceedingly careful.

At length, Chuck led Ralph to his study, a nine by twelve room with a battered metal desk and bookcases piled with *Journals of the American Association of Petroleum Geologists* and *Bulletins of the Society of Exploration Geophysicists*. Dozens of copies of *Oil Weekly* were stacked neatly on a side table. Structure maps of areas in Louisiana and Texas issued by the state geological surveys covered two walls. An old leather swivel chair caught Ralph's eye. Despite signs of wear and tear, it looked well constructed, expensive, and vaguely familiar.

Chuck noticed his interest. "You've seen it before," he said, smiling. "It's one of the set that used to be in the Texoil board room. The company replaced them ten years ago and sold them as surplus. Cost me fifty bucks and well worth it." The smile left Chuck's face. "Sometimes I think me and that chair have a lot in common."

Ralph walked to the journals and ran his finger over one. "Quite a collection you have here, Chuck."

"Just trying to keep up with the new computerized seismic technology. It isn't easy from the outside. I pick up a bit at meetings of the Houston Geophysical Society. At least *they* keep me, as long as I pay my dues."

As Chuck sipped his wine, his voice grew wistful. "I hear they've developed a method to find oil directly with the seismograph, not just through mapping structure. Can't quite believe it. Nowadays, they record all the data on tape, so they can just push a button and the computer prints out sections so simple that even a company vice president can see the structure. Lucky for me a lot of the old seis records are still around. I can usually dig something new out of them that might find an oil field, especially in the case of deep structures. I'd like to think I can get more out of records than any computer can. But me and the computer together, we make quite a team. I want to prove it on this Gillette thing."

Chuck's voice went soft, and his eyes dropped to the floor. "Without a pension from Texoil, the Gillette project is about my last hope."

Ralph was astonished. "What do you mean 'without a pension'? You had over twenty years. You were vested. They have to give you a pension."

Chuck's eyes stayed on the floor. "They threatened to prosecute, said if I signed a paper giving up the pension they wouldn't."

Ralph started to say that Texoil would never do anything like that, but he stopped himself. Of course they would. Some slick, hard-hearted personnel man had bluffed Chuck out of his pension. Ralph could hear him telling his boss now, "Taught that sonovabitch a lesson all right. I'll see that word gets out to the others. That'll teach them not to buy royalty. Saved the company a tidy sum, too."

"I'm sorry things worked out that way," said Ralph. "Let's see if the Gillette deal can make it up for you."

Chuck beamed. "You mean you'll help?"

"I'll try," said Ralph.

"I understand," said Chuck, still beaming.

"I've checked the files," said Ralph. "Texoil has released the Gillette acreage, all right. I'm overdue for a visit to the Lake Charles office. I'll see Maude Gillette and try to get the lease."

Chuck nodded enthusiastically.

Ralph continued, "If I get it, then I'll have to convince an operator that your structure maps are based on good data *without* being able to show it to him. That won't be easy. It'll have to be someone I know well." Ralph started to look at the maps on the wall. "It might be a good idea for you to take me through your data so I can answer questions. If I can't convince anybody, then we'll have to rethink. You might have to show your records."

At Chuck's concerned look, Ralph added, "But we'll cross that bridge when we come to it, okay?"

For the next hour, Ralph examined the records and listened to Chuck's commentary. With the computer, Chuck had produced seismic cross sections, vertical slices showing the position of the various reflecting horizons mapped down to twenty thousand feet. The shallow structures at ten thousand feet, where Texoil had found oil, were clearly delineated. Then there was a void of four thousand feet with no reflections, and finally, the large, clearly defined domal structures below the unconformity at fourteen thousand. They looked like they had been pushed up by deep salt intrusions. Multiple reflecting horizons indicated many sands, which had been arched up over the domes and could provide traps for oil. Chuck's subsurface maps showed three large structures, each covering about two thousand acres. Even with his limited technical knowledge, Ralph understood that the Gillette property looked very promising . . . promising enough to take a chance.

When Ralph left, he carried with him the key structural maps of the deep horizons. As he walked to his car, he noticed a man sitting in a parked car nearby. Am I being tailed? he wondered suddenly.

Ridiculous! he chided himself.

But what if the whole thing was a setup? What if Texoil was using Ames to test his loyalty before offering him the big job? Equally ridiculous, paranoid. He'd known Ames for years. Ames' situation was genuine; the man and his wife weren't making it all up.

Still, Ralph's hand was shaking when he tried to put his key in the door lock. Driving away, he glanced in the mirror and was relieved to see that the other car wasn't following. When he got home he immediately hid the maps under the shirts in his closet, and locked it. Then he felt his face color. He'd have made a lousy spy. He hoped Anne hadn't noticed.

9

Anne

Tuesday morning Anne was restless. The day, week, perhaps years stretched before her like a gray plateau, and she sat at the kitchen table with her third cup of coffee after Ralph and the children had left and wondered what in the world was the matter with her.

By all rights she should have been feeling jubilant. The night before, Ralph had told her all about his meeting with Ames and had assured her that the data looked good, very good in fact. He had promised to approach Jack during the weekend they were to spend at the Sanderson ranch, and that as soon as he had Jack's consent he would go see Maude Gillette about the lease.

"How long will all this take?" Anne had asked.

"A week or two to get the paperwork done."

"I mean, to drill the well?"

"That's something else again. Months."

"How *many* months?"

"I don't know, a lot. It depends on all kinds of factors you wouldn't understand."

"What makes you think I wouldn't?"

"Because *I* don't, for one thing. The point is, I've agreed to go ahead. Isn't that enough for one day?"

"Oh, I don't know," she'd sighed. "I'm sorry, darling, I guess I'm just anxious. I want to know when we're going to be millionaires."

Life is waiting, she thought later, moodily sipping cold coffee. Men are the lucky ones — at least they're doing something. Women can only wait and hope what they're doing is right.

At exactly 10:00, when she had just about decided to go get her hair cut off or buy a dress she couldn't afford, the phone rang. A female voice asked briskly if she were in a position to accept a personal and confidential call. Intrigued, Anne assured the woman she was.

"Anne, Bill Butler here. How are you?"

"Fine, I'm fine," she said carefully, smiling, surprised, enjoying a decidedly pleasant sense of vindication. "And you?"

"Contrite, very contrite. I've spent days trying to think of a way to make it up to you for pinching your table the other night and ruining your evening."

"Nonsense, you didn't ruin my evening. We had a wonderful time!"

"Nevertheless, you must let me atone. See how this strikes you. How about lunch and a cruise on the bay on my yacht tomorrow, just the two of us?"

"Well, that does sound very attractive. Should I be on my guard?"

There was an explosion of laughter on the other end of the line. "Lady, do you always say what's on your mind?"

Anne chuckled. "Practically always. Don't you?"

"Practically never. Seriously though, will you come? I assure you, the arrangements will be very discreet."

"It's not the arrangements I'm worried about."

He laughed again. "I'm sure you can take care of yourself."

"I'll bring my hatpin."

"Then you will come?"

"Okay, I accept," said Anne crisply. "But how do I get there without all of Houston knowing about it? I don't want to be compromised before I'm compromised."

"Let's meet at the boat then. If you wouldn't mind driving your car to the Southwest Shopping Center — that's Exit 22 off the Gulf Freeway — my limo will meet you in front of Bryan's Hardware store at 11:30. My driver will identify himself."

"I doubt he'll have to. How many limos can there be in front of Bryan's Hardware?"

"Don't worry, no one we know ever goes there."

"Sounds very clandestine indeed. I'm writing all this down in invisible ink. Okay! I'll see you at the boat. Can we count on good weather?"

"All ordered," said Bill. "Goodbye, dear."

What should I wear? Anne thought immediately, then, what *am* I doing?

Like most pretty women, she prided herself on being able to handle men, and in the years of her marriage she had carried on several harmless flirtations. If she had not been happy with Ralph, that might not have been as easy as it in fact had been. She liked men and their attention, and, she admitted to herself as she rinsed her coffee cup and put it into the dishwasher, she had only flirted with nice, safe men. Bill Butler was not exactly safe, and it remained to be seen how nice he was. She was accepting Bill's invitation to help Ralph. Sure, that was it, wasn't it?

And now that she had said yes, she was very excited about going. This was not the same excitement one got from giving a good party, and it was a feeling she had missed for a long time. Part of the trouble was that she had been excited about moving to Houston. Life in Washington had become monotonous; she had gone about caring for Ralph and the children, doing the requisite volunteer work, going to and giving parties. Four years in Houston and she was still doing exactly the same thing.

Anyway, what could be more innocent than a lunch in broad daylight on Bill Butler's boat?

She had always told Ralph about her little escapades. "Guess who I had lunch with today," she'd tease. "Bob Morris. He took me to Normandie Farm, can you imagine? He said he wanted to ask me about a present for Ellen's birthday, but Normandie Farm's a bit far from Garfinckel's." She would chuckle, and Ralph would say, "One of these days you're going to get into trouble," but he would laugh too.

She knew, however, she would not say to Ralph, "Guess who I had lunch with today," after seeing Bill Butler.

Never mind, she rationalized, nothing will happen. And I deserve a little fun. It'll put the roses back in my cheeks. And if the Ames thing doesn't work out, it will be good for Ralph's career with Texoil to have an in with Butler.

This reasoning didn't work very well, but she didn't care.

Once she made up her mind to do something, Anne never looked back.

On Thursday morning Anne threaded her way through traffic on the Galveston road, feeling attractive and liberated. At the shopping center she parked her car, locked it, and headed for the only long black limousine in the ranks of Toyotas, Ford Escorts, and pickup trucks. A uniformed chauffeur stepped out and asked politely, "Are you Mr. Butler's guest?" No names, please, she thought, amused. All this precaution was beginning to seem silly.

In the dark, cool interior of the limo she settled back comfortably and watched the flat country race by the shaded windows. What if Butler had invited her to the Petroleum Club for lunch? But he hadn't, and the privacy of the boat offered a greater challenge. It might be fun to see if her usual technique for quelling manly ardor — a hearty laugh — worked on someone reputed to be dangerous.

In less than an hour she saw the waters of Galveston Bay shimmering in the brilliant sunlight. The car turned into a drive of crushed shells and, waved on by a guard, they entered an enclosed area and parked between a boathouse and a dock. Anne got out, and the driver escorted her to the gangplank of a long, sleek, white yacht with *Southwind* emblazoned across its stern. Waiting for her on deck was Bill Butler, sporting a blue yachting jacket and white cap bearing the insignia of the New York Yacht Club. Big, ruddy, and still handsome at fifty-nine — Anne had made a discreet inquiry — he beamed as he grasped both her hands and kissed her lightly on the cheek.

"How lovely you look!" he exclaimed.

"Thank you. I feel like a flag." She wore a white sleeveless sweater under her blue suit, and at the last minute she'd added a floppy red hat with a white streamer. "What a beautiful boat!"

"Thank you. It's my favorite toy. Seventy-five feet and can sleep up to twelve good friends."

"I didn't know you had that many."

"Oho, you've been reading my press releases. Can I get you something to drink?"

"Campari and soda, please," said Anne, watching the Filipino crew take up the gangplank and cast off.

Butler called to someone, whereupon a young man appeared,

received his instructions, and left. "Let's sit in the stern," he suggested. They settled down on comfortable cushions as the boat slid smoothly away from the dock, its diesel engine throbbing faintly. In a few minutes the steward returned with the drinks. On the tray lay a flat beribboned package which Bill handed to her, saying, "A small souvenir of your visit."

Anne was delighted. She loved surprise gifts. She opened the box and took out a bright red, white, and blue Hermès scarf. "You must be a mind reader!" she said, flashing Butler a radiant smile as she took off her hat and tied the scarf over her hair. "It matches perfectly. I don't know why I wore this silly hat in the first place. One stiff breeze and it would be overboard."

"I'm sorry to say I didn't select it myself, but I can take credit for the idea," he said. "Why the face?"

Anne had taken a sip of the bitter Campari. "I don't really like this drink very much, only its gay red color. But my mother always said, 'When in doubt, order something you don't like.' "

Bill threw back his head and laughed. "Are you always this candid?"

"Practically. It gets me into a lot of trouble."

"Fine. I'd like nothing better."

"Why, Mr. Butler, are you flirting with me?"

"I'm doing my damndest," he replied.

The throbbing of the engine had ceased, and as the boat rocked gently in the bay, two crewmen ran up a huge white sail which caught the slight breeze, billowed out, and drew the boat forward. Anne caught her breath. I will remember this forever, she thought. Whatever happens. But, of course, nothing will.

They glided past the distant, misty mirage of the great Baytown refinery, and as they got farther from shore, the breeze increased and they were soon cutting through the choppy water at a fast clip. Anne got up and moved to the bow and took hold of a cable, lifting her face to the spray.

"You've sailed before," said Bill, coming up behind her.

"Oh yes, every summer when I was a child. We always went to Fisher's Island. My father had a catamaran. Actually, I learned on a Sunfish. But that's a different sort of sailing, of course. This is lovely — nice not to be working at it. Posh."

"I never learned to handle small boats, I'm sorry to say. Maybe you could teach me."

"I don't know, I somehow don't think you'd be very receptive to taking orders. Especially from a woman."

"Hmmn. Come to think of it, I've never tried that either. It might be fun — depending on the woman. Try me at lunch, you can tell me which fork to use."

"No thanks. That's mama stuff. I get enough of that at home."

"Ah, I forgot — you have two children, don't you?"

"Now how did you know that? In Washington the politicians all have files, and before parties their secretaries check out all the guests' kiddies, so the senator can say, 'And how did little Jenny survive the mumps?' Do you have a file on me?"

"Not yet — I'm usually not that interested, but when I am I have ways of finding out everything I want to know."

"I'll bet you do at that," she said, feeling a sudden chill.

"Another drink, or lunch? There's wine."

"Oh, lunch, please. The minute I get near a boat I get hungry."

They ate in the salon, which was twice the size of Anne's living room. The conversation, to her relief, subsided into amusing anecdotes served up by Bill as deftly as the steward served the shrimp remoulade and eggs Florentine. She reminded herself that she was being subjected to a charm that had been developed over years of practice and tested on countless women. But she couldn't help being impressed.

Over the lemon ice, Bill said, "I can't remember when I've had such a good time. One bad thing about being the boss is that everybody feels obligated to tell you what you want to hear. With you, I never know what you're going to say."

"I haven't said anything for some time. I've been too busy eating."

"That's another thing. Most women just pick at their food and complain that they're on diets. You — you *eat*."

She laughed. "I hope that's a compliment."

"You bet it is. Ah, Anne, you remind me of my youth, of those smart and sassy girls from Vassar and Radcliffe I dated when I was in college. They kept me on my toes, brought me up short every time I said something stupid. Actually, I was scared to death of them."

"You were? Oh, I can't believe that."

"No, really, they made me feel like a hick."

"Nonsense, you're one of the most sophisticated men I've ever met."

"Wait till you get to know me better. Hayseed in my pockets and oil under my fingernails."

"Sounds interesting."

"Well, I hope you continue to think so. How about coffee over there on the sofa?"

Anne hesitated for a split second. "Could we go back on deck instead? It's so seldom I get to see all that lovely water."

"Of course. Just watch how good I am at following orders."

In fifteen minutes they had had their coffee and were back at the dock. Anne suspected that the trip would have lasted longer had they stayed below.

Bill escorted her to the waiting limousine. "We'll do this again," he said, his hand planted firmly in the small of her back. "I'll call you." Then he kissed her before she could resist or respond, opened the car door, and helped her inside.

"Thank you for the lovely sail and the scarf," she managed before he closed the door. As the car pulled out of the lot, her mind was already in turmoil.

Was what she had done really to help Ralph or just herself? She had grown up with money, not the kind Bill Butler had, but more than her marriage had so far provided. Although she prided herself on making do with what she had — she was always a good sport — she was beginning to worry that her husband had reached the limit of his powers. Her response reflected her roots.

Anne was a New Yorker, with a New Yorker's competitive spirit. New York, banking and marketing center, seat of great corporations, home of culture and the arts, headquarters for the media and publishing world, offered all things to all people — that is, if you could afford them. The struggle for wealth and power, or just mere survival, had created in the New Yorker a new breed. And it was through the eyes of a New Yorker that Anne looked at Houston — and now at Bill Butler.

A New Yorker took nothing for granted. Every day, every act, was a part of the competitive process. First, there had to be enough money to support the lifestyle of a very materialistic society. It was great if you had it, and you had lawyers and investment counselors to help you keep it. If you didn't, you had to dedicate yourself to getting it. If you were a man, you had to fight the long hard battle up the corporate ladder, or the pecking order of a legal firm. Or you had to be the best investment man, winning wealthy clients with your shrewdness and self-confidence; or a real estate developer, nurturing your capital while borrowing increasing sums at great risk to provide for the insatiable demands of New Yorkers for apartment houses and offices.

And you had to succeed, otherwise you might as well drop out of the competition and go back to Kalamazoo. For the breed of people attracted by the high stakes of New York, failure was intolerable. The symbols of success: a co-op on Park Avenue in the sixties; the right private schools and Ivy League college; the right clubs, Cosmopolitan for the woman and Racquet and Tennis or Lynx or Brook for the man; a summer place on Fisher's Island or East Hampton with sailing, golf, and tennis; trips to Europe; and later, if you reached the summit, a home in Greenwich with a winter home in Hobe Sound.

These were necessary props for the "in" New Yorker. For a girl like Anne it had meant the Junior League and a debut at the Pierre. Later came endless rounds of charity balls and getting one's picture in the *Times* as a member of the committee, with a comment on your dress or dancing partner. It meant constant practice at tennis or golf, keeping your waist down and your tan deep. It meant being invited to the chic parties and being seated with the right people. Not many New Yorkers managed to pull themselves up to the top. Most just couldn't make it, got tired and fell off the ladder. Others quit because they didn't think it was worth it.

Anne met all of the qualifications with ease. Her mother was from an old New York family which had for two generations helped set the standards. Her father, though unfortunately from Cincinnati, a fact seldom referred to, had been sent to Princeton by his soap-king father and had graduated with an excellent academic record. While in Princeton he had accumulated a letter in golf, the best club, and a host of friends who later proved very useful when he entered the investment world. It was natural that he would meet and fall in love with Anne's mother. As a couple they had everything it took to be successful New Yorkers.

Anne, as her mother before her, had gone to Vassar, high over the Hudson, protected from non-conformists and, apart from weekends, from men. Vassar had impeccable standards, particularly in the field of Art History in which Anne majored. As a reflection of its New York origins, Vassar was a comfortable but highly competitive world. Although she had many suitors, some more persistent than she would have liked, Anne put off any serious idea of marriage as long as she could. And then, on a weekend trip to Washington, she had met Ralph, who had been living there for three years, working for Texoil. Although as a Southerner he was different — more reserved and gentlemanly than her New York beaus — he was from a fine old Virginia family and well educated; most important, he fitted into her world. After a few weekend dates in Washington and New York, she was very much in love with him. It wasn't long before they had a large, elaborate wedding in a church on Fifth Avenue.

Anne's and Ralph's early years together in Washington had been happy ones. They had both enjoyed the pleasant Georgetown social routine, small dinner parties at their Federal townhouse, waltzes at the Sulgrave Club. Ralph's professional life had centered around the staid Metropolitan Club, their tennis and social life, at the Chevy Chase Country Club. The museums and the symphony and the opera offered ample diversions. They went to New York often and occasionally took a house for the summer in the Hamptons. But when the time had come to move to Houston, Anne was ready. Houston was on the move and so was she. She did not look back.

Anne had over the years acquired a pleasing veneer of confidence and sophistication. She always said and did what would be the right thing in her New York world. She had an open, engaging manner, a "Hello-there, Who-are-you?" approach to life. Armed with a ready smile, she was attractive to men and knew it. She also knew how to handle them. Having been raised in a protected environment, she felt no insecurity, but wanted to preserve what she had inherited. She also had an unwavering instinct to keep going up the ladder. New Yorkers take a long view, and hers, optimistic from the first, now included Houston.

The Ames deal seemed just what Houston had to offer — and in a way, so did Bill Butler. There's no harm in it, she reasoned. If it starts to get serious, *I* can always call a halt.

10

Jack

Over the years Jack and Janet Sanderson had never allowed business or social affairs to keep them from spending their weekends at their ranch in Central Texas.

As Jack pulled into the drive after the Harrison party, Janet said, "Well we can always sell the ranch."

"No way," he said firmly.

"Well, we haven't lost it yet. Something will turn up."

"How I wish I had your confidence," he sighed, taking her in his arms. "I was so damned sure about the Terrebone well."

"You know you're right about that. There's gas down there. Just bad luck, that's all."

"Don't know how much more bad luck I can take."

"C'mon, guy. We've had dry holes before."

"But I wasn't sixty."

"Don't be ridiculous. You're a lot smarter and better than you've ever been. You know more about the business than anybody. You'll do fine."

"You go on in," he said. "I think I'll sit here and think on it for a while, okay?"

On the weekend following the Harrisons' party, they were expecting the Harrison family to join them. They had visited before, and Jack and Janet particularly enjoyed having them because they all seemed to love the "Hill Country" of Llano County, and to appreciate the unique geology of the area and Jack's interesting collections based on its natural history and early settlements. Ralph had a special appreciation for the oaks and hills and streams, which reminded him of the Piedmont of Virginia.

Anne and Ralph were to arrive late tomorrow. Jack and Janet had driven up Thursday, when a shipment of minerals from Mexico was due. For years they had always flown up in the company plane, but since Jack's recent financial difficulties, they'd reluctantly sold the plane and let the pilot go.

This visit was overshadowed by these difficulties. By cutting back his expenses sharply and agreeing to pay the bank a larger percentage of his income against his debt, Jack had obtained on a short term note the two million dollars he owed for the dry hole in Terrebone. He still faced, however, a renewal of this note in six months. The farm produced no income — indeed, it was run at a considerable loss, but it was by now a valuable property and bore its share of Jack's overall indebtedness to the bank. If the bank demanded payment, there was a real threat now that he would have to sell the ranch. This was very difficult for him to face.

In many ways the ranch was more important to Jack than his life in Houston. True, he owed everything he had to the oil industry and to Houston. But his roots went deeper, to East Texas. He loved his state and what it stood for. He considered this more important than whatever the new city of Houston stood for, more fundamental, more lasting.

All of these issues were running through Jack's mind now. The sun was setting over the granite knob to the west of the farm as Jack finally began unloading the car. Tom and Gladys Pickens, the faithful couple who served as rancher and housekeeper, waited now, drinks in hand.

Jack revelled in the familiar sounds of the cattle and the wind rustling through the trees; the smells of the green earth and the barnyard and the fresh air; and the views of the low-slung ranch house and the rolling hills beyond. As was his custom he roamed, drink in hand, through the cattle lot, down to the Llano River which ran swift and clear in front of the house, through the rock gardens Janet had worked on so devotedly over the years, and through the various projects in which he had taken such a keen interest: his ranch museum, his geological collection, and his Indian artifacts, each housed in a separate building. He couldn't wait to unpack the mineral shipment and add its contents to his collection.

The Harrisons arrived shortly after sunset on Friday, Kate and John already brimming with excitement. The Sandersons, whose own children were grown, took great pleasure in having young children on the ranch again to enjoy the pony ring and tennis court and swimming pool.

Kate and John were given an early dinner and allowed their (supervised) choice of TV programs, but the two couples put Gladys' supper on the hot plate and lingered long over Scotch and bourbon before a small fire, even though the weather was mild.

Anne was in particularly high spirits. She talked of her early days in New York, particularly her summers on Fisher's Island. "Lord, I'm glad I don't have to get up in the morning to take tennis lessons and play in a tournament anymore. Ralph and I would love to play you two, though, if you would like." Then the talk switched to families. Anne expressed concern about the influence of other children on her own, and asked about the Sandersons' children and how their attitudes had changed with age.

"It depends on when they grew up," said Janet. "We've gone through every phase. At this point Sarah has become a fanatical mother. Motherhood seems to have fulfilled her. She is perfectly square, does all of the right things in Houston. She wants to be a respected member of the community. Jim and Sally are still very much the Sixties generation. I doubt if they ever will change, particularly Jim. He's an anti-social, anti-marriage, anti-big business, vegetarian, back-to-nature ecologist. He keeps talking about 'keeping his options open,' which seems to me a way of avoiding any commitments.

"But Julie, our youngest, has surprised us. She didn't come this weekend because of her dancing class. She wants to go to Radcliffe. And she actually wants to make her debut. It's really pretty bewildering to be a parent these days," she finished.

"That sounds hopeful," Anne commented. "The thought of all that sex and pot scares me to death. I hope our two will just learn to drink martinis and worry about their reputations, the way we did when I was growing up. I must say, though, that my generation isn't setting a very good example at the moment." She recounted some of the current Houston gossip about people both couples knew. "Most people seem to take a little philandering as a matter of course, as long as it's done discreetly," she said with a shrug.

"Maybe I'm old-fashioned," Ralph interjected, "but I don't

see how anyone can take their morals so lightly. If the marriage is a good one, why risk it? And if it isn't, well, how do you call the thing off? It's rarely so easy. And the children usually bear the brunt of their parents' peccadilloes. Such things usually become public knowledge even if they don't trigger a nasty divorce."

"The Europeans seem to take extramarital affairs for granted," said Jack. "Makes you glad to be an American."

"Come on, Jack," said Anne, emboldened by the drinks, "don't tell me you've never been tempted."

"Oh, I like to look," he said, raising his glass to her.

"But he's not allowed to touch," said Janet comfortably.

Something about the conversation troubled Ralph. He couldn't put his finger on it. It was not just what Anne had said. He worried that it had to do with Bill Butler. Butler had sent them a formal invitation to a dinner party to be held at his home the following week. The invitation could, of course, have something to do with his possible advancement at Texoil, but it had also occurred to him that Anne might have wangled it somehow. She had not appeared the least bit surprised, had accepted it matter-of-factly. And then he pushed it from his mind; after all, they were at the ranch to relax.

Both couples were up at dawn, and Ralph and Jack helped Tom with the animals. Jack liked to be considered a guest on his ranch, but he enjoyed helping out. After a hearty Texas breakfast, including steak and fried eggs doused with strong Mexican jalapeno sauce, Jack took Ralph and Anne on a guided tour to show them the changes that had been made since their last visit.

The ranch house itself was a hundred years old, a line of single rooms extending from both sides of a central breezeway. In order to preserve the house's original character, Jack and Janet had expanded further, as the Sanderson wealth and family grew, by building smaller guest houses nearby in the same style, using old lumber.

A large area had been set aside near the house for an outdoor ranch museum, where Jack had moved and restored old ranch houses and barns, a one-room school, a railway station, and other old structures from the surrounding area. He had found them by following up what might be displaced by new construction. He also had a fine collection of barbed wire and farm tools.

"Someday," said Jack, "these buildings will be the only old ones left around here. Then I'll open them to the public. It's important that Texans maintain their links with their past, meager as they are. If there were no structures left between Mount Vernon and the latest Hilton Hotel, we'd lose all feeling for the contributions of the intervening years. These buildings aren't important architecturally, but they sheltered people from the wilderness. Think of the effort they required! The character of Texas was formed by the people who built them."

After dinner that evening the two couples sat for a long time on the terrace facing west, sipping their drinks as the drama of the sunset unfolded before them. Texas sunsets can be spectacular, and this one didn't disappoint. "Where else," said Jack over his second nightcap, "could you see a better show, and for free?"

They watched almost spellbound from the time the first rays of the setting sun lit up the underside of the low cumulus clouds drifting over the horizon. Eventually the yellow rays of the spectrum emerged, breaking through and turning to gold the thin cirrus clouds high above. As the sun set, its red rays were intensified by the scattering of the blues as they penetrated more and more of the dust-laden West Texas atmosphere. The finale came as a flaming brilliant crimson. No one spoke as they watched the end of the spectacle that had lasted, including the afterglow, for over two hours.

"Did you ever see such a sunset in Houston?" Jack snorted. "I haven't. I wouldn't know where to look for it. Too many distractions."

Later, after their wives had gone to bed, Ralph and Jack took a walk by the river. Ralph explained, without naming Chuck Ames, how he had come into the possession of a deep structure map of the Gillette lands in Louisiana, stressing how much confidence he had in the man who had interpreted it. He was particularly careful as he elucidated the legality of the situation, and more than once emphasized his need to remain in the background as long as he remained with Texoil. Then he brought out Chuck's deep map and mentioned Chuck's requirements.

Jack, who'd been silent throughout, finally laughed. "It's a funny thing. A month ago I would have taken your deal like a shot. I know the Gillette lands very well, and the presence of deep structures there seems quite reasonable to me. There's a big 'but' though. No one else knows but me and the bank, but I've recently gotten into a pretty tight financial situation. I'll work it out, but it means I have to be careful."

"That's a damned shame," said Ralph, disappointment weighing heavily on him now. "And I don't mind telling you how much. There's no one else I'd care to trust with this information."

"Well, let's not give up yet." Ralph brightened at Jack's response. "I'll see what subsurface I have on the Gillette area, study the deep logs on that trend, and take a look at my financial hole card. Let me call you at home in a couple of days. Don't worry. If I don't take it, your friend's secret will be safe. If I do take it and we hit, I'll find some way to conceal your interest until you're ready to reveal it."

"Whew," breathed Ralph, and immediately announced he was going to turn in.

It had not taken Jack long to grasp the possibilities of Ralph's proposal. He understood it, of course, much better than Ralph did. But it involved the risk of losing the ranch. Could he face it? Maybe this was the only way to save it, he thought. Also, there was a certain irony that appealed to Jack almost as much as the money. Suppose he, the Independent, drilled and found oil where Texoil had given up — Texoil and Bill Butler, the quintessential company man. What a capstone to his career that would make! There on the tail ends of the old records might be a vindication of his whole life as an oil man, his methods, his attitudes, his philosophy — Independent versus Company in a classical confrontation.

He knew sleep was out of the question for at least another hour and turned, retracing his steps along his beloved bend of river.

It was generally recognized in oil circles that Independent wildcatters are a very special breed. In the early days they considered themselves swashbuckling buccaneers, gamblers on a grand scale, willing to risk everything on a single well. And they were inordinately proud. They wanted everyone to know just how successful they were.

At the top were the legendary "greats" among the wildcatters, moving in and out of big deals with an aura of romance and mystery. Like Tom Slick of Oklahoma, often called "King of the Wildcatters," a reserved, handsome man with prematurely snow-white hair, who had no scientific training which was in his time meager anyway. But Slick developed an uncanny instinct for finding oil fields. A millionaire at twenty-six, he retired and travelled around the world. Bored, he returned to Oklahoma and discovered another thirty-five million dollars worth of oil before his death at forty-six.

Paul Getty of Oklahoma, H. L. Hunt of Dallas, Sid Richardson of Fort Worth, and Jim Abercrombie of Houston trod the same path. And Houston still teems with would-be Tom Slicks, some hitting it one time and losing it, others amassing huge fortunes. Some, like Glenn McCarthy, rose high as a meteor, only to sink quietly into oblivion.

As a group, Independents feel vastly superior to, even contemptuous of "company men," which they use as a term of derision. For them, company men were emasculated drones, part of a ponderous timid bureaucracy, making safe bets with other people's money. Since he made his own decisions, the Independent knew he could run circles around a company in a fast-breaking play. But the companies, with their vast resources, usually won in the end. The company could afford the expensive lease, drill the deep well, and survive long losing streaks. They could, if they failed, still buy out the Independent who had made a good strike.

In recent years the most successful Independents have tended to be the quiet odds players, carefully counting their odds as they make their moves. And despite their surface animosity, the Independents and company people really get along better than either will admit. Each needs the other. Social relationships provide the inside track for drilling deals. The Independent who can afford the expensive duck hunting camp likes to play host to the top company men. This gives the host not only a chance for inside dope, but a foot in the company door.

Independents have always been a varied group, ranging from unskilled hucksters to Ph.D. geologists. Some peddle drilling deals, others speculate in leases or royalties. There are pure charlatans among them who profit whether the well they drill produces or not, taking their cut up front, receiving kickbacks from the drilling contractors, even deliberately overselling leases in expectation that the well will be dry — which, statistically, is a good bet. A producer creates more problems for them than a dry hole.

There are also countless insiders operating on the fringes of the companies, some no more reputable than racetrack touts, trying to steal information and exploit it for their own gain. Many have wormed their way into society seeking tips from company men in unguarded moments at cocktail parties. Their lease broker is off at dawn the next day, his wallet stuffed with hundred dollar bills, to get first shot at the farmers for their leases or royalty.

Among the Independents, those who, like Jack, were professional geologists and geophysicists were respected, but were not always the most successful. Often they were shy on capital. After accumulating enough experience and files from companies to break away, they inserted their cards in the professional journals — the only advertising permitted — and waited for clients among the Independents. This was how Jack had gotten his start. Some, accepting percentages of the prospect instead of fees, get lucky and become full-fledged Independents. Others eke out a precarious existence as consultants, regretting they ever left the company.

There were now 20,000 Independents in Texas, and competition was increasingly fierce. In 1976 world oil production was expected by experts to peak in the middle 1980s and to decline and then be exhausted before 2100. In a period of about two hundred years the several billion peoples of planet earth would have used up the estimated two trillion barrels of recoverable oil it took nature three billion years to make from the life of the ancient seas. Of this, 400 million had already been produced and 600 million had been discovered and was being produced. To find the trillion barrels still undiscovered, a vast international oil industry had been created involving executives, geologists, geophysicists, petroleum engineers, and a myriad of other supporting professional personnel and services.

The search for oil had by the mid-1970s been intensified with the higher prices forced by OPEC. U.S. oil production had, however, peaked in 1970 and was inexorably coming down. Texas oil production, which had reached 3,500,000 barrels a day in 1972, was down over ten percent, with oil reserves down 50 percent from a peak in 1955. Nature had created just so many oil fields to find and they were going fast.

The very big oil fields, like the ten billion barrel North Slope of Alaska, were already found. The last trillion barrels would come from smaller and smaller fields, making it difficult to keep up the production of the 50 million barrels of oil a day the world had grown used to. Finding costs were up and success ratios down. The best of the virgin territory left was deep offshore Texas and Louisiana, but drilling in water beyond a thousand feet was expensive. There was also virgin territory to drill on land below 15,000 feet, but only gas existed at this depth. In 1976 the overall percentage of wildcat wells which discovered a new field was about 17 percent, or one in six. But many of these were too small or too expensive to produce to be profitable. The chance of finding a really profitable field, producing at least a million barrels, was only one in fifty-five.

When the price of OPEC oil after the Arab oil embargo of 1973 rose from $3.00 to $10.00 a barrel, and reached $34 a barrel in 1979, the search for new fields had proceeded at a faster pace. Houston, the center for mid-continent oil, had become the capital of world oil, with which its whole future was inextricably linked — with production of oil in Nigeria, and the price in Saudi Arabia. Investors from all over the nation, taking advantage of favorable tax laws, poured their savings into drilling deals. Fortunes were being made overnight, by company and Independent alike. Houston was the center of the biggest oil boom ever, a veritable "dance of the billions." Texas was producing 3,000,000 barrels of oil a day, worth 100 million dollars.

Until he received the crushing letter from the bank, Jack had felt sure of staying on top of this heady situation, and when he thought of it at all, he felt assured of a place in history among the Independent greats. Now, however, his confidence had been sorely shaken. He had to make at least one more discovery, to save not only his financial skin, but his reputation. This deal with Ralph and Ames just might be it. Somehow he had to find a way to bring it off.

11

Ralph and Jack

"We've taken some rough blows, old gal," Jack remarked to Janet when they had their evening drink after driving back to Houston. "For the life of me, I never thought I would ever get us into such a box. I guess things just went so well for so long that I assumed it would never stop."

"Don't worry," Janet soothed, patting his hand. "Life is no respecter of the well-being of individuals. Dry holes hit the good as well as the bad. We've always come back, and we sure will this time. I just want to be sure we keep our chins up — and treat our people fairly."

"We've done that," Jack said. "We haven't had to let anyone go who's been with us very long. I'll find places for the others. No one at the Petroleum Club would ever know I wasn't still riding high!"

In his office the next day, Jack took stock of his situation. After cutting his expenses sufficiently to pay the bank the increased percentage of income they required for interest and amortization, truly he was strapped. Moreover he knew the bank could — any time they wanted to, since his loans were on demand — force him to the wall. If put up for distress sales, his pledged real estate and oil-producing properties would be heavily discounted; some wouldn't provide a return allocated under his loan.

However, he felt sure he could pull through, that his oil and gas reserves would ultimately prove adequate to pay the bank back. But his margin could be wiped out by increased interest rates, a reduction in oil prices or allowables, or the premature depletion of an important field.

The first instinct of a wildcatter is to hold onto his oil reserves, and to drill any good prospect he can get his hands on. Jack knew that the Gillette lands were a good prospect. He had followed developments in this area for years, and the seismic interpretation Ralph had shown him fitted his ideas of the way the structures there "grew." The structural "highs" should shift south with depth, and sands should overlie the deep structures, which provided a trap for sands that would otherwise have been washed away. He reached for the telephone.

When Ralph answered, he told him he would take the deal. If Ralph could get a new lease from Maude Gillette on terms Jack specified, he believed Ralph was entitled to a fifteen percent interest in the deal. This would be free of cost, like Chuck's interest, after Jack had recovered his initial investment. Jack also told Ralph that he would like to offer Randy Simpson, whom he normally operated with in this area, a ten percent interest in the prospect, Randy paying his share of all expenses. Ralph liked Randy and knew he could be helpful with the local police juror, an important man in Louisiana. Once Ralph got the lease, Jack knew it would be up to him to do the rest, starting with raising the money. He sighed, and thought to himself, I'm spoiled — I haven't had to do that for years.

Two days later Ralph was on Eastern Flight 62, tourist class, bound for Lake Charles, Louisiana. Thirty minutes after landing, he was behind the wheel of a rental, driving through Lake Charles.

How it had changed! The old Pioneer Building, once the only tall building in town, had been joined by several new skyscrapers.

Ralph had telephoned Maude from Houston, whereupon she had invited him for lunch. Now he had no trouble finding the road to the Gillette mansion overlooking Calcasieu Lake. Remember, you're not just a broker, he told himself as he drove along streets lined with the familiar pine and cypress trees. You are a lawyer about to engage in a negotiation which could change your whole life. History repeating itself, he hoped; the original Gillette lease had been his first big success with Texoil.

Ralph pulled into the circular drive of crushed shells shimmering in the noon sun and stopped in front of a white-columned mansion straight out of "Gone With the Wind." He climbed the steps and walked across the broad veranda, which, he noticed, could use a coat of paint.

Maude herself answered the door, as spry and sharp-eyed as ever, looking exactly the same as the independent, crusty woman he remembered from six years ago. She was truly a worthy opponent, and Ralph was sure he was in for the negotiation of his life.

There was no air conditioning, but the enormous house was pleasantly cool inside. As before, Ralph felt he'd stepped into a museum. The somber oils on the walls, gleaming antiques, sunlight streaming in through eight-foot-high windows, and floorboards creaking softly underfoot transported him back in time and imagination to what he knew must have been the glory days of the Old South. Maude led him across the wide reception hall into a smaller room with bow windows looking out over a magnificent lawn. Here the impressive vases of roses and magnolias gave off a lush fragrance that mingled with the faint, musty smell of history. This was gracious living on a scale that any Virginian would appreciate.

After a polite kiss on the cheek, Ralph exclaimed, "Well, ma'am, let me have a good look at you! You look just the same — wonderful!"

But somehow it was not quite as he remembered it. Emptier, he thought. A more careful look revealed a blank wall where he remembered a painting. He also recalled an exquisite seventeenth-century desk which used to face the garden, now missing from the room.

But there was no time to reflect. With the ease of a lady who was a renowned hostess before he was born, Maude handed him a chilled mint julep, then slipped her arm in his and led him for a stroll through the formal gardens.

Captivated by the beauty of the surroundings, Ralph began to imagine himself lord of the manor, an illusion which he found intoxicating. Perhaps it was the julep. Lunch intensified the illusion. The heavy old silver and crystal, antique Limoges china, the impeccably dressed elderly black man who served them, Maude's charming and witty conversation — all served to draw Ralph deeper into the fantasy world of the Old South.

Only when he was drinking his coffee did he have the strength to focus on tactful ways to bring up the oil lease. Just thinking about it made him feel deceitful and ashamed. At Maude's suggestion, they moved to another room and shared a small love seat.

In front of them, a beautiful small oak table held a decanter of brandy and glasses. Before Ralph could make his opening gambit, Maude spoke.

"I'm going to do something," she said gravely, "which is very difficult for me. Fortunately, it has rarely been necessary, but it certainly is now. I'm going to impose on you as a friend, Ralph."

Ralph was astonished at the swift change in Maude's appearance. The glint was gone from her eye, the animation from her features, and he now saw that she was a shriveled old woman.

"Maude," he said gently, "anything I can do for you would be an honor, 'deed it would."

Maude's twinkle made a momentary comeback. "I knew I could count on your Virginia chivalry."

"Not at all," protested Ralph, grinning broadly. "Subjected to your charms, why a gangster would say the same."

"To be blunt," Maude went on, "I'm in desperate need of money. I'm in the midst of mortgaging the house. Just a few days ago, Texoil dropped their lease. I made the mistake of mentioning it to the banker and now he'll only lend me half of what he previously offered. As I understand it, the potential for oil on my land was an important asset."

"I'd be glad to help — "

"Nonsense. I wouldn't take your money, nor would it be enough. What I need is for you to find someone to pick up my oil lease. I need it for those silly people at the bank."

Evidently, years of experience as a poker-faced negotiator had failed him, for Maude said quickly, "I didn't mean to shock you. My situation is only temporary." She sighed. "I've told you this much. I might as well tell you the rest." She reached for her glass and drained it in a gulp. Looking at Ralph, she smiled. "Shocked you again, I see."

"No," stammered Ralph. "Not at all. I'm sure — "

"Pardon me for interrupting," said Maude, "but I've been thinking about this since you called. Let me get it out of my system and then you tell me what you think."

Ralph nodded and reached for his cognac.

"This oil business has been more a curse than a blessing. My son Bobby has his father's sense of adventure but not his luck. As you probably know, our oldest, Richard, was killed in Korea, so I guess I spoil Bobby. In any event, on the promise of oil, all kinds of people lent Bobby all kinds of money. His promise, as we both know, went largely unfulfilled. Bobby squandered his money and is now in serious financial difficulty. Unfortunately, most of our assets are in trust." She paused briefly and looked away. "Bob knew his son's character as well as I. In time, this will sort itself out, but for the moment, I must have two hundred thousand dollars. The house is worth far more than that, of course. The bank was willing enough to lend it before the leases expired, but now the best they'll do is half. Can you help me get a lease?"

Ralph was flabbergasted. The object of his visit had fallen into his hand like a ripe apple from a tree. His incredible luck was unnerving.

"I think I can help," said Ralph, speaking slowly, "but there's one condition."

At her look of apprehension, he added quickly, "I'm an employee of Texoil, of course, who don't want your lease anymore. Technically, I'm not supposed to do anything personal involving oil without their knowledge and approval. I gather there's some urgency here to find someone else who will drill on your land."

"Damn right," said Maude, again surprising Ralph.

"In that case, ma'am, I need your word that no one will ever learn of my involvement."

Maude's smile was full of relief. "Of course, you have it."

Ralph decided to come directly to the point. "You know Jack Sanderson?"

"Sure," she said, the glint returning. "One of the most successful oil men I know, *and* a gentleman."

"Well, just the other day, he told me he was looking for good prospects in Southern Louisiana. I'm sure he knows a lot about the geology of your land. I'll bet he'd take your lease on the same terms Texoil had. How about it?"

"It's a deal," said Maude, quick as a flash, holding out her hand. "Sign Jack up. And don't worry, mum's the word."

It was three in the afternoon before Ralph got behind the wheel of his car. Still a bit under the influence of the cognac, he drove with great care. He could still make an appearance at the Texoil office before closing, but decided against it. Better not to show up than to show he had been drinking. He would do his Tex-oil business the next day.

He checked into his hotel and called Jack with the good news, then lay down on the bed and considered his good luck. In a sense, he was disappointed. He had wanted to give value, to earn whatever he might gain from his share in Chuck's deal. He hoped fate was not setting him up for some cruel joke.

As soon as he finished talking to Ralph, Jack went to work. As a young Independent, he'd usually had to scrounge the money to get a well down. In his affluent days he had drilled his wells straight up, first class, with his own money. Now, strapped by his obligations to the bank, he knew he had to raise much of the money the hard way — by selling interests to others.

He figured that the total cost of drilling the well to 14,000 feet, and completing it as a producer, would be at least two million dollars. Even if it was a dry hole it would take about a million. The payment to the drilling contractor for the hourly cost of the rig was the one great cost, about a third of the total.

Jack picked up the phone and punched out the number of an old friend, Joe Banks, a reliable Houston drilling contractor who'd drilled many wells for him.

"How's business, Joe? All your rigs running?"

"Oh, fine, Jack. We're not booming but doing pretty well despite the stiff competition. As a matter of fact, I've got a deep rig coming off Old Ocean next month. Could you use it?"

"I just might," said Jack, "but I'd like you to consider putting something in it yourself, like you did with me at Neale a few years ago. You know, drill it in exchange for an oil payment? That worked out well for you, as I recall. If your rig is going to be idle, it wouldn't cost you much more to have it drilling. I'd like to stay out of the banks right now as much as possible. It's a top prospect I've got, or I wouldn't drill it."

Jack wondered what he would do if Joe asked to see his geology, but he needn't have. Joe knew Jack well enough to know he wouldn't drill a dud.

"Oh, I trust you on the geology, Jack. You know that. It really depends on whether I have another job for the rig. What terms did you have in mind?"

"Well, the same basis as our deal at Neale. You drill me a well to 14,000 in Louisiana coast marsh on your usual footage basis for an oil or gas payment out of an eighth."

"Let me figure what it will cost me and you can tell me what odds you can offer me out of oil. O.K.?"

Jack knew that apart from rig time, the other big expenses for the well would be his mud bills, and the string of protection casing he would have to run just below the 10,000-foot Texoil producing sands at Gillette. The casing had to be run before he knew whether he had oil below; if the well was dry, this would be a dead loss. He'd have to have his best engineer on the well to watch the mud weight like a hawk and keep the mud cost down.

There was still, of course, the problem of the 14,000 feet of casing he would have to run for production, but this would be done only if the Schlumberger log showed oil or gas in the deep sand. If he had production, he could finance the casing, the testing, the completion costs, the control valves or "Christmas tree," — and anything else. These costs could add up to an additional million, but good oil or gas sand was money in the bank. No problem.

But there was the problem of paying for the 10,000-foot protection string, about $250,000. In good times he'd ordered pipe casually from the most convenient supply company. Now he needed a pipe dealer who was willing to gamble — and, again, he knew one. Jack detested "Freddie the pipe man," but he knew Freddie would make deals. He braced himself, called Freddie and went almost immediately to his sleazy office and pipe warehouse in Houston's industrial district.

Freddie wore a Houston T-shirt. His trousers were held up by bright red suspenders, and he sported a tattered felt hat indoors as he chewed a big unlit stogie. Jack felt soiled by being there, suddenly embarrassed that he had come to such low straits as to have to deal with such a man.

"How would you like to gamble pipe for an oil payment for a well I'm drilling?" asked Jack casually. "It's a top prospect that I'm drilling straight up, but I'm trying to conserve cash. I'd want good pipe, of course — inspected — but I understand you're willing sometimes to be paid out of oil. I'll be glad to negotiate out with you an oil payment — say out of a sixteenth. I think the well's a cinch."

"Well, Mr. Sanderson, I know your reputation," said Freddie, removing his cigar. "When I don't get cash, I need good odds." He spat out a large wad that splattered on the floor. Jack winced. "I'll need to know a little more about your prospect, of course, but I usually shoot for a five to one payment on a good structure." He grinned, exposing a row of brown teeth.

"Here's my block," said Jack, and handed Freddie a map, "Five thousand acres solid. Naturally I have deep shooting. This is a seismic map that shows the deep structure I'm drilling for. I need a 7-inch string for the shallow zones at 10,000 that have been depleted."

Juggling technicalities, Jack and Freddie negotiated for an hour and a half, reviewing the odds against dry holes, and the narrow margins in pipe prices. In the end they struck a deal, and Jack winced again as he shook Freddie's greasy hand. He'd had to accept what he thought was a rough deal — four to one return out of one quarter of the oil — on pipe priced ten percent above the prevailing list. Jack felt cheated, but then again he had saved $250,000 in up-front cash. He still needed almost a half million dollars more.

Jack knew by heart all the honest tricks to financing a well, and there were many. Since he was starting out with only a sixty percent working interest, he wanted to hold on to all of it if he could. He figured he would come out better if, in raising the cash he needed for the other expenses, he sold an overriding royalty, to be paid out of a fixed percentage of production free of expenses. Normally there would be a lot of people asking him to cut them in on such a deal. Now he asked one named Arnold Pollack to lunch.

"I've decided to sell some overriding royalty under a well I'm going to drill soon," said Jack, after cocktails and small talk at the Petroleum Club. "You've often asked me to let you in on a deal, and I'd be happy to on a prospect I'm drilling in the lower tier of counties in South Louisiana. It's a 14,000 foot test on a 5,000 acre block with good sands to shoot at."

Pollack, a congenial new arrival in Houston, represented Eastern money and had learned just enough about the oil business to think he knew everything. As Jack talked, Pollack's manner changed noticeably from the social acquaintance who would be honored if Jack would just let him in on any deal he might have around. "Overrides are pretty risky compared to royalty, of course," he said. "If you lose the lease, the royalty's gone too. Two hundred dollars an acre seems a little steep. Also, as you tell me, you have only a few seismic lines. Is that enough to prove up 5,000 acres? Tell me, Jack, why is it that after being so aloof to me on deals for so long, you offer me this one?"

Jack realized that Pollack had become the hard-nosed investor, the inquisitor, who had to be suspicious of any deal offered him. He was mortified to have put himself in such a position. Now he was in the same class as all the other Houston promoters! He didn't have the heart to make a hard sell to Pollack on such a basis, and in the end the deal was left in the air. Pollack promised to call.

Discouraged, Jack tried one or two other possible takers, this time by phone to save embarrassment — with pretty much the same results. He began to fear that word might spread. Once upon a time he didn't mind being rebuffed. One early well he had sold only after calling on forty oil companies. But now he was at the peak of his career and too proud to grovel to the carriers of the money bags.

He thought it might be less conspicuous if he tried to sell his override in New York where he had many old friends and clients. Maybe they wouldn't ask so many questions.

He stayed at the Brook Club, where Ralph had put him up as a guest, and pounded the pavements. Every call he made hurt him. To his dismay, he found that the casual New York investor, burned so often by the Houston oil syndicates, had grown wary. Most were polite, but they didn't sign on.

One day, he was sitting at the common dining table at Brook when a young man with whom he had had a very favorable deal took a seat beside him.

"Hello, Jack! It's great to see you. I saw your name on the room list and hoped I'd find you. After that great little gas field we got in Goliad County, I've always hoped you'd let me in on another play."

"Well," said Jack carefully, "it's good to see you, Frank. Just like old times." He told Frank about how well their field was producing, and the good prospects it had for deeper production. "I haven't taken in partners for a long time, Frank. It's quite a responsibility. But just by chance I'm drilling a very good deep prospect in Southern Louisiana and might sell you an overriding royalty if you still like that kind of play. As you know, it's a neat package — all or nothing and a quick answer. In this case, I believe it will be all, or I wouldn't be drilling it straight up." He almost held his breath, but in the end Frank signed up for $250,000.

All his other efforts struck out. He hadn't given up, but time was running out. He still needed another $250,000 to see the deep sand at Gillette.

He thought about it a long time before he picked up the phone and called Tom Pickens at the ranch.

"How's everything going, Tom? How're the cattle?"

"Just great, Jack. We've had rain and the grass looks awfully good. We're all looking forward to your being back up here soon. Anything I can do for you?"

"Well, I haven't decided, but I may want to sell some cattle. The price is pretty good, and the market in Llano next month might be right. Why don't you feed the stock up and get them ready just in case."

Jack sensed the change in Tom's voice; he seemed to choke a little before replying. "O.K., boss," was all he said, but Jack knew he was startled, not to mention worried.

But no more so than Jack. To sell the herd he'd built up so carefully over the years was almost like cutting off his right hand. But it *would* get him that last $250,000.

He scowled, passed a hand over his eyes, and let his mind drift back to the early days in Austin and Houston.

12

Jack

With his mother's strong backing and precious little else, he decided to get his degree in geology at the University of Texas. For the first two years, he just barely scraped by working at two part-time jobs and in the summer. He never knew whether he would be able to pay the meager bills that sustained his spartan life. He had no car, no money for dates, and had trouble coming up with dimes for cokes at the college shop, which proved a constant embarrassment.

But he managed to make good grades, earned his letter in cross-country, and gradually his situation improved. During his junior year his fraternity gave him room and board in return for tutoring the freshmen. In his senior year he made Phi Beta Kappa, his letter in track, and was elected president of his fraternity. He had made an outstanding record in the School of Geology, and on graduation felt fully prepared to enter his chosen profession.

He had decided to marry Janet almost as soon as he met her. She was the sister of the ubiquitous Sam Johnson, his East Texas oil field friend. Sam, who was in Wyoming at the time, had asked Jack, a sophomore, to look after Janet when she entered Texas U. Jack had found her to be exceptionally pretty, with an easy, winning smile. She didn't say much, but when she did she revealed a good sense of humor, sound judgment, and a healthy skepticism. In his junior year he had given her his fraternity pin. She had gone to summer school to catch up with him, and shortly after graduation they were married in her sleepy hometown of Lufkin, with her minister father officiating. Janet was another decision he had never had cause to regret.

Nor had he ever regretted his decision to head for Houston after the wedding. There had never been any debate over where they would go. Houston had been a leading oil center ever since the discovery of the Spindletop field and was fast becoming the oil capital of America, and indeed, the world. Tulsa, Dallas, Fort Worth, Oklahoma City, and New Orleans were regional outposts of the oil kingdom, but Houston was its heart and soul.

Jack and Janet didn't know the city; they'd been there only once, for a wedding, two years before. But they were too naive to be intimidated. They arrived one Saturday afternoon, their possessions piled into Jack's battered Chevrolet, and put up in a tumbledown motel on South Main that charged only five dollars a night. That first evening, in their dark, tiny room tinted green by the flashing Rest Haven sign outside the window, Jack held Janet close and promised, "This is going to be our town, my girl. I'm the best darned geologist that's ever hit this place, so don't you worry about anything!"

It was not until weeks later that concerned friends told them that South Main was a dangerous, violent neighborhood. Jack and Janet simply hadn't noticed. For them, all of Houston, even Skid Row, was still radiant, enchanted, the land of their dreams.

On their first Monday morning in Houston, Jack put on his best suit, Janet selected his most elegant tie, and he went forth to confront the Personnel Director of the mighty Coastal Oil Company, with whom he had been put in contact by a friend from school. Within an hour he had been offered a job as a subsurface geologist, at two hundred dollars a month, a rather princely salary in those Depression days. After talking it over with Janet, Jack accepted the offer the next morning. He might have tried his luck with Texoil, Humble, Gulf, Mobil, or the scores of other smaller oil companies in Houston, but Coastal seemed as good as any; it offered opportunities for education and advancement, and he saw no reason to look further.

In those first busy, exciting weeks, Jack was caught up in his new job, while Janet was just as busy searching for a home for them. She read the real estate ads, talked to friends, took daily excursions to various neighborhoods, and in time advised Jack that they might do best to settle in one of Houston's burgeoning suburbs. The commute would be a nuisance for Jack, but houses closer to town were expensive and their tiny yards looked terribly confining. Both of them wanted space and trees, such as they'd grown up with in East Texas, and they wanted children.

They soon made a down payment on a small brick cottage on a large lot in a live oak grove in a popular suburb called Bellevue. Several of Jack's new friends at Coastal lived there, and almost all their neighbors were connected with the oil business in one way or another. Before long, Janet was teaching a Sunday school class at the Bellevue Methodist Church, and their weekends were filled with square dancing parties, cookouts, and an occasional Sunday at the beach in Galveston.

The first thing Jack realized, in his new life at Coastal, was how much he had to learn. His education up to that point could not compare with the mass of information resulting from exploration and research by a major oil company. He was given intensive training in the use of the powerful new tool, the Schlumberger electrical log, which enabled geologists to tell from electrical measurements made in a well if the strata of the earth they had drilled contained oil or gas or salt water. These logs could also be matched with one another to map the "structure," or configuration, of the underlying rocks, giving tantalizing clues as to where traps of oil might be found.

As one of their duties Jack and the other young geologists spent many exciting, sleepless nights "sitting" on wells out in the field. They assisted the petroleum engineers in the drilling and testing of the wells and trying to predict the chances of production. These trips to the field might last four or five days, usually spent in tents or shacks near the well, and if part of Jack hated the separation from Janet, part of him still savored the romance of oil exploration.

The second thing Jack learned at Coastal was that he was part of a huge, and sometimes cumbersome, bureaucracy. He was, to be precise, one of the eight geologists in the Geological Section of the Exploration Division of the Department of Exploration and Production.

This was, to be sure, the most glamorous part of the company, for the discovery of oil provided the bulk of Coastal's income and, in effect, subsidized its pipeline, refining, marketing, and other activities. Even in those depression days, with oil selling for $1.25 a barrel, substantial profits could be made. But everything depended on outwitting the other companies in the endless competition for finding new fields.

Most of Jack's immediate associates, the other geologists in the Section, were about his age, with backgrounds much like his own and too excited about their work to worry much about getting ahead of one another. There was an easy camaraderie among them that often extended to weekend cookouts and beer parties.

Jack's first real problem came one step up the bureaucratic ladder, with the director of the Exploration Division, a man named Clarence Willens. Called "Doc" to his face, because of his doctorate from Harvard, he'd been dubbed "Old Ironhead" behind his back by junior geologists who considered him stubborn and dogmatic. Jack was soon among that number. "Doc" Willens was a proud, sensitive man who, at fifty-five, knew he would rise no higher in the Coastal hierarchy. He had been responsible for the discovery of several major fields on the Texas and Louisiana coasts, and he knew he was secure in his present job. As the years passed, however, he'd become more and more withdrawn, suspicious, and hostile to new ideas. It seemed incredible to Jack, innocent then of bureaucracies, that a man with such a closed mind could hold a key position in an expanding new industry, where every year saw great scientific revolutions taking place.

By the time Jack had been with Coastal a year, his special flair for finding oil was recognized. This, most oilmen agree, is as much an art as a science. Jack and a dozen other geologists could study the same ambiguous data, but more often than not it was Jack who would find the proverbial needle in the haystack. He scored several early successes, coming up with geological interpretations that led to several good fields. And yet he was frustrated in his dealings with Old Ironhead.

One continuing issue was where Coastal should concentrate its exploration. Because Coastal had been born amid the great Spindletop oil boom, the company had for nearly thirty years focused on the prolific Texas-Louisiana coastal plain, with its fabulous salt dome structures which could produce as much as a thousand barrels of oil per acre foot of rich Miocene sand.

Yet with the discovery of more and more oil along the coast, it seemed to Jack only logical that Coastal should explore more inland, where competition was not so fierce and leases could be had, and more cheaply, in what amounted to virgin territory. Jack was convinced that important discoveries were awaiting the company there. He worked on his own time, nights and often Sundays, studying all the available data, until he had pinpointed what he believed to be a promising area centered north of Beaumont. He documented his case as fully as he could and recommended that Coastal shoot a broad reconnaissance seismic survey over the area.

As Jack made his presentation to "Doc" Willens, the veteran geologist listened grimly, a scowl on his face, his eyes unblinking behind his thick glasses, his big head twitching impatiently. When Jack had finished, Willens said gruffly, "I don't know where you young fellows get your ideas. Is that what they taught you at the University of Texas? This is a great company we work for, and it's great because we've been finding oil in those thick lush Miocene sands along the coast for a long, long time. You start going north and you run out of big structures. There aren't any shallow salt domes there; the ones you find are deep and don't amount to anything. Those thin Oligocene sands up there are so tight your recovery will be half what we're used to down south. Young man, as long as I'm sitting in this chair, we're staying south. I'd suggest you get back to your maps."

Jack stormed out of the office, went home, and poured out his frustrations to Janet.

Then the news of Texoil's discovery of a new field in Newton County swept through Houston one Monday morning. The *Houston Post*'s story carried the declaration of Bill Butler, District Geologist for Texoil: "Once again, Texoil leads the way in its important new Texas oil discovery north of Beaumont. We have opened up an entirely new trend in a new producing formation, the Marine Oligocene, about which you will hear more."

Jack could hardly speak when he heard the news. That was *his* field, the one he'd all but begged "Doc" Willens to shoot. Of course Texoil had to find it. He wasn't the only bright young geologist in town. Others were studying the same logs, reaching the same conclusions. If Coastal wanted to drag its feet, to live in the past, others would reap the inland treasures.

The Exploration Department held its weekly staff meeting that afternoon. Jack gritted his teeth and kept silent as the various reports were made. The meeting was about to break up when Henry

Hewlett raised his hand. An office man, a scholar by inclination, and blessed with a biting sense of humor, Henry said, "Say, wasn't that Jack's field that Texoil brought in last week? The one Jack was telling us to shoot four or five months ago? Am I right, Jack, or does memory deceive me?"

Before Jack could answer, "Doc" Willens spoke up. His face was red, but his voice was steely. "That so-called field is a fluke. Texoil will lose their shirt there; it will never pay off. Let's get back to work!"

But Texoil did not lose its shirt. For weeks, the papers were full of stories on the dimensions of the new Newton County field. It looked like the discovery of the year, and there was talk around Houston that it might spark a wave of new inland exploration over a large area. Doc Willens hadn't relented, but his boss recognized this opportunity, and Jack was offered the job of Chief Geologist for Louisiana in Lafayette, to follow the new exciting trend on the Louisiana side.

Lafayette, Louisiana, in 1939, was a sleepy college town that was fast becoming an oil center. Most major companies and a dozen Independents had offices there. Famed for its annual Azalea Festival, Lafayette lay on the northwest edge of Louisiana's bayou country, an area of lakes and swamps, pine and cypress thick with Spanish moss.

Most of the residents were of French descent. In the late seventeenth century, their ancestors had settled in what was then Acadia, in eastern Canada, now known as Nova Scotia. After the British seized Acadia in 1713, many of the French there made their way to the French settlements along the Gulf Coast around New Orleans, where they maintained their own culture long after the Louisiana Purchase in 1803. They were called "Cajun," an abbreviation of Acadian.

Jack, Janet, and their two-year-old twins moved into a comfortable house in Lafayette complete with a Cajun housekeeper named Marie. She was soon delighting them with filé gumbo, crawfish bisque, jambalaya, stuffed shrimp, and countless other Cajun treats. Through her, they met their neighbors, who dropped by with gifts of food and drink, a Cajun custom.

Before long, their new friends took them on tours of the bayous, where the original Cajun settlers had hunted and fished and trapped. They traveled on small narrow boats called "pirogues," which they claimed could sail on the dew. Each year brought the Rice Festival, the Crawfish Festival, and the Sweet Potato Festival. These were capped, of course, by Mardi Gras, when men in clown suits and fiddlers went about kissing the girls, playing tricks on the men, and drinking lots of the local wine. The celebration climaxed with a huge gumbo dinner, with much drinking, dancing, pranks, and laughter.

Jack still remembered his first Cajun joke: In the midst of Mardi Gras, a Cajun husband found his best friend in bed with his wife. The dazed husband wandered out of the bedroom and told the others, "My friend Pierre, he is so drunk he t'ink he is me?"

On their way home from their first Mardi Gras, Janet was nestling sleepily against him as he drove. "I've never had that good a time anywhere," she said. "They treated us just like family."

"They really let themselves go," said Jack. "Most of them are poor but it doesn't seem to matter."

"Making money isn't the most important thing in life," said Janet.

"What's the phrase they use?" asked Jack. *"Joie de vivre?"*

"Joy of living," murmured Janet. "Let's hope we keep ours."

Jack's main aim in life was finding oil, and the Louisiana assignment provided him with his first big opportunity. The more he studied the geological data, the more confirmation he got of his belief that other promising structures lay in a belt of country lying to the north. Jack found areas where the pull of the earth's gravity was less, instead of greater, than normal as under shallow salt domes. This could mean salt domes much deeper than those to the south. And salt domes signified structures that could contain oil.

Jack eagerly worked up maps showing possible structural traps for oil-bearing strata at different depths overlying deep domes. The Louisiana area he was interested in was on the same geological trend as the Texoil discovery in Newton County, Texas. They were both traversed by the same east-west major fault. Surely Willens would listen this time.

Jack was at a hotel in Lake Charles when he called Houston. "All I want," he pleaded, "is to send a crew up north and do a little shooting."

"The oil is along the coast," insisted Willens. "A lot of idiots have wasted their time and money up north. Well, we won't."

Angry and frustrated, Jack walked down to the hotel's dark, cool bar. He was on his second beer when a pleasant-looking man in his early thirties, wearing silver-rimmed glasses, approached.

"You Jack Sanderson with Coastal?"

"Right," said Jack, his tone distinctly uninviting.

"I'm Randy Simpson," persisted the man, taking the next stool. "I'm an Independent working out of my office here in Lake Charles." With an outdoorsman's tan and dressed in dungarees, an old flannel shirt and work boots, Simpson looked like a roustabout. But his eastern accent, obvious intelligence, and good sense of humor bespoke a good education. The time passed pleasantly and when Simpson suggested dinner at his place, Jack readily agreed. Outside, on Lake Charles' main street, several passers-by hailed Simpson. Jack took note: such a popular man might be useful in negotiating leases with stubborn local landowners.

They climbed into Simpson's dusty old pick-up and rattled out of town. Jack assumed he was heading for a bowl of chili in some backwoods bungalow, and that suited him. But at sunset, Simpson turned down a long lane, lined with flowering magnolias, and stopped in front of a house like no other Jack had ever seen — modern architecture, all pecky cypress and glass, overlooking a lovely bayou.

Jack stopped gaping long enough to ask, "This yours?"

"Yep," said Simpson, smiling broadly.

"Looks like one of . . . what's his name . . . Wright. Frank Lloyd Wright's houses."

"It should. Built for me by one of his students in '35. That was a good year. Thank God, it's paid for."

Randy's wife, Mary, a striking, dark-haired woman with alert hazel eyes, was charming and hospitable. While Randy mixed a pitcher of martinis, measuring the vermouth with an eyedropper, she made Jack feel relaxed and welcome. Several children ran about the house until a servant in a white jacket led the youngsters away to their dinner.

They dined by candlelight on a delicious bouillabaisse, accompanied by a fine French wine. Soft classical music played in the background — Grieg, said Mary. The meal and the Simpsons' spirited company made Jack forget about Coastal Oil's stupidity.

After thick Cajun coffee had been served and Randy had produced aromatic Cuban cigars, Mary excused herself to see to the children.

"I hear you're interested in Acadia Parish," said Randy, lighting his cigar.

"Where'd you hear that?" Jack's tone was deliberately casual. No one outside Coastal was supposed to have that kind of information.

"Oh, I've got my sources," said Randy, letting smoke drift toward the cathedral ceiling. "I hear you think there may be some deep domes up there. Well, I've mapped some good gravity minima there and I think so, too."

"Oh," said Jack, cautious now, wondering where the conversation was leading.

"I've got a thousand-acre block up there called Bayou Bleu. Haven't got the capital to drill myself, so I'm looking to make a deal. I hear you might be a good man to talk to."

"You mean Coastal?" said Jack, not bothering to hide his disgust. "Only this afternoon, Doc Willens turned down my request to send a crew up there."

Randy shook his head. "Doc'll bankrupt that company yet. Heard how he stopped you from checking out the Newton County field that Texoil brought in. I'm sure Texoil is ready to drill along the trend, but I'd rather not deal with Butler."

"I'll need something to change Doc's mind," said Jack.

"Look at this," said Randy, who stood up and produced a gravity map from a side table. "I've covered Bayou Bleu with a torsion balance and I'm sure there's structure under there."

The torsion balance, invented some years earlier by German scientists for measuring the horizontal pull of the earth's gravity, had been outdated by the seismograph. Still, it was a useful reconnaissance tool if properly employed. Randy's data strengthened Jack's belief that deep salt structures existed in the north.

"Looks like a long east-west structural trend," said Jack who had carried the map to a lamp. "Seems to be related to a major fault." He straightened and looked out the window into the black Louisiana night. "Might be enough to convince Houston. What kind of deal are you proposing?"

After ten minutes of good natured wrangling, Jack summed it up. "Okay. I get Houston to send a crew up there and run a couple of lines across your picture. If nothing shows up, we quit. If we find north dip, you want a half-million dollar oil payment, out of an eighth override, plus your landowner's royalty on your own fee land."

"That's it," agreed Simpson, stubbing his cigar in a huge crystal ash tray.

"Will you give me a verbal sixty-day option on that basis?" asked Jack.

Simpson grinned and extended his hand. "You've got it."

After a half hour's pondering in his office the next day, Jack called Willens in Houston.

"Doc, I've got evidence of a good structure in Acadia Parish and I'd like to send a crew up to shoot it."

"Acadia Parish?" Willens' tone was scornful. "Hell. That's halfway to St. Louis. Did you get lost?"

"No, Doc, I — "

Willens' booming voice cut him off. "Damn it, Sanderson! We're looking for oil on the coast, not hundreds of miles inland. Why can't you get that through your thick skull?"

"This is an extension of the Newton County fault," said Jack exasperatedly. "Texoil will be after it pretty soon. An Independent, Randy Simpson, has been over it with a torsion balance and found a good minima."

"A torsion balance?" roared Willens. "Why didn't he use a forked stick?"

"But I've seen Simpson's data," Jack insisted.

"I know all about Simpson and his land up north. His old man lost a fortune drilling the area and the son's been trying to sucker others into the place ever since."

Controlling his rage with difficulty, Jack said slowly, "I'm sending a written request for permission to send a crew to Acadia Parish."

"Send away," said Willens coldly. "I'll have the denial typed and ready to go this afternoon. Good day."

Jack found himself holding a dead phone. He slammed it into its cradle and was still fuming when Coastal's seismic crew called in that they were idled by lack of permits from landowners. The hell with Willens.

The next day, he and Randy Simpson joined the fifteen-man crew at Randy's block. The land had been cleared and irrigated for rice, where a slight natural elevation had caused Bayou Bleu to flow around it. On the coast, salt domes could arch the surface twenty or thirty feet, but a dome 20,000 feet deep, Jack realized, might only cause a rise of a few feet. He thought the area looked promising.

Jack and Randy showed the crew where to lay out two parallel north-south lines about a half mile apart across Randy's minima. Each line would be about seven thousand feet long, requiring seven one-thousand-foot "spreads" of seismometers and connecting cables. First, the surveyors laid out the lines, marking the shot points at thousand-foot intervals. Next the drillers, using a small rotary drill, put down fifty-foot holes at each shot point, a total of sixteen holes to be shot in two days.

The shooter, shirtless in the summer heat, pushed down a quarter pound of dynamite to the bottom of the hole with a long, hinged pole. Then he filled the hole with water to keep the explosive energy in the ground. A wire ran from the dynamite fuse to the hand detonator he carried.

The recorder, holder of a Ph.D. in electrical engineering, was field crew leader. He supervised the complex equipment in the recording truck which would detail the reflected sound waves from the blast. Jack and Randy watched impatiently as the recorder issued his last-minute instructions to his helper, while warming up the amplifiers.

"Are you ready?" the recorder finally shouted.

"Ready!" yelled the shooter, now standing fifty feet from the hole, his detonator poised.

"Shoot!"

The dynamite exploded with a dull thud, sending a geyser of water and mud out of the hole. The men standing nearby shielded their faces from flying debris. In the recording truck, a camera recorded moving beams of light on an oscillograph, electronic signals representing the first arrival of sound coming along the short surface path at 3,000 feet per second. Then came the waves which had gone straight down at over 10,000 feet per second. Within three seconds, reflections from these waves had been recorded from many beds of rock down to 15,000 feet.

Standing at the door of the recording truck, Jack heard the recorder say, "Looked good. Lots of reflections." His helper immediately took the long roll of film into the tiny darkroom. A few minutes later, he emerged with it still dripping from the "fixer." The recorder studied the wet film to adjust his instruments for the next shot, while his helper moved the shooting truck the thousand feet to the next hole.

Both Randy and Jack understood the dangers of trying to force conclusions on skimpy data. Impatiently, they waited until midafternoon when five spreads had been shot. Then they crowded into the truck for their first look at the records.

"There it is," cried Jack, tracing the outline with a finger. "North dip." A quick look revealed that all five records had the wave form of the reflection from the top of the Marine Oligocene at 8,000 feet. "It comes up from the south dipping south," said Jack, "a little steeper than the regional dip, just like it should. And at the top of your minima, it flattens and turns over to make a north dip, about twenty thousandths of a second."

"That should mean about a hundred feet of closure," said Randy. The closure indicated the height of the trap for oil. "Enough. We've got a structure here, an oil field."

The next day at his office, Jack found a Telex from Doc Willens ordering him to report to Houston immediately. Evidently Willens had gotten word about the unauthorized visit to Acadia Parish. But Jack wasn't worried. Not even Old Ironhead could ignore the hard evidence of the north dip at Bayou Bleu.

Five months later, the first well came in at Bayou Bleu at 8,300 feet, producing three thousand barrels a day. Ultimately, the field had thirty wells and would produce twenty-five million barrels. Jack received a five thousand dollar bonus, a raise, and a promise of promotion. Randy Simpson would eventually receive in the neighborhood of five million dollars.

His discovery of Bayou Bleu, for which Jack had received so little while Coastal had made so much, was the final straw. Jack was determined that the next field he found would be his own.

A few months later, despite Coastal's warnings that no oil company would take him back, Jack left Coastal and turned Independent.

Oil companies lived in fear that an employee would leave with information that was worth millions. When it happened, it was bad for morale. Part of his settlement required Jack to sign an agreement that he would not explore for oil for six months in any area where he had been working for Coastal. This pleased Jack no end; after six months he was free to look *anywhere* for himself. Jack had his eye on some promising land near Bayou Bleu, which Coastal had turned down. He was giving Coastal six months to find it first.

13

Ralph

So high were Ralph's spirits on his return from Lake Charles that he nearly forgot about Bill Butler's dinner party. Anne, of course, had not, and as he listened to her worrying out loud about what to wear, he wondered whether the invitation had anything to do with his possible advancement. Now that the Gillette lease was in hand he found he didn't much care. It was a feeling he liked.

The Butler home, which was also in River Oaks, wasn't far away, though it was in a section that definitely lay beyond Ralph's means.

The house was famous, having been designed by a world-renowned architect and written up in all the architectural journals. Ralph thought the exterior resembled nothing so much as a pile of building blocks of different sizes, stacked one upon another as though by a child at play. The blocks had been chosen, however, because of Bill Butler's insistence on privacy, but they didn't begin to suggest the elegance, and comfort that lay within. The interior emphasized again and again that nothing was too good for Bill Butler.

Anne and Ralph arrived precisely at eight. Traversing an immense square foyer, they made their way into the high-ceilinged drawing room which was baronial in scale. It was large enough, Ralph had kidded Anne, to take a long walk in on a rainy Sunday afternoon. The windows, doors and mantels were massive, the woodwork that framed them imposing yet classic. The russet leather furniture blended beautifully with the Philippine mahogany and stood imposingly at hard right angles to everything else. It was, above all, a man's room. The only feminine touch were the masses of flowers but even these were arranged in square wooden tubs. Bill Butler's surroundings matched him.

Their host excused himself from the only other couple there and strode across the room. A hefty six-foot-two, he put body into whatever he did. "Welcome, Anne, Ralph," he said warmly, taking Anne's hand in both of his, Ralph was quick to notice. "How good of you to come! Alicia is away as usual, in our place at St. Tropez, so would you mind acting as my hostess, Anne?" His eyes twinkled. "It'll be a small group, only sixty." Without waiting for an answer, he turned and summoned the other couple. "Here, I'd like you to meet Frank and Vera Wood. Frank owns the Oilers, you know. We're celebrating his birthday tonight. Care to join us in champagne?"

Ralph marveled at just how much Bill seemed at one with his setting. He stood out, exuding energy and bigness and confidence. Although he worked hard at presenting an image of the rustic, hometown, self-made Texan, he was none of these. Even during his years at Yale, Ralph had heard over the years, Bill had cultivated friendships with young men from families of great wealth and power. This was what he wanted.

He could be utterly disarming, but the charm only masked for a while his absolute insistence on getting what *he* wanted. He knew where to get the best geological information, he always knew the lawyer who could help him make the best deal, and a slip of the tongue by a rival over drinks about an oil concession would find Bill on his plane at dawn and in the Persian Gulf that evening, negotiating with this Sultan or that.

At fifty-nine Bill Butler stood at the peak of his power, in perfect health, immensely wealthy, and in full control of his company, whose board he scorned and seldom convened. No director dared question his decisions or stand up against him. Texoil produced two million barrels of oil a day, four percent of the oil of the free world, from fields in fifteen countries. A Texoil well had discovered the first oil in the North Sea. Three jet planes, one a converted B707 with three bedrooms, were always at Butler's disposal. Although he didn't need it, he saw that his own salary and bonuses were always the highest in the industry, currently over one million dollars a year. His need to be first was rapacious.

Among businessmen he was a natural leader. He had been President of the Business Council, Chairman of the Roundtable, and was currently Chairman of the American Petroleum Institute, the trade association of big oil. He had been adviser to every President since Truman. During the summer encampments at the Bohemian Grove among the redwoods of Northern California, he held court daily at luncheon for the great and near-great of industry and government. Texoil was his base. He had made it fourth among the oil companies of the world. He had used it to achieve his own personal goals and lifestyle. From his New York office, which was his cockpit, he could fuel the illusion that he, as much as any other man, ran the world.

Ralph turned his full attention to Frank Wood now, even though he'd never paid much attention to professional football.

"It's the Oilers who put Houston on the map," Wood was saying. "You ask any man what he's most proud of in Houston, and he'll tell you the Oilers. The team represents the fulfillment of the manhood of every red-blooded Houston man. Same goes for women and womanhood. The Oilers are paid gladiators representing all of us, fulfilling our secret ambitions. When the Oilers win, we all win!"

"I agree football's a fine sport," said Ralph carefully, "but it's really a spectator sport. Most of us can't play it. I like tennis and golf."

"Those games are for sissies," said Wood dismissively. Ralph doubted he was even aware of the insult. "Professional football is hard and tough. Anyway, Houston's too damn hot for that stuff. A man is better off coming out to the air-conditioned Astrodome for a real contest. When you've seen Joe Glasscock hit the line, you've seen it all. Football is Houston's sport. And it makes lots of money," he said with a wink.

"Obviously because you field such good teams. So how do you do it?"

"I've got plenty of money to spend," said Wood proudly. "Unless I earn money, big money, I can't pay the prices and salaries for the best players." He lowered his voice. "Listen, I just paid a cool million for Ernie Steel. Houston wants winners."

Ralph finally excused himself and moved among the other guests, about half of whom he knew. He had lost sight of Anne, even though the room did not seem at all crowded. He watched Butler playing the perfect host and stopped for a moment to listen to the string quartet playing at the far end of the room.

"You work for Bill Butler?" asked an older man Ralph knew only by reputation. "Quite a man. I've known him all my life, his father before him. Rather different from what he appears. Toughest man I've ever seen in a deal. A lot of people are scared to deal with him, afraid they'll get run over or end up in a lawsuit. But he keeps his word — once you're sure what his word is."

"Well, as a Texoil lawyer, I get quite a different picture," Ralph smiled. "As chairman of Texoil, he has to stand behind his word. That's the only way you can stay in the oil business. The whole company is behind his deals. That puts a lot of assets at risk."

"O.K. I'm sure you know where you stand, but watch out. I wouldn't like to get caught crossing Bill Butler. He's above the law and responsibility to other men. He fought to make it and no one is going to take it away from him. No one. At the level at which he operates there is no higher authority. He slips in and out of countries as fast as his planes can carry him. He's got them all wrapped around his finger, you know, those gnomes in Zurich, the kings and sheiks of the Middle East. The world is his oyster."

As the man moved away, Ralph wondered if he should start worrying.

Ralph finally caught up with Anne, who stood talking with a group of women they knew. "I deal only with Lord of London," said one dowager whose accoutrements confirmed her assertion. "They have this dear fellow there, you know, Robert Blair. If I see anything in his catalogues I like, he has it flown in from New York or London the next day. Often he flies off to make the rounds of their shops just looking for things for me. And what a charming boy. It's sad he doesn't like the Houston girls, but then he wouldn't have so much time for me. Tsk, you know what I mean."

Suddenly Bill Butler materialized next to Anne. "Dear," he said, squeezing her hand, "would you mind finding our birthday boy and see that he gets to his place? He's on your right."

Innocuous enough, Ralph told himself, perfectly natural. He was finding jealousy very demanding.

Anne, seated at the far end of the large table, was a conspicuous and attractive balance to the host. She'd had a few glasses of champagne by now and was especially witty and charming. She turned to Frank Wood and put her hand lightly on his sleeve.

"I'm ashamed to admit I'm not much of an Oilers fan," she said with a big smile. "Ralph has taken me to a couple of your games, but I usually let him find another man to go with. Frankly, I can never quite figure out what's going on. And all those people sitting in those luxurious boxes never seem to pay attention anyway. They're too busy talking and drinking."

"Shame on you," retorted Frank Wood, shaking a finger. "We need pretty girls like you to make our games more interesting. You should give parties before the games. Everybody's doing it. Get some of your friends together. If you can't get the Texoil box, have your party in mine. The first one will be on the club. We're creating a women's support group, the Oilerettes. Every member gets a diamond pin from me, gives at least three parties a season and sells twenty-five season tickets to friends. Join up!"

Anne wondered if the man's enthusiasm ever waned. "That's very kind of you, but I'm not sure I'm your girl. But I promise you I'll come when I can. I understand Texoil is spending a million dollars redecorating their box. Perhaps I can persuade them to give it a more feminine touch so we girls will feel more at home. I'll certainly speak to Bill about it."

Since the meal had not been served until ten, everyone was in high spirits, courtesy of all the drinking. Bill Butler, as always, dominated his party. Gesturing, laughing, shouting across the table, he kept alive a party spirit that was infectious.

After the first course, he announced a film showing highlights of the Oilers' games during the last season. When he clapped his hands, a large screen descended the wall behind him.

When the film ended there was boisterous applause, and the dinner resumed, five more courses of it, meticulously prepared, with the best French wines. With dessert came champagne and Butler rose to make his toast, a little unsteady but still in control.

"I ask you to drink a birthday toast with me to a real man, Frank Wood, owner of the Houston Oilers. I like a man who fights to win, who fights with everything he's got, who never quits. Frank is that kind of man. He would be a success in anything he took on, whether sports or oil or whatever takes a fighter. Frank's a real fighter. His teams win. On the football field you don't ask for or give quarter. You hit hard, you squirm, you kick, you bite, you do everything you need to do to get the ball down the field. The only important thing is to win. Frank's my sort of man. I'm proud to call Frank my friend. He's the man who put Houston on the map. He's a man with guts. I drink to him, and so should you all. Many more birthdays, Frank!"

Ralph wondered if he was the only one not having a good time, the only one who winced at the fulsome toast. If this was Houston society at its best, he wanted no part of it. And he thought there was something inherently improper in Butler's naming Anne as hostess. Surely he had a sister, knew a widow, at the very least a best friend of his wife's? He took a sip of his brandy and a glance at his watch, wondering how soon they could escape. As "hostess," however, Anne would probably expect to stay to the bitter end.

To cries of "Hear, hear!" Frank Wood rose to his feet, smiling broadly. "Bill, I'm speechless," he said, and immediately disproved his statement. "Thank you for a great evening and for those kind words. I want the world to know I'm proud to be your friend. I only wish I were in your league." He paused at the burst of laughter. "There's no one I know who deserves better what he's got. The oil of the world was there and you took it with your bare hands. I wish I had you on my team, a running back to hit the opposing line. You'd get through. No one will ever be able to stop you. Keep it up. And thanks to everyone here." He swept his glass in a semi-circle, slopping a little brandy in the process. "You represent the spirit of Houston. My boys are out there fighting for you. We'll never let you down. A toast to our host, Bill Butler!"

When dinner was over, Ralph noticed that Bill Butler headed straight for Anne and guided her to a corner sofa, where they remained deep in conversation until various guests sought out their host to say goodbye. By then Ralph was thoroughly irritated, hardly able to follow the conversation of the lady with the jewelry, who had cornered him beside a tub of oleander. Nor was he assuaged when he overheard Frank Wood telling Bill in a loud voice how much he had enjoyed Anne's company. "She's great!" he exclaimed. "Make her come to the games. We need girls like her on our team." Ralph was beginning to feel like a distinct fifth wheel.

When Anne and Ralph finally took their leave, it seemed to Ralph that Bill held her hand a lot longer than was necessary. When he turned to Ralph he added, a twinkle in his eye, "I've got something I want to talk to you about real soon, young fellow," and clapped him heartily on the back.

Neither spoke on the drive home, but once they were in their house Ralph ventured, "You seem to have made quite a hit with Butler."

Shrugging, Anne sighed, "I guess. He asked me to be his hostess at the party he's giving before the pre-season game."

"What did you say? He didn't mention anything about it to me!"

"I'm sure he meant to, Ralph. Anyway, I didn't promise anything."

"I'd really rather you didn't."

"O.K., boss," she said, casually enough, but Ralph took little comfort. This wasn't like her. Of course, he had no business questioning Anne's right to the admiration of other men, or to a little harmless flirtation. His own record over the years had not been so good that he could take a holier-than-thou position. But Butler was a powerful as well as an attractive man. The combination might be irresistible.

The last thing Ralph wanted to do was give Anne the impression he was jealous. It was a matter of pride not to show any lack of confidence in her. That he worked for Bill Butler made it worse. Suddenly he wanted more than anything in the world to find oil on the Gillette lands. He'd no longer be beholden to Butler — or anyone else.

When he arrived home the next evening, Anne, in giving him a rundown of the day's events, said casually, "By the way, I called Bill's secretary and left word that we can't join his party next week."

Ralph said nothing, but he knew his wife well enough to recognize that this hadn't been easy for her — and that she was by no means convinced she'd done the right thing.

14

Anne

Anne pulled into the vast expanse of asphalt surrounding the Lone Star Mall and parked opposite the Neiman-Marcus entrance. She was making a last-minute check of her makeup and hair when the limousine silently appeared in her rear view mirror. Quickly, she shoved everything back in her handbag, donned dark glasses and a floppy hat, got out and locked her car. Still, she couldn't resist looking around as she trotted over to the big car, a part of her terrified that someone might recognize her.

And then, perversely, she felt the slightest twinge of disappointment that she hadn't seen anyone who might have recognized her. Silly! she admonished herself as she settled into the spacious back seat and turned to greet her host.

"It's so good to see you again," Bill said, taking her hand and not letting it go. "You can't know how much I've looked forward to this."

Though his smile was dazzling, she could see fatigue around his eyes and was instantly reminded of the vast realms of his life and the strain that went with it. Sympathy and understanding stirred within her, but she said nothing and contented herself with looking at the suburban landscape flying by. Being able to see out when outsiders couldn't see in gave her a sense of security — even superiority — and "if only they could see me now."

She felt Bill's eyes on her. "I can remember when all this was prairie," he said. "Five thousand acres of it belonged to my father, a sort of weekend place where he raised cattle. I learned to ride here, wouldn't be surprised if I galloped where that shopping center is more than once." There was an unmistakable wistfulness in his tone. "Twenty years ago, I developed it and made a small fortune. Over thirty-five hundred houses. Beginning to wonder if I made a mistake."

Anne smiled. "I doubt if you had any choice. Houston grew, people needed houses. If you didn't develop it, someone else would."

"Suppose so," he sighed. "You know, the older I get, the more I remind myself of my father. Toward the end, he started questioning progress and extolling the old values. Frightening to see yourself become what you once scorned."

"Or feared." It popped out before she could stop it and instantly she regretted it.

"Beg your pardon?"

"Oh, nothing," said Anne, forcing a bright smile. "Let's quit being so serious."

"Of course," said Bill, leaning forward and opening a door in the back of the front seat to reveal a small refrigerator. "If you'll pull down that table," he motioned toward a small handle in the back of the seat on Anne's side, "I believe light refreshment is in order."

Light refreshment proved to be a split of Möet champagne. Bill popped the cork, bouncing it off the plexiglass divider separating them from the chauffeur. He clinked his glass against hers. "To the future of two kindred souls."

They sipped champagne, from time to time looking into each other's eyes, then looking away quickly. At one point he took her hand. "Look over there, Anne. That's the Alvin oil field." His face and voice glowed with pride. "My first big success with Texoil. Produced over a hundred million barrels."

Anne saw only rusting derrick skeletons dotting the flat, barren land. The suburbs were more attractive. "Where did the name Alvin come from?"

"From the small town that used to be there, as most fields are named, now grown into a city. The field still dribbles out about a hundred barrels a day. Should close it down, but somehow I never seem to get around to it.

"Maybe you shouldn't," said Anne slowly. "Maybe that field

represents something special to you. It was *your* discovery."

An expression she couldn't fathom flickered across Bill's face, and he quickly looked away. After some moments he said in a low voice, "You're very perceptive."

They rode in silence until the limousine turned off the main highway and crunched along a crushed-shell road which wound for several miles through typical Gulf Coast marsh. Ahead Anne could see a tall chain link fence and a heavy metal gate, which swung open as they neared. Anne turned in time to see the gate close behind them.

"Radio controlled like a garage door," said Bill, his voice back to normal.

The marsh lay on both sides of the elevated road, flat and shiny like a mirror but for the tall grass and water hyacinths, and occasional stands of cypress trees.

"What a lovely sight," murmured Anne.

"Except for the road," said Bill, "it's unchanged since the beginning of time."

"Oh!" Anne cried. "That gray bird standing there! He's so close. Doesn't the car frighten him?"

"That's a blue heron," said Bill. "He's fishing for dinner. Cars don't seem to scare the wildlife nearly so much as people."

Anne rolled down the window just as three ducks flew low overhead and settled onto the water amid a chorus of quacks.

"Only the female quacks," said Bill. "The male makes that hoarse, raspy sound."

"Hmmn. The ducks I like best have orange sauce on them."

Bill chuckled as the car entered a wide circular drive on what must have been an island. It stopped in front of a long, gray low-slung hunting lodge built of logs of uniform size. Its very simplicity was notable, and Anne sensed the hand of a famous architect. But for the road, the lodge was surrounded by water.

"This is it," announced Bill.

When the chauffeur opened Anne's door, she stepped into an eerily quiet world of bright sunshine. Bill's voice beside her was soft. "If you look over there, you'll see an osprey nest on top of that dead tree."

She shaded her eyes and squinted. The dead tree had a bunch of sticks piled at the top and she could make out the form of a fairly large bird. "Is an osprey some kind of seagull?" she asked.

116

Again, Bill chuckled. "More like a sea hawk, a hawk that lives on fish. They're getting scarcer all the time. The Texoil directors wanted to fill in some of the marsh and expand the lodge. You should've seen their faces when I told them we couldn't because it might disturb the osprey family. They were mad as hell until I came across with a few more season tickets to the Oilers' games."

"You took on your board of directors over a bird's nest?" asked Anne, making no attempt to hide her amazement.

"Of course," Bill replied. "If I didn't do things like that once in a while, I'd have no fun at all."

It crossed Anne's mind that his seeing her might be one of those "things," but before she had a chance to formulate a question, Bill ushered her toward the lodge. She reached out and touched one of the logs, which were dotted with worm holes.

"What kind of wood is this?"

"Pecky cypress," said Bill. "The holes were pecked by small insects. Grows all around, lasts forever."

They stepped into a huge room panelled in knotty pine. Colorful Mexican blankets were draped over padded rawhide chairs and couches. There were three walls of picture windows looking out over the marsh and the fourth bore a huge flagstone fireplace, next to which stood a large glass-fronted case filled with shotguns. A huge dining table, which could easily accommodate twenty, occupied the center of the room.

"Most of the year," said Bill, "there's very little going on here. Come hunting season, it gets pretty lively."

Anne was looking at the mounted specimens of Gulf game and fish that filled the remaining wall space. Then she glanced up at Bill's profile, too rugged to be handsome in the conventional sense but attractive nonetheless. Her reaction surprised her; she'd always preferred finely chiseled features like Ralph's.

She didn't resist when Bill put his arm around her, smiled down at her upturned face, and kissed her. It was so casual, seemingly so natural and right. What shocked her was the fervor of her own response. And it was Bill, not she who pulled back.

She searched for something to say, a suggestion for something to do, to relieve the tension. "Any place we could take a walk before lunch?"

His grin was lopsided. "There's always the road."

"Let's explore a bit," she said, taking his hand and leading

117

him outdoors. Hand in hand, they walked back along the road to the next island, which Bill explained had trap-shooting facilities. Along the way, he pointed out herons, cranes, ducks, geese, and a variety of smaller birds Anne had never heard of.

They were standing by a muddy embankment where Bill had found some raccoon tracks, when Anne said, "Look, a whole family of turtles sunning themselves on that log."

"Could be," he said, smiling.

"What do you mean, could be? Those are turtles, aren't they?"

"Depends," he said. "You know the difference between a tortoise, a turtle, and a terrapin?"

"I like games, but science is not my strong point." She frowned. "A tortoise is a land animal and turtles are water animals, but I don't know about terrapins."

"Not many people do," said Bill. "Turtles live in salt water, terrapins in fresh. This marsh is fed by a slow-moving stream emptying into the Gulf. The water is brackish."

They headed back to the lodge, Anne trotting beside Bill, taking two steps for every one of his.

"I like your lodge," she said. "It doesn't spoil that primitive, lonely feeling you get from the marsh, doesn't break its spell."

"I wanted you to see it," said Bill. "I'm sorry it isn't duck season. Our boats would take us out to the blinds. We'll do that some cold November day. You'll find them very comfortable. They're made of concrete sunk in the marsh floor, each with its own stove. But today we'll shoot skeet from the high-low houses. I have a 410 which I believe will just suit you."

At the traps nearby, which operated electrically, Bill explained to Anne how they shot the clay pigeons, one thrown high and the other low, sometimes in turn, sometimes together. The marksman progressed through numbered stations in a semicircle. Bill loaded Anne's gun and placed her at the first station.

"On your mark, get set, shoot," he said gaily, pressing the low button. "Bravo!" he congratulated as Anne demolished the pigeon with her first shot. "Good shot! I didn't know you were such an expert. Where did you learn?"

"Oh, during summers on Fisher's Island," Anne replied casually. "My father hunted. Since he had no son, he wanted me to practice skeet with him. And I've always shot a little, mostly small birds. We often hunt duck with friends in lodges along the Texas and Louisiana coast. It's great fun. I love being on the marsh at dawn . . . but also at noon." She smiled impishly.

After two rounds, Bill suggested lunch. He had, of course, shot better, but he had been surprised at how well Anne had done. As they drank a martini in the lodge, he complimented her on her skill.

"I'm like you, Bill Butler. Anything I do I try to do well. I too want to win."

"Can two people who both want to win get on?" Bill asked. "A man and a woman, I mean?"

Anne smiled at him over her drink, deliberately provocative. "In the case of a man and a woman, I think Nature has ways of seeing that both win," she said.

Bill laughed with delight. "Come," he said, "let's have lunch before I get serious."

The meal was served by the same Filipinos who had been on the boat, in a small paneled room hung with hunting prints and gun racks. Bill regaled her with witty tales of safaris in Africa, and tiger-hunting in Nepal. Anne had little to do but ask interested questions, and Bill grew more expansive.

After lunch they sat with coffee on a long, low divan facing the marshland scene. When Anne was offered the brandy, she accepted readily.

"To you," said Bill, "you lovely lady. I can't tell you how good it feels to be here with you, away from everything. I'm . . . comfortable with you. I hope you know that's a great compliment. I hope you're as happy here as I am."

"It's hard to say how I feel," said Anne seriously. "The marsh is so lovely and wild, another world, and in here we are so safe and close. There's something about the contrast. You make me feel, well, protected."

Their hands had found each other, and they sat for a long time, silent, gazing out of the window. How strange, thought Anne. Who would believe we could sit here like this just holding hands? What did it reveal about this powerful man? Was it more important to him to sit quietly, sharing the beauty of a place he loved with her than to make love to her? Would that come, she thought drowsily. Did she want it to? Maybe this was just his way of softening her up, a "line" without words. But she dismissed the thought. No, it must be more complicated than that. She let her head rest on his shoulder.

The Texoil car did not start back from the hunting lodge at three-thirty as scheduled, nor did it start at four. When it did leave, Anne realized that she would arrive home after Ralph, and that there would have to be explanations. But she didn't care. She was in that other world as she sat silently, hand in hand with and very close to Bill Butler, on the ride back to the real world, which all of a sudden she was not prepared to face.

15

Ralph and Anne

One evening in late August, Ralph and Anne met Diane and Brad Compton at the club for tennis at six. The plan was to have drinks and dinner at the club and do whatever might occur to them later.

They were evenly matched. Both couples played good, hard driving tennis. Each couple took a set, and as twilight approached they decided to go two out of three for match and dinner. Brad, the weakest of the four, failed miserably at his serve, and Ralph and Anne won two-one.

"That was a beautiful party the Hardwicks gave at The Warwick," said Anne companionably over dinner. "We had a wonderful time. And what a guest list!"

"I've never seen such a buffet, or so much champagne." Ralph shook his head. "Be assured the government paid for it. There was scarcely a soul there that wouldn't have qualified as a business deduction. You can bet, though, that nobody cared. At 2:30 I cared very little except the girl I happened to be dancing with."

"Well, I had more fun at your party," said Diane. "I really prefer small affairs. But you're right. Not many people do their parties as well as Tom and Lucy, even the ones who can afford to. So many of the big parties are so obviously planned to impress, so blatantly business-oriented. The younger guys, most of whom are fresh out of the oil fields, just stand around. They have no idea how to dance or make small talk except for 'Who does your husband work for?' "

"Poor things," clucked Anne.

"We go to lots of the parties given by the older set," Diane went on. "The people are rather dear. They're so relaxed now. They've made it. They want for little, they have lovely homes, they've traveled widely, and they keep up with everything that's happening in New York and London and Paris. They were the ones who introduced Houston to the East, to New York, Newport, Southampton and Palm Beach society. They read all the good books, and they're extremely well informed on international affairs.

"Dear old Mrs. Bates, for instance. There's always a crowd around her after dinner. And not just because she's considered the grande dame and everyone wants to be invited to her parties. She's invariably the liveliest, most interesting person in the bunch. She's interested in you, who you are. 'Won't you come to see me sometime? I'll send you a card,' she says.

"No one though, will ever equal our dear Ima. You really never knew her, did you? She was marvelous. You know, her home's a museum now. It has twenty-six rooms full of priceless early American and English furniture and decorative arts. Will Hogg, her father, was Texas' first native governor, and she was his hostess. Such parties Miss Ima gave! She had an extraordinary memory for people and was the leader in establishing the original Houston charities. She died in London at the age of ninety while looking for furniture there."

"I'm sorry we missed her," said Ralph.

They all agreed, however, that the number of charity balls in Houston had become excessive, even though Diane and Ralph were very involved with the annual Museum of Fine Arts Ball. "They're usually very good parties," said Anne equivocating, "but there are just too many of them. Still, Ralph and I go to as many as we can. Thank God not all of them are annual affairs."

The clock on the wall of the club dining room showed nine-thirty as they were finishing dessert.

"Speaking of parties," said Brad, looking at his watch, "we have a beaut for you, if you're interested. Count and Countess Rezzoli are having one of their bashes tonight, and they asked us to bring you. They're this Italian couple who came here about five years ago, rich as cream. He's from an old Roman family, about sixty, I'd say, a real smooth operator. He came here ostensibly to invest the family money in oil, but he's acted as a funnel for other

Italian investments. He's in everything, all honest, supposedly, but there are rumors."

"She's indescribable," said Diane excitedly. "Much younger than he, beautiful in a slim, willowy way, unpredictable, a bird of the night. Their parties are legendary — you've probably heard of them, and you *can* believe everything you hear. We've been to a few. They can get anyone they want, although a few of the real squares of Houston stay away. You'd never catch Jack and Janet Sanderson there, for instance."

"You can see some real weirdos there, too," added Brad. "I don't know where they find them. Wops with wives dripping with diamonds, A-rabs, Indians. There's always pot around, and they say there's a room with a silver bowl full of cocaine, but if you don't go in for it, and we don't, you'll never see it."

"You needn't worry about your reputation," Diane said quickly. "You'll see a lot of people you know there. I think it would be educational for you. Also, you just might enjoy it. What do you say?"

Anne and Ralph looked at each other and nodded.

"Might be a good idea to go home and take a nap," said Brad as he signed for the round of drinks. "These shindigs never get rolling until midnight. Formal dress, would you believe? Come by our house about eleven-thirty. You'll need us to get by the bouncers in monkey suits at the door."

The Rezzolis' ten-acre estate was ensconced behind a high brick wall in a fashionable area that boasted one of Houston's most prestigious country clubs, the Bayou Club. Its long drive wound through woods, past a stream, and emerged in front of an enormous, twenty-foot high, one-storied structure that stretched in both directions as far as the eye could see. As an attendant whisked the car away, Ralph stared at the house, which seemed more like a modernistic fortress, with clean straight lines, gleaming white-painted stone, and an occasional slit for a window.

At the door, they were vetted by a muscular-looking young man who ushered them through a small foyer into a huge hall that was a riot of bright colors. Even Ralph, who had little enthusiasm for modern art, recognized a huge canvas as a Picasso. Another looked like Jackson Pollack's dribbly work, and the rest belonged to what Ralph categorized as the vast trove of undifferentiated abstract art that he had been exposed to over the years. Scattered about the thick bright blue carpet were clusters of white leather sofas and chairs. Man-high potted plants stood on either side of huge plate glass windows that looked over a vast expanse of illuminated formal garden, complete with sheltered benches and bubbling fountains. A dozen or so formally-dressed guests completed the scene.

With a crook of a finger, their guide summoned a waiter bearing a silver tray with glasses and a bottle of Dom Perignon, 1929. While the waiter offered glasses all around, the major-domo, in a pleasing but unidentifiable accent, said, "If you desire anything else, please ask."

"Champagne's fine," Brad assured him.

The major-domo continued, "The bar is at the left of the patio, hors d'oeuvres are being served in the Gauguin room on the right, and at one, omelets and salad will be available in the Monet room, which is behind me. Starting at two you will find crepes and sweets in the garden."

"What do you think of the place?" said Brad in a booming voice that made Ralph wince.

"The champagne is worth the price of admission," admitted Ralph. "As for the place, it looks like an adult Disneyland."

"Come on," urged Diane, taking his arm. "Let me show you around."

They strolled into another room, large by any standard other than that of the immense entry hall. An expanse of thick white carpet was broken by several pink marble tables and chrome and pink leather chairs. From a distance, the six paintings, hung two to a wall, seemed inadequate against the delicate pink background, but before Ralph had taken two steps, the vivid earth tones of Gauguin's dark-skinned island women and lush tropical foliage seized his attention, and he saw how the pink somehow enhanced their primitive sensuality.

"Luscious, aren't they?" said Diane, squeezing his arm.

"They're superb! Any museum would be thrilled to have these."

"Thrilled is right. The one you're looking at is the most interesting. No one knows its background, or its value. The Count has never allowed his collection to be examined by experts. Rumor has it most of them were stolen during the war. How he came by them is anyone's guess. That one is the most valuable, probably worth all the rest put together. Say ten million, give or take a few."

Ralph whistled, then, seeing the way she was looking at him he said, "You wouldn't be pulling my leg?"

"No way, honest Injun."

Brad's voice interrupted. "Let's get something to eat, honey. All this culture's hard to take on an empty stomach." He draped an arm over each of them and steered them toward a table in the middle of the room. Covered with white damask, it held a dazzling array of silver, candles, and food that was a work of art in itself. A sinfully large mound of black caviar was flanked by masses of shrimp, crab claws, and smoked salmon. These in turn gave way to plates of tiny puff pastries and silver chafing dishes, kept warm by flickering candles.

Anne appeared, carrying a small china plate. "Did you notice these?" she said in an awed voice, holding up a fork. "The handle's gold filigree. Absolutely exquisite."

"Glad we came?" Ralph teased.

"I wouldn't have missed it! Everything's fabulous! Have you seen the fish pond?" She gestured toward oversized French doors which led to a huge atrium, resplendent with orchids, palms, and a waterfall cascading into a shiny black pond. It flashed with gold and silver as large carp broke the surface and disappeared again.

"Everything's gorgeous, but I keep wondering where they actually live," said Ralph.

"Don't be such a fuddy-duddy. People like that don't just 'live' like the rest of us. Have some caviar. Diane says it's Caspian."

"Have you seen anyone we know?"

"Not yet. Did you see the garden? Come on."

Holding yet another glass of champagne provided by yet another attentive waiter, they drifted outside, trailed by Diane and Brad. Violins were playing somewhere to the left. The atrium patio was surrounded on three sides by a series of rooms, several as large as the room they had left, all lit. Each seemed to have some special function for the evening. In one, people played cards boisterously, apparently gambling at Twenty-one. Another room appeared to have been reserved for dancing. A quintet was tuning up. Looking across the patio they saw several couples walking among the trees while others sat in the dim light afforded by the lanterns.

And then, Bill Butler appeared. At his elbow was a delicate

and beautiful woman, her blonde hair piled high, wearing a pale green silk robe that clung to her like a second skin. The Countess Rezzoli bestowed a rather fey smile on Diane and Brad, then greeted Anne and Ralph in a low, husky voice. She hoped they had been taken care of and was so happy the Harrisons could come. She had heard such nice things about them.

Butler greeted them warmly, bussing both ladies on the cheek. Actually, he kissed Anne twice and whispered something in her ear.

As they all strolled along, Ralph was beginning to feel as if he were moving underwater in the company of some extremely color-ful, exotic, and languid fish. He resolved to forego the next glass of champagne.

Although the Countess nodded occasionally, she made no ef-fort to introduce anyone else, except the Count, whom they met on a winding path with a particularly attractive, very young girl in a low-cut gown.

"Bill, darling, you take this lovely lady," she said presently, indicating Anne. "Get her a drink or show her the rest of the gar-dens. I want to talk to this delightful man." She took Ralph's arm, and the group separated, Diane going off with a couple she knew, and Brad heading for the bar.

The Countess took two champagnes from a hovering waiter, gave one to Ralph, who had decided that he needed it after all, and attached herself to his side. "Call me Carlotta," she murmured. "I am so long waiting to meet you. Shall we walk a little?"

As they entered the shadows she took his free hand and held it to her body. She had nothing on beneath her silk robe. Startled, Ralph drew back, but she seemed not to notice.

"Great party," he said lamely. "It's hard to believe we're in Houston." He laughed, feeling the champagne. "Where did you learn to live like this?"

With an intriguing accent which Ralph thought might be Aus-trian, the Countess replied in a sensuous monotone, "My husband, of course, is from Rome. As a young girl I lived in Venice. It was the heyday of life in the great Venetian palazzos. They were full of wealthy and foolish and charming people from all over the world: Peggy Guggenheim, the Archduke of Austria, faded Polish and Russian royalty. It *was* another world. The palaces of the Doges were for us islands of pleasure amidst the canals and lagoons. Like the firefly, people lived for the evening, which was timeless. Everyone tried to outdo the other in the extravagance and novelty of their parties."

"Most of us have to get up in the daytime and go to work, though," he said, feeling like a clod. "Hard to make a firefly out of a drone."

"Perhaps," purred Carlotta, "but in the evening I try." She signaled for more champagne as she led him to a sheltered alcove. His hand, which she still held, she placed around her waist. He left it there. She continued in the most seductive voice he had ever heard, "In everyone there is someone else that wishes to escape the prison of the day-to-day world they live in. For most, this world is drab and boring. To survive in the modern era men must do the dull things men must do: they must find oil, build buildings, buy and sell things. The woman must do her woman's chores. In this house I give people a chance to escape for a brief moment into a world of fantasy. I myself am a realist, an observer. This is not my world. I simply arrange the illusion and I do not intrude on the fantasies of my guests. Inside these walls I permit them to leave their inhibitions behind, and do what pleases them.

"The only rules here are not to bore or harm others or tell what happens here. Those who break the rules are not invited back. I provide what you call props, yes, for my guests' role-playing — interesting conversation with people from many backgrounds, music, food, drink, and other stimuli, dancing, gaming, what have you. In the bar there can be arguments, in the garden repose, or lovemaking. You can find here both the erotic and the intellectual. Whatever you choose."

"That's a lot of choices," said Ralph uncomfortably.

"They are easily narrowed down. Just now, for example, I find you very attractive, very masculine, very warm. Perhaps later we might choose to make love, perhaps not. There are places here for that purpose."

Equally captivated and repelled, Ralph fumbled for something to say. "My dear Carlotta, that's pretty strong stuff for an ordinary mortal like myself, even when the mortal is full of champagne. I'm not sure I'm capable of so much, ah, illusion. Unfortunately, I *do* know I'm in Houston. Can you really make Venice out of Houston?"

"Why not?" she asked, and kissed him. He found it impossible not to respond. "Do you now?" she asked, quite seriously. She clung to him for a moment during which the prospect of accepting her invitation grew increasingly compelling to Ralph. But he wavered too long. As though dismissing him as not worth the effort, Carlotta rose and undulated through the garden. He followed sheepishly.

Already embarrassed at what she must see as his lack of manhood, Ralph suddenly spied something that upset him even more. True, he had just kissed his hostess under circumstances that had aroused his full ardor, but that did not prepare him for what appeared to be a similar tete-a-tete in the arbor between his wife and Bill Butler. Her head was on Butler's shoulder, his arm was around her. He remembered Anne's comment about getting into Butler's circles. This, he thought, was scarcely the way. But what could he do? Tap Butler on the shoulder, then hit him in the jaw? Not in this company.

Carlotta had slipped away. Rattled, he sauntered on alone, accepted another glass of champagne, and found Diane in a small group.

"Can we get out of here?" he muttered to Diane. "This place is beginning to get to me. I'm not sure I understand what's happening. What with the champagne and a talk I've just had with our hostess, I'm rather confused. I believe she'd like for all of us to get drunk and find someone to make love to, or perhaps get naked and throw each other in the pool, or beat each other with chains. Are you a candidate for anything?"

"I wondered how you'd react. Brad and I have been here several times, and I've never really relaxed. I'm always a little afraid that something terrible will happen."

"If it did I suspect Carlotta would throw seven veils over it and turn it into a pumpkin. I don't know what I'm saying, do I?"

Diane chuckled. "You're fine, just shocked. Let's find a place to sit down."

They threaded their way through what was by now a crowd, finally encountering the bar, a monstrous affair offering drinks of every nationality imaginable. As a lark they each took a Turkish Raki. Its licorice taste offered a welcome contrast to the sweet champagne. They settled themselves on a comfortable sofa well back in a dark room nearby. Ralph, stimulated by the champagne, the Countess, and the general air of wantonness, not necessarily in that order, now had a strong inclination to kiss Diane.

"You're lovely," he whispered, taking her hand. "You know that I've always been attracted to you." He put his lips to the palm of her hand, then he set his glass down and put his arm around her, drawing her to him. "Why do things have to be so complicated?" he said, "raising so many questions that have no answers." He leaned over and kissed her mouth, holding her close. She did not resist, but neither did she encourage him. When he finally drew back, she put her hand to his cheek and said gently, "You're sweet, and I love being here with you, but I'm afraid I don't know the answers either. Maybe we'd better go back."

As they left the room, they heard loud male voices nearby. Ralph thought he saw a gaming table. Several of the men had their coats off. Someone shouted, "Get me a drink, nigger." Ralph froze. It was Brad.

"Wait here. I'll take care of it," he said to Diane, and he began to push his way through the by now curious crowd. Brad, his tie loosened, was holding out his glass to a black man in a dinner jacket, who said quietly, "I am sorry, but you have made a mistake. I am a guest here like yourself. I would have been glad to get you a drink but not under orders."

Brad threw the glass down and slapped the man hard on the cheek. "Guest, hell! You're nothing but a God-damned nigger! You get me a drink!"

The black man drew back, his control admirable. "I could knock you out with one blow," he said, "you sodden fool, but you're not worth it. I have respect for my host, if you don't." Brad was making a feeble attempt to raise his fists, blubbering incoherently, when Ralph and a few others interceded. "Come on, Brad, let's go home," coaxed Ralph. "I'll take you." But the two men from the front door were already there, and Brad went quietly between them.

Ralph and Diane went in search of Anne and found her walking along the terrace with Bill Butler. They said goodbye to Butler and decided, under the circumstances, to leave without a farewell to host or hostess, who were nowhere to be seen.

Brad let Diane drive; he slept all the way home, then lurched out of the car and into the house.

"Need any help?" Ralph asked Diane.

"No, no. You two go on. It's been a long night."

Long and confusing, thought Ralph, when he and Anne were

at last in bed. He was still rather drunk. His head was in a turmoil. He was angry with Anne, but what could he say? He really had little to go by. Just as he had been taken in tow by the Countess, Anne had been paired off with Butler. She obviously wouldn't have wanted to offend Butler if she could avoid it, for Ralph's sake. And yet he was jealous. He suspected that Anne might see in Butler the opportunity to get ahead that he knew she wanted. Butler was a glittering target. Finally, furious that she could lie beside him quietly as if nothing were wrong, he lashed out.

"Listen, I want to know what you think you were doing out there in the dark with Bill Butler! I saw you, you know! So did God knows how many other people! How do you think this makes me look? What will people say? I'm mad as hell at the way you acted. I don't like it one damned bit."

"For God's sake, I was nearly asleep!" she said thickly. "And look who's talking! What do you know anyway? You were busy smooching with your Countess. You've got a nerve, accusing me! And you don't give a damn about me, just how it looks! I have a right to make friends with Bill Butler if I want to. I'll tell you this: He likes me. And he knows how to treat a woman. Leave me alone. I want to go to sleep."

"You're damned well not going to sleep until we settle this! If you think I'm going to put up with your playing around with Bill Butler, you're mistaken. By God, you're my wife!"

This was met with silence, and in a few minutes a black wave full of gold carp engulfed him.

The next morning she was lying still, looking at him intently when he woke. He felt awful. He stared back awkwardly.

"I just want to tell you that I won't accept the horrible things you said last night. I've done nothing to deserve your abuse and I won't take it. You've never talked to me like that before. I hope it was the alcohol."

Ralph's hangover was preventing him from thinking very clearly. "I'm sorry, I was wrong," he said. "I *was* drunk. I didn't mean what I said. It was just the crazy evening. I wish we hadn't gone. I apologize."

"Nothing happened," Anne said sullenly.

"I know," said Ralph, and he held his hand out as a peace-making gesture. Anne took it reluctantly, whereupon Ralph turned over and went back to sleep.

Anne, who had been awake for a long time, was appalled at how easily she had turned his attack — all too justified — against him, and how readily, even eagerly, he had accepted the blame. She knew she had embarked upon an itinerary of lies, destination unknown. She knew Ralph would believe her lies because he believed in her and in their marriage. He was not a modern man. He would never understand, let alone condone, what she had done, what she might be going to do.

The simple solution was to stop seeing Bill Butler, but the truth was, she didn't want to.

She was remembering something that had happened when she was twelve, something she had diligently avoided thinking about for years, but which had shaped her life, her choice of a husband — and should shape her behavior now.

They were summering on Fisher's Island, and her father was away. She had wandered into her house early from a cancelled tennis lesson, and had seen her mother in the embrace of a neighbor. They hadn't seen her. In that instant all the hints and rumors and jokes and moralistic passages in books her reticent mother had bought her coalesced into one brilliant shock of understanding. She had run out onto the beach and thrown stones and shells into the water until she saw the neighbor's car drive away.

She had no one she could tell.

Her father must have known something. She had eavesdropped for weeks, and one evening her father told her mother he had had lunch with the neighbor, and the neighbor said he was going to sell his house and move to Watch Hill. Her mother had cried.

She had blamed her mother more and more over the years. Now her own actions were throwing a different light on her mother's behavior. For the first time she could understand why a supposedly happy wife and mother would be tempted by the attentions of another man. So many did this — was it really so wrong? Or was it only wrong to get caught?

Her father had failed her in a different way. He was a senior partner in a brokerage firm. During a recession he had used the capital of a client to save his firm. Later the money was repaid, but he was spared going to jail only through the efforts of the best legal counsel in New York. It was in the papers and everyone knew. The children at her school knew; she could tell they did by the way they looked at her.

She could never forgive her father. In the blind scramble for wealth he had gone too far. And yet he had survived, gone on, provided well for the family. Maybe you had to take risks. The things his wealth had bought for her as a girl were important; she wouldn't have wanted to miss them.

So where did you draw the line? Ralph, sleeping beside her, drew answers from the past. Anne's past just raised more questions.

16

Early in September Ralph was in his office trying to concentrate on routine Texoil business. The initial excitement produced by his securing the lease had waned. Now he found it hard to believe anything had happened. From his experience with Texoil he knew very well how many months would have to pass before the Gillette well would be proven either productive or dry. But this well was *his*, not the company's, and the thought of the delay made him edgy and restless.

As he left for an afternoon meeting of the Art Museum Board, over which Diane would preside, he realized he'd pretty much put what had passed between them at the Rezzolis' out of his mind, but all of a sudden he found himself dreading seeing her again. What might she expect of him? Did he really want to continue his flirtation?

But then, as he drove past the chic Maxim's Restaurant, he saw something that shook him to the core. Bill Butler, with Anne at his side, was emerging from the restaurant in apparent high fettle. Ralph's foot faltered on the gas pedal. A cold sweat broke out on his brow. He looked back, hoping it had been a mirage — or someone else. It wasn't. He drove on, and it wasn't until he reached the museum that he wondered how he'd actually gotten there, such was his mental state.

Diane greeted him as if nothing had ever happened. "Sorry about Brad's performance the other evening," she said quickly. "He gets that way sometimes. He wrote a note of apology to the Countess and asked her to convey one to the guest he offended. He was really quite contrite. He's been at the ranch for the last few days. Would you mind giving me a ride home after the meeting? My car is in the garage."

"Sure, I'd be delighted," said Ralph, grateful that she had put him at ease.

She presided beautifully over the meeting, and watching her skill and poise, he almost forgot about Anne. The group contained many of the leaders of the city: a bank president, the head of an insurance company, six elderly members of old families that had always given generously to the Museum, a professional or two, and several young matrons, two from the East, whose husbands were rising stars in the Houston business world. Alastair Crane made his report as Director.

Under Diane's leadership the Houston Museum of Fine Arts was coming into its own, thanks also to the generosity of her family and the Comptons and other older oil families. Most of them had traveled widely in Europe and the Orient and found it natural to want to bring to Houston the art they admired. Indeed, they felt it their duty. They also liked the recognition.

Few opportunities escaped the roving eye of Director Crane. He was good and he knew it. His contacts in London and Geneva brought him top Greek vases and Russian icons. He concentrated on the best, whether it was pre-Columbian textiles or Luristan bronzes. And for every good find, Crane could usually locate a donor.

The Museum's problem, as always, was budget. Several important capital bequests had been received recently, one for a new $7,000,000 wing and another for a complete renovation of the main building. Both had been memorialized in the name of the donor. But gifts for the operating budget were more difficult, and for this purpose the Board had voted to seek an endowment fund of $10 million. With the income from endowment, together with regular annual giving in categories from Contributors at less than $500 to Patrons at $10,000, they hoped to assure a more stable future for the Museum, including substantial sums for acquisitions.

Diane had been responsible for the whole plan; tactfully and persuasively she had brought the Board to the point of launching the campaign. Today they were to set their goals for individual donors. The newly elected President of the Museum, who was actually the chief fundraiser, sat beside her.

"Our professional advisors tell us," announced Diane, "that to reach $10 million we must have at least two gifts of $1 million, six of $500,000, twenty of $100,000, a hundred of $25,000 and so on. Brad and I want to start the campaign off with a million. We hope members of the Board will do what they can. We understand that not many are as fortunate as we, and we certainly don't want anyone to feel embarrassed. Many people will be limited," and her words seemed tinged with pity for those benighted people who were limited by their company salary, even though it might be $500,000 a year. "Remember, contributions can be paid over five years.

"One of our problems is that everyone thinks we get vast sums from Houston companies, particularly the oil companies. I wish we did. Actually, the sum raised by the Combined Arts Corporate Campaign is only about a half-million dollars for all of Houston's competing arts organizations. The CACC was formed to protect the companies, not get more money from them. I wish the companies could be approached individually. If they could, I'm sure Ralph could get a lot more from the oil companies."

Diane asked everyone to write down on a pledge card what they could do. She wanted to announce first not individual gifts, but a total for the Board. Unless it was impressive, others would not feel such a strong obligation. Experience had shown that people only gave as a result of personal solicitation. She asked everyone present, on a confidential basis, to indicate other potential donors, with the size of gift that might be expected. Among them they knew most of the people in Houston.

There was, of course, considerable discussion. In the end, Ralph was embarrassed that his own pledge was only $1,000. The Board members present had pledged $4,500,000.

On the way home, Ralph congratulated Diane on the way she had conducted the meeting.

"Thank you," she said. "It's nice to be appreciated. Actually, I take my job very seriously. I think it's important to give people a link with the past, especially since Houston hasn't got much of a cultural base. Outside of a few early houses they've rebuilt down by the interchange, we're more or less an instant city. People need access to the artistic heritage of other cultures. Europe, the Far East, the ancient civilizations — I want to see them all represented. And I'm really proud of our Mayan and Aztec collections. You know what really gives me a kick? To see a bunch of school kids going through. Most of them look bored to death, of course, but once in a while you see one that's all eyes.''

"Even the bored ones will remember something," said Ralph. "You think so?"

"Well, at least they'll get the idea that something happened before they were born besides Conestoga wagons and oil rigs."

"That's what I mean! It's hard to explain, because most people think of the museum as by the rich for the rich, and working for it as some sort of a social plum."

"Nonsense, if you were on salary you'd earn more than I do."

"You're certainly good for a girl's ego," she said, laughing. "Come in for a drink?"

"Love to."

They had reached the cobblestone drive to the spacious Compton residence on Hiawatha Lane. It was part of the sheltered enclave, laid out by the founding Houston oil hierarchy, that surrounded Rice University, of which they were so proud.

Century-old live oaks protected the neo-Georgian brick residence, blotting out the city with their huge canopies that provided perpetual shade.

Diane opened the door with her key, then rang the wall bell in the marble entryway. She walked ahead to the long porch bordering the swimming pool, now deep in shade. As they passed through the spacious rooms, Ralph marveled at the treasures of furniture and art. Each time he came to the house he was more impressed. There were priceless paintings, mostly Impressionists, and two magnificent Van Goghs from his Auvergne period. The furniture was mostly French, Louis Seize chairs, ornate cabinets, sofas that were museum-quality.

He noted that every piece of furniture, every painting, every *object* played an important part in the general composition of the room. Flowers from the Compton greenhouses were everywhere. A few lights had been turned on, but the lighting came mainly from the indirectly lighted paintings. The atmosphere was one of complete calm and repose. Ralph could not help but contrast it with Brad's recent performance at the party. This house was all Diane.

When they reached the porch, she rang the servants' bell again. Still no one came. "How stupid of me, I forgot that the servants are off this evening!" she said. She looked at Ralph. "I guess we're alone. Why don't you fix us a drink? The bar is at the end of the porch. I'd like a gin and tonic."

"How does Brad fit in with this?" Ralph asked as he brought the drinks. "It doesn't seem to fit him."

Diane laughed shortly. "Oh, he tolerates my taste. Sometimes I even think he likes it. He has his own rooms, of course, with his things, including a large den in the basement I don't even enter. This was my parents' home. The French furniture and Impressionist paintings reflect my mother's taste as well as mine. It's my escape from Houston, sometimes my escape from Brad. Will you excuse me for a moment?"

When she returned she had on a long silk hostess gown in a pleasing Japanese print. She lay back across the wide sofa against a pillow, drink in hand. Ralph had never seen her look so desirable. Her gown accentuated her lovely breasts, and the silk clung to her beautifully proportioned body. He got up from his chair and sat beside her.

"I hope I didn't offend you the other evening," he said gently. "What happened was a natural impulse and it had nothing to do with the drinks. I think you know how I feel about you. Of course, it makes no sense at all. As we said, it raises too many questions for which there are no answers."

"Nor will there ever be," she said. "You know I'm attracted to you, Ralph. It's probably better not to talk about it. Words don't help. Logic doesn't help. Most of our friends in Houston in such a situation would have had their affair a long time ago without giving it a thought. The fact that we gave it a thought is what complicates it.

"The trouble is, I know myself too well. I couldn't get involved in a chance affair. It would have to really mean something to me, it would have to mean too much. And for reasons that may not be apparent, I don't want to break up my marriage. I'm sure you don't want to break up yours either. And I certainly don't want to hurt anyone. Brad, with all his faults, deserves better than that.

"There is, though, something you don't know that makes me especially vulnerable. Brad is impotent. Except for a brief period at the beginning, we haven't had any sex life. That's why I have no children."

Ralph was surprised, then shocked. "Oh, lord . . . Diane," he managed. "How can someone like you . . . All these years, and with such a good grace, never letting anyone know!"

"Well, it's not the kind of thing you go around mentioning at dinner parties."

"I'm touched that you confided in me. I must say it gives me an even stronger sense of respect for you."

"I've always been afraid to . . . let myself go with anyone . . ." she smiled sadly, "in case I can't get back, you know? Oh hell," she said, her voice catching, "why don't you just kiss me?"

They were facing each other. He looked at her for a long moment, then cupped her face in his hands. She smiled at him. He leaned forward and kissed her gently. She remained very still, expectant. He pulled himself alongside and held her close. He kissed her full and forcefully on the lips, and she put her arms around him and pressed against him. He was aroused as he could not remember having been for a long time.

She was pulling at his tie, which he realized was strangling him. "Wouldn't you like to get rid of this?" she murmured. "Make yourself comfortable."

Awkwardly he got up and started to unbutton his collar. "You could put your things in there," she said, pointing to a door. His mind was teeming as he headed for it. It was past the point of discussion now. If she had decided, he couldn't abandon her.

And yet, as he walked away from her, he wished he could just keep on going. He thought of Anne, the children, their happy life together. As in a brush with death, his whole life seemed to be passing before his eyes.

His head felt as if it were on fire when he reached for the door handle.

And then all hell broke loose. He had set off the second tier alarm system which Diane had failed to clear as they entered that part of the house. They could hear the pre-recorded call to the police going out, the loud clang of the alarm in the servants' house.

"There's nothing we can do," cried Diane, jumping to her feet and coming to where he stood, stricken with shock and embarrassment. To his further horror, she started to laugh. "I'm sorry, I can't help it," she said. "It's just — we've been so *serious* about it, and — Better go now, hurry! They'll be here in five minutes. If anyone sees you, you just brought me home." She kissed him quickly, and he left, stuffing his tie in his pocket.

Now he had his way out, but did he really want it? It was not as if he had never made love to another woman before. Maybe this was his last chance with Diane. He thought bitterly about what a poor show he had made.

By dinnertime, he was in a state, utterly out of sorts with everything, but he managed to restrain himself until Anne served coffee. "Funny thing," he said finally. "As I was going to the Museum board meeting today I thought I saw you coming out of Maxim's with Bill Butler."

Anne didn't even flinch. "You know I had lunch with Sally Crane today. When we were coming out of Maxim's we ran into Bill. He'd been giving a luncheon there for a bunch of Arabs. He was very friendly and insisted on seeing me to my car. I certainly hope you're not getting paranoid about Bill." She raised her eyebrows.

Ralph almost choked, so glad was he that he hadn't made a blatant accusation. Relief flooded through him, relief that his suspicions were groundless, relief that nothing had happened with Diane.

Anne's feelings were less simple. At the moment Ralph had spotted them, Bill had been making another appointment to see her. She was appalled at how easily she had assumed the role of injured party, deflected the accusation which was all too justified, dissembled, pretended, yes, lied, while sticking to a particle of truth. But there was no point in upsetting Ralph, she told herself. It was a harmless flirtation; it might indeed help their marriage for her to get this restlessness out of her system, because of course this wasn't going to last long, she knew, nor was she going to get seriously involved. She knew Bill was a notorious lady's man. She could handle it.

Yet she felt a softness creeping over her when she thought of Bill Butler. She knew she was not his ordinary conquest. He had as much as told her so. "You're different, you make me feel at ease, I can relax with you," he had said. It was just so exciting to be near all that power and wealth. Where Bill walked people gave way before him. Perhaps she could guide Ralph to be someone important and forceful, someone to be reckoned with. In the meantime it was tempting to find out what Bill Butler's life was all about.

17

Jack

Jack was trying to get the drilling of the deep test on the Gillette lands under way. It had been four months since Ralph had made the proposal to him — four very busy months. He had, after a Herculean effort, raised the million dollars of risk money he needed. The drilling contractor who was sharing his risk had at last freed up a rig that could go easily to 16,000 feet. The 10,000 feet of protection pipe, without any upfront cost, had been lined up and tested. Jack had just enough cash left to cover out-of-pocket expenses until he saw the log at 16,000 feet. He had gotten the necessary permits, surveyed the well location, built the shell road, and prepared the mud pits.

All these things he had done hundreds of times in his life as an Independent, but not for years had he felt the sense of risk and exhilaration. It was almost like starting all over again, and though at his age this should have taxed him, it didn't. In fact, if he had been superstitious, it would have been easy to convince himself that this well would be a success, so many parallels could be drawn between it and his first big strike at West Bayou Bleu — the association with Randy Simpson, the previous rejection of the lease by a major company, even, he thought ruefully, the connection with Bill Butler and Texoil, whom Jack had gotten to drill it. He yielded himself to memory.

After leaving Coastal Jack opened a small office in the Esperson Building and put his card in the Geological Society Bulletin as a consulting geologist. Soon he had work coming in from a number of Independent oilmen. He would do the necessary subsurface work to determine whether a particular prospect justified drilling. He charged modest fees, worked hard, and soon received credit for finding two good fields.

He was also starting to work for himself. Night after night, while Janet and the children were asleep, he shuffled electrical logs searching for the elusive evidence that would indicate oil in some new area. It was the same old search for a needle in a haystack, but Jack didn't mind now; he knew the black gold was there and he believed that in time he would find it, and for himself.

Once six months had passed, Jack began what he had been waiting impatiently to do: start exploration of a swampy area five miles west of Bayou Bleu that he had always considered his prime prospect. He was sure Coastal had made a mistake in not looking more closely at that area. During Coastal's original seismic survey which led to Bayou Bleu's discovery, the bayou was in flood. The swampy land to the west was under water and had not been shot. Jack had later recommended that a crew be sent back to survey this area, to see whether the west dip off Bayou Bleu continued to go down, or came up to form another structure. Randy's original gravity survey had indicated the possibility of such a structure.

Doc Willens, as usual, had vetoed this. On the day his commitment to Coastal was up, Jack drove to Louisiana for a talk with Randy Simpson. Randy knew the lease situation in the area better than anyone.

The influx of wealth had not changed Randy at all. He and Mary still drove a pick-up truck and dressed in jeans and work shirts. When Jack revealed what he had in mind, after a long evening of good food, good wine, and good talk, Randy was not surprised.

"I've always thought there was another structure to the west," he said. "The wells on that side of Bayou Bleu showed very little west dip. The A.A.P.G. Bulletin has an article on the discovery of Bayou Bleu which shows a gravity minima out there and no dry hole west of the field."

"Well," Jack said, "I want to take the leases west of Bayou Bleu, all I can get, and I'd like you to help me. If we can get a big enough block. I'd like to shoot it, and if we find something, get someone to drill it."

"What did you have in mind?"

"It's difficult for me, as an outsider, to buy the leases. You know those Cajuns living there and could do that a lot better. I'd like you to take a percentage of the deal, take the leases, see about the legal work, and find someone to drill us a test well."

"What percentage did you have in mind?"

"What would you like?"

Randy frowned. "I'm a little short on cash just now. I'd say a quarter would be enough for me."

"Fine with me," Jack said delightedly.

"Then you've got a deal," Randy smiled.

The two friends shook hands. Neither then nor later did they ever enter into a formal contract. That was the way oilmen did business.

In two weeks, Randy had leased nearly a thousand acres, at a cost of not much more than five thousand dollars. The next step was to make a seismic survey of the area. Jack hired a crew by the day and directed it himself. He was in the recording truck when the records were taken out of the "soup," and he studied them carefully, while they were still dripping with developing fluid. After only two days' shooting, Jack was convinced he had been right. The seismic records showed that the oil-bearing strata over Bayou Bleu, although they dipped down to the west to form the structural trap for the field, started up again further west on his new leases. This meant that everything higher structurally than the water level in Bayou Bleu, would also produce to the west. To save his limited capital, Jack terminated the shooting.

The next step was to get someone to drill a test well for an interest. The well would cost close to a hundred thousand dollars, and Jack, of course, did not have that much cash. Nor did Randy, despite his income from Bayou Bleu. Jack's plan in starting out as an Independent was to spend his own money on leases and seismic work. If he found nothing, he would accept the loss. But if he found a good structure, he would seek a partner to pay for the test well, in exchange for a half interest in it. An investor who was willing to risk a hundred thousand dollars on Jack's judgment had a chance of making millions.

Investors, however, were not readily found. Texas and Louisiana were full of fast-talking oil promoters with surefire deals, the vast majority of which turned out to be dry holes. But Jack and Randy were in luck. Randy had an old college friend from the East now living in Houston, Cy Farrell, who had made money with Randy on drilling deals in the past and gladly took his word that West Bayou Bleu was a good prospect. Farrell and some of his Eastern friends were willing to take Jack's deal, putting up the cost of the test well. At that point, Jack's 75 percent interest in the block was halved to 37.5 percent, and Randy's quarter interest became 12.5 percent.

To improve their odds, the location for the well was made as close as possible to the production at Bayou Bleu. Finally, in the summer of 1941, drilling began. The log of the well as it went down showed it to be running structurally just as the seismic line had shown — high enough to produce. Jack and Randy and Farrell were on hand when the well reached the critical depth, poised for a celebration. Randy, as usual, had the champagne on ice.

But there was to be no celebration. The well struck gas, not oil as expected. This proved it was on structure — a geological success, but the sand was thin and gas was then priced so low it was all but worthless. As they drilled deeper, looking for oil, the bit got stuck. Jack and Randy paced about the well impatiently, until it became clear that the stuck well could not be drilled out except at prohibitive expense.

"Damn, damn, damn," Randy muttered.

"What does this mean?" Farrell asked. Cy, champagne in hand, still had high hopes for the well.

"It means we have to abandon the well and drill another one," Randy said.

"It's just rotten luck," Jack added.

"This means another $100,000, doesn't it?" Farrell asked.

"That's right," Randy said tonelessly.

"I'll see how the other fellows feel. I don't know. Money's tight. We've earned our half interest in the block, of course, with this well. I don't think we want to drill another."

"That's right," Jack assured him. "You've earned it even if you don't spend another dime. But I'm damned sure that Randy and I want to get another well drilled, one way or another, and that you do, too. We've got to define our structure better to the west, so we can persuade someone else to drill it for us on the same basis you came in on."

"Say, Randy," Cy said. "That champagne you brought for the victory celebration? Let's drink it anyway."

They did, but in the days ahead Jack felt little cause for celebration. Randy got the investor group to agree to continue with more seismic work, but that cost money, and Jack had to bear his share. His initial stake was now almost gone, and he was so pressed for cash that after a long talk with Janet, he mortgaged their house to raise the extra money needed for his share of the shooting. He still believed there was oil west of Bayou Bleu, but another foul-up like the first well would wipe him out. It happened every day.

The group leased more acreage farther west and carried out a more thorough seismic survey. To their delight, it revealed an even larger structure than Jack had imagined. With this strong evidence in hand, Randy and Jack went forth once more to find someone to drill another well.

Jack first offered the deal to Coastal, as a courtesy, to repay them for their generosity to him.

Willens, however, declined. "Coastal wants nothing to do with anything west of Bayou Bleu."

"Why not?" Randy asked, when Jack reported back to him. "Didn't you show them our seismic maps?"

"Willens wouldn't even look at the maps. He wasn't willing to admit that Coastal could have overlooked a major field two miles from one they discovered. So, if we don't find oil, they'll say we're damn fools. And if we do, you may as well realize this, they're going to say I pulled a fast one on them."

"Pulled a fast one!" Randy raged. "You told them to test there."

"I know that," Jack said. "But that won't stop them."

"Well, don't worry," said Randy. "I think I've got us a deal!"

"Great!" Jack exclaimed. "Who with?"

"Texoil."

"Texoil?"

Randy shrugged. "Look, partner, I know you don't like Bill Butler. Neither do I, and I know him better than you do. But leave him aside for a moment. They're a big company and a good one. They've done a lot of exploration in Louisiana along our trend, and they're eager to follow up their Newton County discovery over in

Texas. I had an informal talk with their Vice-President for Production in Houston, and they're ready to talk."

"What's the deal?"

"The standard one. They'll drill a well for a half interest."

Jack sighed. His original 75 percent, now reduced to 37.5 percent, was about to become 18.75 percent. But those were the breaks of the game. The boys with the big money usually ended up with the big interest. Besides, 18.75 percent of a major field would still not be chicken feed.

"That's not good enough," Jack declared.

Randy looked at him sharply. "Why not?"

"They've got to agree to drill two wells," Jack said, "a second one if the first is dry. We got burned bad when we lost our first well. We can't survive another fiasco like that."

"They'll fight it like hell," Randy warned.

"Then we'll go to Gulf or Conoco. We've got the structure. It's two wells or no deal."

Texoil's lawyers strongly opposed this. For two wells, they demanded a 60–40 split, which Jack refused. The negotiations broke down, and Jack and Randy were about to approach Gulf, when they received an eleventh-hour call from Texoil's chief negotiator. They accepted the deal, but bitterly. Even at the outset, it was clear that no love was lost between the Sanderson-Simpson team and the company in which Jack's old nemesis, Bill Butler, was playing an increasingly important role.

The preparations for Texoil's first test well were interrupted by an act that stunned and changed the world: the Japanese attack on Pearl Harbor. That "day of infamy," and the immediate U.S. declaration of war, left Jack confused and troubled. He had for months ignored the war in Europe and the signs of unrest in the Pacific.

The reality of war left him with an even greater sense of urgency. He would have to go fight, he knew that. In time he would be called up, unless he claimed exemption for being in a necessary industry. He knew he couldn't do that, and that Janet would never expect him to. His first impulse was to enlist, but he knew he was too old to be a foot soldier. Someone had told him he could apply to the Navy for a commission as an Air Combat Intelligence officer. He would do that, he thought, as soon as the well came in. His only thought now was to complete the drilling west of Bayou Bleu before he was called away.

Jack was back in Houston when Randy called to tell him about Texoil's plans for the first test well.

"I don't understand it," Randy said. "They've located it on the east end of our block, on the smaller of the two hickeys. It looks like a lousy location to me. There's a better structure further west."

Jack had a sinking feeling. "Hold on," he said, and made a quick study of his maps.

"It's on structure and a possible place to drill, but not the best location according to our seis picture," he said bitterly, after the maps had confirmed his fears. "What's wrong with them? A first-year geology student would have better sense than that!"

"I can tell you the rumor I've heard," Randy said.

"Go ahead."

"I've heard that Texoil officials bought up royalty on the east side of the area, and that's why they decided to drill on that side."

"No, no, no," Jack groaned.

"It would be impossible to prove," Randy said.

"Should I go talk with them?"

"Under the circumstances, it wouldn't do any good. The decision is theirs. After all, we can't lose. They have to drill a second well if it's dry."

Jack felt drained. "Well, do what you can," he said. "It certainly puts a new light on things. I have an appointment with the Navy Recruiting Office tomorrow. I guess that'll have to wait."

But finding the field they were expecting was not to be so easy. The well encountered only slight shows as it went down. It was a blow to Jack when Randy called him in Houston to tell him that Texoil's well had found only a thin non-commercial oil sand, where they had placed most of their hopes.

"A duster, as they said in the old days," Randy added ruefully.

"Well, at least they'll have to drill the second well on top. They've no place else to go."

"Partner, I've heard another unhappy rumor."

"What this time?" Jack demanded.

"I heard they don't plan to drill a second well. They're asking us to let them off the hook."

"Don't plan to drill it? We've got a contract!"

"Yes, and Texoil's got a lot of high-priced lawyers, too."

"Who's behind this?"

"Bill Butler, I hear. He's their head man for Louisiana."

"My God, that guy's like a bad dream! I'm going over to tell him he's got to drill."

"You could try, but I doubt it'll do any good."

"We'll see about that!" Jack slammed down the phone, jumped to his feet, and strode the five blocks to the Texoil Building.

Soon he was confronting the Texoil receptionist. "I want to see Bill Butler right now," he declared, panting from his walk. "I'm Jack Sanderson."

"I'm sorry, he's busy," said the crisply tailored young woman.

"Busy, hell!" Jack snapped, and marched past her into Butler's corner office. He found the Texoil heir on the phone, with his feet up on his desk.

"And what might you want?" Butler asked, as he ended his phone call.

Jack studied Butler's handsome, arrogant face, realizing that Butler would not remember him from their boyhood encounter in the East Texas field. Jack tried to control his temper. "I'm Jack Sanderson," he said. "What's this I hear about you wanting to get out of drilling the second well at Bayou Bleu?"

Butler grinned. "Ah, Sanderson. You've good sources of information. Yes, I think our first well proved your structure is worthless. Another dry hole would be just a waste of money."

"The first hole was dry because you drilled at the worst possible location. I've heard some rumors why you did that, too, which I hope aren't true. But as long as you honor your obligation to drill the second well, I won't complain."

"I don't see it," Butler said. "Let's face it, two dry wells have been drilled on your block already.'

"Dammit, Butler, you know you're committed under your contract to drill two wells and you'll drill that second well or I'll sue you for all it's worth. You've got your nerve. A big company like Texoil, to ask me, an Independent just starting out, to *give* you something, to give up a well you owe me. The answer is 'No.' "

Butler stood up and faced Jack across his desk, menacingly. "Look here, you two-bit hick promoter, maybe you can force us to drill the second well, but you'll live to regret it. An Independent who doesn't play ball with the majors is asking for trouble. He doesn't get deals. The word gets around fast. Better think about it."

"Just drill me my well," Jack said. "I'll take my chances as to the consequences. And this time drill on top even if your brass doesn't have any royalty under it." Jack stormed out of the office, leaving Butler scowling at his desk.

As an act of faith that Texoil's second well at West Bayou Bleu would come in, Jack went to the Navy Recruiting Office and put in his application for a commission. He was told there might be a delay of two months to a year, which information produced in him a mixture of frustration and relief.

Butler dragged his feet over the drilling of the second well west of Bayou Bleu until Jack had his lawyer call Texoil's general counsel. But the well was finally spudded and Jack got his departure for the Navy delayed until he could see it down. It was a hot night in June when the well reached 8,400 feet, where oil was expected, and an electrical log was to be run to see what they had.

A half dozen Texoil men were gathered on the derrick floor, set among the pine trees at the edge of the slow-moving Bayou Bleu, awaiting the results. A bar had been set up, courtesy of Bill Butler, and his men were drinking. There had been shows of oil and gas in the mud during the last day of drilling and an air of excitement and tension had been created, the feeling oilmen get that "this one will be it." Randy, Jack, and Cy Farrell stood to one side, sipping beers and waiting. Uninvited, they had made no move to join the Texoil group. Mary Simpson and Janet were waiting, too, in a car parked nearby.

Texoil was the operator of the well, and its men were, therefore, in charge. Texoil's officials, led by Bill Butler, were crowded around the Schlumberger truck, awaiting the electrical log that would reveal their success or failure. Butler and his associates ignored Jack and Randy.

Jack was tired, angry and nervous. He was due to report for naval duty in California in three days, and if this well was a failure he would be leaving Janet and the children with little money and huge debts. He didn't mind going to war, but the thought of leaving his family was very painful.

The minutes ticked by. Butler's crowd laughed and drank whiskey. Jack and his friends made small talk and sweated it out.

Finally, well past midnight, the door to the truck burst open and an excited Schlumberger operator handed Bill Butler the log they had been waiting for.

Butler studied it intently as his friends crowded around. The seconds seemed like hours to Jack and Randy, who were pointedly excluded from this climactic moment.

"Rude bastards, aren't they?" Randy muttered.

"I wouldn't put it past them to try to make some last-minute royalty purchases before the news gets out," said Jack.

"If it's good news," Cy Farrell grumbled, mopping his brow.

The news looked good. A couple of men began to nod gravely. One geologist let out a low whistle. Finally Bill Butler spoke.

"Gentlemen, Texoil has done it again!" he declared.

The others began to cheer. Butler raised his glass high. "To Texoil!" he declared, and the others joined in the toast. "To Texoil!" To Bill they sang, "For he's a jolly good fellow."

For Jack, the suspense, and the rude snub, had become unbearable. He marched over and confronted Butler.

"We'd like to see the log, too," he said coldly.

Butler laughed in his face. "Oh, I imagine we'll send you a copy next week," he said, and his Texoil friends roared with laughter.

Jack stuck out his hand. "Butler, give me that log. I found this field. You people would never have drilled here if I hadn't threatened to sue you."

Butler scowled. "Then maybe you'd better sue to see the log," he snapped, rolling it up.

"That does it!" Jack roared. He swung a roundhouse right to Butler's chin. The Texoil heir staggered and fell back, and the log fluttered to the floor. While Butler's friends helped him to his feet, Jack seized the log. He and Randy studied it anxiously. Their trained eyes quickly saw a number of sands — they counted eighteen — that should produce either gas or oil.

"What the hell does all that mean?" Cy demanded.

Randy grinned. "It means this is one monster of an oil field, my friend!"

Suddenly Bill Butler grabbed Jack by the shoulder, spun him around, and punched him in the face. Jack fought back as Randy and some of the Texoil men tried to come between them.

Janet came running up from the car where she had been waiting. "Jack, for heaven's sake, why are you fighting?" she cried. "Stop it! Don't be crazy!"

The other men finally succeeded in dragging the two apart.

"Let's get out of here," Randy said under his breath.

"Okay," Jack muttered, feeling his jaw.

"Yeah, and don't come back," Butler snarled.

"Just send our checks on time, Butler," Randy said, and Jack and his friends headed for the car.

They dropped Cy Farrell at his hotel in Lake Charles, then drove to the Simpsons'. There, the four of them sat up talking and drinking coffee.

No one spoke the numbers, but they all knew that if the new field was as big as it appeared to be, Jack's share of the profits could run to many millions of dollars.

Mary put the Brandenburg Concertos on the phonograph, and the music filled the house with a serenity so often missing from their daily lives. They were all a little dazed; later Jack would say that he had been in shock for several days.

"I think clothes will be my main extravagance," Janet confessed, "if I can overcome my guilt. When I was growing up, my mother never had any new clothes. She was the preacher's wife, of course, and had to go to church every Sunday. She had only one plain black dress that she must have worn for fifteen years. I grew up hating that dress. And embarrassed by it, too, because the other mothers would come in their new spring or fall outfits, and my mother was still wearing that same black dress. I'd beg her to get a new one, but she'd always say she had better things to spend her money on. She was such a beautiful woman, too, so gentle . . ."

Tears came to her eyes, and Jack reached for her hand.

"I'm sorry. Just forgive me if I disappear and they find me in Neiman-Marcus or Sakowitz up to my ears in fancy clothes."

"You can have whatever you want," Jack vowed. "You've earned it."

"You'll splurge at first," Mary said. "Everybody does. Why not? It's so wonderful to know the money is there, and there's so *much* of it. But you're like a kid in a candy store. You get your tummyache and then you learn to use some sense."

"If you're smart you do," Randy added. "Some of our colleagues don't learn the virtue of moderation. I know a fellow in Baton Rouge who'd always wanted a Cadillac. Really lusted for one. Then his well came in and he went down and bought himself a big red Cadillac. Paid cash. But he still had the itch, so he went back the next day and bought a blue one, a convertible. Next day he went back and bought a black Fleetwood. You'd better believe there was one happy Cadillac dealer in Baton Rouge, because this fellow felt it was beneath his new dignity to haggle about the price. Anyway, to end this tale, my friend bought fourteen Cadillacs before he realized the awful truth. You can't buy all the Cadillacs. You can't romance all the ladies, drink all the booze."

"I, for one, don't even want to try," said Jack smugly.

"Well, that's the strange thing. Money doesn't really change fundamentals," Randy said. "What was good before gets better, and what was bad gets worse. But you're the same people with most of the same problems. Money solves a few little ones, but if you're not careful it replaces them with some real whoppers."

He got up and poured himself another brandy. Mary turned the record over. The first pink light of dawn hung over the bayou.

"The important thing is your children," Jack said quietly. "They need stability, and values. And they have to know how to work; no child of mine is going to grow up living off a fat allowance. Janet and I have worked hard all our lives, and that's the secret of all the success and happiness we've had. We can't let our own success spoil our children."

Janet smiled. "Children have a way of getting away from you," she said. "You draw up your master plan but somehow they ignore it."

"Well, first there's the matter of this war we've got to win," Randy said. "What's your status now, Jack?"

"I leave for California in three days."

"Then what?" Mary asked.

"I'll go to Pearl Harbor first for training and probably be reassigned somewhere in the Pacific."

"And I might just follow you out there," said Randy, to everyone's surprise. "The sidelines are getting sort of uncomfortable."

"I've always expected you would. Remember the poem, 'I could not love thee, dear, so much, loved I not honor more'?" Mary said.

"What's that from?" Randy asked.

"It's called 'To Lucasta, on going to the wars' by Richard Lovelace," she explained. "It still applies today, three hundred years later, doesn't it? Come on to bed, you sentimental old fool."

Mary and Randy stood up, embraced their friends, and went off to bed. Jack sat with his arms around Janet, wanting to comfort her, but not knowing what he could say. The great oil field he had found now seemed quite insignificant when compared with the war that had to be fought and the family he must hold together in a time of danger and change. They sat there for a long time, whispering words of love and comfort, and watching dawn creep across the silent Louisiana bayou.

18

In 1945, when the war was over, a new life awaited Jack in Houston. A million dollars a year was pouring in from West Bayou Bleu. No longer was he just a geologist serving as a consultant. Now he was an Independent oilman, with the knowledge and capital to search for oil on his own. He quickly opened an office in the Continental Building, hired a geologist, a draftsman, and a secretary, and set out to make up for lost time.

Many people brought *him* deals now, prospects they wanted him to shoot or drill or invest in, and sometimes he entered into these ventures. Most often Jack created his own deals. Once again, he pored over maps, Schlumberger logs, and seismic records for days on end looking for the clues that would lead to oil. Others had studied these same data, of course; practically every likely piece of land in the Southwest had been shot a dozen times. But Jack had faith in his ability to see what others had not, to spot the "hickeys," or structures that could lead him to the new oil fields so many sought.

During his years in the Pacific, Jack had often thought about an area in Louisiana about ten miles east of his West Bayou Bleu field. Some early seismic "leads" he recalled, but it was an instinct based on a number of different clues that convinced him the oil was there.

Early in 1946 he was back there, shooting in another dismal swamp, and by the spring he was drilling. He might have brought in partners, but he chose to finance this well himself; even if he got a dry hole he could use the tax write-off against his Bayou Bleu income. Alas, his first well had shows but was, indeed, a dry hole.

Disappointed but not discouraged, he shot the area once more, this time with a closer coverage. With this and knowledge gained from the dry hole, he drilled again, a half-mile east. This time he found a field that, while not as big as West Bayou Bleu, would ultimately produce five million barrels and would be just as profitable for him, since he was its sole owner. He also learned from this discovery the danger in drilling, which was expensive, on insufficient data, which was relatively cheap.

To take care of his Louisiana operations, he opened a Sanderson Production Company office in Lafayette, and to celebrate, he brought Janet over for a week's reunion with the Simpsons, Maude Gillette and their old Cajun friends.

He and Janet also celebrated by buying a house.

River Oaks was, of course, the logical place for them. Most of Houston's successful Independents and oil company executives lived there. It was impressive, even awesome, to drive block after block past those imposing mansions, those monuments to wealth that Houstonians had created. And the area *was* lovely with its quiet streets, and old oak and pine trees.

A real estate agent, an energetic, well-dressed woman in her forties, escorted them through three houses on that first afternoon. Each was huge, formal, and designed for entertaining on a grand scale. Each was, like a Cadillac or a sable coat, calculated to create a certain aura about its owner.

The real estate agent bubbled with enthusiasm. She had done her homework — she congratulated Jack on his recent success in Louisiana and his new office there — and she mentioned the various oilmen who would be their neighbors. At the third house she whispered that Bill Butler lived just two blocks away. She had no way of knowing, of course, that this held no attraction for Jack.

"What do you think?" Janet asked as they drove away.

"I don't know," he admitted. "They're fine houses, but . . ."

She gave him a long look. "Let me show you one more," she said, and directed him to an older neighborhood near Rice University.

They turned onto Caroline Street and stopped in front of a large Southern Colonial house with white fluted columns and set back among pine trees. They went through the big old house for nearly an hour, entranced. Although it would require some restoration and considerable painting, the house possessed something inviting, a lived-in quality.

Finally they walked out and sat in their car.

"A penny for your thoughts," Janet said softly.

"It reminds me of home," he replied. "The fine old Southern mansions in Tyler."

"Me, too."

"It has dignity without being pretentious."

"And look at the neighborhood," she said. "It looks like real people live here. Kids who ride bikes. People who do their own yards. Oh, Jack, don't you love it?"

"I do," he said. "It's elegant, or can be, but it still seems to be part of the real world. River Oaks is like another planet, all refined and picture-perfect. I don't want my kids to grow up cut off from reality. I want them to go to public school and — "

"Excellent school right down the street."

". . . and know ordinary people, like we are, in spite of all the money that we've got now. That's the real point — we can't let the money cut us off from people."

"I'd love to do a real job of restoring this house," Janet said excitedly. "We could find good early American furniture — "

"I think we've found a home," was all Jack said.

They paid cash for the house and in the months ahead Janet was busy with its restoration.

Jack's success made them more and more in demand socially. Invitations poured in, until Janet had to learn to decline politely the vast majority of them, as hard as it was for her to say no to anyone. When they entertained, it was usually at small dinners at home, for both of them disliked big, noisy cocktail parties.

Soon they joined the Houston Country Club, the oldest and most prestigious of the city's country clubs. And then came the River Oaks Club, where many of the successful newcomers of the oil and business fraternity did most of their entertaining; many of its members became close friends. Jack was invited to join the city's most elite luncheon clubs, including the Ramada Club. Their members were not only leading oilmen, lawyers, bankers, and businessmen, but members of prominent old families, many of whom had political interests. It was said that the executive committee of the Ramada Club "ran Houston," but Jack had no idea. He was still trying to understand Houston and had not the faintest notion who or what ran it.

He was aware, however, of how highly conservative most leading Houstonians were in their political thinking. To many of them, labor leaders were all Reds, Roosevelt and Truman had been Ultra-Liberals, and even Eisenhower was increasingly seen as the dupe of a left-leaning White House staff. At the local government level, he discovered that the businessmen completely controlled Houston's politics, and as a result the city had no zoning, low taxes, and inadequate public services.

At the other extreme were the city's labor leaders and a few liberal activists, many of whom taught at the local universities. A vocal and bitter group, they exercised considerable power and were often able to control Houston's congressional seats. Jack had met many of them and, while he believed most were sincere, he thought some were frustrated, disgruntled people who had achieved little success in life and were bitter toward those who had. Jack resented seeing such men make business, particularly big business, their political whipping post. Houston, whatever its faults, was thriving, and business was largely responsible.

The need, Jack felt, was for the extremists of both left and right to stop fighting one another and cooperate, so the city's prosperity could be extended to more people. Philosophically, Jack was a moderate, a pragmatist of the political center, and it was hard for him to understand why some people preferred to shout extremist slogans rather than seek solutions.

Jack and Janet both played tennis at River Oaks, and Jack played golf. One day he played a round with a man named Jason Rowland, a Houston Independent who turned up deals for several of the major oil companies.

"I've specialized in the Gulf Coast," Jack remarked, "but recently I've been branching out. I've gone into Southwest Texas, shallow Frio gas mainly, and also into the Rocky Mountain area. I've opened a small office in Denver and fly up for a few days whenever I can."

"That's good to know," Rowland said. "I've just put together a block west of Scott City, Kansas, based on some old magnetometer work. It will need some seis work before a drilling, but I'd be happy to show it to you."

"Great!" Jack said. "Why don't you meet me for lunch Thursday at the Ramada Club? Bring your map and we can look it over in one of the private rooms after lunch; they don't like maps on the lunch tables, you know."

The lunch went well. Jack liked Rowland and thought his block was an excellent prospect. Their meeting was marred only by the fact that Bill Butler was sitting across the dining room with two of his vice-presidents; Jack was convinced a lot of angry glances were coming his way.

After he had had an opportunity to examine Rowland's map, Jack took it back with him to check it against his own data. He had promised his friend a quick reply, but he had no more than entered his office the next morning when Rowland was on the phone.

"Jack, I hate like the devil to tell you this, but I must withdraw that deal I offered you. I'm terribly embarrassed, but I have no choice."

"No problem," Jack said easily, "but I must say I'm curious. What changed your mind?"

He heard the other man sigh. "I shouldn't tell you."

"You certainly don't have to."

"No, I owe you an explanation. I just got a call from Arch Calhoun of Texoil. He and Bill Butler were lunching at the Ramada Club yesterday. They saw my map and realized we were discussing a deal. What Arch said, in a nutshell, was that if I did business with you, I wouldn't be doing any more deals with Texoil."

"That's outrageous," Jack exclaimed.

"I do half my business with Texoil," Rowland said quietly. "I can't buck them. I hope you'll forgive me, Jack."

"Don't give it another thought," Jack said. "Call me when you're ready for another round of golf."

He briefly considered some sort of legal action. What Butler had done was certainly unethical, if not illegal. A lawsuit was not out of the question, or a protest to the American Petroleum Institute. But he quickly dismissed those alternatives. Butler would plead ignorance, Arch Calhoun would deny all, and Rowland would only be embarrassed and hurt professionally.

Jack wasn't afraid of Butler. Although he didn't run a major oil company, his income was now running about ten million dollars a year, which put him in the dozen top Independents in Houston. Jack was too big and too respected for anyone, even Bill Butler, to push around. Still, Jack resolved to play it cool. Butler was obviously looking for any move he could make to hurt him.

Jack's natural inclination, as he savored his growing success, was to expand his operations; indeed, the income tax laws almost forced him to. As long as an Independent kept drilling, he could manage it so his expenses and deductions, which included all of the costs of drilling except materials, equalled his income, so he paid no taxes. But if he stopped drilling, he was taxed like anybody else. In the highest bracket, which Jack was in, the tax was 92 percent of the marginal dollar of income. This was, however, after deduction of the depletion allowance of 27.5 percent on gross receipts from oil and gas, limited to 50 percent of net income. Being greater than the actual annual rate of depletion of oil reserves, this was in effect a government subsidy to encourage more wildcat drilling. It was the depletion deduction that provided the cash flow for the Independent to live on, and to drill more wells. There resulted a kind of treadmill, but one few oilmen complained about as they raced from one deal to the next to find wells to drill to use up their tax money. This was not difficult for Jack, who was trained to find prospects.

Jack's office in Denver had also proven profitable, and its success led to another in Calgary, where he hoped to get in on the fields being discovered in Alberta and Saskatchewan provinces. He liked the Canadians and their free-wheeling ways; he felt as much at home there as in Houston. He soon had three seismograph parties at work in Canada, and quickly they found five new fields. Jack's income went up so high that, for the first time, his bank loan went down. Finally, his income exceeded his expenses and the interest and amortization of his loans.

But Jack was still determined to find new oil plays.

"Offshore," his chief geologist, Ed Swanson, declared one evening. "We're in every big play from the Gulf Coast to Saskatchewan. The only thing missing is the offshore, and I say that's the way of the future. Being able to drill in deeper water is opening up a lot of good virgin oil territory. I'm telling you, Jack, it's time we got our feet wet."

"I'm ready," Jack responded. "But where? Show me a plan. How do we finance it?"

"I've got one," declared Jack's number one geologist, an excitable man named Chet Beasley. "The Department of the Interior is putting up a good block of leases just south of Aransas Pass. We know that part of the Gulf Coast as well as anybody. I've got some old structural leads there, so let's do some reconnaissance shooting over them and see what we find."

"Go to it," Jack declared.

Jack personally oversaw the seismic work, which was quicker and much less expensive at sea than on land. The recording boat simply dragged behind the seismometers, which picked up reflections from seismic impulses created under water with compressed air.

The shooting turned up a good medium-sized structure that Jack hoped might be good for ten million barrels of oil. His sealed bid of $15 million, submitted to the Interior Department along with other sealed bids, got the lease. He could tell from the other bids that he hadn't "left much on the table," meaning his margin over the next highest bid.

Jack's first well offshore proved to be on the wrong side of the fault he had mapped, and produced only a dry hole, but it was followed by three producing wells that Jack's staff estimated would bring in at least five million barrels. With oil selling at $3.50 a barrel, that meant a profit of at least $7.5 million — not as much as Jack had hoped for but not bad either.

The moderate success of Section 10, as the first field was called, only whetted Jack's appetite for a bigger success in the scramble for offshore oil. As the operator of this field he set out to learn more about the area than anyone else. He immersed himself in studying structure maps and seismic work and other data he had on the Aransas Pass offshore area, until a combination of hard facts and instinct convinced him that he had pinpointed a real bonanza, a large structure beneath the bright blue waters of the Gulf of Mexico not far from Section 10.

"I think Section 10 has given us a lead to something much bigger to the west," he told Chet Beasley one morning. "We got a lot of unexplained north dip in the shooting when we found Section 10, that means more structure than we are producing from. I don't think anyone else is onto it. Those leases are coming up soon. I want to shoot that area carefully, but I don't want anyone else to know about it. Any ideas?"

Both men were aware that in the hotly competitive world of oil-finding, "intelligence gathering" was carried on constantly by the other operators, particularly the major companies, and outright spying and stealing of data were not unknown. Their big competitor in the Section 10 area was, it so happened, Texoil. They had been exploring and producing there for five years and knew it well.

At length Jack came up with what he thought was the best plan for shooting the area they were interested in, which they referred to by the code name Tortuga. Under this plan, they would carry out a routine decoy survey, concentrating south of the Tortuga structure. Their recording boat would also shoot the Tortuga area, with a series of individual, apparently random, lines, while going and coming from the decoy area. These, in the end, could be put together to comprise a thorough survey of Tortuga. Only Jack, Chet, and a handful of technicians on the boats would know what was actually happening.

The secret shooting went ahead as planned, and the results were beyond Jack's wildest dreams: a structure under Tortuga that might produce 200 million barrels of oil, if not more.

Jack decided that, to be safe, he would make a bid to the Department of Interior for $50 million for the Tortuga parcel. That might be high, particularly if no one had observed his concentration of shooting there, but he'd rather be high than risk losing this prize. He decided to put up half the money himself, which the bank was willing to lend him, and he brought together a group of three Houston Independents, all close friends, to put up the other $25 million. These investors were given seismic maps of the structure, but were not told its exact location, and they were sworn not to discuss the upcoming bid with outsiders. In short, they had to trust Jack.

Jack took elaborate precautions to ensure secrecy. All seismic data, maps, and correspondence were kept in his own personal office safe. An elaborate code was devised for all references to both the structure and the proposed bid. He wrote all checks through a New York bank, rather than risk a leak from his Houston bank.

Two days before the bids were to be submitted in Washington, Chet called in from their office in Port Aransas.

"Jack, something's up," he shouted over the scrambler. "Something that smells bad. Two days ago a speedboat followed us while we did our diversionary shooting. They could have seen us shoot our final line over Tortuga on the way in."

"It could be nothing," Jack said. "Probably just some joker out for a spin."

"No, there's more. This morning, half a dozen recording boats were all over Tortuga. They're still there, shooting like crazy. No one knows who they are or where they came from. I think you'd better get down here right now!"

"I'm on my way."

He headed for the door, pausing long enough to tell his secretary to call the heliport and warm up the helicopter he often rented for quick trips. A half-hour later he was over the Gulf.

The shining water was a glorious deep blue, and there was unlimited visibility. From miles away, Jack could see the intruding boats crisscrossing the patch of ocean he had hoped was his alone. When he was directly above the five recording boats, he could see the men scurrying across their decks and the seismic lines they dragged behind them. What he could not see was any evidence of whose boats they were.

Then the pilot touched Jack's arm and pointed to the west. High above them, silhouetted against the afternoon sun, a second helicopter was circling the Tortuga structure.

Jack seized his binoculars and gazed at the mystery chopper. With a sudden chill, he recognized the Texoil markings. In the front seat, wearing a jaunty naval cap, was his Texoil rival, Bill Butler, grinning as he surveyed the scene beneath him.

Jack yelled to his pilot to go up for a closer look. Soon the two choppers were barely thirty yards apart, two dots far above the choppy gulf.

Jack, beside himself with rage, found himself shouting abuse at his rival. Butler, his binoculars fixed on Jack now, saluted before his craft raced away toward the mainland.

Jack shook his fist, and then told his pilot to return to base.

Back in his office, Jack placed a conference call to his five partners in the Tortuga venture. He used his "secure" phone, reflecting bitterly that he really had no idea what was secure anymore, not after this disappointment.

"Someone was shooting our area this afternoon," he told his partners. "Shooting it very expertly. I suspect that the recording boats were from a major company." He decided not to tell them immediately about Bill Butler's presence. "They're just in time to make an informed bid. This changes everything. I suggest that we raise our bid to Charlie level."

That was their agreed-upon code for a $30 million increase, to a bid of $80 million.

One man whistled. "That's a helluva lot of money," he sighed.

"Sorry, it's over my limit," another said.

"That's okay," Jack said. "I'll take your cut. Is everyone else in?"

Everyone was, and the new bid was rushed to the Interior Department in Washington in time for the deadline that evening. The bids were to be opened the next afternoon.

Jack did not sleep that night. He gave up trying, and went down to his study and paced about. Luck and skill had led him to the Tortuga structure. He had imagined it as the crowning achievement of his career. It had been within his grasp, so close he could taste it, and then Texoil had charged into the picture. What had gone wrong? Who had leaked? Some low-level employee, for money? Or one of his partners, in a moment of whiskey-induced boasting? To do everything right, and then to be cheated out of his prize, was almost more than he could bear to imagine.

Or would his $80 million bid hold up? It was one hell of a lot of money, over half of it his, and Texoil would have a hard time beating it in the few hours available for analyzing the data and preparing their bid. That was his advantage, he told himself: he was an Independent and could move fast while the big companies held their endless meetings.

But Texoil was Bill Butler's show and he could bypass all the committees. Jack remembered Butler's arrogant grin in the helicopter that morning; it was not the grin of a man who thought he could lose.

Was $80 million enough? At dawn, Jack was still wrestling with the maddening question, not to mention the more frightening prospect that Texoil knew his group's bid, and was looking down his throat like an opponent in poker who knew your hole card. If this were the case, Jack knew he was beaten.

The Interior Department officials opened the bids at 1:00 P.M., Houston time, and the results went out over the wires immediately.

Jack waited in his office alone, watching the news on his private news ticker.

Block 620, bought by Coastal for $10 million.

Block 736, Gulf, $32 million.

Block 187, Coastal, $17 million.

There were twenty-odd leases being bid on.

Suddenly the numbers 625 danced across the ticker. That was

it, the Tortuga block, and Jack's heart skipped several beats as the machine began to click again.

Texoil, $82 million!

Jack sank back into his chair in utter despair.

Butler had not only found out about his structure, but he'd clearly known of his $80 million bid and deliberately topped it.

A great sense of futility swept over him. How could an Independent buck a rich, ruthless major like Butler's Texoil?

He poured himself a drink and began to call his partners with the bad news.

Later, at home, he continued to drink while Janet watched anxiously, bringing crackers and cheese and fruit into the study. As he was raging his way through the story of Bill Butler's sabotage for the fourth time, she suddenly got to her feet, stood in front of him, and grabbed his glass.

"I'm not going to let you make a drunkard of yourself over a few measly dollars — or even a few measly millions of dollars. Go to bed."

For a moment he was angrier at her than he had ever been in his life. He lunged to his feet, ready to roar at her, then felt himself sway and knew she was right. "Sorry," he said. "If it just wasn't Butler."

"You're making an obsession out of that man, Jack," she said pointedly. "Wouldn't he be delighted to know that?"

"He gets my goat, all right."

"Well, don't let him, hear?"

"I won't," he said. "Damned if I will."

And, over the years, he hadn't. But when he started his well with Ralph on the Gillette land, he knew Bill Butler was still there, looking over his shoulder.

19

Ralph and Anne

"We should have some news today from Jack about the well," said Ralph brightly. "It spudded ten days ago. They set surface casing, and it's been drilling away for a week. It's exciting to know that the pipe is turning and won't stop until we know what we've got."

"I try not to think about it," sighed Anne. "I guess I'm superstitious."

It was now November. Ralph, who had just come downstairs, went to the front door to get the morning paper. Then he seated himself at the breakfast table, poured a cup of coffee, and opened the paper. There were no big headlines, but it didn't matter. What he saw had the same sort of impact: "Bill Butlers Seek Divorce." The piece bore a Paris dateline and quoted a French lawyer's press release: Mr. and Mrs. William Butler of New York and Houston, after thirty-three years of marriage, had reached an amicable agreement for separation leading to divorce. She would continue to live in their home in the south of France, he in their home in Houston and their apartment in New York, where Butler was at present.

Brief, dry, right to the point, Ralph mused, knowing full well that the owner of the paper was a close friend and neighbor of the Butlers. Ralph read it again, then looked up as Anne and the children sat down.

"You'll be interested in this," said Ralph lightly and turned his attention to his scrambled eggs. At first he had not been concerned, but now he experienced a foreboding as she read. He needn't have worried. She was cool, as she usually was.

"What's it about, Mom?" asked John, his mouth full of toast.

"Nothing that would interest you," Anne replied with a small smile.

"Why not? How do you know if you don't tell me?"

"Don't be sassy," said Kate. "Can I have more toast?"

"May I," said Ralph automatically, handing her the plate.

"I wasn't being sassy! Was I, Daddy? I just asked a question, didn't I? Can't I even ask a question?"

"Hush, both of you and eat your cereal or you'll be late," said Anne, handing the paper back to Ralph.

"I'll bet this'll be the only topic of conversation at the museum dinner tonight," ventured Ralph.

"Well, I doubt anyone will be very shocked. They've really been separated for years," Anne replied.

"What time is the party tonight?" asked Ralph.

"Cocktails are at 6:30. Try not to be late, O.K.?"

Of course Anne wasn't surprised. She'd been in the kitchen when the call came yesterday. Bill had told her about the divorce and his schedule. He wanted to see her when he returned to Houston next week. It was all rather perfunctory: arrangements were made, nothing more was said — no indication that there was to be any change in their relationship.

After Ralph and the children had left, Anne sat at the table and stared at the paper. Bill's call had excited, then frightened her. "I just thought you should know . . ." he had said. She had mumbled some cliché about being sorry that had made him laugh. "Don't be," he said. "This is long overdue. We just never got around to it until now." She had almost expected him to say something about not having a good reason until now, but he had not.

What did I expect? she thought angrily. What if he had said, "I'm getting a divorce so I can marry you." Then what? Am I ready for that? Is that what I want?

Or did she really just want what she had — Ralph and the possibility of oil millions, and Bill to flatter and divert her with his power and wealth. She had read somewhere that women needed three husbands — a lover, a provider, and a handyman. She remembered how she'd laughed and handed the article to Ralph, who had kissed her and said, "You can always hire a handyman." It seemed a long time ago, when she was happy and wanted nothing else.

But what choice did she have now, except to break it off?

Ah, but she didn't want to! There was something about Bill that thrilled her, and not just his fame and the trappings of his position. It was because he thought *she* was important, preferred her to all others. He had told her so. "Things come out more clearly when I'm with you," he had said the last time they were together. He had taken to telling her about his business problems, seeking her judgment, complimenting her on her common sense and business acumen. "Texoil should hire you," he said admiringly. "You're better than my board members."

But all this time he had been a married man — and now he was free. The implications were so far-reaching that Anne felt staggered — except that he had said nothing about any change between them. I should be glad, she thought scornfully, since I don't want things to change.

Ralph was suspicious, she knew. She had been careful, gotten so good at it and at lying that she sometimes astounded herself. She thought she had handled the newspaper story of the divorce well.

The odd thing was that she still loved Ralph, along with the guilty knowledge that she was deceiving him, even if he didn't know it. Besides, she was pretty sure something was going on between him and Diane. Ever since the Rezzolis' party she had felt this, even hoped for it. She wouldn't blame him, of course. He was only human, too.

Ugh, what flimsy rationalization!

She badly wanted to talk to someone, which made her realize that she had no real friends in Houston. The girls she had known best in college, or her friends from their years in Washington — well, a phone call wouldn't do, not after all this time. Suppose she confided in Janet — Janet's hair would stand on end — or Diane. But what if Diane said, "Well, there *has* been talk . . ." or Sally Crane said, "My dear, what *is* he like — you know, you lucky dog!"

As if on cue, the phone rang. It was Janet. "Would you mind stopping for us tonight?" she asked. "It's always so hard to park at the Museum, and we're on your way."

"Sure, we'd love to pick you up. How's Jack? How's the drilling going?"

166

"Jack says we're down to nine thousand feet. Too early to tell anything. I'm a finger-crosser, but don't tell him that. He says inside of another month we'll all be richer than Croesus."

Anne laughed. "I could live with that."

"I'm sure you could. Some people can't. Well, see you tonight then."

The party was in full swing when the Sandersons and Harrisons entered the pre-Columbian rooms of the Museum where cocktails were being served. Diane, as Chairman of the Board, was at the head of the receiving line, followed by Brad, Alastair Crane, and Dr. Jules LaCoeur, a professor from Rice University who was the featured speaker.

"How are you?" murmured Ralph, kissing Diane on the cheek.

"Frazzled," she whispered. "We've been having some work done on the house — revising the security system."

Ralph felt his cheeks color. "Ah, we don't have one," he said lamely.

"Lucky you. It can be a real pain sometimes."

Everybody but the waiters seemed to be talking about the Butler divorce. "I've seen this coming for a long time," said one dowager proudly. "Alicia was always away, in Paris or the Riviera, the children are long since married and gone, so why not? Good for them for having the guts to make a break. I know plenty of people who should and don't."

"I don't know, I still think it's sad after all those years," said another. "And it makes it so uncomfortable for their friends. I hate being put in the position of taking sides."

No one seemed to doubt the possibility of another woman being involved. However, they all admitted that after his early peccadilloes Bill had been very discreet, in Houston at least. Time would tell. Ralph listened to all this with interest, and some trepidation. He could see Anne occasionally as she went from group to group. He thought she seemed a little gayer than usual, drinking a little more.

When dinnertime came, Ralph found Diane on his right. For some reason he felt compelled to say something about their recent experience, but managed only, "I'm embarrassed at what happened." She shrugged, then smiled. "Don't give it a thought."

Ralph escaped into a long talk with an elderly woman on his left about the "new" people in Houston, those who had lived there less than ten years. "It's just not the same," she said plaintively. "They're so pushy. They're always showing off and in the most vulgar ways. The jewelry their wives wear would sink them. But you're such a nice young man. Who did you say your father was?"

Later, when Ralph found himself dancing with Diane, she murmured, "I've thought about you so often. We must find another time to be together, if only to talk."

Ralph held her closer, but he didn't know what to say. He was grateful she did not take him for a fool after he had bolted and that she didn't seem to mind that he had not called her, as he had been sorely tempted to do. Twirling through a Viennese waltz with Diane, a dance they both loved and did well, he felt a new surge of desire. But his life seemed beyond his control, at the mercy of powerful forces — Butler, Diane, and the outcome of the well which was turning, turning, night and day, below the swamps of the Gillette land.

"We're getting pretty close to the target depth," Jack had remarked to Ralph earlier. "I'd say another two weeks will tell the story. Everything's running pretty much as expected up to now, but we really don't know anything definite."

"As long as we're drilling we can still hope. Anything is possible," said Ralph. "I sometimes wish we didn't have to get the final answer on the well, that it would just keep drilling forever. If it's dry, hope is gone. But we can't think of that."

"Like a horse race," commented Anne.

"Something like that." Jack smiled.

But now that the long waiting would soon be over, Ralph thought about it more and more as a reality, not a dream. If the well hit, he would be rich. Not as rich as Bill Butler, but rich enough to be his own man. Anne had said little or nothing that evening when the conversation had turned to the Butlers' divorce, and he didn't know how to interpret her silence. It certainly was not like her *not* to have an opinion.

20

Anne drove herself to the airport; it was safer that way. There she asked for Hangar 5 and parked alongside. She located Texoil 71X and walked up the gangway where Bill Butler was waiting to receive her. He greeted her at the top of the ladder with a light kiss and drew her inside.

As always his supreme confidence and abundant energy gave Anne a new feeling of assurance. Still he made no reference to his divorce. In due time, she thought.

"I've missed you," he cried. "Come sit down, have a martini — I made it especially for you. How do you like my plane?"

"It's gorgeous! I'm impressed."

"I designed this window. I hate those little windows they usually have on planes. This one lets us see the whole world, and today you're going to see my chunk of it." He raised his glass to her. "To us."

"And where are we going, may I ask? I've never had such a view from a plane before."

"We're going down the coastline to Laredo at eight thousand feet. You'll be able to see the yacht and the hunting lodge, the oil field I found at Bay City, our refinery at Corpus Christi, and my ranch near Duval. At Laredo we rise to thirty-two thousand feet for our return, so you can see it all together, and half of Texas to boot. Ready?"

"Ready as ever," Anne grinned. "I've never seen this part of Texas before. This is very exciting!"

The plane taxied out, turned into the wind and took off as Bill held Anne's hand. As they proceeded down the coast Bill pointed out the sights, telling the pilot by intercom when he wanted to circle or go lower. As he talked he drank martinis, while she nursed her one.

"The Texas-Mexican coast is where we started," he said. "My father came from Corpus Christi. He didn't have much education; he made his start the hard way as a roustabout, then a drilling contractor. Later he was an Independent, a wildcatter, fighting Lord Cowdry and Shell Mex and the other majors in Tampico's Golden Lane. Those were tough days, a lot of violence and Mexican politics. The best wells flowed a hundred thousand barrels a day, which made big money, and my father got his share."

"Your father must have had a great influence on your life," Anne commented.

"He did. A decisive influence. Father always felt at a disadvantage because of his lack of education and because, without refineries and markets, he was at the mercy of the majors who bought his oil. That's why he wanted me to get the best education. That's why he wanted to build his own integrated oil company, which became Texoil. I had to go to the best school and university. I had to study everything I would need to run Texoil. I didn't just study one subject at Yale, I studied three: law, geology, and engineering. I took majors in all three. I had to excel, in my grades, in athletics, I had to win. I won three letters at Choate and four at Yale.

"And I had to learn the oil business, from the ground up, the hard way. I had to do this with obstacles put in the way by my father to toughen me. I spent one summer as roustabout on a drilling rig, with more than my share up top on the crown block stacking drill pipe. Another summer I 'hustled jugs' on a seismograph crew, burying the seismometers in the earth, stripped to the waist in the broiling sun. I never asked for any favors."

"Knowing all this makes me understand you better," said Anne. "After two generations you must have oil in your veins. It's a shame your father couldn't have lived to see what you've made of Texoil. He would be very proud of you."

"I hope he would," said Bill. "But I'm talking too much — it's because you're a good listener. Let's have some lunch. The gumbo is from the recipe of an old restaurant in Lafayette, Louisiana, Don's, the best creole restaurant in the world. And I ordered champagne. This is a festive occasion!"

He served the food himself, on trays that fitted onto the chairs in front of the window.

As they ate he pointed out particular places of interest. "There's the Bay City oil field, a hundred million barrels that will earn Texoil five hundred million dollars in profits. It was my idea. I shot it. I drilled it. By itself it could supply the free world for twenty days."

When they were over Corpus Christi, Bill pointed out the Texoil refinery. "That's the most modern refinery in the world," he said proudly. "It can turn two hundred thousand barrels of oil into gasoline and other products every day. I saw to it that it had the latest technology, the best equipment. I wanted to be sure Texoil would always have a market for our oil, not be cut off like my father was. I built it in Corpus as a tribute to him.

"And that's the King Ranch, a million acres, twice as big as mine, which you can see coming up on the horizon. But the King Ranch has a lot of heirs and my ranch is all mine. See those dots clustered around the windmills? Those are my cattle. There's my house. You can't see it well, but it's a real ranch house, Spanish style, low and rambling, surrounded by live oaks. I want to take you there, ride the trails with you. You'd love it."

When the plane turned at the international border at Laredo, Bill pointed south along the low Mexican coast. "You can almost see Tampico down there," he said. "It has never been much of a place. In my father's day it was a hell-raising oil town. But I have the feeling that some of my roots are there." He paused and looked away. "And now let's turn back. I've asked the pilot to go up to thirty-two thousand so we can see more, the whole state. Let me take your tray. Would you like a brandy?"

Anne accepted, though she intended to hoard the last drink. She was already giddy from the martini, the wine, but most of all the vision of his life Bill was showing her.

"Everyone develops his own philosophy of life," he said expansively. "I believe a man should do and take what he wants, that he should recognize no limits to his achievements. He should not be bound by the petty rules made by weak men to protect themselves from their weaknesses. At Yale I read Nietzsche for the first time. I'll always remember what he said. 'I teach you the superman.' 'Man is a thing to be surmounted.' 'Man is the bridge between beast and superman.' That was pretty heady stuff for a kid from

Texas. I opted for Nietzsche's philosophy of life instead of the sloppy, sentimental Christian ethic. I shot for the stars. I wanted everything.

"And this is the result. This is my world," he said, waving his hand. "Everything you've seen is mine. But I need someone to share it with, someone who appreciates me and understands me. Alicia was so cold. She was New England. She had always had everything. She was never interested in what I was doing, never gave me credit for anything. She didn't like oilmen, wouldn't give them the time of day. She never came with me to the API or the Business Council. She was always in Paris or London with her literary friends, tiddly weak people, chasing butterflies they never caught." Bill took another sip of brandy and shook his head. "I was never happy with Alicia. We should have called it quits a long time ago."

Anne's head was buzzing with the drink, anticipation, or perhaps apprehension. Bill seemed to be leading up to something for which she was not sure she was ready. I should say something, she thought.

But Bill was not waiting for her encouragement, he was gazing as if spellbound out the big window. Now they could see half of Texas; the former objects of Bill's interest became tiny specks as they merged with the panorama of the great state. Caught up in his own ego, Bill leaned forward and said, "Higher, higher," into the intercom.

"Look, Bill," Anne said finally, "I'm as flattered as I can be by all this and I'm touched that you've confided in me, but I'm confused, and scared too, I guess. I just don't see myself as part of all this. I don't know what you want me to be."

"I need you," said Butler. "With you I can do anything. I'm worth 500 million. It can be a billion. I want you to share it with me." He got to his feet unsteadily and swept his arm over the vast horizon before them. "Higher, higher," he said as he downed his brandy. "See all that? It's all mine. I control this state. I own the governor. With your help I can run the country."

Bill hadn't seemed to expect her to say anything. Why should he, she thought with dismay; he hadn't asked her anything, just told her — told her everything except what she had been expecting, that he loved her and wanted to marry her.

"Descending for landing in Houston," came the pilot's voice

over the intercom. "Please fasten your seat belts."

Ralph had gone to meet a friend from Virginia between planes, and had taken him to lunch at the airport restaurant. On his way back when he was passing the private hangars, he spotted a car ahead that looked like Anne's. He watched her turn out of the Texoil gate, then saw Bill Butler, getting into a black limousine marked TXL.

Ralph was stunned. Anne, always a fast and impatient driver, was quickly lost to view, and he drove back to his office in a fog, creeping along as if he'd had too much to drink. Why would Anne meet Bill at the airport? It didn't make sense — or rather, it did.

He spent the afternoon in a state of shock, staring out the window, totting up the evidence as if preparing for a murder trial. He had been a fool. Why hadn't he had the sense to face up to his suspicions? Perhaps because he so hoped they were unfounded.

But now everything fell into place. The seemingly chance meetings, the Butler divorce, Anne's cool reaction — how could he have been so stupid? More to the point, how could she have lied to him, deceived him, betrayed their marriage and their children? He had to confront her now, and he was afraid.

When the time came to go home, he drove the familiar route without seeing it and arrived home surprised to find that he was there. He greeted the children and Anne as if nothing was wrong, and got through dinner somehow, and a National Geographic special about whales that had been assigned as part of Kate's homework.

At last the children went up to bed and he was alone with Anne in the living room.

"I wonder how the teacher is going to deal with the sex part," said Anne.

"Probably skip over it."

"I don't know — they're pretty determined to be modern about everything these days. I think they're going too fast for Kate. That movie about birth scared her to death."

He just looked at her. After a moment she said, "Is something the matter?"

"I saw you today."

"Saw me?"

"At the airport."

She flushed. "Were you following me?"

"No, of course not. I met Chuck Snider for lunch between planes. Would you like to give me your explanation?"

"Bill Butler invited me to fly down to Laredo and back with him."

"And you didn't think to mention it to me?"

"I didn't think you'd understand."

"You were right — I don't."

She was silent.

"Is that all?" he said.

"What do you want me to say? That I wasn't there, that there was nothing to it? Would you believe me?"

"Why not? I did before."

"I know, and I regret — I can't tell you how sorry I am that I've lied to you."

"I'm not concerned with the lying, only with what you lied about. There's something between you and Butler, isn't there?"

"Yes."

Ralph took a deep breath. "How long?"

"I don't know. A few weeks, months — "

"You don't even know?"

"Oh, I know. It's just that . . . You don't really want details, do you?"

"No. Yes. I don't know. I can't believe that you . . . Is this serious? Does he want to marry you? Is that why he's getting a divorce?"

"I don't know."

"You don't know? What the hell is going on, anyway?"

She began to cry. "I don't know. Today, he — You don't want to hear all this!"

"You're right. All I want to hear is that it's over."

"Would that satisfy you? If I said that, then what?"

"Then — Anne, you can't expect me to just swallow this and forget it! You must have known I'd find out sooner or later! What did you expect me to do?"

"I honestly didn't think that far ahead."

"Well, think now! Are you willing to break up our marriage over this? How important is he to you?"

She got up and began to walk back and forth. "I don't know, I don't know! I can't make you understand how — He's not what you think, you know. He's a gentle, even vulnerable man — "

Ralph snorted. "Spare me!"

"Please," she said. "He's made me feel . . . important, appreciated."

"And I haven't?"

"It isn't that — "

"Look," he said, suddenly terrified. "I know I'm no competition for a man as rich and powerful as Bill Butler, but I love you! Damn it, I don't know whether or not I can forgive you, but I do know I don't want to lose you. Especially now, with the well coming in. Don't you know a whole new life is opening up for us? Why in hell couldn't you wait?"

She stopped in front of him. "It has nothing to do with that," she said quietly. "And I can't even ask you to forgive me, because I can't stop now." She made a little noise that could have been a laugh.

Ralph stood up, feeling hollow and cold. "You can't mean you expect me to condone all this?"

"No, of course not."

"Well, for God's sake, are you telling me you intend to go on seeing him?"

"I have to."

"What am I supposed to do?"

"I don't know." She sounded and looked miserable. "It's like the flu, don't you see? I have to let it run its course."

"To see whether you can land him or not?"

"Oh, Ralph, please don't."

"You realize I can't stay here, don't you?"

"I — You could, you could. After all, until now you didn't even know — "

"My God, what do you take me for?" He was shouting now. "On top of everything else, the man is my boss, I'm in line to be his personal lawyer! Or pimp, as the case may be."

"Ralph, please — "

"Oh, Anne! Anne! How did you get into this mess? I'm going to have to quit my job, move out, don't you realize that?"

She took a deep breath, and her mood seemed to change. "I'm sorry. I guess you do have to do that. What about the children?"

"This is your idea, you explain it to them!"

"All right. But I think we'd better get our stories straight."

175

"Just tell them I've been called away on business."

"Where will you go?"

"I'll let you know when I decide."

"Are you going tonight?"

"I guess I can sleep in the guest room."

"Maybe it won't be for long."

"What do you mean by that?"

"Just that I don't really know how I feel, and when I sort things out I will. Would you come back if I asked you?"

"Ask me later," he said.

In the night Ralph woke in the guest room to find Kate standing over him.

"Daddy?" she said softly, as though she had been saying it for some time.

He struggled to sit up, tasting the sour residue of the brandy he had drunk to go to sleep, aware that he must stink of it. "What's the matter? Bad dream?" She sometimes came to him in the night — to him, never to Anne.

"What are you doing in here?"

The gulf between parent and child had never seemed so deep, the lies one told so ethical. "Mom thought she was catching cold, and I have a trip to make tomorrow so I wanted to make sure I didn't catch it." Remember to tell Anne this in the morning, he thought.

"Where are you going?"

A good question. "Ah — it's just a business trip."

"Why didn't you say so before?"

"Somebody called after you were asleep. My boss. I was going to tell you in the morning."

"When will you be back?"

She was leaning against the bed in one of his old T shirts that she preferred to the pretty nightgowns Anne bought her. He reached over and drew her in beside him, averting his poisonous breath, positioning her head under his chin. "I'm not sure," he said, making it up as he went along. "A week or so." It would never be possible to tell her *never*. He would never do that. He would think of something. "What did you dream about?"

"Dinosaurs again," she said. "Isn't that silly?"

She had been dreaming about dinosaurs off and on ever since the trip to the Sandersons' ranch.

"No, dreams are never silly. They're messages."

"Well, I wish this one would just send me a letter instead. I'm too old to dream about stuff like that."

"No you're not. I dreamed a bear was chasing me just the other night."

"You did?"

"Indeed I did."

"What did you do?"

"I ran and my feet stuck to the ground, and then I woke up."

"I'm afraid I'll keep dreaming about it the rest of my life."

"Well, you might for a while, when something else is bothering you. It's a message in code. Maybe you're scared of something else right now. That movie at school?"

"About having a baby?"

"Did that scare you?"

"Sort of. The baby was all wet and the mother was happy and all that, but her face was wet and her hair was all messed up."

He hugged her to him. "Maybe you should ask your mother about it."

"I did. She said they call it labor because the mother has to work hard to push the baby out, and she said it hurts but not too much, and that when the baby is born it's worth it and you forget all about the labor."

"Well then, see?"

"But Mommy hasn't forgotten."

Ralph sighed. "She didn't mind though, did she? She went ahead and had John, didn't she?"

Kate thought for a minute. "It's too bad you can't take turns and the husband have the next one."

Ralph laughed. "It's not fair, is it? But if it's any consolation to you, fathers hurt too — different kinds of pain, perhaps . . ." He was on the verge of self-pity. "Maybe I should get you a book about dinosaurs," he offered. "The more you know about something, the less you are afraid of it." That was perhaps the biggest lie yet, he thought.

"Get it for Johnny. He likes them. He never dreams about anything."

"His time will come. What would you like, then?"

"The new Judy Blume?"

"Okay. Now we'd better get back to sleep. Have to get up early in the morning."

"Okay."

He walked her back to her room and tucked her in, burying his face in her warm neck instead of kissing her, and returned to the unfamiliar emptiness of the cool bed.

21

In the morning Ralph dressed and took the bag he had packed the night before downstairs before anyone was up. He made some coffee and was pouring a cup when John came down. "Mom says she has a cold and could we manage," he said sleepily. This evidence of marital telepathy oddly cheered Ralph. "What's the suitcase for?"

"I've got to fly to Washington on business," said Ralph, who had refined his story while shaving.

John poured Cheerios into a bowl and was patting them down when Kate appeared. "Dad's going to Washington," he said.

"You didn't say Washington," she accused Ralph, as if he and John had shared a secret.

"I guess I forgot to mention where."

"You'll be back by next Friday, won't you?"

"I'm not sure. What's next Friday?"

"The dance recital. I *told* you!"

"I'm sorry, sweetie, I forgot all about it. But I would have remembered," he hastened to add, as he saw the hurt spread across her face. "It's on my calendar at the office."

"But you won't *be* in the office!"

"No, but I'm going there first today, and I always check my calendar before I go away."

"You will be back, won't you?"

"I'll try my very best, but I can't promise absolutely. There's something I have to straighten out and it may take time. I'm very sorry. Now I really have to go. Give me a kiss."

"Aren't you going to say goodbye to Mom?" said John.

"I already did."

John was indifferent, Kate angry, and Anne was hiding. As Ralph left, he wondered why he should be the one who felt guilty.

At the office he called Harry Colt and told him another invented story, this time about a family emergency. Harry was just on the point of leaving for Louisiana and paid little attention. Ralph told the same story to his secretary, asking her to hold his mail and telephone calls, since he wasn't sure where he'd be for a few days. He had lunch at his desk, finished what work he could during the day, and parceled out what remained. Somehow, without thinking about it, he had realized where he could go.

At five, from the telephone booth in the Texoil lobby, he called the Simpsons in Lake Charles. When Mary answered, he barely identified himself before blurting out, "I'm afraid I need help. It's Anne and me. I really can't talk about it over the phone. Nothing's settled, but I need a place to get away to, and I need to be with friends and have time to think this through. Could I hide out there for a few days? I won't be any trouble."

"Come straight here," ordered Mary. "Our home is yours. Tell us only what you want to. We don't need to know anything except that we love you both. Here you can do exactly as you like."

It was seven when Ralph drove into the pine-covered grounds of the Simpsons' place. Mary greeted him with a warm embrace, Randy with a hard slap on the back. Mary showed him to his room. "There's the makings of a toddy on the bureau," she said. "And why don't we dress for dinner just for old times' sake?" She had put out Randy's extra dinner jacket. Ralph stood looking out of the window at the view he and Anne had seen so often, lovely white pines and cypresses hung with Spanish moss on the bluff by the river. His only thought was that Anne should be there with him.

At dinner there was champagne. No one referred to Anne's and Ralph's difficulties. There was only comfortable talk about old friends and experiences and Randy's report on the drilling. Neither Mary nor Randy said a word about Ralph's plans for the future, for which he was grateful.

However, when Ralph announced that he was going to turn in, Mary followed him a little way down the hall and said, "When and if you want to talk, I'm considered a very good listener by the gardener and the maid and the man who fixed the circuit breaker who has a wife with asthma and raises Siamese cats."

180

He laughed. "I think I'm embarrassed."

"I know. It can't happen to me. It does, though, you know. It's like bursitis, too — if you get it you're amazed to find out how many people you know have had it."

"Thanks — thanks for everything. Maybe tomorrow."

"We'll be here."

The night passed in a sort of hallucinatory daze that just missed being sleep. Ralph got up early and went for a walk in the pines along the river, in an effort to shake off a dream Kate would have been proud of. He was trying to fly a plane, but he was on a highway and it wouldn't leave the ground. He sat for a while on a grassy knoll endeavoring to think things through; but all that occurred to him was a mess of practical problems in an assortment of sizes: where to find a Judy Blume book for Kate, would he have to get an apartment in Houston, had he left Anne enough money to pay the water bill, what would Bill Butler be like as a stepfather, could oil lawyers handle their own divorces, what if the well came in, what if the well didn't come in.

When he was about to return to the house, Mary appeared and sat down beside him. "Bad night?" she asked.

"I've had better."

"You want to talk about it now?"

"I don't know. I seem to be saying that a lot lately. The trouble is, I don't like to talk about my personal problems. That's one of the problems, I guess."

"I don't know many men who do, not about personal things, that is. Men don't even talk to each other about personal things, do they?"

"I'm not sure." They laughed. "I guess we're ashamed. To admit you have personal problems seems to be to admit a character flaw. You should be able to handle them."

"Not when it involves other people. You can't write the script and expect them to follow it."

"Too bad. I could write a good one."

"Is there another man?"

"Are you clairvoyant?" His voice was light, but he felt shame flood through him.

"No — it's just that it's not unusual. Does she love him?"

The question stunned Ralph. "I — I don't know!" he said. "She never actually said that, but — "

"But what?"

"But if she doesn't, why . . .?"

"Boredom. The need to feel that she counts for something."

"Of course she counts for something! I — Mary, I can't live without her! And how could she be bored? She's busy all the time!"

"Maybe that's why she's busy — to keep from realizing. Look, Ralph, I'm not saying it's right or that there's anything you've done wrong. I just know how I used to feel at that age, when my children were young and Randy was up-and-coming. I was angry all the time because he was the one who got to go out and control our lives, do things people besides housewives were interested in, while I was supposed to be 'fulfilled' raising children and managing a household."

"Even if that's the reason, what can I do about it? I can't give the children away. Anne has never wanted to work."

"I'm not sure there's much you *can* do except try to understand."

"I'm not certain I can. I'm angry too. If what you say is true, even angrier than I was. Do women really want to trade places? A man's life at work is not always what you call 'fulfilling,' you know. Is she justified in betraying our marriage just because she's bored?"

"I used the wrong word. It's not that simple. It also has to do with marriage itself, the loss of excitement, romance, call it what you will."

For an instant memories of Diane flooded Ralph's mind. "I admit I've never been much good at figuring out what is most important to a woman — and how to help them fulfill themselves. I've never been perceptive enough to get beyond the narrow bounds of self and ego to come close enough to a woman — even one I love and am married to."

"Oh, come on. I can still remember Anne telling us about the weekend you planned for your fifth anniversary — a trip to a little country inn outside of Washington, a topaz ring in her napkin on the breakfast tray!"

Ralph snorted. "Do you know what I gave her for her birthday this year?"

"What?"

"A word processor."

"Ah."

"I thought she could keep household accounts in it, and her records for the thrift shop sales —. Oh God, listen to me!"

"Never mind, it happens to the best of us. What did she say?"

"She seemed pleased."

"That's where she made her mistake. The time Randy gave me a Cuisinart I fed him frozen dinners for three weeks."

"The trouble is, I don't know what to do. She said she needs time to make up her mind. It's all up to her, you see. And I know I'm not the most exciting or successful husband — I hesitate, I'm careful, I keep my own counsel. But she knew that when she married me, didn't she?"

"No. No one ever knows the person they marry. Dr. Johnson said, 'Men do not understand women so they marry them.' That's what gives it what excitement it has, finding out as you go along."

"What shall I do, Mary?"

"I can't tell you except to come in and we'll have breakfast."

Randy was waiting in the dining room with the news that Jack had called. The well was nearing a critical depth, and unless something unexpected happened in today's drilling, they would run the first deep electrical log that night. They hadn't encountered any sand so far, but should pick it up any time now.

"We must all go out to the well!" declared Randy. "Jack's here, of course; he's staying at the Majestic as usual. And Mary never misses a logging. This is going to be a particularly exciting one. It means a lot to all of us."

When they met that morning in Randy's office, Ralph took Jack aside and explained his situation. Jack was completely sympathetic, and it helped Ralph to be able to confide his troubles to such an old friend. "I'm awfully sorry about this, Ralph," Jack said. "Janet will be, too. But I'm not going to give you two up. I know you both too well. You've got to work it out, but just remember that we're rooting for you."

Ralph spent the day with Randy and Jack in Randy's office looking over the information on the well. The anticipation of the impending logging took his mind off the almost insuperable problems he faced. This well was of desperate importance to him. No matter what happened between Anne and himself, he knew he could never go back to work for Texoil. He couldn't ever work again for Bill Butler. He thought with some irony how close he had come to becoming Bill's personal lawyer — to helping him with his divorce case, he thought bitterly.

During the afternoon, Jack and Randy got a call from the field that was very disturbing. The well had not encountered the deep sand they had expected at fourteen thousand feet. "There's nothing to worry about yet," said Jack hastily. "We'll get it. It's just a little deeper than we thought." He didn't want to admit the possibility that there was no sand, not on top of Ralph's other troubles. But the possibility existed. That was what Texoil had predicted, why they had abandoned the Gillette leases. Ralph called Chuck Ames to let him know how things stood. Chuck had expected the sand by now, and he too was apprehensive. There was no trip to the well.

The next day Jack and Randy were at the well, but Ralph, of course, couldn't risk being seen. The time dragged interminably; he took a walk, tried to read, surprised himself by taking a nap, fought off a late afternoon compulsion to call Anne. Mary said once, "It might help to talk about it," but all he could do was shake his head, hoping she didn't notice the tears that suddenly stung his eyes and closed his throat.

When Randy came home that evening, Ralph sensed that the news was bad. "I'm afraid we still haven't got the sand," he said glumly. "No one can understand it. We're two hundred feet below where we expected it from the seismic survey. Anyway, we've got to run the log tonight when we come out of the hole to change the bit. Even though we've had no evidence of sand, we have to try to find out where we are."

Randy and Ralph met Jack at the well at midnight. This time Mary didn't come. This was not the occasion for any celebration. Ralph stayed in the car, parked off the plank road behind the mud pits. The Texoil scout could very easily drop by.

Jack explained the situation.

"Our first electrical log showed the upper sands at ten thousand feet which have produced for Texoil elsewhere under the Gillette lease. These sands were, as we expected, well developed but low on structure and wet. As you know, we made the choice to drill the best location for the deep sands expected at fourteen thousand feet. But even if there is structure there, and I am still sure there is, it won't produce without sands. It all depends on the sands. So far we haven't found any, but we're drilling ahead and we should know pretty soon whether they're there or not."

184

So they waited. By eleven that evening there had been no break, the bit had become dulled, and to replace it the fourteen thousand feet of drill pipe had to be taken out, three joints at a time, and stacked in the derrick. It took a long time — for Ralph and Jack and Randy an excruciatingly long time. Then it was time to log. The big Schlumberger truck, the focal point of the drama being enacted on the intensely lighted derrick floor, moved into place. The chief of the truck, like a star actor waiting to go on stage, checked his equipment.

The Schlumberger crew placed the long slim logging tool in the hole and started reeling out the almost three miles of cable. Occasionally it would go slowly, particularly when they got to the uncased hole, but it got down. Jack was in the truck watching the light beam in the Schlumberger camera. The log would be recorded only coming back out of the hole, but Jack paled when it reached bottom without the familiar sand kick. There was no sand. They passed word to Ralph in the car.

An hour later when they had the log it was a sober group who were searching it for some evidence of what had happened. The Schlumberger chief shook his head somberly. "Not a trace," he said. "Below ten thousand there were only two or three small kicks, nothing to indicate a sand of any interest. Frankly, I don't know where we are at bottom." Jack and Randy and their geologists compared the logs from the closest wells, but they provided no help. There was nothing to correlate with. There had never been a well so deep in this area before.

They huddled. Jack was the operator and the most experienced. "Well," he said, "it doesn't look too good, but we haven't lost the game yet by any means. We'll go back in and drill ahead. In the meantime we must try to figure out what happened, why we didn't get the sand. I'll speak to the seis people who ran my lines." To Ralph, he said, "Let's see what we can find out from the old records."

It was a subdued group when they parted. The hint of failure hung over the enterprise they had begun with such high hopes. They all knew the odds in finding oil. Even with the best possible evidence, the risk is still great. The possible reward is so high, it's almost always worth the gamble. But failure, by any name, is hard to face.

Ralph was particularly downcast. He had started out the evening in comparatively high spirits. He had been caught up in the performance he could watch on the derrick floor — the booming voice of the great mud pumps, the clicking of the drill pipe as it was being stacked, the bright lights that made the surrounding rice fields as light as day, the suspense as the Schlumberger crew went through its act, and then, when the log did not wiggle, the pall that fell over everyone.

Each man reacted differently to this development, according to his temperament and involvement. Randy, a wealthy man with a minor investment in the prospect, took it philosophically. But Jack had placed all his hopes on this well. He had drilled a lot of dry holes, but this one could break him. He tried to shrug it off, but for the first time he was afraid he might not make it. Ralph had no money in the well, but he had no job, maybe no wife, and in any case great responsibilities ahead. The well meant everything to him.

Ralph went into town and called Chuck Ames, since it was a matter too sensitive for the car radio. He told him where the well stood. Would he look over the old records and see if he had some explanation? Chuck was still too scared of being discovered to come to the well.

Later Ralph went to bed, and lay in the dark thinking about what Mary had said the morning after he arrived. He tried to discount it as women's lib cliches, but the alternative explanation for Anne's involvement with Butler was even more painful than the admission that he had failed his wife. Failed her he had, and failed himself when, true to his character as a procrastinator, he had not heeded the warning signals and asked her what was the matter. True, he had confronted her after the Rezzolis' party, but as a drunk and jealous husband, not as a deeply loving friend and helpmate. An old fashioned word, that, and one to which he wished he had paid attention.

But how did he know she needed help? *Anne?* Anne was always so self-sufficient, so gregarious, so interested in everything. How could he have helped her if she had come to him and said, "I'm bored and restless, I want to feel part of what you're doing"?

She had, he realized suddenly, and with a shiver of recognition. The time he had finally told her about Ames, they had nearly got into a fight because he was holding back. He had accused her of thinking she could do his job better than he did. How she must have felt, how impotent to move him, make him go, wind him up, how she must have wished she were in charge!

But that's the way I am and she knows it, his stubborn ego insisted.

And how she must have been chafing during all this waiting, wishing she could do something.

He wondered what she was feeling now.

The days following Ralph's departure were very difficult for Anne. For the children's sake, she went through the pretense of Ralph's business trip and carried on with her normal activities, although she begged off a couple of dinner parties citing Ralph's absence. She was not in touch with Bill Butler and doubted he was aware of Ralph's leave of absence. Ralph was not that important at Texoil.

Ralph had left on January 18. Anne had not heard from him for ten days. Nothing of sufficient importance had occurred to make her try to reach him through the office. He had called the office only once to say that he was traveling and could leave no fixed address or telephone number. His secretary had called once to see if Anne knew how to get in touch with him. She didn't.

Anne was not used to being alone, and she hated it. After the children were in bed nothing stood between her and her anxiety over the mess she now saw she had made of what any sane woman would regard as a happy life. She took to drinking wine and watching TV late into the night, stumbling into bed at one and two and out of it in a fog when the children got up. In the night many times she thought she would have called Ralph if she'd known where he was, but in the mornings she knew she would not. Something had been wrong all along of which Bill Butler was the symptom. Maybe he would, after all, somehow prove the cure.

But even though she made any excuse to be near the telephone at the time he always called, it never rang. It was as though Bill sensed she needed him and was deliberately staying away.

Finally she called him, something she had never done before, using the procedure they had agreed upon if ever she should have to cancel a date.

"Well, Anne," he said, sounding businesslike. "What can I do for you?"

Just save my life, she thought. "I'm sorry to bother you," she said quickly, aware that the apology put her at a disadvantage and angry that she should have to think in such terms, "but I really need to see you. Would it be possible for me to meet you at your house this afternoon sometime?"

After a moment's pause which did not escape her attention, he said, "Certainly, dear. What time? Unfortunately, I can't do lunch, but I could be there by four. Would that suit you?"

Anne said that it would, but as she hung up she couldn't help getting the impression that Bill had not seemed quite so eager to see her as when their meetings had been on his initiative. The implication had always been "Don't call me, I'll call you." Did the hunter sense he was now the hunted? Anne knew enough about male psychology to detect the difference. Now there was something *she* wanted. Still, she didn't know how she felt, except that she was close to panic. And yet she knew the next move with Ralph was up to her and couldn't be long delayed. She must find out where she stood.

Bill arrived at home shortly after she had been discreetly admitted to his library. He embraced her warmly. "I'm so happy to see you," he said. "I've wanted to call you, but I'm up to my ears in work right now. Is anything wrong?"

She felt like blurting out that her husband had left her, but she knew better. The fact that she knew better told her more than all her twistings and turnings since Ralph had gone. "I've had time to think," she said, "and maybe I have no right to question you, but I'm uneasy about where I stand with you. We've been plunging ahead, taking risks; we're getting reckless, and I don't know what for."

"My dear girl, of course you have every right! And I'm ashamed that you have to ask me. I'm afraid I've been so caught up in the delight of our getting to know each other, getting close, that I haven't paid enough attention to the problems this raises for you. I know you need to know where we stand, and believe me, I have thought about it, and I think I've come up with something that will be comfortable for everyone.

"I know you're aware that Ralph is in line to become my personal attorney, and I think we can start with that. If he assumes that position, it will mean about half time in New York and quite a lot abroad. I already have a townhouse on 64th Street in New York that you can use as a *pied-à-terre*, with a full staff, all expenses, and a limousine at your disposal. When Ralph comes to New York you can come with him, and you can stay there alone whenever you like. After all, you are a New Yorker, so it would be natural for you to make occasional trips.

"Sometimes when he's there I'll be here and you needn't go with him. When you have children there's always some excuse. Also, a personal attorney works very closely with his principal. No one will comment if we're often together and traveling together. Sometimes there will be two of us, sometimes three. And you can fill in as my hostess, as you did at my party for Frank Wood. I no longer have a wife, so why not my attorney's wife, an old friend?

"You see, it's an open arrangement that reflects Ralph's new job. No one will ever raise a question."

He looked as if he'd handed her a diamond necklace, pleased and expectant of gratitude. Anne had listened with mounting rage, outrage, disbelief — surely he was kidding — and now something approaching suffocation. She got to her feet and stared at him, speechless.

He had never suggested to Anne anything so precise about their future before. Although he had made clear his strong attachment to her and his need for her, he had never asked her to marry him. And he hadn't now. Was *this* what had been in his mind all the time? Or was this a way out when he felt cornered? No matter which, Anne was sickened at having put herself in a situation that could result in such an insulting proposal, insulting even less for herself than for Ralph, whom Bill seemed to have cast as a willing cuckold.

"My God, I asked for it, didn't I? But where you end up is asking me to become a high-priced whore! Do you really think for one minute I would be willing to do *that*, to ask Ralph to do *that*, to give up everything for *that*?" In her fury, and to her astonishment, she slapped him on the face hard, so hard he winced and his cheek reddened.

"Come now, Anne," Bill said calmly, getting to his feet. "Aren't you being a little dramatic? We've gotten on very well together. I think I've made you a reasonable proposal. You can have your present life and one with me. I believe it would work. And if you're careful, why should Ralph have to know?"

"You must think he's as insensitive as you are!" She flung off the hand he extended to her and headed for the door.

"Anne, dear, don't go off like this," he said coaxingly. "We can work something out."

"Never!" she cried. "What do you take me for? You may be a great man, Bill Butler, but you're a fool!"

She did not allow herself to cry until she was locked in her own room at home, and there she cried long and hard, in shame and grief. After a while she stopped, got up and washed her face and forced herself to think it through.

Bill Butler's performance had been so repugnant, so revealing, so egotistic, that for her there could be no doubt. For one thing, she would never be in awe of him again. He had not once asked her what she wanted.

In his various descriptions of what their life would be together he had mentioned yachts and ranches and hunting lodges and apartments and limousines in New York, but he had never mentioned love or marriage. It was clear that Bill only wanted to use her as a hostess and adornment to his parties and, when it suited him, his mistress. This probably explained his offer to Ralph to become his personal attorney. To Bill, Ralph would be an asset rather than a problem. He would shield Bill from outside criticism and any embarrassment with her about not marrying her.

What a fool she had been! She had cheapened herself. She had put Ralph in an intolerable position. When it became clear to her that she had risked losing Ralph over a man who was nothing but a rotter, she realized how much she really loved her husband.

Ralph had retired after a quiet dinner with the Simpsons and was reading when the door to his bedroom opened gently. "May I come in?" Anne said shyly.

"Anne!" He jumped to his feet and took her in his arms. "Oh my God! You're here! I've been half crazy."

"Join the club," she said shakily, then started to laugh. There were tears in her eyes. "Oh, darling, I don't know what I thought I was doing. Playing out some fantasy left over from my adolescence, I guess. But something has happened that woke me up. I want to tell you about it."

"It doesn't matter! I don't want to hear it. I don't care about anything except that you're here. I never realized before how much I love you, how much I need you."

"I only want you and the children and a chance for us to lead a happy life together," said Anne. "And we'll do it. You can count on me."

"All I want is to be a good husband and to be good for you, to do things for you, to make you proud of me. You'll see. I love you very much." He kissed her long and deeply.

"Before it's too late," she murmured, "what about the well?"

"The well is still drilling," he said, "and as long as it turns there's hope. Nobody knows why we've reached fourteen thousand feet and not found any sand. Chuck was sure it was there. Jack was convinced. We've asked Chuck to go over the records again, and he said he'd call us in the morning. In the meantime, I can't present you with a very optimistic hope for the future. Naturally, I can't go back to work for Texoil. But," and he looked at Anne tenderly and held her close to him, "none of that really matters to me now. The important thing is that we are together again. Our well will come in. If not, I'll find something. I'm not worried. I have you."

"I don't deserve you," said Anne. "I can't believe what an idiot I've been. Of course you can't work for Bill again. My God, when I think that you almost became his lawyer! But don't worry, well or no well we'll be all right. I'll help. This will be a good time to dip into my little inheritance. I'll be a good manager, I'll show you! I'll make this up to you if it takes the rest of our lives."

22

Together

In the morning Chuck called Jack. "Everything's all right," he said excitedly. "I've found out the cause of our problem, and I'm surprised I didn't see it before. I've been at this all night, and I'm sure I'm right.

"I was always certain the sand was there, and I still am. The reason we haven't found it must be that the velocity of sound I used in my calculations was too slow. The calculated depth of any reflection increases directly with the velocity used. At fourteen thousand feet a five percent velocity error would be seven hundred feet. No fourteen-thousand-foot well has ever been drilled before in the general area of the Gillette lands, so we've never been able to get a direct velocity measurement by lowering a seismometer in a well. I've always applied a standard Time-Depth Chart that everyone uses for this area, called Normal Gulf Coast. I won't go into it now, but with my seismic records there's a way of calculating velocity from the time differences of the reflections from a single horizon as they move out on the record. We could have measured the velocity more accurately by lowering a seismometer down the well, but unfortunately I didn't think of it when we had the drill stem out.

"Well, since you called I've re-calculated every record I have from the Gillette area. The velocity I come up with is three percent faster than the one I used. The sand should be at 14,420 feet. The seismic work you did in checking the structure won't provide enough data to make a velocity calculation. You should hit the sand today or tomorrow. They'll know by the drilling time, then you can run a new log. It will show something quite different. *Believe me.*"

After Jack shared this news with the others, Anne and Ralph stayed on with Mary and Randy while he went out to the well. The two couples tried to distract themselves. They drove through the bayou country, they picnicked along the Bayou Teche under a tremendous swamp cypress tree covered with Spanish moss, they recalled the day they'd spent on the "Whiskey Cheater" River, as they called it, when they'd waded miles up the river and floated down on logs, drinks in hand.

They got back to Lake Charles at dusk to find Jack waiting for them. "We've been in sand since 14,510 feet," he said, his eyes sparkling. "Chuck's dope was right. So far we've dug fifty-five feet. The mud is kicking gas, but we've been able to control it. I want to drill into the sand a little more before running a log, to be sure we've got enough to justify setting casing. That means we could be coming out of the hole as early as tomorrow afternoon. Keep your fingers crossed!"

After dinner they all went out to the well, their hopes rising as the drill went down. The difference between this evening and the one wherein the log showed nothing was palpable.

From the rate the bit was penetrating, they knew they were still in sand. Small chunks of sand came up with the drilling mud. The pit where the mud went for conditioning after emerging from its long trip up the open bore was bubbling gas. The continuous measurements being taken showed no increase in the salt content of the mud. The sounds of the mud pumps and the turning drill stem were as background music for the drama now unfolding.

Randy broke out a bottle and they all had a drink in the portable hut where Jack bunked when he spent the night at the well. An ebullient Mary danced a jig to "Frère Jacques": "Where's your well? Where's your well? Great oilmen, great oilmen! Wanta see a well come in, wanta see a well come in. Where's your well? Where's your well?"

Ralph was euphoric. With Anne again at his side, he felt secure and confident about the future. For the first time he felt it in his bones: this well was going to be a whopper, and he had earned his share.

Anne looked around her, at her husband whom she loved, at

193

the others she knew so well, all of them brimming with the kind of excitement she'd never witnessed in them before. But she felt strangely distanced from them, as if she knew better than they the significance of what was taking place, that it was something *she* was a part of, and that something would have a profound effect on all their lives. At that moment, the champagne in her hand untouched, the restlessness that had disturbed her sleep the night before was replaced by an exhilarating sense of personal power. It was *she* who had persuaded Ralph to take Chuck's deal, and Ralph gave her full credit. Bill Butler would never have done that.

Later, everyone but Jack went home. He would not sleep much that night. The bit was turning, cutting sand. Did it bear oil or gas or water? Only the log could tell. The dice were rolling. No one knew how they would come to rest, but the odds were steadily improving.

Jack had sat on many wells, but he sensed this one was different. This one could be the jackpot, he could almost smell it! But still he was cautious. The gas could be coming from a stringer. Jack remembered his confidence at Terrebone — and how abandoning that well left him owing two million dollars. He shook off the unpleasant recollection and went to his bunk to lie down for a while. But he couldn't sleep, he was too keyed up. He arose and went outside.

Although Jack had been on many drilling rigs, the scene before him never ceased to fascinate him. A modern oil rig for deep drilling, with its looming 120-foot derrick, is a spectacle. Such a rig cost about eight million dollars and rented for nine thousand a day. It was lit up to the extent that darkness was banished, its huge diesel engines generating enough power to light a small town. Its four crews kept it going twenty-four hours a day, seven days a week; they worked eight-hour tours, offshore twelve hours on and twelve hours off, a week on, a week off. At all times the rig emitted ominous noises, from the turning rotary table, the clanking of steel hitting steel and the rhythmic chug-chug of its powerful mud pumps.

The basic task of the rig was to thrust the great turning bit at the end of the drill stem as deep as twenty thousand feet or more into the earth. The pipe, rotated endlessly by the turntable, was lubricated by a column of heavy mud, which also held back the rock face of the open hole and brought up the drill cuttings. As the well deepened, drill pipe was added. The pipe's huge weight helped the rotating diamond bit cut the hard rock. When a bit had to be changed or a test or some other operation performed, the whole drill string had to be raised, disjointed three thirty-one-foot lengths at a time, and stacked in the derrick, then put back in the same way.

The drillers had to monitor constantly a myriad of gauges showing engine temperature and oil pressure, pump pressure and strokes per minute, drilling penetration rate, mud weight, and gas and salt content. They had to keep the brakes and blowout preventers in working order. They had to condition the mud constantly and, after each joint of drill pipe was added, collect, wash, and analyze the cuttings samples. The drillers had to assist in running logs and getting sidewall cores. They had to set protection pipe to keep the well from caving in. In the end, they had to plug and abandon the well if it was dry or, if it was a producer, set the production string, perforate it so fluid could come in and then run the narrow tubing and complete the well, putting in place a "Christmas tree" of control valves on top as a conduit for the fluid and to hold back the pressure. An oil rig was a busy place, for all the monitoring a place where the unexpected could happen — and usually did.

What would happen with this one, Jack wondered. Everything depended on it, in a sense, his whole life.

Jack decided to run his log at 2:00 A.M. of the second morning after they had struck the deep sand. He wanted to see as much of the sand as possible, but he was reluctant to carry more open hole that might contain gas or oil. He didn't want to risk a blowout. He was also anxious to avoid losing the hole before determining what the deep sand contained.

Drilling time indicated that the bit had penetrated about a hundred feet of sand with only minor breaks. In addition to gas, the drilling mud carried into the pits bubbles of beautiful live green oil. The well then seemed to go out of sand for ten feet, and then come back into sand. Jack consulted Randy and Ralph, but it was he who had to make the decision. The drilling stopped. Except for the mud pumps the rig was quiet. The long process of withdrawing the drill pipe began. The Schlumberger truck had been ordered. Casing had been lined up for delivery on short notice if production was indicated. The casing would be set on the shale break between the sands.

This time, in addition to the two couples and Jack, Janet had flown in from Houston, and Maude Gillette was invited. Chuck Ames, still cautious, waited by the phone in Houston. Maude brought sandwiches and a case of Taittinger champagne, which were laid out in Jack's shack.

As usual, there were delays, 4:00 passed, then 6:00, and then the electrical logging tool was lowered into the hole. It went down fast. Although considerable gas and oil had been liberated when the pipe was coming out of the hole, the outcome of the impending test was still not clear. The shows could have come from inconsequential sand streaks above.

The women were sipping champagne in the shack when Randy burst in. "The curves looked good in the camera going into the sand! They're on bottom now and will be logging as the tool comes up. Come with me to the truck. And bring your drinks!"

They were all watching as the light beams on the Schlumberger recorder both deflected out, which means good porosity with either oil or gas. Both beams stayed out as the log came up through the sand. All of it looked good. Mary was dancing around with her elbows raised, resting her hands on her hips, to mimic the Schlumberger lights that both kicked out when they topped the oil sand. "Stay out, you lights," Mary crowed, hugging Randy. The others joined in. The feeling of apprehension that had pervaded the group evaporated and gradually, the sense that something momentous was about to happen, something that they would never forget, took over.

When the recorded log was taken out of the photographic "soup" and hung up to dry, they crowded around, trying to see what the curves revealed. Jack had the log in his hand, holding it high, squinting at it with the expertise that had come from inspecting thousands of logs. Then he said quietly, his voice shaking ever so slightly, "Well, that's it. It's all good, mostly oil with a thirty-five foot gas cap. Let's run the other logs." Later the truck would shoot retrievable pellets into the formation for sand samples to be analyzed for gas and oil and water content. But the outcome was clear. It was a major find!

There were shouts of joy, whoops, hollers, stomping and impromptu victory dances. "We made it!" "It's a well!" "Gillette field does it again!" "And this time it's a big one!" "Whooo-eee!" "I'll drink to that!" Maude Gillette put it best; raising her glass of champagne to the ceiling, she said, "Thank God!"

The Schlumberger truck would be running additional electrical logs the rest of the day. Jack was busy giving the necessary instructions for the logs, seeing that the mud was conditioned to hold back the oil and gas, ordering the quarter of a million dollars' worth of seven-inch pipe that would go into casing the hole, ordering the Halliburton crew that would cement the pipe, and another to shoot the casing for production, run the tubing, and install the Christmas tree. He would be completely occupied for the next twenty-four hours, almost without a break. This was what he had been trained for. He knew what to do and he relished it.

"What good's an oil well," drawled Maude, "producing that greasy, smelly stuff? What do you get out of it? Nothing but a goddamned lousy fortune!" They all drained their glasses, laughing like children, and, like children, held them out to Randy for more.

To each the success of the well meant something different. All of them had known wealth before; all except Anne and Ralph had participated in oil discoveries; but no one had ever found a field as big as this. There was one reaction common to all, however: now *everything* was possible.

Ralph hurried to the nearest telephone to call Chuck, who was almost overcome with emotion. He called Bess to the phone so she could hear it from Ralph. "Are you sure it's all right?" asked Bess anxiously. "No chance for a slip?"

"None," said Ralph firmly. "Believe me."

Chuck, cautious as ever, immediately burned all of the old Texoil records.

Back at the well Ralph discovered a real party in progress. Someone had brought in a bucket full of oil-cut mud from the slush pit. "I annoint you Queen of the Wildcatters," said Anne gaily, as she daubed some of the smelly stuff on Maude Gillette's forehead and then on Mary's and Janet's. "You're ladies in waiting." They all thought this hilarious and smeared the mud over their faces and Anne's.

"But what about us?" protested Jack, laughing. "What do we get?"

"You are King of the Wildcatters," proclaimed Anne, "and this is your kingly mustache." Ralph and Randy got the same treatment. Over and over they toasted each other and long life.

"By now I should be falling down drunk," said Ralph incredulously. "But I'm just — just — "

"Happy?" said Janet.

"Happy," he agreed.

The party went on until the champagne ran out. They sang, told naughty Cajun jokes, and made an attempt at a circular Greek dance.

"Sun is up," said Mary, stretching. "Let's hit the road before we turn into a pumpkin."

Later, the three men gathered in Randy's office in Lake Charles. They knew they had found a very important field. In the first hundred-foot sand the gas cap, which was rich in distillate, was underlain by sixty-five feet of oil with no water. They had penetrated ten feet of oil in a second sand without running through it.

"So how does it look, Jack?" Ralph asked eagerly.

"It's very big," Jack replied. "And it's wide open. It's a major field! There could be many sands below total depth. We know there are seismic reflections, which must come from sands. There can be oil off-structure in the gas sand we've got on top. As you know, oil, for the same acre-foot of reservoir, yields much more revenue than gas."

"What happens next?"

"When we run seven-inch and are protected from a blowout," said Jack, "we'll drill ahead until we are out of sand. Then we'll run a log and decide whether to quit and set smaller pipe, or drill ahead."

"All this is going to cost a lot of money."

"Sure, but that's no problem. The oil and gas down there is like money in the bank. When we've drilled enough wells to be sure where the top is, we'll take a well down very deep — maybe 25,000. And remember, this is only one structure. Chuck says there are three. The other two will each take a wildcat, but they should be cinches after our discovery well. He paused to take a deep breath. "Friends, we're looking at hundreds of millions of dollars. I don't see any real problems ahead. If you're willing for me to operate, as called for in our agreements, I'll set up a local office. We'll be drilling and producing wells on Gillette land for many years. I don't believe any of us need worry about financing the development of this baby. Any of the banks in Houston will lend us whatever we need, with plenty to spare for our personal use. I can arrange it for all of us, or you can deal with your own bank. Just let me know."

The three of them sat and stared at each other, then broke into cheers. "I don't know what your plans are, Ralph," Jack said later, "but my guess is you wouldn't want to continue working for Texoil. I really don't think there's any danger of you ever being accused of conflict of interest. After all, Texoil gave the Gillette lease up. So far as the world knows, I just came along and took it, shot it, and found the structure I drilled. But you must realize how much this is worth to you. I figure you have a future profit at the very minimum of thirty million . . . in the long run probably much more.

"Also, unless you want to sell out, which you really shouldn't do until the fields are developed, you don't have much choice but to stay in the oil business. Otherwise your profits will be eaten up by taxes. You'll be cushioned for several years by development costs here, but someday you'll have to drill more wildcats to avoid paying all of your income to Uncle Sam. You'll want to think this out, but why don't you consider going into partnership with me? I need a good lawyer. This would also provide a reason for your leaving Texoil and a cover for your new wealth. No one has to know it all came from the Gillette lands. I have interests in other fields. Think about it."

"Whew! I am so grateful to you, Jack! Let me talk it over with Anne. What you say makes a great deal of sense. I'd be proud to be your partner. I'm not sure I will contribute enough to justify it, but I'd like to try."

23

Ralph and Anne

The very suddenness with which a successful oil well can impart to the consciousness the image of vast wealth has an indescribably exhilarating effect. This is particularly true when it displaces a suspicion of failure.

Ralph and Anne Harrison had, through their families, known modest wealth, they had lived well, and they had close friends who possessed great wealth, so they had had ample preparation for what lay ahead. Ralph's sixty-thousand-dollar-a-year salary at Texoil just hadn't provided enough to fulfill their desires. Now they could buy almost anything they wanted. Back in Houston with Kate and John, who were not aware of any of the turbulent events of recent weeks, their modest home at the entrance to River Oaks became the cocoon from which they would burst into their new world.

Ralph had returned quietly to the office, had managed by hint and innuendo to link his recent leave-of-absence to an inheritance that had changed his financial situation. He had a long talk with Harry Colt and explained that he felt he should make a change. He would like to take a little time to chart his future. He might join a law firm, or join up with some Independent producer.

Ralph called next on Ray Pickering with somewhat the same story. He told Pickering that he felt obligated to let him know about his plans in light of Ray's recent proposal to Ralph about becoming Bill Butler's top lawyer. Secretly Ralph felt that Bill Butler would be relieved to learn of his departure. Pickering did not appear surprised. Ralph immediately wondered how much he knew. After all, he was Butler's personal lawyer.

When he told his secretary he was leaving, she didn't seem surprised either. Did she and others know about Bill Butler? Butler had a secretary, too. Ralph would never know.

Harry Colt threw a farewell dinner in a private room at the Petroleum Club, with a dozen of Ralph's closest associates present. There was much drinking, certainly more than Ralph was used to. They presented him with a new tennis racquet. Then Harry cleared his throat and raised his glass. "We're going to miss you here, Ralph, old boy. The place won't ever be the same. We're all roughnecks here. Sure, we make good money and wear ties and try to control our language. But at heart we're just roughnecks. We'd be more at home spitting tobacco on a derrick floor. You're different, Ralph. I remember you telling me that you weren't really an oilman, that you had pretended long enough. Maybe you're right, but you were good for us. You gave us a little insight into where we came from, what the past means to the present, what it's all about out there. In addition to missing your title opinions, we'll miss that. Here's to you, Ralph. Good Luck! Keep in touch!"

Ralph was genuinely touched. He knew he had never been as close to these men as they were to each other. Some were crude, some even venal. But there was an honesty about their relationship that he envied. He knew that he had kept them at a distance, but when he rose to answer Harry's toast he felt a rush of affection for all of them.

The party rolled on until the Club blinked the lights at midnight. As Ralph stumbled down the steps arm-in-arm with Harry, he had just a twinge of regret at leaving Texoil, that is, until he thought of the life that lay ahead. He knew one thing. Much as he had enjoyed his work and the companionship of Texoil men over the years, he had never been cut out to be a company man. The narrow tube it represented, the mixture of fear and loyalty, the crowding out of personal relations by rank and duty, had suddenly, by the lifting of his own horizons, been brought sharply into focus. "If you have to, you have to," he thought, "but no more for me."

Ralph had not wanted to announce his association with Jack too quickly. Better let his quitting Texoil and Jack's Gillette discovery recede into the background. But Jack needed him, so the announcement was made just before Christmas. Jack had insisted that both of their names appear in the new firm title: Sanderson and Harrison, Oil Producers. Very large loans, perhaps a total of two hundred million dollars, would be required to drill the many wells required to produce the new Gillette field. Ralph's training as a lawyer gave him just the right background to take this over. The amounts were so large that Ralph thought they should seek their loans in New York, possibly in London.

Early in May, Ralph and Jack made the rounds of the big New York banks, flying up in the new jet the company had bought. Anne and Janet went with them. Anne and Ralph introduced the Sandersons to some of their friends in New York and enjoyed quiet dinners at Twenty-One. The women shopped and toured the museums, and Ralph tried to interest Jack in joining his New York club, but Jack demurred. "I appreciate it," he said, "but I can't see spending that much time here. Place makes me feel as if my fly is open."

Throughout this time Ralph and Anne carried on a running dialogue about their future. They were both eager to begin what they regarded as a new life. The discovery well was producing five hundred barrels a day, and three more wells were nearing completion. With increased world oil prices forced by OPEC, their income, over and above what must be set aside for drilling, would be more than a million dollars a year, more than they could conceivably spend. They had the tax cover of the depletion allowance and intangible drilling costs. They could do anything they wanted.

"It's funny," mused Anne. "Once everything seemed so difficult, so unattainable. I always wondered how it would feel just to be able to cut loose and buy everything I wanted. Now that we can, I've already come to consider it quite normal. It's not so much fun because it's not wicked anymore. How do I make it seem wicked? I already take for granted all those Sakowitz and Neiman Marcus clothes in my closet!"

"Well," Ralph replied with a twinkle, "there are some much more wicked things we could do. For instance, as soon as it becomes known what a successful oilman I am, Houston won't understand our living where we do. Why not build a house? We could rent a nice place while we decide what we want. Suppose I have the people at River Oaks Realty look around?"

"Oh, Ralph, could we? I'd love to!" The feeling that she had sensed was encroaching on her, which she refused to identify as boredom, fled with the prospect of moving, designing a house. It also chased away for a while the one flaw in her nice new life.

After they'd returned from Lake Charles, Butler had tried to talk to her. At ten o'clock on the day after she got back, there had been a call and a familiar voice had said, "Mrs. Harrison, please." When Anne replied, the voice had said, "Are you in a position to take a call?" Anne said "no" and hung up. This was repeated.

He didn't stop. Finally, Anne thought it best to make her position clear. She accepted the call, and immediately he came on the phone and asked her to lunch on his yacht.

"Bill," she said firmly, "I won't, and I want you to stop calling me. I'm sorry about what happened. It was as much my fault as yours. But I don't want to see you again. And I can't believe you really care about me anyway. You were never interested in me as a person. You never asked how I felt about anything. I was supposed to be your hostess, the prop for your act. Frankly, I can't believe you ever cared enough about me that you can't find a substitute. I'm very happy with my husband and I don't want to change anything."

"Anne, dear, listen to me. I don't give up," said Bill, an edge creeping into his voice. "Everything you just said is true. I know how foolish and insensitive I was. I drove you away. But it's different now. I'm not thinking of you with your husband as my lawyer. I want *you*. I want you for my wife. And I mean that in every way a man can."

Anne was too stunned to reply.

"And there's something else you should know. It had nothing to do with you, of course, but my lawyers have evidence that Ralph is involved in Jack Sanderson's takeover of the Gillette field from my company. If they can prove it, it will break both of them. They won't ever be able to do business in Houston again. Think what that would mean for you. You wouldn't like that, Anne. I wouldn't like that. I would like to spare you that."

She thought he sounded downright vindictive, then felt as if she were choking. "Are you threatening me?" she managed.

"No, no, of course not," he purred. "I just think you should know all the facts before you make a decision."

"How can I make you understand? I have *made* a decision!"

"No, Anne! Think it over and let me have one more chance to persuade you. My car will be waiting at noon a block to the right of your home to bring you to me on the yacht. If you'll marry me, I'll call this whole investigation off. Ralph can go right along as if nothing ever happened. Think what you'd be saved."

"Not a chance," said Anne, her voice steely. "You can wait on your damned yacht till hell freezes over. If you attack Ralph I'll stick with him to the end. We'll fight you with everything we've got. And what's more, we'll lick you. Don't you *ever* call me again." She slammed down the phone.

When Ralph came home that evening she told him the whole story. "I'm sorry," she said at last, running her hands through her hair. "I'm afraid I may have made everything worse. I'm sure Bill is going to do everything he can to prove you were in with Jack in getting the Gillette field away from Texoil."

"Don't worry," said Ralph, putting his arm around her. "I'm proud of you. You did just right. Jack and I can take care of ourselves."

"Do you think you ought to tell Jack?" The thought of anyone else knowing about this episode in her life, which seemed to her increasingly sordid and inexcusable, made Anne shrivel inside.

"I can't see why. Whatever Butler is going to do he would have done with or without you."

"You sure?" she said, not pacified.

"Of course. Not to deny your attraction, but Bill Butler is interested in his business, first and foremost. Everything else takes a back seat."

Nevertheless, Ralph was worried.

Ralph and Anne had no way of knowing what Butler was up to, though both continued to be apprehensive. But as the weeks wore on, and he didn't show his hand, Anne began to relax. "Is there anything he could do, any way he could find out you were involved?" she said one night.

"The only connection is Ames, and he certainly isn't going to spread the news."

"But surely there are records somewhere, and information as to who worked on that seismic crew."

"Oh, buried somewhere, but what would they show? That the decision to drill the Gillette well was based only on a shallow map and that the records had been cut short, probably because there was nothing on them."

"But those tail ends that Chuck took — someone else knew about them, right?"

"A guy named Jerry King was the supervisor, but in ordering the records cut he was just following orders. The chief geologist was the one who made the decision. Neither knew that Chuck took the deep ends."

"Yes, but this Jerry King . . . Is he still working for Texoil?"

"No, he's long gone."

"Could they get in touch with him?"

"I doubt it would occur to them. Not unless they stumbled onto Chuck. We've pretty well taken care of that."

"Then I can stop worrying?"

"You can stop worrying."

As summer approached Anne began to take Ralph at his word, and they made less and less effort to conceal the change in their fortunes. In June, after a search made enjoyable by the fact that money was no longer a consideration, they found a stately house in River Oaks. They took a year's lease and put their own things in storage preparatory to building on a large lot nearby. It was the best one left in River Oaks, which they purchased for slightly over a million dollars. Since Ralph was increasingly busy, the plans for the new house became Anne's responsibility. She flung herself into the project with gusto, finding a compatible architect, studying and researching possible plans, and visiting other homes he had designed. She seemed always on the run, often arriving at home breathless just minutes before the children were due home from school. Although she had now acquired a full-time housekeeper, she was determined not to leave the children's care to anyone else.

Ralph's work was even more engrossing and demanding. The firm had kept three rigs drilling on their Gillette lease, two extension wells that would pretty well tell the whole story on the size of the deep field. He juggled contracts, leases, loans, and projections for the future, often arriving home at nine or ten at night, and was frequently out of town. "Since we're rich I'm working harder than ever," he said wryly.

"All for a good cause," retorted Anne, grinning.

After they had settled into their new home, the Harrisons planned a small housewarming party. It would be catered, and

205

they wanted to invite only guests they liked, but discovered they had ended up including only those who lived very much as they were now doing.

"I feel pretty hypocritical about this," said Ralph uncomfortably, as Anne was licking the last envelope for the reminders.

"Why, what do you mean?" She looked up, puzzled.

"I don't suppose we could still have the Colts?"

"Oh, Ralph, we went all over that! We decided it was even more hypocritical to show off in front of friends who don't have as much. We'll have them another time, to an outdoor barbecue or something."

"It's not your fault. I went over the list with you, and I agree it's too late to change it now. I just get the feeling sometimes that our values are changing."

"Well, I guess they're bound to in some ways. But the point is, we're not going to lose touch with old friends; it's just that a good party depends on bringing people together who are comfortable with each other."

"Okay. Just so you're happy."

"I am! It will be a great success, I promise."

On New Year's Eve Anne and Ralph gave a glittering white tie party at their rented home in River Oaks. They had become used to it and felt easy entertaining there. Their guest list shone as brightly as the holiday decorations Anne had so lovingly created, and the next morning there was a full-page spread in the morning paper, as the party consultant had assured Anne there would be.

The whole thing worried Ralph. It seemed to him that they'd become the very thing he and Anne had once ridiculed. But Anne appeared excited and pleased. "My mother had a scrapbook of clippings of her parties, and parties she went to," she said. "I always turned up my nose at it, but now I think I understand. It's like the review of a play you've put on — you want some evidence of success after going to all the work and trouble."

"And expense," grumbled Ralph. "We used to live for a year on what that cost."

"Oh darling, what's the matter? Do you think all this money is going to my head?"

"Going to a good cause if it is," he said, kissing her. "As long as we've got it we might as well enjoy it. I'm just a little worried about the publicity, though. I don't think it helps our image, whatever that may be. It makes us look typically "big rich," even if we are. There'll be twice as many salesmen and charities after us."

"Oh, I can handle *them*," Anne sniffed. "But if it will make you feel better, I'll tell Carol not to alert the press next time we give a party."

The truth was, everything was coming their way, and Anne was thriving on their new life. She had headed the highly successful Houston Symphony Ball; they had joined every club in town, including the posh new riding club in the suburbs; they were invited to every party, and scarcely a day went by that their names were not mentioned on the society page in connection with some function or other. Eventually, if the truth be told, Ralph was tired and Anne, frenetic.

It did not escape Ralph's notice, however, that he was never mentioned in press stories about the oil industry. He was still not accepted as an oil man. And, as the days passed his sense of foreboding, a feeling that he and Anne were living on borrowed time, intensified. He knew Bill Butler was pursuing Texoil's investigation of how they lost the Gillette field. And he knew Butler well enough to know that he would never give up.

24

"I think the partnership with Ralph is working out very well," Jack commented to Janet over breakfast one day. "He's a good oil lawyer and knows a lot about the business side from his experience with Texoil. He fills in a number of my own gaps. After all, it's been a long time since I worked for a big company. He's been really great at lining up the loans we need. It must be inflation — the amounts are incredible, especially when I think how recently I was turned down for a lousy two million dollars." He shook his head, then shrugged. "Every fraction of a point Ralph can squeeze out of interest rates means savings of hundreds of thousands. That's why his London trip is so important. There should be good rates there from the Euro-dollar market."

"He's a blessing, all right, especially because you have more free time now," said Janet. "You ought to take advantage of it, do some of the things you've always wanted to do."

"Well, at the moment," said Jack, "things do seem to be going well, but frankly, I'm a little worried."

"Nonsense, what could go wrong?"

"I don't know, but Ralph and I are producing lots of oil out of Texoil's old Gillette lease. Things are too quiet. I have a feeling Bill Butler has another shoe he's getting ready to drop."

In August the Harrison family flew to England in the company plane. They were met at Heathrow Airport by a man from Hartwell Brothers, the London representative of Ralph's Houston bank, and the London manager of the oil well supply company who handled his and Jack's business.

Two chauffeured Bentleys spirited them to Claridge's, where they had reserved a suite with three bedrooms. An urbane assistant manager in pinstripe suit and silk shirt saw their eleven pieces of luggage to their rooms and promised to arrange tickets to the theater. The rooms were impressive, each with a different decor. Anne wondered what the hotel's flower bill looked like, such were the vases of blooms in their rooms. Bottles of assorted spirits awaited their choice, surrounded by mounds of fruit. Ralph couldn't help remembering the boarding house in Bloomsbury where he had stayed during his first visit to London years before. Quite a change.

That evening the Harrisons had an early dinner and saw a play at a theater just off Piccadilly. Later they walked about a bit, followed discreetly by their Bentley, among the throngs of young people who had taken over the area. They seemed like a swarm of insects fluttering around a bright light, without order or discipline or purpose. Occasionally one would lie down on the sidewalk until some passerby moved him, or her, to one side. Ralph was repelled, Anne half-amused, half-distressed, the children fascinated and a little scared.

The next day Anne took the children shopping at Liberty's while Ralph called on Hartwell Brothers in the City where young men in bowler hats, runners and clerks from the financial houses, scurried along the narrow street.

The Hartwell partners, Sir Ian and Harrold, made every effort to impress him. Sanderson and Harrison were seeking a line of credit for a hundred million dollars to drill their proven locations in the Gillette field, a sizable loan even for London. Ralph had with him the appraisal report by a geological consulting firm in Dallas, the best in the business. Hartwell Brothers had a report by a London firm. They were not far apart on reserves. The questions were the length of the loan, the terms of repayment, and the interest rate.

Business was not entered into precipitately at Hartwell Brothers. Instead, the partners took Ralph on a brief tour of the premises, showing off the firm's library, the original counting room, and paintings of Hartwell partners going back more than two hundred years. They made little progress before lunch, which was served in a Jacobean paneled dining room. There were dry martinis before and an excellent claret with the roast beef and Yorkshire pudding, all of which duly impressed Ralph. Only after brandy, as they withdrew for coffee and cigars to a smaller room, did the senior partner get down to the business at hand.

Jack and Ralph had already received a loan proposal from Citibank in New York, which had agreed to put together a consortium of banks for their loan. The Citibank geologist had not, however, given them their ultimate full proved reserve, preferring to earmark funds but to commit only by advances well by well as additional geological data became available. Jack and Ralph had no particular problem with that. They were confident that the new wells would substantiate their interpretation as to the size of the field.

It did, however, create an uncertainty. Hartwell Brothers did not hesitate to commit the full amount, subject only to review if the drilling encountered highly unexpected geological conditions. They were very flexible, too, on length of payback, leaving Jack and Ralph enough free income after meeting their debt service to live on and finance a sizable exploration program for new fields. The real issue, the lifeblood of the private banker, was the rate of interest.

Ian Hartwell explained that the Euro-dollar market was in a state of flux. The OPEC countries had become alarmed at the amounts they had put into the market, and had put on the brakes. Ralph found it hard to believe that the situation had changed drastically from that given over the phone to him two days before from New York; however, he had not had time that morning to read the *Financial Times,* or the financial section of the *London Times.*

"We'll both watch the situation closely," Ian Hartwell stated, "and we can discuss it further when you and the family come to us for the weekend at Southhaven. Daphne and I have been looking forward very much to having you and your wife and children. In the meantime our lawyers can go over the title work you have brought. This is not to say, of course, that we expect to find any deficiencies. The law was, I believe, your original field?"

On Friday they drove to Southhaven, arriving promptly at 6:00 P.M. "Welcome to Kent," said Sir Ian. "We're so pleased to have you in our home. Now you must have a quick cup of tea before going to your rooms. We'll meet for drinks at 7:00, with the Bensons, who've also joined us for the weekend. Sir Geoffrey has just retired from the diplomatic service. You'll find him and Lady Astrid a delightful pair. Don't bother to change. Come this way, children."

After dinner the three couples sat over brandies in a small cozy drawing room.

"You have a fine way of life here," said Ralph. "I'm sure the country weekend will go down in history as England's greatest contribution to civilization. We haven't quite caught up with you yet in America. In Texas, most weekends in the country center around hunting at ranches. It's all very pleasant in a different way. We've spent some great weekends on ranches near San Antonio hunting wild turkey and deer, really strenuous affairs — up at dawn, late evenings, and drinking. My partner and his wife have a lovely ranch in Central Texas where things are more relaxed — no hunting, very leisurely. I gather English weekends are more like that.

"Indeed, yes!" said Sir Ian. "And they're not special occasions, but a regular part of our lives. Daphne and I haven't missed a weekend here in years, except when we were abroad, or visiting friends. I don't believe I could face the week in the city without a weekend to unwind."

The conversation shifted to the world scene, and Sir Geoffrey who had served as British Ambassador to Saudi Arabia and was now an advisor to Hartwell Brothers on Middle East oil, gave his views on the situation in the Middle East and the prospects for future oil production there. "Barring a new Arab-Israeli crisis, I believe Saudi Arabia will continue to sell us oil at something like present levels," he began. "High though the Saudis' income is for their small population, they seem to have committed themselves to spending more than they make. Saudi reserves are great, as you know — almost two hundred billion barrels — and these can be increased by additional drilling. Within a few decades, when the oil from Iran and Iraq and Nigeria is largely depleted, the world will be getting almost all of its imported oil from the Saudis. Other countries will have to keep what oil they have for their own needs.

"But you probably know more than I do about all this, coming as you do from Houston. I'm very interested in your city. In Saudi Arabia, Houston is considered their other capital. Most of the procurement, engineering, and financial and managerial services for your Arabian American Oil Company come from Houston. This should assure you a solid base for prosperity for several decades. You're fortunate to live where you do."

On Sunday evening, after a quiet dinner, Sir Ian and Ralph at last discussed business. Again he told Ralph that interest rates were going up and he named a figure. Ralph calculated it to be a half point over what Citibank had offered rather than the point lower he had anticipated, which would have saved a million dollars a year in interest. He excused himself to call Jack in Houston, from whom he got a different story: the New York market was softening. Was the gentlemanly Sir Ian lying? Ralph suggested they delay until they could talk to Citibank again.

Before retiring, Sir Ian mentioned to Ralph that their lawyers were satisfied with the title of the Gillette lease. They had found the Texoil assignment back to Maude Gillette in good order. And then he mentioned something that sent a chill through Ralph. They were delayed in their search because Texoil was making copies of all the parish records on the Gillette lands. This could mean only one thing: Texoil was pressing its investigation of how Jack Sanderson had got the Gillette lease.

The next morning the Harrisons' car returned them to Claridge's. Three of them spent the rest of the day shopping while Ralph worried.

On the following day they made a scheduled trip to Oxford. When they got back to Claridge's Ralph found a cable from Jack saying that a suit against them by Texoil over the Gillette field was imminent and that he felt it best for Ralph to return to Houston to start preparing their defense.

Ralph was almost relieved; what he had long dreaded was now at hand, ready to be dealt with.

"I hate this more than I can tell you," he said somberly to Anne. "I had looked forward so to seeing our favorite places in Europe with you and the children. But there's no reason you can't finish the trip without me. There's really nothing you can do at home."

Anne, though worried and disappointed, was very understanding. She and the children went out to Heathrow to see Ralph off on the Concorde.

"Don't worry, dear," Ralph whispered as he kissed her goodbye. "We'll take care of Bill Butler."

But when Ralph got back to Houston, he found the situation to be much more threatening than he had anticipated.

"Of course, we've always felt a little uneasy — a little guilty, to be frank — over the way we got the Gillette field," said Jack. "We always knew we were vulnerable there. I still don't feel, however, that we have done anything illegal — or even, by oil business standards, anything unethical. And we've done everything possible, in our internal records and accounting procedures, to make it difficult for Texoil to prove anything."

Ralph nodded, wanting to believe that it would come to nothing, but the hammering of his heart told him otherwise.

25

Conflict

Two days later, at 2:30 in the afternoon, as they were busy working in the firm's plush quarters on the fifteenth floor of Pennzoil Place, three burly U.S. Marshals from the Federal District Court paid them a visit.

"We are sorry to disturb you, but I must advise you that on this day, Texoil has filed suit against you in the U.S. District Court for the Eastern Division of Texas for return of the Gillette lease and fields as having been acquired by you illegally. Pursuant to this suit the judge of this court has issued a subpoena duces tecum which requires us to padlock and seal all of your relevant files. Although this would normally have required a hearing of the motion, because of the sweeping allegations made by Texoil, including possible fraud, the court has directed that the files be seized by ex parte action." The chief deputy rattled this off as if he said it every day.

"That is all I am in a position to tell you. We hereby served the subpoena on you and your company. I have a statement for you to sign certifying that we have been given access to all of your various papers on the Gillette field which are necessary for us to carry out our orders. You will also, I believe, be hearing from Texoil directly." The men in dark suits went about their task.

The office, of course, was plunged into a state of turmoil as the designated company files were sealed. The office manager made arrangements to obtain access to papers needed to carry out the company's day-to-day operations, under condition that they not be destroyed or removed.

Ralph and Jack, stunned by the harsh and unexpected development, began an instant analysis of what had happened and what they could do about it. Ralph was outlining a legal counterstrategy when Jack was notified that he had a visitor. "A Mr. Ray Pickering of Texoil is here to see you, sir."

Jack and Ralph exchanged looks of surprise, conferred briefly and called to the secretary to show him in.

"I'm sorry to surprise you this way," Pickering said by way of greeting. He offered his hand, then quickly withdrew it. "I hope you won't take it as anything personal, since we've always been good friends. May I sit down?"

"Now, gentlemen, you must have realized that the Gillette field is such a valuable property that Texoil could not let its loss go by without the most exhaustive inquiry, which has been taking place ever since your discovery there. We're convinced, and we believe we have the evidence to prove it, that Texoil dropped the lease and you took it as a result of a conspiracy between you and certain of our own employees, who planned to benefit through payoffs from your company. The U.S. District Court here has at our request subpoenaed your records on the field."

"That's absurd," said Jack angrily. "Nothing like that took place and you'll never be able to convince anyone it did. What are you after?"

"We demand full recovery of the field and the rights to develop it, leaving open for the moment the question of damages we have incurred. I realize that our subpoena places a burden on you; however, I hope we can resolve this matter as soon as possible. I'm prepared to negotiate with you so we can take over the field with the least possible difficulty for you. We are willing to assume any legitimate financial obligations you have taken in your development of the field to date."

"Very generous of you," said Jack sarcastically.

"Be assured, however," Pickering continued unfazed, "that Texoil will put every resource at its disposal into winning our suit. Our investigation has gone much deeper into the actions of the people involved than you would think possible." He paused to clear his throat, and Ralph got the distinct impression that the performance was all scripted. "I can't negotiate with you today; for one thing, I'm sure you want to talk this over. Ralph, since you were a Texoil employee at the time Texoil gave up the lease, you are, of course, involved both personally and as a partner in your firm. You'll want to give particular thought to our charges, I know." There was no missing the snide note in his voice now.

Jack's response was cool, his voice even. "This is a real sledge-hammer blow you've dealt us, Ray. You've filed suit before giving us a chance to respond to the questions you've raised about our Gillette field. Of course we'll answer all your charges at the proper time. The idea that there was conspiracy within Texoil is patently absurd. You misjudge your own employees. A company like Texoil is too big, and there are too many people involved, to permit them to engage in a conspiracy against the company's interest. You have plenty of evidence as to why the company made the decision to assign the Gillette lands back to the owner.

"Our position is very simple and very clear. I knew, as everyone who reads Lockwood oil reports knew, the moment you dropped your lease on the Gillette land. I knew Maude Gillette, and I've always thought there was a good chance for deep production under her land that your company for some curious reason didn't follow up. I took a new lease from Maude on the same basis as the one you had, shot it, found a deep structure, and drilled it. You're embarrassed by your mistake and you're trying to punish us for doing what you failed to do. But it's the weakness of your bureaucratic organization that led you to such bad decisions."

"Don't underestimate us, Jack," Pickering said testily. "That would be dangerous."

"Come on, Ray, we all know who's behind this. Bill Butler thinks he's a big man, that he runs Houston, possibly the country. But by God, we'll show him. He doesn't. Independents still have some rights around here! You big companies can't push us around. I've been in this business a long time. I've fought for everything I have. You can rest assured we'll fight this suit with everything we've got. Ralph is, as you know very well, an expert in the law involved, and we're going to do everything possible to prove you have no case."

"For starters," said Ralph easily, "we're going to file tomorrow in the District Court here for a restraining order on the action you took today. We'll also file, as you have, for a subpoena of your files connected with the Gillette field. We'll ask for a similar order in a suit to be filed tomorrow against Texoil in Lake Charles. Later we'll raise the question of damages against Texoil, which will include those caused by your interruption of our operations, as well as to our reputation as a result of publicity in this matter."

"Well, lots of luck," said Pickering with a nasty smile.

Jack got to his feet, put his hands on the desk, and leaned across it menacingly. "You must be very pleased that you've done the boss's dirty work so well, you miserable little lackey," he spit out. "But then, you're used to it, aren't you? And well paid? You know something? Whatever he pays you, it isn't worth it. And now you can get your ass out of my office, you little shit. You make me sick!"

Whereupon Jack went to the door and flung it wide for Pickering.

Pickering looked shocked; no one had ever heard Jack talk this way before. He retreated in some confusion, muttering, "You'll regret this. This isn't the way to handle this problem, if you expect to come out with your shirt. Good day, gentlemen — I retract that. Good day."

Jack and Ralph sat for some time without saying anything. Ralph had been amazed by Jack's performance. Although he had known him well for many years, he had never seen him so angry, never heard him use such language. He himself hadn't challenged Pickering as Jack had. It was natural that Jack speak for both of them. Nevertheless, he was ashamed of his reticence. There was no way he could have spoken back to Pickering the way Jack had. He was too aware of the weakness in their position and the possibility that the Texoil charge could be sustained — but then, so was Jack. The truth was that he, Ralph, wasn't strong enough to fight Bill Butler. He just wasn't made that way.

"Well, Bill has finally let us have it," Ralph broke the silence. "I'm glad it's all out on the table. It clears the air. We know now exactly what we face."

"We do that," agreed Jack, "and we have a lot of work to do. You know the legal steps we must take, Ralph, and I propose we get about it. Get in anyone you want to help you. Spare no expense. This thing is big enough to justify an all-out fight to the end."

"We both know our point of vulnerability," said Ralph. "However, I think we can win. In basing their case on a conspiracy among their own employees, Texoil has, of course, a non-starter. We know there was no conspiracy; they just made a stupid mistake. The District Geologist in Lake Charles didn't conspire with his

District Manager, and with Harry Colt in Houston, to drop the lease. I know them too well."

"Well, don't worry about *yourself*," said Jack, clapping Ralph on the back. "You're in the clear. The Texoil records will show that you had no knowledge through company channels that the lease had been dropped. From a geological point of view, you had no way to judge whether the lease was good or bad, and you could not have influenced Texoil's technical decision. Even if they can prove that you receive a considerable income from our firm, your ownership is spread over all of the properties of the company and could easily have resulted from your investment or my compensation to you for services since joining the firm. Texoil may contend that the remuneration to others in the so-called conspiracy is something promised in the future and has not yet become apparent. We know, of course, that this isn't the case, so we should have no fear of their being able to prove it."

"I agree," said Ralph. "I'm not really worried about myself. The only weak link in our case, if they knew it, is Chuck Ames. Apparently they don't know about Chuck, that we are in contact with him or that he had anything to do with our taking the Gillette lease. From their point of view, it would be incredible that a man fired so long ago would be able to discover under their own leases an oil field that their geologists and geophysicists couldn't. Rest assured they've forgotten about Chuck. Since he's not a current employee, it would be difficult to prove he was a part of the alleged conspiracy."

"Well, though we did it to protect him, it's a good thing our payments to him are made indirectly and he pays taxes on those payments," said Jack. "Assuming the worst, even if Texoil discovers Chuck's income is from us, it would not necessarily establish any wrongdoing. Our payments are carried as compensation for consulting services. What do you think?"

Ralph had, of course, been mulling over the situation for a long time. The counter restraining order was his idea, also their filing for a subpoena of the Texoil records. This would show the internal communications and data on which the Texoil decision to abandon their Gillette lease had been based. It should prove there was no conspiracy.

"Yes," said Ralph wearily, "we're lucky they've missed Chuck so far. He's a discreet man. We've had very little contact with him, and I don't believe his role in the matter will ever come to light. The trick with the cutoff ends of the seismic records which led him to discover the deep structure at Gillette is too bizarre to be credible. No one in Texoil would ever think of it. Well, if you'll excuse me, I have a lot of work to do. I'll probably be here all night. And don't you worry. Insofar as the law can protect us, I'll do everything possible to see that it does."

Jack took off his coat and tie and rolled up his sleeves. "I'm not going anywhere either." He had to prepare the necessary instructions to the company employees to prevent any breakdown in operations. He also had to inform their bankers and drilling contractors. He called for two secretaries to stand by so he could start dictating.

He got home at four in the morning, and the headlines were glaring at him when he joined Janet for a quick breakfast at eight.

"Texoil Demands Return of Mammoth Oil Field. Charges Conspiracy of Own Employees." The article mentioned the serving of the subpoena on Sanderson and Harrison, and referred to the fact that Ralph was a former Texoil employee. Although it could not specify the retaliatory steps Sanderson and Harrison would take, the article predicted a bitter battle over the field, reputed to be worth five hundred million dollars.

Jack read the paper carefully and explained the whole affair as well as he could. Despite her efforts to take it all in stride, Janet was alarmed. Neither of them had ever been involved in such a public controversy before. Everyone would know that Jack was being charged with stealing the Gillette field from Texoil; the tongues of Houston would wag that night.

"Don't you worry," said Janet. "I know they won't be able to prove you did anything wrong. You'll come out of this stronger than ever." She smiled and took his hand.

"You bet," he said, but his words suddenly lacked conviction. Texoil was Bill Butler, and Bill Butler had been waiting for something like this for a long time.

"In a way it's a relief," said Ralph to Anne that evening. "I've been feeling uneasy for months. At least now we know what we're dealing with."

Anne hugged herself. "I wish I had your confidence. Right now I don't know whether I'm cold with fear or whether the thermostat's broken."

"There's really nothing to be afraid of," he said hastily. "We'll win in the end, I'm sure of it. When all the evidence is in, and we have their papers just as they now have ours, there will be no proof of a conspiracy."

"Even so, a lot of people are going to think there was some hanky-panky involved."

"Does that matter so much, what those people think?"

"No," she said thoughtfully. "As a matter of fact, the ones who spring to mind would admire you for it — Brad, for one, and Bill, when you come right down to it."

Ever prudent, he proposed that they take stock of their situation in view of the possible financial consequences of the Texoil charge. "About the new house," he started.

Anne winced. The reference to the house touched a sensitive spot. The planning itself had become for Anne such an important part of her life that it was difficult for her to consider the matter objectively. The house was inextricably linked to Anne's whole future in Houston.

"I'll ask the architect to tell us where we stand," she said calmly. "But nothing must happen to the house. We've put too much of ourselves into it. It means too much to us."

Then she sighed. "I wonder where Bill stands in this matter now. He told me once that he would call the suit off if I'd agree to marry him, can you believe it? There was no way in the world he would ever do that once his attorneys told him he had a case. He would never let anything personal stand between him and a half-billion-dollar oil field. No way. Bill has to do this to prove nobody gets the better of him or Texoil. Before he could give up an oil field for sentimental reasons, he would have stepped down and let somebody else run the company."

"I think you're right," said Ralph gravely. "In any case I would never, under any circumstances, have asked you to appeal to him. Jack and I can take care of ourselves."

During the next week Pickering twice sent an emissary to Jack with an offer. The second improved on the first, but went no further than allowing Sanderson and Harrison to retain a small override on production after payout. This would yield them an ultimate return of only two to three percent of the profits they expected to receive. "You want to take our field away from us and toss us a tip," Jack told the Texoil man tersely. "Tell Pickering to quit wasting our time and his. We'll see you in court in two weeks when arguments on our motions begin."

Indeed, Jack had long ago concluded that he could not compromise. He was fighting not just for the large financial stake involved, but for his reputation. Of course, he was risking his whole future. If Texoil proved its charge, Jack was finished. The Houston papers had hinted as much in the many articles already written about the case. "Local Independent Charged in Oil Conspiracy." "Did Sanderson Steal Mammoth Field from Butler?"

Considering every aspect of the situation, Jack was confident that he had done nothing immoral or even unethical. Texoil had itself thrown away the field. Jack also saw a possible opportunity. The press had played up the unequal struggle between the giant Texoil and the smaller Independent firm. If Jack could beat Texoil it would be David defeating Goliath. He could see in his mind's eye a cartoon showing Jack, with his sling, hitting Bill Butler with his rock. What satisfaction that would give him, and it wouldn't hurt his reputation in Houston at all.

After weeks of discovery and argument on the multitude of motions filed by both sides, the case was set down for trial without a jury before Judge Jonathan Browne of the U.S. District Court in Houston on April 3, 1978. It was a little over a year after the first deep Gillette well had come in. The courtroom was jammed and the air was electric with tension.

Jack and Ralph had agreed to waive their rights to a jury because of the relevance to the case of geological and geophysical data of a highly technical nature not easily understood by an ordinary juror.

Although Ralph managed his and Jack's case, the court work was done by outside trial lawyers. The Texoil employees involved had been subjected to exhaustive discovery and required to make statements of personal income and expenses: how much they spent on their homes, on travel, and what debts they had.

Harry Colt was, of course, a prime target. Bill Butler considered Harry, as head of the Exploration and Production Department, the principal culprit for having dropped the Gillette lease.

Indeed, in a sense he was, although he had made a reasonable decision in view of the information he had available. Bill also knew that Harry was a close friend of Ralph.

The Texoil attorney asked Harry a few perfunctory questions to establish his position in making the decision that lost the company the field.

"Is it true that you are a close friend of Ralph Harrison?"

"Yes, I am," Harry replied. "He reported directly to me on most matters as Assistant General Counsel, responsible for all legal work for my Department."

"But you and your wife are also quite close to Mr. and Mrs. Harrison socially, is it not true?"

"Yes, it is," said Harry. "We are good friends. And I have had a very satisfactory working relationship with Ralph. He's a fine man."

"But it went further than a normal business relationship, did it not? You saw each other on many social occasions. Did you and your wife not have dinner with the Harrisons on May 6, not long before he quit Texoil?" the attorney asked.

"Yes, we did. Nothing unusual about that," replied Harry.

"Did you have any occasion that evening to discuss the Gillette lease?"

"Not at all. There were several other couples there. The conversation was general."

"Tell me the extent to which you and Harrison discussed the Gillette lease in your office."

"In fact we didn't," said Harry. "The decision to drop the lease was a production, not a legal, matter. The drafting of the papers reassigning the lease to Maude Gillette was a routine matter done in Lake Charles."

The Texoil attorney paused for effect and resumed in a harsh, accusatory tone, "I want you to tell this court why you decided to drop the lease, Mr. Colt. You are an experienced production man. How could you have made such a grave mistake, a mistake that cost your company a major oil field?"

"I admit a mistake was made. I acted on the recommendation of our head production man in Lake Charles. Our last producing well in the Gillette field had reached its economic limit. We had drilled a deep, expensive, dry hole there. The evidence I was shown revealed no place else to drill," Harry replied.

The Texoil attorney was silent, with his back to Harry, fumbling with some papers. Suddenly he faced Harry and thundered, "How is it, Mr. Colt, that the total of your personal expenditures last year as shown by your checking accounts, exceeded your salary, minus taxes, by a hundred thousand dollars? You make $250,000 a year from Texoil. It would seem to me you and your wife could live in your lifestyle on that. But you spent much more. You must have been encouraged to spend by a windfall income — say from the Gillette field. Where did you get that extra hundred thousand dollars?"

As Harry paled and hesitated, his lawyer was on his feet, objecting. "This is a very personal matter, Your Honor. My client should not be forced to answer that question. It is both irrelevant and prejudicial to him."

"Objection overruled," said Judge Browne firmly. "The witness must answer the question."

After consulting his attorney, Harry continued reluctantly. "I resent very much having to reveal that I had to borrow the money in question. I did not volunteer this information to your investigators because they didn't ask me and because Texoil is very hard on employees who borrow. They don't have much confidence in us. They say going into debt makes us more vulnerable to being bribed. The extra money you refer to was spent for hospital bills for one of our children, who has been crippled since birth. It's not something we like to discuss publicly. Do you want me to show you my checks to doctors and hospitals?" Harry asked testily.

"Question withdrawn," said the Texoil lawyer. But the hurt to Harry and to his wife, who was crying, remained. A wave of sympathy rippled through the audience.

Ralph, who had been subpoenaed, testified for two hours on the following day. Anne was there, sitting in the front row. Well but conservatively dressed, she held her head high. The Texoil attorneys concentrated on proving that Ralph had conspired with his former boss, Harry Colt, and others in Texoil, to get control of the Gillette lease. Why, otherwise, had he been rewarded by a partnership with Sanderson Production Company? Why, otherwise, had he come into such a large income? Ralph had been forced to admit how much rent he paid for his house and his and Anne's living expenses. For people who valued their privacy, this was extremely embarrassing.

"You are, are you not, a close friend of the Colts?" the Texoil attorney asked.

Ralph's reply was straightforward. "My wife and I are good friends of the Colts," he said. "Harry Colt is the best production man I know and a loyal Texoil employee. It's a shame Texoil doesn't appreciate him."

The lawyer winced. "As a close friend you saw him often socially, as well as in the office, did you not? You had ample opportunity to arrange for the Gillette lease to be dropped so Sanderson could take it. Your large income makes it clear that you are now receiving your payoff, as could be the others who were involved."

Ralph's defense lawyer leaped to his feet and objected to this question, which was sustained, but Texoil was allowed to file records showing the many conferences and telephone discussions Ralph had had with Colt during the period involved, and the dates of the evenings the two couples had been together, including the dinner at River Oaks.

"All of this information is completely irrelevant," said Ralph when he was allowed to make a statement. "You can't produce any evidence from intracompany files that I even knew in advance that the Gillette lease was to be dropped, since I didn't. I never discussed the matter with Harry Colt, or any other Texoil employee. I never saw a piece of paper dealing with this matter. The legal work was all done in Lake Charles."

"How can you explain your resigning from your position at Texoil at about the same time the lease was dropped, and how do you explain the fact that you entered into a lucrative partnership in Sanderson Production Company at that same time?"

"I had every right to quit Texoil and go into partnership with Jack Sanderson. I was at a dead end at Texoil. Promotions in the Legal Department had been discussed with me, but I had no opportunity to progress to executive positions in the Production Department. Plenty of other company men have gone out for themselves. It's not unusual, either, that they acquire an interest in the company they join and make more money than they had earned before."

The Texoil lawyer was unable to shake Ralph's statement. Ralph had been very convincing, showing himself to be strong and confident, someone to be reckoned with in the trial.

By this time considerable public interest had been aroused.

Sympathy in Houston up to this point seemed to run in favor of Jack and Ralph, as the underdogs, over Butler. Everyone knew the devastating consequences a decision in favor of Texoil would have on the future of the two men. Prosecution for the State would be pressured to bring criminal charges against Jack and Ralph. Oil men compete hard, but they don't like to get indicted. The whole system under which men found oil fields was at stake, the integrity of the oil industry, the very life blood of Houston. You might press your luck in your business dealings, but you didn't step over the line. More important, if you did, you didn't get caught.

On the following day, Bill Butler took the stand. In response to a question by his attorney, and over the objections by the attorneys for Jack and Ralph, Butler stated that his suspicions had been aroused when a major oil field had been found on land which had only recently been released by Texoil. Texoil had the best Exploration and Production Department in the industry. They had explored and operated oil fields on the Gillette tract for many years. It was incredible to him that the company officials involved would give up such an important oil reserve, unless the facts in the case had been deliberately misrepresented by someone who had sold out to Sanderson.

Butler said he was familiar with the evidence that had been presented in support of Texoil's case and considered it conclusive; however, it was quite easy for the steal to have been made without leaving any trace. All that was needed was a verbal assurance by Sanderson that a given reward would be made at some future date in some agreed way. The opportunities for such a payoff in the oil business were unlimited.

"By God, my people don't give away oil fields. Their whole lives have been spent finding oil for Texoil. There is no way they would release the Gillette lands unless there was a Judas in there concealing or falsifying information, somebody who rigged test results and drew crooked maps. I'll stake my whole reputation as an oilman on it."

Butler's attorney asked Bill when he had first met Jack Sanderson. Would he review their relationship over the years? Was there anything that would arouse the suspicion that Jack would be capable of bribery to take over some other company's oil field?

"I'm a company man," replied Butler. "Sanderson is an Independent. He left his company at an early age. To me the company is the key to the successful operation of the oil industry, indeed of industry generally in this country. By attracting public investment the company raises the immense sums required. The company is in the business for the long haul. It is not hit-and-run. It is accountable for its actions. It is the companies who basically produce and refine and market the oil that fuels our economy. Independents play a small role. They find the small fields the companies don't want. Occasionally they luck into a good field, usually with the experience they got from the majors, more often with information they stole from the companies."

Jack's attorney was on his feet shouting, "Objection, objection! The witness can't throw these words, bribery and stealing, around without any proof. This is very serious business!"

"Sustained," said Judge Browne. "Mr. Butler, please be aware that you are verging on a criminal accusation here."

"I'm speaking of Independents in general," said Butler, unruffled. "Sanderson is like the rest of the Independents. They're all a bunch of jackals preying on the majors. I've had considerable experience with Jack Sanderson. Texoil took a prospect from him in the forties just after he left Coastal and started out for himself. It was a good one. We found a good field and he made a killing. Where did he get the information that led him to his prospect? Where else but Coastal? The circumstances speak for themselves."

"Objection!" protested Jack's attorney.

"Sustained," said the judge. "I don't intend to caution you again, Mr. Butler."

"What I'm saying, Your Honor, is that Independents like Sanderson are in our offices every day, hobnobbing with our geologists and land men. They have all the opportunity in the world to lay their hands on our own dope. Unless the law can stop this hemorrhaging of information from the companies, and its use to take our fields away from us, we won't be able to stay in the business. Our investors won't put up the money that's needed. I say, set an example. Give us back our oil field."

"These statements are without basis; they are opinions and conjecture and will not be considered as evidence. You may step down, Mr. Butler. Court is adjourned for lunch."

After lunch it was Jack Sanderson's turn to testify. He was first questioned by his lawyer.

"Mr. Sanderson, will you tell the court the background of your relations with the Texoil Company and with Mr. Bill Butler in particular?"

Jack replied, "Judge Browne, as he has told you, I've known Bill Butler a long time. When I was making my start as an Independent he was District Geologist in South Louisiana for Texoil. Our backgrounds were, of course, quite different. I had only the small nest egg I had saved working as a geologist. His position in Texoil could just possibly have been related to the fact that his father was chairman of the company. The prospect he referred to was a good one. It helped Texoil build up its Gulf Coast reserves and made me a fortune.

"The prospect was not one that Coastal was interested in. If they had been, they could have taken it. Under my terminal contract with Coastal I had to wait six months before buying leases in any area I had been involved in for them. The Bayou Bleu prospect was altogether my own idea. If Coastal has never raised an issue about it, why should Texoil? I've had some tough dealings with Bill Butler, but I deny very strongly doing anything unethical, either in connection with Bayou Bleu, or in the Gillette field. I did not bribe. I did not steal."

"Can you explain how you as an Independent with limited resources could find fields the large companies didn't?" asked Judge Browne.

"Independents can beat the majors at their own game because we work harder. We have the powerful incentive of owning what we find," replied Jack. "The company geologist spends most of his time coping with the big bureaucracy which hogties him. He worries about his place in the pecking order, the decorations of his office, his pension, his time off, his expense account. He will avoid or fudge decisions so he can't be pinned to a mistake that would endanger his career.

"I get my information about prospects from many sources, wherever I can. I get ideas from talking with other geologists, in the office and on the golf course or in a hunting blind. I get it by spotting from the air a suspicious bend in a Louisiana bayou that might be the result of structural uplift. I get it by reading all the published geological reports and oil journals and studying Schlumberger logs for hours at a time looking for evidence of faults and pinchouts and reverse dips that could provide a lead."

"Now can you tell us which of these techniques led to your discovery on the Gillette lands?'' said Browne.

"My taking the Gillette lands was based on the cumulative experience of a lifetime of study in the lower Gulf Coast area, from talks with those who worked there in the early days, from old maps and records, from the latest articles about the growth of structures and their relationship to the sedimentary environment that leads to the accumulation of oil. I *live* oil finding. I don't just do it from nine to five. It is for me a way of life. And I'm willing to bet my last dollar and go broke for it.

"Bill Butler talks about protecting our free enterprise system. This is only his attempt to justify taking away the field I found and giving it to Texoil. I don't consider Butler or his geologists a part of the system. They don't risk a dime of their own money, only the company's. The essence of free enterprise is risk-taking. The men who take the risks are the Independents. I found the Gillette lease open. I shot it. I drilled the well that found the deep pay that Texoil failed to find. And, by God, no one, not even Bill Butler, is going to take it away from me without a helluva fight!''

A murmur ran through the crowd as Bill Butler stiffened and reddened.

"Please confine your remarks to answering my questions, Mr. Sanderson," directed the judge.

But Bill Butler was on his feet. "Are you so sure you found the deep Gillette field with your own information?" he shouted. "Or was it mine?" He waved away his lawyer who was trying to restrain him. "Produce your seismic maps and prove it! I am aware that seismic surveys by agreement have been privileged and that we have not shown ours, but I challenge you to show yours."

"Please sit down, Mr. Butler! Remember you are in a court of law," ordered Judge Browne.

Jack reached into his briefcase and brought out the seismic report on which he had drilled his well. Jack knew, of course, that Texoil had no map. They had cut off their deep records. He also knew that his seismic survey had been pretty meager, more a confirmation of structure than a discovery, but that he wouldn't have to show his bluff. "I'll show it to you," Jack said, "if you'll show me Texoil's deep map, with the information you said I stole."

A hush stole over the small group of Texoil lawyers and engineers, but they made no move to get a map. No one had dared tell Bill Butler that they had none. They whispered among themselves and to Butler, who scowled with obvious disgust. "Apparently we don't have one," he acknowledged painfully to Judge Browne.

"Well, that seems a little strange to me," said the judge. "I thought the majors had all the information and the Independents stole it from them and took their fields. Very strange. Well, Mr. Butler, Mr. Sanderson. This has been a very enlightening exchange. We will proceed with no more interruptions from the audience."

26

The next day the Houston papers outdid themselves in ridiculing Bill Butler. "Major Accuses Independent of Stealing Their Seismic Maps — Finds Out Texoil Had None." "Bill Butler Finds His Geologists Outmaneuvered by Independent Sanderson."

Back in the Texoil executive suites blood flowed. Harry Colt was spared as Chief of Production; however, the head of the Explortion Department, who should have had a deep seismic map of the Gillette lands, was summarily demoted and ordered to the Denver Exploration office. Butler, who had been humiliated before the entire oil industry, doubled the number of private detectives assigned to tracing possible leaks. No one who had ever had access to geological and geophysical information on the Gillette lease was missed. He had to find out why there was no deep map.

And so it was they came to Chuck. The private detective who located him was skilled in his trade. He knew enough about Ames to know that he had been in charge of the seismic work that had led to the shallow Gillette field. He knew that Ames had been a friend of Ralph Harrison's, and the circumstances under which Ames had been fired. He knew that Texoil should have had a deep seismic map and didn't. In his view, a man who could buy royalty under a company play could very easily steal a map. The detective assumed that Chuck would have a guilty feeling which would make him insecure and easily frightened. He also knew how to take advantage of all that. Mostly he bluffed his way, but without much success, for Chuck Ames gave no ground.

Ralph had arranged with Chuck to trigger a meeting in case of just such an emergency. And now the call came, from a pay phone, Ralph knew, per their plan. Late that night found him walking in Herman Park with Chuck, both fairly certain they'd not been followed.

"I think you did just right," said Ralph when he had heard Chuck's story. "This Fletcher was obviously bluffing. The only thing that really bothers me is your supervisor, Jerry King. Do you have any idea what happened to him?"

"The last I heard he was in Venezuela. He left soon after I did. I have the feeling he didn't like what happened any more than I did. He was pretty hot-headed, didn't like to take orders."

"Even if he should turn up, there's nothing much they can prove, but it could be an embarrassment. In any case, the next move is up to them. Either Fletcher will try to talk to you again or he will have you subpoenaed. We'll have to wait then, to see what evidence they come up with. The fact that they have no deep map doesn't mean you stole it."

"And if King should turn up?"

"Even assuming the worst — that he would be on their side — the fact is that he told you to get rid of the deep map. If you make a clean breast of it, there's still nothing illegal about what you did. Unethical, according to their standards, but not stealing. And there's another angle that occurred to me that might help our case. It has to do with the royalty setup. Try not to worry too much, I think we're going to come out of this just fine."

Ralph, however, was not so sanguine when he and Jack explored the possibilities of this latest bombshell the next day. "I hope Fletcher is bluffing," he said nervously. "If he weren't, why would he go to Chuck in the first place? Why not just subpoena him?"

"True enough, but if they're onto Chuck it won't be long before they're onto King. I think we'd better check into his whereabouts. I'll call Doug Blount and get him to run a blind ad in the *Petroleum Journal*. Every oil man from Oklahoma to Kuwait reads the Journal."

"What's to prevent Texoil from doing the same thing?"

"Nothing. Let's just hope he's gone into chicken farming."

"Or has a bad memory."

"Or both."

Ralph and Jack knew full well what a gamble they were taking. King might attempt to protect himself, or as a result of either threat or inducement by Texoil, support the company's position. Ralph knew King was hardheaded; he was, however, gambling that he was honest.

In the meantime, Texoil geophysicists had to search the vast Texoil seismic warehouse with its millions of seismic records for three days to find the pine box full of records labeled "Gillette Prospect." It didn't take them long to find that the deep reflections were missing, cut off.

New allegations, which Texoil leaked to all of the Houston papers, instantly became headlines. "Texoil's Seismic Data For The Deep Gillette Field Stolen." "Texoil Employee Cut Texoil Records And Gave Deep Results to Sanderson And Harrison." "Independents Accused of Theft."

The papers reported that, according to Texoil sources, Chuck's role explained why the company had no deep map at Gillette, and how he had been able to make a deep map of his own from the deep reflections denied Texoil. Since Ralph Harrison was a fellow Texoil employee and good friend of Ames at the time, this also explained how Ralph was able to obtain the map which led him and Sanderson to take the Gillette lease.

When the court process server came to Chuck's house with the subpoena, he told Ralph, he refused to accept the Texoil check for his testimonial time. He threw it on the porch floor as Bess peered through the shades.

"I'm afraid this is a new ball game," Jack said to Ralph the next morning. His frown lines seemed to have deepened overnight. "We're up against the wall. Theft of geophysical data and its misuse strikes at the heart of the oil business. It's done all the time because it can seldom be proven. But when it's pinned on someone cold, there has to be a general reaction of moral indignation. Every oilman in Houston has been guilty of making use of other people's dope at one time or another, but they won't admit it and they don't want to condone it in others for fear it will result in their own data being stolen."

"I realize that," said Ralph, "and I don't believe we can get Chuck through the grilling he will be put to by Texoil without his admitting what he did. It will be hard with King missing to prove he acted under orders. Chuck's not really capable of lying, even if he wanted to. Pickering and his people will tie him in knots; he

232

won't know what's happened to him. If he is forced later to recant his testimony, his guilt will be self-evident. After all, we didn't think he did anything illegal, even very unethical. Otherwise we wouldn't have dealt with him. It was the appearances that worried us, and the despicable double standard between the top and the bottom that pervades the oil business.

"I believe Chuck must come absolutely clean, tell everything, including the fact that he gave us a deep map of Gillette. It's not the only course he is capable of taking, but it happens to be the right course. His lawyer can show that it all stemmed from a wrong decision by his Texoil supervisor, which led inevitably to everything that happened later. What will seal his case was the great injustice done to Chuck, which resulted in the ruin of his professional career and later life because of a little thing like that small royalty purchase. I want this brought out in the starkest possible way, showing the great injustice done to the little people in this business who can't fight back, while the big tough boys like Bill Butler get away with murder.

"Do you remember the Texoil Royalty Pool? I was offered a membership in it. You remember that because of it Texoil needlessly drilled a dry hole at West Bayou Bleu. The Pool is cheating in tens of millions. Would Bill Butler like to have us spill it all to the public, to his stockholders? If we get in trouble with Chuck's testimony, I would like to take this matter up quietly over a drink with my former boss Pickering. I believe we might have an ace in the hole."

"You've got something there," said Jack, a smile creasing his face. "Bill is the biggest participant in the Pool. I don't think he would like to have that story told."

When Chuck finally appeared in the courtroom it was filled to capacity. He had been built up in the press as Texoil's secret weapon, the mole who had been brought out of hiding so Texoil could show how the Gillette field had been stolen.

The Texoil attorney led Chuck through a long series of questions concerning his education and early career with Texoil. He was admitted to be one of the outstanding "record men" of the seismograph business. This had led him to the middle level position of Chief of Party with control over the operations of the party and the final interpretation of its results. But Chuck was not, as a true professional should be, content with the very good remuneration he received. He had wanted more. Even before he shot Gillette, although he knew it was against company regulations, he had secretly bought royalty which the data Texoil had paid for showed was favorable for oil.

This dishonest greedy streak, the Texoil lawyer continued, also evidenced itself by his cutting from the seismic records reflections from the deep structures Chuck, with the experience Texoil had provided him, knew to be there. He had stolen from Texoil the key to the discovery of a great oil field. When Texoil had depleted the shallow field, all that was left for them to drill after Ames stole their data, they had dropped their Gillette lease. Ames then connived with his friend Ralph Harrison to obtain these leases. Harrison and Sanderson had then found the field on the basis of Texoil's own data. Obviously Ames had been cut in. The very integrity of the oil business was at stake. The Gillette field must be returned to Texoil. Thieving could not be rewarded in the oil industry — the very heart of Houston economy.

When Ames was asked to reply he told his story exactly as it happened, and he told it well. He had, he said, as a scientist, been disappointed at not being allowed to do more seismic work to bring out the deep reflections he thought he saw there, which would reveal the deep structure. He was more offended when, in spite of his protests, he was directed by his supervisor to cut from the records even the poor deep reflections that had been obtained. He had merely picked up and saved the discarded records because he considered them valuable scientific information. He testified that it was only by chance that he was later able to interpret them, too late to take them to Texoil because of the fear that they would accuse him of stealing them. Also, he deeply resented the great injustice he thought the company had done him in firing him. In any event, he had doubted that they would believe his interpretation any more than they had originally. Later, and only after Texoil had abandoned the Gillette lease, he had told Ralph about his ideas as any professional man would. He felt he had done nothing wrong.

The opposing attorneys went back and forth over his testimony, sometimes in Chuck's favor as a scientist, sometimes against him. Texoil tried to show that he had a professional, if not a legal obligation, to take his findings of a deep structure at Gillette to Texoil, for whom he had worked in producing the seismic data. The reaction of the courtroom seemed to be on balance, sometimes favoring Chuck, sometimes Texoil. The questions of the judge showed his concern at the precedent that might be set in condoning the misapplication of seismic data.

Ralph was called to testify first. He had been the link with Ames. If he and Jack were guilty of having stolen data from Texoil, he was the one most immediately involved.

"My original instinct, when Ames first told me about the deep maps, was based on a desire to help him," said Ralph. "I believed he had been badly treated by Texoil. Originally Ames had no deep map on Gillette, and Texoil refused to accept his recommendation for further shooting for the deep structure. I did not, therefore, feel that I was injuring Texoil in helping Ames. I'm not a geologist. If, with all of the masses of data Texoil had on the Gillette lands, they decided to withdraw, how could Ames and I persuade them otherwise? I thought that Ames should have his chance."

In his testimony Jack admitted that Ralph had conveyed to him Ames' tip about Gillette. "Tips in Houston, though, are a dime a dozen," he said. "I get them every day. I knew more about the Gillette lands than I got from Ralph Harrison from my own studies and from talking with other geologists and geophysicists who, like Ames, had worked there. Neither Harrison nor Ames had ever shown me any hard data, which was why I insisted on shooting the lease myself before agreeing to drill a well. I have offered to show the map I drilled on. Texoil, as one of the largest oil companies in the world, has access to every type of information. If Texoil had abandoned the Gillette lands," Jack said, "it made me look foolish to drill there. Maybe I was lucky."

That night Jack and Ralph talked back and forth, trying to assess where they stood. There was no question that the introduction of Ames into the trial had been a setback, one that they had tried hard to overcome but with mixed results. Should they play their last card? Maybe it was their big chance to gain the sympathy of the audience — and the judge. The Pool was not directly involved in the issue of the trial, but raising the issue could only be related to the fairness of Texoil's general approach to the whole trial.

The general attitude of the Houston press, and knowledgeable Houstonians, which had wavered during the trial, now seemed to favor Texoil. Although Ralph and Jack had not lied, they had obviously been caught trying to cover up their relationship with

Chuck. Since they had so far assumed the role of injured innocence, the naive little Independent against a ruthless major, Chuck's testimony made them look like hypocrites, if not liars. Most people seemed to believe that it was a simple case of Chuck's having stolen Texoil's data and sold it to Ralph and Jack. Chuck had no proof he was ordered to cut off the end of the records and discard them.

The trial was nearing an end when the lawyer for the partnership addressed the judge. "I would like to reintroduce a previous witness, Your Honor. Before I do that, I would like to make a statement for the defense." The judge assented. Bill Butler, who had attended few of the sessions of the trial after giving his own testimony, happened to be there.

"Texoil," the lawyer said in opening, "is seeking to take the deep Gillette field away from Sanderson and Harrison, who discovered it. In doing so Texoil relies entirely on their accusation, which we do not believe they have proved, that it resulted from a conspiracy on the part of their employees to give their company information which enabled them to discover the field. In making such an accusation they have done a great injustice to their employees, since none have been shown to have been guilty of anything more than bad judgment. They have now included Charles Ames, a former employee, in their accusation.

"I admit that my clients discussed the oil-producing possibilities of the Gillette lands with Ames, a fact that they were not questioned about and chose not to volunteer. The record will show that they did not lie. Ames had not, of course, been a Texoil employee for ten years, ten years during which he had to live with his career shattered by a small indiscretion of buying royalty, which harmed the company not at all. This has paid him and his wife over ten years a pittance, twelve thousand dollars, which has helped them eke out a living. Texoil during this period has denied Ames the pension he was legally entitled to, by threatening to sue him for having bought a little royalty. I would like to recall Mr. Harrison, to put this matter in perspective." A hush fell over the audience instantly.

Ralph rose, looked squarely at Bill Butler, and began speaking slowly. "Texoil fired Chuck Ames, took away his pension, and ruined his career for buying a piddling little oil royalty. At the same time Bill Butler and his top executives were and have since been engaging in the secret purchasing of royalty on a very large scale, unknown to the Texoil Board and their stockholders, which is not only unethical but a conflict of interest inimical to the interests of the stockholders of the company. I know because I myself was sounded out on the opportunity to share in the Pool and refused."

But the last of Ralph's words were not heard because Texoil's head lawyer had jumped to his feet and shouted excitedly, "Objection, objection! I demand this extraneous charge be withdrawn and what has been said be stricken from the record. It has nothing to do with this case." There was pandemonium in the courtroom, which Judge Browne did his best to quell.

There ensued a long pause while the Texoil lawyers conferred, then sent one of the members for a bench conference with the judge. After considerable deliberation, although it was an unusual request, the judge asked the principals in the trial to join him in his chambers. When the group had reassembled in privacy, the judge asked Ralph to proceed in describing the new charge he had made.

"I know of the activity I spoke of because I was sounded out by Texoil on an advancement which included participation in it — and turned it down." Ralph turned to Bill Butler and pointed an accusing finger. "I speak of the Texoil Executive Royalty Pool, of which Bill Butler has the largest interest. This pool includes producing royalties, bought surreptitiously in and around Texoil, plays on Texoil information which, I learned while in Texoil, now has a value of $50,000,000.

"And this pool is no innocent endeavor, else why should its existence be such a carefully guarded secret? If purchasing royalty is so profitable, why wasn't it done in behalf of the company, who paid for the data its purchases were based on? The purchase of royalty at the time leases are taken helps drive the prices of leases up. The ownership of royalty by the top executives of a company distorts decisions to lease and drill.

"I am familiar with an example which occurred during Texoil's discovery of the Bayou Bleu field. Texoil drilled as its first location one that would drain the pool royalty but which was to any geologist a bad location. That cost Texoil $100,000. Would some Texoil stockholder who knew that not be likely to sue the company for that loss? Maybe they would like to sue Bill Butler. The real issue of this trial, Your Honor, is whether justice in the oil business is on a double standard — one for the small man and another for the big bosses. I demand of this court that that issue be faced."

The Texoil lawyers, at this juncture, bitterly assailed Ralph and his accusation. All of this, they contended, was utterly false and irrelevant. If Ralph wanted to pursue this accusation it would mean another trial since it was entirely unrelated to the one underway.

The judge was silent for a long time. Finally, he said, "I rule that this new accusation against Texoil by Mr. Harrison is not relevant to this trial and cannot be introduced. There is, however, every possibility, in light of what Mr. Harrison has said, that he or others influenced by him will raise this issue as a separate case, since it appears to involve serious questions concerning Texoil stockholder rights." Bill Butler had been silent, but he was now seen whispering furiously with Pickering. "The hearing will be resumed," said the judge.

Pickering jumped up and cornered Ralph before he could reach the door. "I can offer you a deal," he muttered. "If you will lay off the Pool, both in this trial and later, we won't challenge the Ames testimony. We won't cross-examine either him or you, even though you are both vulnerable as hell. What about it?" he snapped.

"And rehabilitate and reinstate Ames in your company?"

"Agreed."

"O.K.," said Ralph. "It's a deal, but as you will see, we didn't need it."

The trial resumed. The judge announced that he agreed that the issue raised by Ralph could not be introduced into the trial in progress. Texoil declined to cross-examine Ralph, which was seen by all present as a damaging admission of weakness. Ralph's and Jack's attorney then called his last witness.

Jerry King entered the courtroom and made his way to the witness stand. Several people in the audience recognized him, and a hum of surprise was gavelled into silence by the judge.

After he was sworn in, the defense lawyer launched an explanation of King's tardy appearance.

"Jerry King had been our missing witness until yesterday," he said. "He has been working in Venezuela since leaving Texoil ten years ago, and it was not until he read our advertisement in the *Petroleum Journal* that he knew of this trial. He arrived in Houston from Caracas only yesterday. We have not attempted to influence his testimony. We have no fear, because we believe he's an honest man and will tell the truth."

The audience buzzed at this new, slightly exotic element that indeed might tip the case in favor of Sanderson and Harrison.

Jack's attorney quickly established King's position as supervisor of Ames' seismic party and the fact that he had discarded the ends of the records which contained the deep seismic reflections. King cheerfully admitted to his lapse of judgment.

"Mr. King," said Judge Browne, "will you tell us why you agreed to come all this way to testify? It would have been very easy for you to ignore the advertisement asking for your presence."

"Well, Your Honor, you're right, it is a long way. But I like Chuck Ames. He's a good man, a good geologist. If he's in trouble, I want to help him out. I feel I owe him — he was right and I was wrong."

"Thank you. Now will you tell us whether you actually ordered Mr. Ames to cut off the records."

"I sure did."

"Did he object?"

"Yes, he did, and strongly. But I told him to cut the end of the records off before putting them into the boxes for shipment. I ignored his objections."

"May I ask the witness why he didn't get larger boxes and save the full records?" said the Texoil lawyer.

"The deep records were damned poor, a real jumble of trash. No reflections at all. If anyone back in headquarters in Houston had taken a look at them, they would have blamed me for not doing better. I didn't reshoot for the deep because I was under heavy pressure from my boss to move on to the new job. That's the way these companies are — they don't give you time to do the work right and they blame you when it's wrong. The fact was I ignored Chuck Ames's suggestions and I didn't make the effort I could have to get better records."

"But didn't you worry that you might have been criticized for having the records cut? After all, it prevented you from making a deep map, which cost Texoil a deep oil field under the Gillette land, an oil field that should rightfully be theirs."

"Christ, I don't know," said King. "No one in Texoil thought highly of the deep prospects. Maybe I figured I could shift the blame to Ames. It's been ten years. I can't remember what all went through my head."

"No more questions, Your Honor."

239

"You may step down — and thank you," said Judge Browne. "Court is adjourned until tomorrow at 10:00 A.M."

The next day the Houston press duly reported all the speculation. Ralph and Jack had made a strong moral case for the little man, but they had been forced to admit that they had received valuable information from Ames. Nevertheless, Texoil had emerged as a heartless bureaucracy; whether that image would count against them legally was questionable. What did it all prove? Sympathy was expressed for the judge in this case.

27

The trial of Texoil vs. Sanderson and Harrison was finally over. Houston had waited weeks for the verdict. And when Judge Browne's decision was handed down, it was in Jack's and Ralph's favor; the judge, in essence, found no evidence of a conspiracy among their employees or between them and the defendants. Texoil had not been able to prove disloyalty on the part of its employees, nor evidence of a payoff.

The internal Texoil records had shown carelessness and bad judgment, but no evidence that the release of the Gillette lands was not the result of a normal decision-making process. There was no evidence that Ralph knew in advance of the release. His secretary had testified that no paper had crossed his desk which could have informed him of it. His initials appeared on no company records to this effect.

Harry Colt's close relationship with Ralph was established, but no evidence could be found that he had conspired with Ralph to give him the Gillette lease, nor that he received any income beyond that from the company. His borrowing had been explained. Harry had, at his own suggestion, taken a polygraph test and was absolved. No evidence could be found, either, against any of the employees of the Lake Charles office, except that a landman who had been spending heavily was found to have purchased royalty under another Texoil lease. Two of the Texoil employees charged had instituted damage suits against Texoil for defamation of character.

The Houston press highlighted the court decision. "Local

Firm Vindicated." "Texoil Humbled by Independents." Jack's and Ralph's telephones rang off the hook with congratulations. Anne was deluged with invitations for dinner. Finally Texoil announced that it would file no appeal to the District Court's decision; they seemed to know they were licked. Bill Butler was reported to be furious. He forced Ray Pickering to retire as Chief Counsel and went off to Africa for a month of big-game hunting. Sanderson and Harrison put out a low-key release expressing gratification that justice had been done in the case, and disclaimed any suit for damages against Texoil. The case was over. Or was it?

Jack and Janet emerged from the trial unscathed; in fact, Jack's reputation in Houston had been enhanced. But the intense publicity had had a profound impact on Ralph and Anne. Was a goddamned lousy fortune worth it? Did the attainment of wealth and recognition and power justify such a price in unwanted publicity, acrimonious conflict and tension? Some people seemed to thrive on conflict; winning was the aim of their game. But Ralph and Anne realized that for them it wasn't.

For once it was Anne who volunteered the doubt. "I'm not sure that we've been going by the right values," she said. "Somewhere along the line of making it in Houston, we got off; I certainly did. I can't believe I ever attached so much importance to society page accounts of our parties. I guess most people would just take the suit in their stride so long as they won, and that's okay — for somebody else. But all those things I wanted to do with our money — I don't know. They don't seem worth the effort now. Maybe having it makes you no longer want it."

"Well, I have an idea," said Ralph. "You know that I stay in touch with Joe Rector, my old real estate friend in Middleburg. When we hit at Gillette, I asked him to keep his eye out for an estate near Middleburg. He called me today. Guess what? That Texas fellow who bought Fairmont is retiring from the government. It's available! Also, I haven't told you but the University of Virginia has been after me to take a year off and act as lawyer-in-residence. I could still keep my hand in the firm by helping Jack with business in Washington and New York — and the firm owns an apartment at the Carlyle in New York." He paused, his excitement mounting. "Anne, let's take the year off to rethink our values. When we come back to Houston we'll live by them."

"Hand me the phone," ordered Anne, looking as if a massive

weight had been lifted from her shoulders, "I'm calling Josh to cancel that monster of a house and send us his bill."

There were many going away parties for Anne and Ralph, the successful outcome of the Texoil suit having made them even more popular than before. Diane and Brad outdid themselves, taking over the whole Warwick Hotel for a glittering bash. Even Josh Fleming gave a discreet little soiree in the Mayan rooms of the museum. But the Sandersons had insisted on a formal dinner for just fifty friends at River Oaks.

"This seems like where we came in," said Ralph, when Jack and Janet greeted them.

After dinner Jack stood up and reached for a glass of champagne.

"To our dear friends Anne and Ralph," Jack said earnestly. "Janet and I want to extend every good wish to them in their return to Virginia for a year's sabbatical. I know they will be glad to be back on their own turf again. We'll all miss them here, particularly Janet and I, who count them among our closest friends. But we know they'll be back in Houston before you know it. They have both demonstrated a deep affection for our city, and after all, Ralph is still a partner in our firm and still has a big part to play. I can assure them that in their absence, we'll all try to keep Houston moving forward so they'll always be proud of their adopted home. So here's to Anne and Ralph!"

Then Ralph got up, surprised at the rush of feeling that forced him to clear his throat. "First time in my life I've been speechless," he said. "And I'm a lawyer! Jack, Janet, thank you for a grand sendoff. Houston has been very good to us, mostly because of good friends like you. We love it here and it's hard for us to leave, even if it's only for a year. We've had the opportunity to buy my old family farm, Fairmont, near Middleburg, Virginia, and I've received an offer I can't resist. I've always wanted a refresher in pure law, and the University of Virginia has offered me a year as lawyer-in-residence. During this year I'll be watching over the Sanderson and Harrison interests in Washington and New York, and I want to thank Jack especially for making that possible. So you see, the combination — plus a permanent hunting box in Virginia — was really irresistible."

Then Anne had her turn. "This is *not* good-bye. We'll be back

243

very soon for keeps. In the meantime, as we say in the South, y'all come see us."

Ralph was seated between Janet and Diane. Late in the evening, after many drinks, he turned to Diane feeling he had to say something. "You know, I'll miss you," he said.

"Oh, you'll see me," Diane replied lightly. "I often get back to Foxhollow. I'm on the board, you know." She winked, then grinned.

"That would be great," said Ralph, but he knew deep down that his heart wasn't really in it.

He looked tenderly at Anne down the long table and silently raised his glass to her. She smiled lovingly and toasted him back. No, there were no real regrets about their life in Houston. Ralph felt that after a slow start he had earned a place for himself in Houston — a place as a man to be reckoned with — a real oilman. He faced the future with confidence.

They both knew they would return to Houston without any misgivings. They knew now that they could live their own life there, on their own terms, without having to prove anything to anybody. The city that had accepted them as they were in the first place would let them go their own way now.

As Janet and Jack drove home, she said, "Now that all our problems are behind us, I have a distinct feeling that something is just beginning."

"Yes, it is," said Jack. "And we're going to make the best of it, old gal. We're going to pay Houston back, whether it wants it or not, for what it's done for us. We'll help make something out of this old town we can be proud of. Have I told you I'm thinking of running for mayor of Houston?"

Afterword

The fabric of modern society is very fragile. Houston was a boom town during the nineteen-seventies; however, it was heavily dependent on a few key industries, particularly oil. The severe setbacks the oil industry has experienced in the nineteen-eighties have imposed heavy strains on Houston's economic, political, and social structure.

Production of oil in the United States peaked in 1971 and Texas production has declined steadily ever since. However, the impetus given to the oil industry by the high prices forced by OPEC after 1973 carried the profitability of oil to new heights, until disastrous inflation hit the whole country in the late seventies. Inflation rose from 4.8 percent in 1976 to 13.3 percent in 1980. Employment in the Texas oil industry fell from 4.5 million in 1981 to 3.5 million in 1984. Migration to Houston peaked at 107,000 in 1978, and by 1984 Houston, for the first time, lost population.

As the impact of the recession spread, building activity in Houston virtually ceased in the face of the highest vacancies in apartments and office spaces in the country. Unemployment in Houston grew to eight percent — over the national average. The decline of the oil industry, coupled with a drastic decrease in real estate values and income, led to severe losses by the key Houston banks. Houston had only just recovered when it received in 1985 an even more serious blow.

Plagued by recession and surplus productive capacity aggravated by new non-OPEC discoveries in the North Sea and Mexico, OPEC was unable to control its members, and in 1985 oil fell within a few weeks from $34 a barrel to $13 — and even less. In many older fields this was below the cost of production. Most Houston Independent oilmen, unable to finance exploration under these conditions and with little expectation of finding profitable oil, simply shut down "for the duration" of low prices, or went broke.

Drilling contractors were forced into a period of unprofitable operation and bankruptcies, with sixty percent of their drilling rigs scrapped or stocked. Seismic field parties were cut fifty percent. Two Houston banks teetered on the edge of solvency.

Then came the testing time for the people of Houston, the time to prove that the great city they had built was not a fluke, and that success did not make them soft. Houstonians have the opportunity to prove that their setback was caused by circumstances over which they had no control — that they can come back. Houston real estate men say that it will take five years, but that Houston property values will return. Oilmen predict a ten-year period of pressure on price by oversupply, but at prices that can see them through.

Houstonians have a chance to prove that the stubborn individualism and determination that started Houston on its upward spiral are still there to do it again. Even though its industrial mix must change, with oil playing a lesser role, Houston's geography, its port, its airlines, its railroads, its vast rich economic hinterland, are still there. Most of its workers are still there, raring to go. Houston has a chance to prove that it was not just a flash in the pan, an historical accident. It can show that Houstonians had really discovered what enables masses of people to live and work together in creating a successful modern city, with opportunity and the basic amenities of life for all.